I0748582

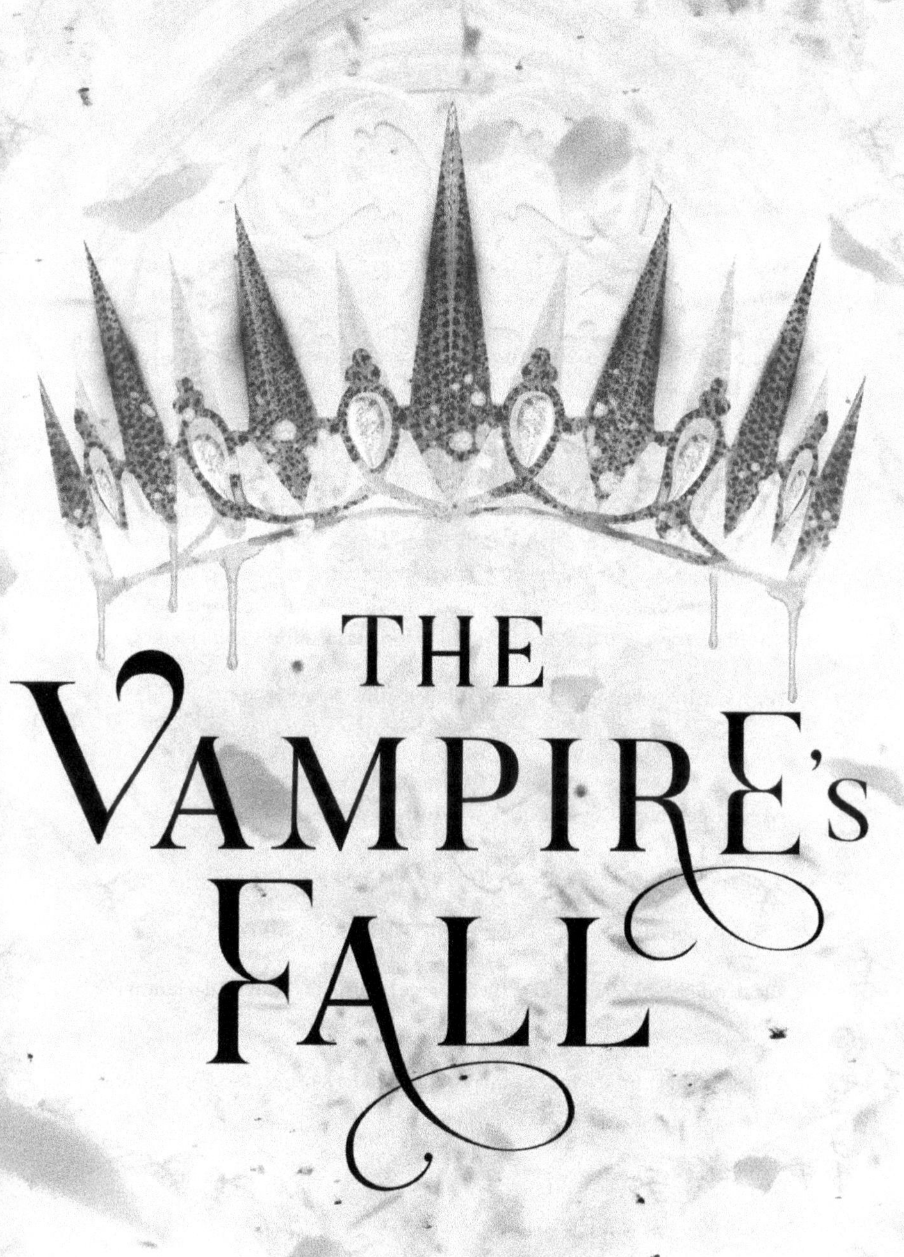

THE VAMPIRE's FALL

CREATORS OF THE NIGHT 1

ELIZA DELMAR

The Vampire's Fall

For more information, go to : www.elizabethduivenvoorde.ca

Louisa Klein (Line Editor), lostinfiction.co.uk/

Alecia Goodman (Copy Editor), www.underwrapspub.com

Jessi Elliott (Proof Reader), www.jessielliott.com/

Cover designed by Selkkie Designs, www.selkkiedesigns.com/

Illustraited by Meri (@cathrine6mirror), cathrine6mirror.deviantart .com

Map Designed by Andrés Aguirre (aaguirreart), https://aaguirreart.c om/

ISBN: 978-1-990224-03-4(Ebook)

978-1-7774478-5-4(Paperback)

978-1-7774478-2-3(Hardcover)

Third Edition: June 2025

In loving memory of my grandfather, Glen Marling,
who introduced me to the world of Dark Fantasy.

The Vampire's Fall contains violence, blood and gore, sexual content, and coarse language. Reader discretion is advised.

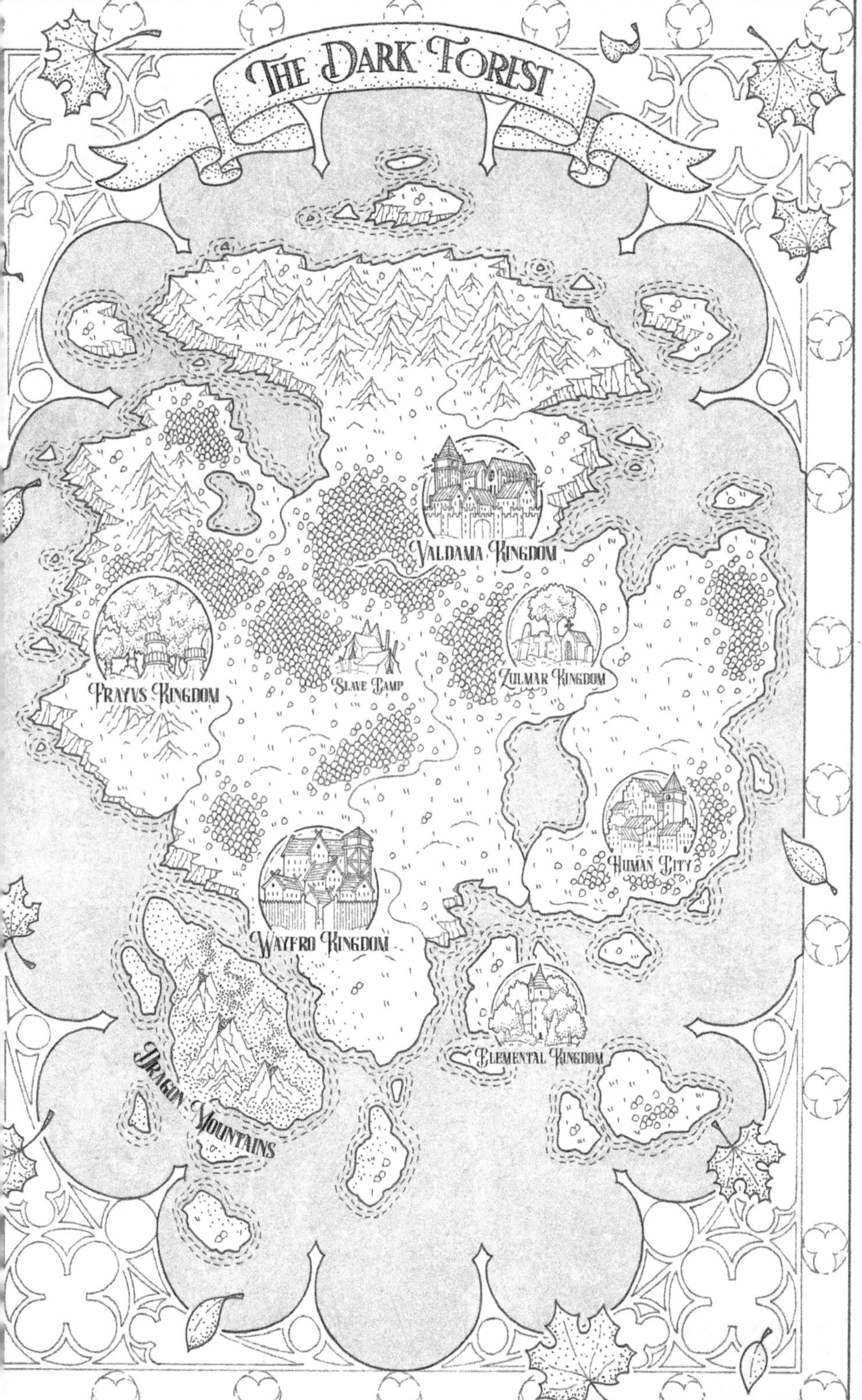

The Dark Forest
Valdama Kingdom
Frayvs Kingdom
Slave Camp
Zulmar Kingdom
Human City
Wayfro Kingdom
Elemental Kingdom
Dragon Mountains

Prologue

Vladimir

MY FIRST DAY AS a royal guard and there's already panic in the castle. I should have listened to my father and taken his place on the King's Council. Instead, I'd insisted on being trained as a guard. And what is my first assignment? To find two princesses hiding.

I round a corner, keeping my eyes focused. The princesses went missing sometime after their early evening feed. The Queen had discovered the younger of the two, Akantha, was missing first, then went to check on the oldest and found her missing as well. She immediately called for a search party.

And I'm one of the unfortunate souls who has to search the halls of the castle.

Another guard, William, slugs down the hall. He pauses a few paces ahead of me. "Find them yet?"

I shake my head. "What about you?"

He sighs. "Not even a lock of hair. Are we even sure they're still in the castle?"

The queen would never allow the two young princesses to leave the castle, would she? "I could search outside?"

William nods, his black hair falling out of its slicked-back manner. "Good idea. I'll comb through the halls again. Maybe try the library too."

With a vague plan, we part ways. I head to the nearest exit and step out into the crisp evening air. Gravel shifts under my boots, sounding almost too loud in the quiet of night.

I pace the castle grounds, but find no one. I'm about to give up when a soft giggle cuts through the air. I stiffen. Hold my breath. Listen.

Another giggle.

Being as quiet as possible, I follow the giggles to the outer rim of the grounds. There's a gap in the stone wall, too small for myself to fit through comfortably, but large enough for a child. I crouch and peek through.

On the other side are two girls in lush gowns. The older one wears a yellow gown and has black wavy hair that's just past her shoulders, she looks to be around four hundred years old, giving her the appearance of a nine-year-old human. The other is younger, looking about four in human years, which would easily translate to her being shy of two hundred. She has shoulder length black hair and is wearing a blue dress.

The older girl kneels in the grass, taking the younger girl's hand and guiding her to follow suit. They kneel together in the grass next to a small patch of flowers. The older girl leans forward and inhales deeply, "Akantha, smell these ones."

Akantha? The younger princess?

The younger girl leans forward and closes her eyes. Her nose twitches as she sniffs. A smile spreads across her lips and her eyes open, "Wow, they smell so pretty."

She turns her head towards me, searching for more flowers. I catch sight of her ice blue eyes and my heart jumps into my throat. A vampire with blue eyes?

The older girl, possibly Princess Callisora, looks right at me. Her eyes flash red, but then dull back to their regular chocolate color. She stands and brushes off her dress: "Come on Akantha. It's time to go back."

Chapter One

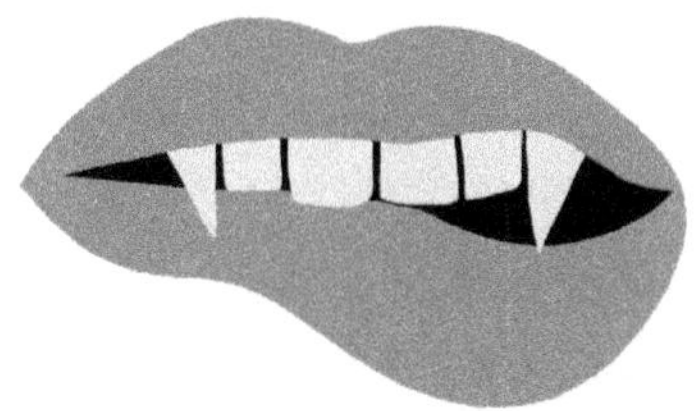

Callisora

My attention is drawn to the faint heartbeat of the man lying next to me—my most recent feed, my mid-day snack. With a deep inhale through my nose, I open my eyes as a breeze rushes in from the window, filling the room with crisp evening air. The wine-colored tapestry hanging from my bed's massive pillars ripples. I pull the blanket off myself and slip out of bed. Stretching my arms over my head, I yawn. The translucent nightdress' sleeves slide down my arms, the soft fabric billowing at my elbows. The night dress was a gift from the fairies. Their style is much more sensual than the vampires' Victorian aesthetic. But I have to admit, the corsets do wonders for my waistline.

Leaning over the unconscious man, I tug at the thin chain that hangs around my neck. A teardrop-shaped vial dislodges from between my breasts and sways above him. The red liquid inside gives off a dull glow, the magic wearing off. I uncap the vial and dump out the contents. It loses its power as soon as it leaves the container, turning a bright red as it falls through the air. It paints a small splatter on the smooth wood floor.

I reach over, taking the man's wrist and drag my nail along his skin. It splits open. Nothing comes. I listen for his barely perceptible heartbeat. With a gentle squeeze on his arm, a little blood oozes from the cut on his wrist. I press harder, sliding my hand down his arm until an adequate pool begins to form. The liquid glows bright, while it's captured in the magical vial. Once full, there will be enough to protect me from the sunlight until my next feed, after which I'll have to change it again. The blood inside becomes rancid tasting and inedible after being confined for so long. There's too much magic in it by then, so unfortunately, I can't just drink it. It needs to be dumped. It isn't much anyway.

A soft knock comes from my bedchamber door.

"I'm awake," I call.

The door opens, and a lean fairy enters. Her skin is a soft pink that sparkles dimly in the darkness, but shimmers more as she passes the moon-lit window. Her hair isn't as lightly colored as her skin tone, bright pink strands blend into a lovely violet hue at the tips. Her matching violet eyes look me over, then shift to the man for a moment, before moving back to me. "Good evening Princess. I trust you had a restful slumber?"

"For the most part." I press the vial back between my breasts. Stepping away from the bed I remove my thin nightgown in one swift motion, grabbing two fistfuls of cloth at my thighs and pulling it over my head. It lands on the floor, discarded and bloodstained. My hand grasps one of the golden handles of my wardrobe. Pulling the door open reveals gowns upon gowns of thickly layered, darkly colored fabric, as if wearing layers could ever warm the cold skin of a vampire! I tilt my head from side to side, considering my options. Not only are the gowns thick, but many of them are bulky and unflattering. I prefer clothes that show off my lady-bits and make men's heads turn. After choosing a navy dress with a close-fitting bodice and reasonable skirt diameter, the fairy dresses me.

My corset is tied tightly. The soft fabric falls around me, hugging my body as it, too, were tied to fit snug against my curves. After stepping into a pair of black heels, I proceed to my vanity. The reflection-less glass stares back at me. I bring my finger to my mouth and press the soft pad against the tip of my fang. A small sting emanates from the newly broken skin. I take my bloodied digit, pressing it against the mirror and my reflection appears.

I lick my finger as the fairy steps up behind me. She retrieves my hairbrush and proceeds to brush out the tangles. Each section of long black hair falls in spirals down my back, bouncing with the joy of being free from knots. The fairy places the brush back on the vanity and styles my hair in a half-updo. I'm accustomed to simple hairstyles and fancy clothes. It's a style I personally find lovely. She then plucks a tiara from the top of the vanity.

The swirling wire of the tiara presses against my forehead, the only jewels on it being a single blood red diamond shaped like a teardrop.

I tilt my head from side to side, appreciating the simple yet beautiful job the servant had done. I give my hair a fluff with my hands, making it slightly less elegant looking, then stand.

The fairy takes a step back, giving me space.

I look towards the blanched face of the man on my bed. "Thank you for the splendid afternoon," I smirk, then turn to the fairy. "Dispose of him," I wave a hand over my shoulder. "And change the bedsheets."

She isn't new to this; she knows how to handle my late-day feeds. I bring one home nearly every day, after all. I fuck them, then drink their blood. The dopamine-induced liquid is intoxicating, and not only does it fill me, but it also gives a most pleasurable high.

I leave my room and head down the long hall. The corridor curves, splitting off into multiple directions. I stop before a rigid-looking oak door. Lifting my hand to knock, I gather my nerves. The door creaks open and I step in. The floorboards groan under my weight. "Evening, sister."

Akantha sits on the edge of her window, one leg hanging inside and the other outside. "Evening Callisora."

She's facing outside, as if she's looking out into the Dark Forest surrounding the castle. She inhales deeply, tightening her grip on the velvet blanket wrapped around her.

"It's a chilly evening, isn't it?" She turns her head to look at me. Her blue eyes send a shiver down my spine. All vampires have brown eyes—when they aren't red with hunger—except for Akantha. Father had become outraged when he first saw Akantha's eyes, thinking Mother had an affair with a fairy and birthed a Youngling. A half-breed. But after the Elder had tasted Akantha's blood and assured Father that the baby was full vampire, we discovered that Akantha's eye color was due to her blindness. Or at least, that's what the Elder had told us.

I step towards her. "Indeed it is," the chill had awoken me not long ago. "Are you coming down for the evening feed?"

She bobs her head and unwraps the blanket. The fabric falls to the floor, revealing that she's still in her nightdress and her hair's in unkempt tangles and knots. She looks like she's never left her bed, never brushed her hair.

I cover my mouth to conceal a small gasp. Her nightdress isn't as revealing as mine. Thick material hides all of her pear-like body shape. The fabric is tight around her wrists and neck, to fall down just above her ankles. Her bare feet look dirty, having never been covered with shoes, but her toenails are somehow just as clean looking as my own. "You can't go like that. Mother will have a fit." Still, the thought of Mother scolding Akantha amuses me, not that it would ever actually happen. Akantha is Mother's little lamb, soft and delicate, in need of protection.

"Why? I never leave the castle grounds. No one will see me."

She has a point.

"You know how Mother is. We have to keep up appearances even when no one is looking." Or caring. I make my way to her wardrobe. The hinges scream with its opening. Thick fabrics fill the space, reflecting the gowns in my own. "Any preference in color?"

Akantha tilts her head, her long black tangles moving stiffly. "They all feel the same when I wear them, so no."

The door opens behind me. "Oh ... Your highness!" The voice is familiar. A glance over my shoulder confirms that Akantha's handmaiden has arrived. I don't remember her name, but her golden skin shines brighter than true gold. Her hair is just as vibrant at the base and transitions to a lovely silver. It's slightly amusing, considering fairies are deathly allergic to silver. She offers me a light smile, "I wasn't expecting you here this early in the evening."

I lift a shoulder in a half shrug, turning away from the wall of gowns. "I thought I'd check on my sister before the evening feed."

The fairy moves towards the fabrics at the same time as I move away.

"That's very considerate of you, but Lady Akantha needs to get ready, so I must ask you to step out."

It's nothing I haven't seen before.

"Very well," I nod my thanks to the fairy, then shift my attention to Akantha, who's looking towards the window again, a strange expression painted across her face. Loneliness? Longing? "I'll see you downstairs."

Akantha's body stiffens, and she swivels her head in my direction again. "Yes, see you there."

I turn to leave the room. At the door, I glance back at the fairy. "Dress her warmly." I head back into the hall.

CHAPTER TWO

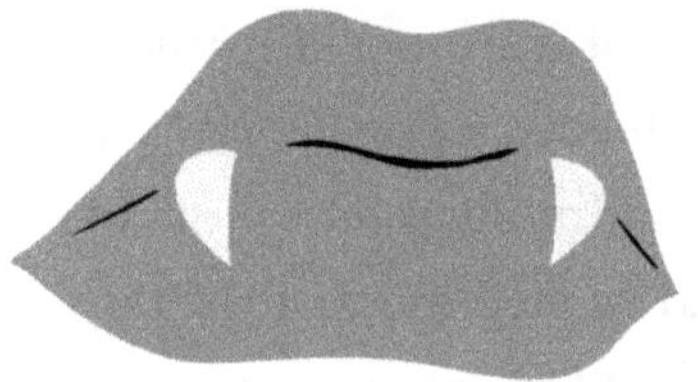

Akantha

CALLISORA'S SCENT HANGS IN the air long after the door closes behind her. Roses and blood. The tangy yet perfumed aroma causes my gums to ache. My adult fangs haven't come in yet, but my mouth doesn't seem to realize that. A strange tingling sensation spreads throughout my mouth. My venom numbs my mouth in case my non-existent fangs pierce anything. I swallow down an alarming amount of saliva.

Callisora had surely fed recently. Why else would the smell of blood overpower that of the roses? However, she always smells that way first thing in the evening. Like she'd just strolled away from a slaughter after rolling in the garden. It is an aroma that feeds my inner beast as well as my outer nature-lover. Though it isn't all good. It's also a reminder that Callisora is more than she appears. Surely, she is beautiful—how else would she lure men into her bed?—but under that beauty is a blood-thirsty beast.

"How was your rest, my dear?" The soft voiced fairy, Helena asks. Even though the darkness consumes everything, I can still see her. Well, in a way. The soft yellow glow of her aura illuminates the blackness around her. Callisora's aura is red with silver swirls, whereas my handmaiden has glints of amber.

"I tossed and turned most of the day." I stroll to my bed and sit. It's taken six centuries, but I've managed to memorize most of the furniture's placement in the castle. My room was the easiest to master. Second was the garden. The library is one of the trickiest, because some chairs and tables are moved around on occasion.

Helena's fingers tip-tap across the gowns in my wardrobe. "I'm sorry to hear that," her tone is always so gentle, yet authoritative. The thicker fabrics rustle as her dainty hands move, whereas the thinner ones make barely any sound. Finally, the sounds all stop. Helena moves around the room, grunting as she lugs a gown from the collection towards me. "This should do nicely. It won't be too hot during your lessons, and you won't freeze when we go for your daily stroll in the garden."

I hold in a sigh. As if I could ever be too hot or too cold. I reach out and touch the coarse fabric—curse Callisora for telling Helena to dress me warm. I am not some human that would break easily. How does one prove they aren't as fragile as a flower?

I stand, heaving the massive amount of fabric up into my arms as I do.

Helena gasps. "Oh, dear, let me help you with that!" Her warm hands brush against my arms as she attempts to get hold of the garment.

My blood boils. The distraction sets me off balance and I fall back.

The bed hugs my body, reminding me of the exhaustion that still plagues my being. Restless sleeps with nightmares of being decapitated. Last night's dream rushes back to me. All the blood. So much blood and none of it appetizing. It had felt so real. Like it wasn't a dream. More like it was a memory.

"Akantha? I'm so sorry, are you alright?" Helena is standing over me, her shaky voice makes the amber in her aura dance. Or perhaps they're quivering with fear. The scent of blood escaping her bitten lip hits me. She's worried. But why? Does she think I'll lash out? I've never done that before. I'd never hurt her, she's too important to me.

"It was an accident. I'm fine."

Rising to my feet, I don't touch the dress.

Helena lets out a sigh of relief, then takes my arm and guides me to the center of the room. She babbles on about today's lessons—history, botany, science, and magic.

Helena has always been like this; overprotective, affectionate, and caring. She was assigned to take care of me when I was very young, so I've had her by my side for as long as I can remember.

"Must I endure another lesson today?" My voice comes off more annoyed than I intend.

Helena fumbles with the clothes. "You need to learn vampire history, my lady, just as your sister has."

I let out a heavy sigh. Callisora is first in line for the throne, which means only she is granted the title of princess. I, on the other hand, am a Duchess. Or at least I will be when Callisora is queen. As such, I need to work extra hard to find a purpose in life. Thankfully, the Elder had offered to take me on as his apprentice in a few hundred years or so. Usually, the Elders don't take on vampires from royal lineage to teach, but due to my blindness, he's willing to make an exception. Father had most likely convinced him to out of worry, and he probably agreed to from pity.

A stiff stretch of material wraps around my torso, and I gasp. Pushing the corset away, I glare at Helena. "No. I refuse to wear that. It's restricting and uncomfortable."

Helena sighs with instant defeat, "It was worth a try. But you know your mother is going to be upset."

I huff in response. It's not like mother would be upset for long. I refuse to wear the thing on a daily basis. It shouldn't be surprising to anyone anymore.

The fairy aids me in dressing and braids my hair. As she fights to get the wire tiara to stay on my head, a shiver runs down my spine. The wind whispers into the room and steals kisses from both my cheeks, leaving them feeling raw and chilled. The breeze carries a scent with it. One I know all too well and yet not at all. It brings a small smile to my lips and eases my frustrations.

Cinnamon.

CHAPTER THREE

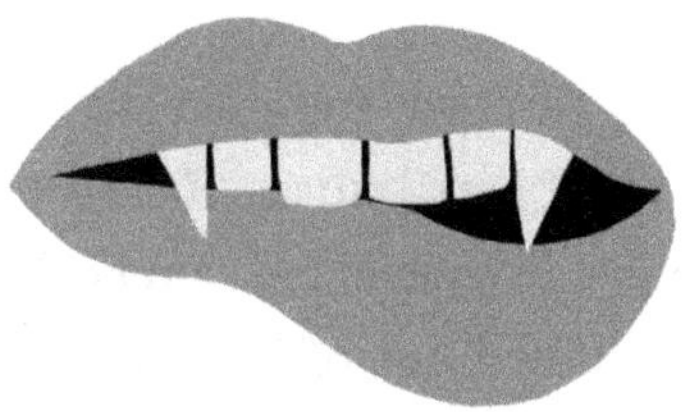

Callisora

THE DOUBLE DOORS ARE open, welcoming me to enter the dining hall. But I don't feel welcomed. Father sits at the head and Mother's in the seat to his right. She's his right hand in ruling the kingdom, so she's always seated on his right side. I've always thought that they were taking it a little too literally.

Mother looks away from Father and to where I'm standing in the doorway. Her black hair is tied up into an intricate braided hairstyle that wraps around itself atop her head. A few long waves escape and frame her narrowed face. A small nose adds to the daintiness of her complexion. Thin eyebrows, small lips, high cheekbones; she's the definition of a beautiful queen. "Good evening, Callisora. Come in. Have a seat."

I inhale through my nose. My shoulders rollback, and I waltz into the room. Mother's eyes follow me as I walk along side the table towards the seat to Father's left.

Smoothing the fabric under my buttocks before sitting, I offer a toothy smile. "Evening, Mother. Evening, Father."

Father grunts, his piercing eyes fixated on nothing in particular. His black hair is slicked back, showing off his round ears. I've never known Father not to have his dark hair slicked out of his face. He wears his usual black overcoat and matching pants. The collar of a burgundy shirt is folded over the collar of his overcoat, giving him a splash of color.

His eyes shift to meet mine, his red orbs drill into me. My stomach twists, and I refocus on Mother, "How was your rest?"

"Excellent. Your father and I had a very productive conversation during the early morning."

The sparkle in her eye adds to my gut's torment.

I straighten my back more than I thought possible. "About?" What could they possibly have talked about that would make Mother this excited?

"We'll talk about it when your sister gets here."

"But–"

"Hush!" Father hisses, "Do not speak out of turn!" His voice bounces off the walls and hits me repeatedly. He's no longer looking my way, but his creased brow and distant glare are clearly meant for me.

My lips press together and look down at my lap. My fingers entwine, allowing me to pick at my long nails. I clean dried blood out from under one.

Mother sighs with delight. I look up to find my sister entering the room.

"Oh, Akantha, you look lovely!"

The pride in her voice causes bile to rise and I swallow it back down. I should be used to this—and in a way I am—but being looked down on by my parents has always left me feeling bitter. I try not to hold it against Akantha, but some days I wish I could be in her shoes and receive a gentle embrace from our mother again.

Akantha's messy hair is now entwined into a long braid, hanging over her shoulder like half a shawl and bringing more attention to her narrow face and lean neck. Her dress grazes the floor, nearly hiding her bare feet. Black lace covers the glimmering green silk that embraces her figure.

Mother walks over and takes Akantha's hand, leading her away from the servant and to the table. It takes Mother longer to notice than it takes me, but when Akantha sits, Mother lets out a shriek, "Akantha! Where is your corset?"

I smirk. If Akantha could see the look on Mother's face, she'd laugh. Mother often overreacts when it comes to such *scandalous affairs*. It took a century for her to get used to Akantha not wearing shoes.

Akantha simply shrugs, "I see no purpose in wearing such things. It is restricting and rather uncomfortable." Her answer is the same as every other day that Mother protests over her lack of corset. I wonder how long it'll take Mother to accept this fashion choice.

Mother places a hand over her heart in shock, "What? But it's customary attire. This is–"

"Scandalous?" I interrupt with a snicker.

"Bite your tongue!" Father's dark voice causes my muscles to tense. He keeps his eyes on me. "Akantha, you are to dress appropriately. If you wish to be wed."

Akantha sits up, her clouded eyes wide. I'm unsure if she's excited or afraid. The only readable emotion is the one she's allowing us to see. Shock.

My curiosity urges me to ask Father what he means. I bite my inner cheek to stay silent.

Mother reclaims her seat, a wide smile on her lips. Clearly, this is the *fantastic* thing she and Father had talked about. Marrying off their disabled daughter. "Your father and I have been discussing your futures."

Futures? As in plural?

Frustration and excitement mix within my chest. "We're too young to be betrothed," I remind them. I'm only nine hundred. One hundred years too young, according to the Royal Law. Akantha is four centuries too young. "According to the law set by the Council," I add, in an attempt to protect myself from Father's wrath.

The Council works with the King to keep order and make sure the crown doesn't go power crazy—although it often doesn't work. Royalty has always been notorious for finding loopholes in the laws—Father included. One law prohibits vampires from sharing a bed with the King apart from the Queen. Naturally, father decided to take the fairy slaves—who work in the castle—on as his mistresses. A dangerous choice, seeing as he could create a child with them and would then have to kill it.

"I rule the Council, Callisora," he snaps. "Besides, I already spoke with them about this, and they ruled in my favour." Of course, they did. But why so soon? Why the sudden rush? "As future Queen, you must marry a noble."

Valdama—the kingdom of vampires—has never had a female heir; the firstborn has always been male. As such, I have to marry a strong male from high society, to sit by my side and help me rule. Since all heirs who don't become the ruling monarch are made into Dukes and Duchesses, it only seems fit for me to marry a Duke, I suppose. We do hail from the same bloodline.

But to think that I'd be queen so soon. It's unsettling. I'm the future queen of a dying kingdom, filled with vampires who want to be here about as much as a mermaid wants to be stranded in the desert.

Even if Akantha had been born a son and I'd wanted to run off to allow her to take over the throne, I couldn't. The Valdama Knights would hunt me down and capture me. I'd probably be tried for treason for abandoning the crown. Even if I somehow did make a home for myself in the Dark Forest, or even in the human world, I wouldn't be able to settle down and have a family. The blood of a royal female—any female related to Dracula—can't produce offspring with creatures other than a vampire. So, I couldn't even settle down with a human. It would have to be a vampire who didn't care that I was a runaway princess.

Although, if Akantha had been born male, or if Mother and Father had tried for a son, I'd probably be forced to marry them instead of finding a suitor. It's not uncommon for vampires to marry their siblings, especially in the higher classes; it's supposed to keep the bloodline strong. It's appalling, in my opinion.

Thankfully, my parents are not siblings. They are first cousins, though that's not much better. From what I've heard growing up, Mother and Father's younger brother grew up together, and were very close. They were even betrothed from a young age. Father took Mother away from my uncle after he became king. I don't know much of the details beyond that, but I doubt he ever loved her.

"And me?" Akantha's voice is barely above a whisper. Her jaw is clenched, brows lowered with uncertainty. Surely, Mother and Father have already found her a suitor. Someone who is strong and capable of protecting her, but isn't a threat to the throne.

Father smiles, showing his favouritism. My blood boils. "I want to end this feud with Wayfro. It's been going on far too long." Wayfro—The Land of Werewolves.

"It's only been ten thousand years," I mutter.

Father shoots me a silent glare. I press my lips together. He continues, "You will be wed to the youngest Werewolf Prince."

Akantha bows her head. "Of course, Father."

Her voice doesn't shake, but her hands do. Though they are hidden from my sight, her green flowing sleeves ripple with the movement.

I clench my teeth, but say nothing. It's not like werewolves are the only threat. There are still the Rogues, Rebels, and Younglings.

The Rebels are a group of creatures who've gathered to overthrow Father. Many think he's an unfit king. From the little I've heard, they aren't too much of a threat, just a small organization of cry babies.

Rogues are creatures who feed off their own kind, killing for amusement and not for hunger. Though, when they do get hungry, their hunger can wipe out entire families. Their bloodlust is worse than a newly changed monster. The thought of ever crossing a Rogue vampire sends shivers down my spine.

And Younglings are creatures born from two different species. They inherit both the independent and common strengths of their parents, but only weaknesses that are the same in both parents.

It's a type of synergy where the traits of the offspring are better than the sum of its genetic contributors. My ancestors have been killing off Younglings since the first one was born. Father sees the act as a sport and finds great entertainment in killing the small children and their parents.

"On a separate note," Father sits up straighter as the servants walk in with plates. Each plate carries a tall wine glass filled with a dark red substance—blood. Unfortunately, the royal vampires have been drinking animal blood for the last few millennia to keep us healthy. Human blood is far sweeter and is very addictive, which is why I adore it. The plates are set in front of us. The servants move away from the table. Father's eyes follow the movements of each woman's hips as she walks away.

He focuses on his glass and continues speaking, "I hear that the Slave Tamer is coming to the castle."

I roll my eyes. It's more likely that he summoned the Slave Tamer. Has he already slept with all the slaves he got last time? It wouldn't surprise me.

Mother lifts her glass off her plate, careful not to spill it even though it's only half full.

"We have enough servants, dear."

Her eyes glow red as soon as they land on the liquid. She opens her mouth slightly, draws out her fangs—even though she doesn't have to—and takes a sip.

I watch the fairies that linger around the room. It doesn't surprise me that we don't have vampire servants. We are the only kingdom that still retains slaves as servants. Other kingdoms had stopped this practice anywhere from one to five hundred years ago. The fairies and werewolves use to have a mix of species that served them. Except they put a stop to that when the fairies and werewolves formed an alliance with one another and decided to employ their own kind. The Zombie King still buys servants just so he can set them free. He's a neutral party, or at least he tries to be.

"Nonsense. We shan't be rude!" He tips the glass back and downs the thick substance, which had been filled to the rim.

I glance at Akantha. She's the reason we use glasses and don't go out to the barn out back or hunt for our meals. She's a late fanger. Her fangs haven't come in yet. She's supposed to get them within her first two hundred years of life. Mother says it's because she doesn't care much for her heritage, so her body hasn't welcomed the fangs.

My eyes drift down to my own blood-filled glass, and my nose scrunches. It smells of cow, dirt, fecal matter, soap, and blood. That's all I can smell. Disgusting.

"I'm not hungry," I volunteer.

Mother lowers her glass, but doesn't place it on the table. Instead, she swirls the liquid around. "Are you feeling unwell?"

"I am well, Mother."

"She eats too much junk food," Father mumbles in disgust. He gestures to a male fairy with blue skin and blue-green hair. My glass is taken and brought to Father. "She plays with her food, too. It's undignified." He's one to talk.

"Oh, Callisora. You aren't a child anymore," Mother tries scolding, but her tone is too gentle. She takes another sip, then licks her lips.

I nod. "Of course, Mother. My apologies," I stand. "Please pardon me."

"No," Father has chugged my glass while Mother and I were conversing. "You are joining your mother and me in the Throne Room."

I close my eyes to control the outburst that hangs on the end of my tongue.

I regain my composure before looking at my parents again. "Of course, Father."

CHAPTER FOUR

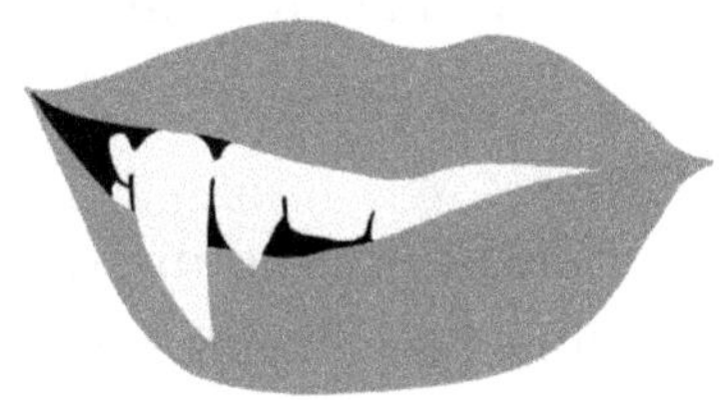

Farran

CHAINS CLICK AND CLACK as bodies shift in the dimly lit tent. The massive space is bordered by stone walls and covered with a tarp ceiling. Lanterns hang from the wooden banisters above, allowing small bits of light to barely fill the space. Moonlight floods in from the open doorway. A breeze rushes in and cools the sweat that clings to my body.

The torn clothes hang off my body, barely covering the important areas that need shielding from hungry eyes. I scratch at a patch of dried dirt on my arm.

A horse cough echoes through the space, drawing my attention away from the dark spot on my body. Four-foot poles stick out of the ground in random places, four to six fairies chained to each one. The fairies' range in ages, some being small, young ones, others being tall and wise.

He's coming.

My gaze shifts to the doorway. The voice is right. He is coming. His scent grows stronger with every step he takes towards the tent—leather and gunpowder.

My hands shake, causing my chains to rattle along with all the others in the room.

Let me kill him.

The shackles tighten around my wrists. No, my wrists are expanding. She's trying to get out.

"Don't," I whisper, "He's our master."

He's no master of mine.

I close my eyes and take a deep breath through my nose, then release it through my mouth.

"Farran?" A small voice chirps nearby.

My eyes open. The little fairy girl at the next post over is looking at me. Her large blue eyes filled with fear.

"Is he coming?" Her voice breaks with a squeak. She's new. Her hair is still blonde, but changing to green, and her pale skin is following suit.

The others who share the pole with her are also young. Newly changed. None of them were born like this. None of us here were born like this. We used to be humans. Used to fear the monsters in the Dark Forest. But now we only fear one man. The man who took us. Who changed us.

The man who's getting closer.

I nod. The girl whimpers and cowers, moving away from the doorway as much as she can, though it's not like she can move far. Her chained hands catch when the chain runs out. The sound of sizzling flesh is followed by the smell. My nose scrunches, but my stomach rumbles. I swallow and move closer, careful not to move the silver around my wrists. The last thing I need is another burn scar. Perhaps it's why Master collects fairies and the odd werewolf? Because we're both sensitive to silver.

Tears stream down the girl's cheeks, but she doesn't let out a sound.

"Are you alright?" I keep my eyes focused on her little face, worried I might lose control at the sight of her cooked flesh.

She nods, though her body is shaking. Shaking from fear or shock, I'm unsure.

It smells so good.

I involuntarily inhale through my nose, taking in a deep breath of the salty crisp scent. My mouth waters. I move away from the small girl. Only now do I feel the hundreds of eyes on me. All blue. All round. All scared. Did they think I would eat her? Who am I kidding? If not for the chains, I might have.

I sit next to my post, leaning against it. The chain grazes my knee, already scarred from a past grazing. It stings, but doesn't burn. My head rests against the wood, my gaze focused on the open doorway. The eyes that had once looked my way move off me and onto new targets.

Being the only werewolf at camp means I get my own post. It's nice. I have all the space I need while sleeping, but it's a tad lonely. Apart from the host of new recruits, no one else is close to me. Perhaps Master doesn't mind the idea of me feeding off small children, but would prefer the older fairies stay in one piece.

The light from the doorway is blocked by a shadowed figure. His wide shoulders and tall figure block the breeze from entering.

He takes a step inside. My stomach clenches, muscles restrict as I fight my inner wolf. The wild creature demands this man be ripped apart and punished for keeping us locked up like this.

Master steps under one of the lamps. Light illuminates his creased forehead, high cheekbones, and pointed chin. Hazel eyes examine the room before landing on me. He approaches, just as he does every time he enters here. Master doesn't visit often, but when he does, he comes right over to me.

He stops. Close enough that I can see the bloodstains on his shirt and the dirt tangled in the fur of his once luxurious wolf coat, but not close enough that I could reach him. "Good evening, pup."

A snarl escapes. My wolf struggles to free herself from my prison of a body, but I resist her. He's just trying to rile us up, any reason to punish us. Resisting is hard. My body wants to change. Every day that I don't makes my wolf restless, my muscles achy, and my gut twist into knots. It's like trying to prevent a flow of water from passing. Every time I block the flow, it gets stronger. Soon enough, it'll be too much and knock me out of the way. But not today.

Master laughs, his belly jiggling at the movement. When he'd first acquired me, he was thin and fit, but he's let himself go over the years. His stomach is round and slowly growing. I've overheard some of the smaller fairies compare it to a pregnant belly. The ones who'd say that in front of him are no longer alive. "It's good to see you're so alert this evening."

His booming voice holds enough authority that it forces my wolf to submit. I bow my head with a whimper.

A soft chuckle escapes his lips. Master turns his back to me when more men enter the tent. He walks toward the doorway. "We're going to the Vampire King. Prepare fifteen fairies." He pauses a moment. "Get the wolf ready too. She's stinking up the place. I'm sure the Zombie King would pay a handsome price to free her."

The men don't respond with words, only actions. They approach the posts and grab onto the fairies. Screams, a mix of pain and sorrow, echo in my ears. The smell of burning flesh makes my stomach ache. Due to the Vampire King's preference, mostly only female fairies are chosen. The odd male is acquired for the Zombie King to purchase and free.

Master always brings more slaves than he needs to. He knows that the Zombie King would buy everyone that he can, only to free them after. Master doesn't care what the Zombie King does with the slaves after, as long as he gets paid.

I've never gone outside this tent, but that changes today. I'm going to meet both the Vampire and Zombie rulers. And I'll be free by the end of it.

Two men come up to me. I don't move. Cowering would show weakness, and fighting would jeopardize my impending freedom. My wolf knows this as well. Rough hands grab at my shoulders while another set unlocks the shackles from my wrists, only to put on new ones. Another silver shackle is locked around my neck, along with one around each of my ankles. They're all connected together by thick chains.

The fresh silver sends a burning sensation through my veins. It heats my arms. My mouth waters, but not from the delicious smell of my own cooking flesh. My tongue is drowning and I fight back the need to vomit. I can endure this pain.

The men tug on the chain, forcing me forward. I follow the line of fairies and leave the tent.

The moonlight Illuminates the path in front of us, even as we step out of the clearing and into the thick forest. The freshly polished silver burns my skin with every step. My foot catches on a rock and I stumble out of line. One of the men comes out of nowhere to shove me back into place. My tongue drowns in saliva again. I spit the excess out. It lands on my bare foot.

I lower my hands to my pelvis, giving my legs a small amount of extra slack, which will hopefully make walking easier. Fairies are tall creatures, standing at a minimum of six feet three inches fully grown, so why would they have such short chains? I'm far shorter than them, and even I'm struggling. There's no way that their awkward hunched walk makes us walk any faster.

We'll be there soon.

For once, I'm grateful for my wolf's intruding voice. We'll be there soon. Be free soon.

CHAPTER FIVE

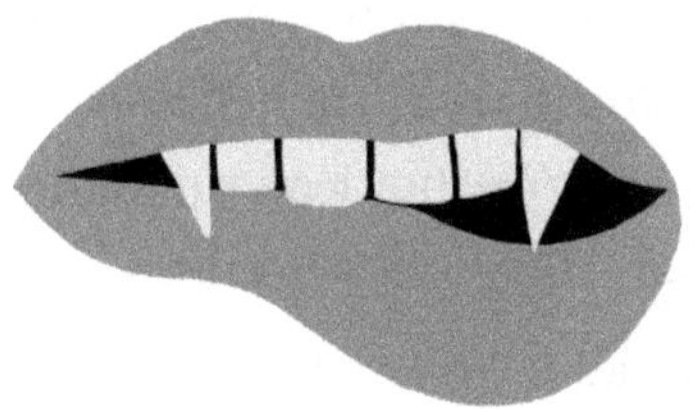

Callisora

FATHER SITS IN THE largest of three thrones. Mother is in the slightly smaller one to his right. I'm slouched in the smallest one, my patience running short. Why must I sit here? I don't even want to see the Slave Tamer. He's a disgusting human who thrives off of capturing creatures of the night for profit. It's demeaning to even be sitting in his presence.

Mother clears her throat. "Straighten up, Callisora."

I groan internally and stiffen my back. "Of course, Mother."

A thunderous knock echoes through the Throne Room, filling the space with brief spurts of sound. The tall walls are decorated with banners of red, which match the plush cushions of the thrones, as well as the long floor-to-throne rug that stretches out along the floor. The tall oak doors open, allowing a breeze to disturb the tapestries that hang along the walls, depicting centuries of history.

A plump human enters. He is followed by a group of chained fairies. Three other humans walk in after the fairies; each carrying silver picks with dried blood at the ends. The plump man stops before us, kneeling on the first of three steps that lead up to the platform the thrones sit upon. The other humans guide the fairies to kneel in a huddled group behind their keeper.

"Good evening, your majesty," The man bows his head, dark locks of greasy hair hide his face. His heart thumps in his chest, "Thank you for welcoming us into your home."

Father lifts his chin, looking down his nose at the human. "What have you brought us this evening?"

The man—the Slave Tamer—rises. The brown blood stains embedded in his fur coat make my mouth dry. Is that wolf fur? *Werewolf* fur? How did he get that?

The fairies follow suit. One struggles to stand and is jabbed in the ribs by one of the other humans. The silver pick pierces their skin. The fairy clenches its teeth. The tangy aroma of blood fills the air. My mouth tingles and I swallow, quickly regaining control.

Mother and Father seem unfazed by the events unfolding in front of us. Mother averts her eyes, looking towards the far wall with an expression of unimpressed boredom. Father stands and walks towards the group, his hands held behind his back. Judging by the horrified expressions on the fairies' faces, he's ogling them. Perhaps even trying to hear their pulse.

All vampires who are a descendant of Dracula have a gift that enhances one of our natural abilities. Father's is influence; he can convince his prey to willingly approach him without hesitation. Most other vampires can't do this as easily and are at risk of their prey being too strong-willed and fleeing. Except this gift isn't limited to only his prey, he can also influence other vampires. It's probably how he got the Council to agree to marrying Akantha and I off so quickly.

I can hear heartbeats, every squeezing ventricle in this room thumps in my ears. Other vampires have to be closer to their kill, but not me.

An irregular heartbeat catches my attention. I stand.

"Callisora," Mother's whispered voice hisses.

I ignore her, my curiosity leading me towards the group. Most eyes are on me now, including Father's. I focus on the heartbeat, ignoring the slow beats of Mother and Father's hearts, the fluttering ones of the fairies, and the even thuds of the humans. The one I'm searching for is faster—quick and strong.

I circle the group like a shark in shallow water. Her scent hits me the moment I see her. It must have been masked by that of the fairies. Approaching, I take in the sight of her tanned skin, short messy brown locks, and ragged clothes. Her brown eyes meet mine, round and glossy. Her body trembles, but her heart doesn't race. The ones around her do. I reach out and grab the chain.

Pain shoots up my arm. Gasping, I pull away. Cradling my hand, I evaluate the damage. The skin of my palm has been burned away, exposing the muscles and tendons normally hidden underneath. "Holy Water," I whisper through gritted teeth. My fingers curl into a fist, nails digging into my healing flesh.

"What was that?" Father appears at my side. His red eyes are on me when I look up at him. I uncurl my fingers and present my palm, mostly covered now in blistering skin. He leans down and takes a deep inhale. His brows pinch together and he straightens, "What is the meaning of this? Soaking the chains in Holy Water?" His voice booms with both anger and curiosity.

The Slave Tamer's heart skips a few beats. "I-I apologize," he stutters, "I didn't think the princess would approach the werewolf-"

"Werewolf?" Mother stands, her interest piqued. She doesn't leave the platform. Instead, she cranes her neck to look over the group at us.

Father hisses, possibly only now seeing the wolf. "Why would you bring this ugly creature into my kingdom?"

"She's being sold to the Zombie King, your majesty," the Slave Tamer sputters. If his heart beats any faster, he might have a heart attack.

I shake my head, thoughts swirling around my brain. "No, she isn't." I smirk at the wolf's trembling body. "You're selling her to me." Father tenses next to me. "She could make a good guard dog during full moons. There's a full moon coming soon." I offer. If this mutt knows what's good for her, she won't attack me or Akantha during that time. Or ever.

Father grunts before going to the Slave Tamer. "I'll take these four," he gestures to four young female fairies, "and the fleabag."

The Slave Tamer visibly hesitates. Father's glare intensifies, and the human nods, stating his price. Father gestures towards the doors, "One of my guards will pay you at the gates to the kingdom."

Shackles are removed from the fairies and wolf who were purchased. The remaining unbought slaves follow their master out.

Father turns to me. All my insides twist and squeeze. I know that look. "Get the slaves cleaned up!"

The order isn't for me. Servants emerge from the shadows, gathering the new additions to our staff and lead them away. Father's gaze never leaves mine. He places a hand on my shoulder and squeezes. My shoulder blade cracks in half. Shards of bone tear through thin layers of muscle. My throat tightens and I clench my jaw.

His gaze darkens. "If that mutt steps out of line, it's your hide on the line." With that, he releases me and turns. "Out of my sight."

CHAPTER SIX

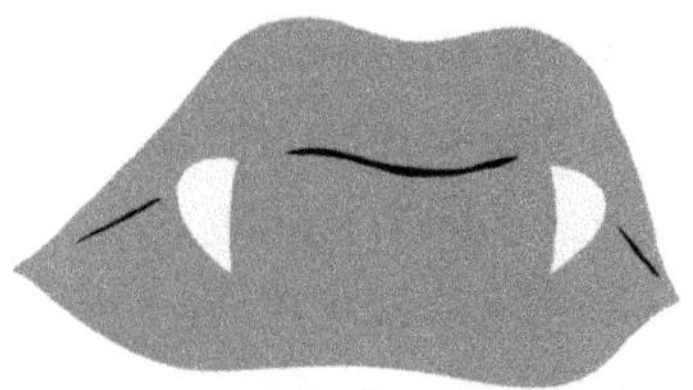

Akantha

THE SOFT SPINES OF books tickle my fingertips. I glide my appendages along the deer skins that bind all of vampire history, from the appearance of the first vampire—Dracula—all the way to my birth. Every law that has ever been written, changed, or erased is accessible in these texts. Deaths and wars are included too. In fact, they're described in great detail. My stomach turns every time Helena reads it to me.

"Akantha, are you listening?" The fairy asks from behind me.

I nod once, then look over my shoulder at her. Helena's aura illuminates the dark void of the library. "Indeed."

"Really?" Her tone is flat, but the way she emphasizes the last letter of the word is enough to give away her annoyance without having to see her face. The book claps closed. "Summarize."

Reaching out my hand, I step away from the wall of books and towards the labyrinth of chairs and tables.

"King Linus passed the official law that permitted the killing of Younglings at birth," the corner of a table jabs into my thigh. I clench my teeth.

She doesn't ask if I'm okay. It's not the first time I've walked into something tonight. "And?" She presses, her fingernail tapping against the spine of the textbook she's most likely cradling.

It's times like this I believe Helena is in a romantic relationship with these books and their history. "He was killed by his younger brother—Arnold—who took the throne and married Linus' widowed wife." The words make my stomach turn. Not only because Arnold married his brother's wife after making her a widow, but also because it reminds me of my own impending wedding. Part of me had always thought I'd be cast aside and forgotten, allowed to be taught by the Elder and maybe someday live freely. But no, every aspect of my life is decided for me, much like Callisora's. At least she has some illusion of choice, choosing between more than one man. I'm being assigned to one, it's not fair. I want to choose my own destiny, decide who I want to marry. Yes, I'm grateful that Father has arranged for me to be guided by the Elder and marry someone strong who'll protect me. But no one has ever asked me what I want. I'm not sure exactly what I'd choose, but having the choice would be nice.

Helena doesn't speak, her silence urging me to continue.

"Arnold fathered no heirs with his queen, but did father one with his werewolf mistress. He tried to lift the law stating his child had to die, but his request was denied. When his heir was born, it was killed. The wolf was so enraged that she later came into the castle and killed the vampire queen while she slept."

Helena takes a small breath. "What happened to King Arnold?"

"He was dethroned by one of Linus' heirs."

"Why?"

"Because his mental state dwindled after he was forced to execute his mistress." He later died of a broken heart, which is briefly mentioned in the text, but isn't gory enough to be part of my lesson.

"No, Akantha. It's because a king is nothing without his queen. The Vampire Queen is seen as the heart of her subjects. She keeps the king's intentions pure and his missions clear."

Doubt nips at the back of my mind, but I'm not sure what is wrong with that phrase. Have I heard it so many times that it feels fake? Or is my subconscious trying to tell me something?

"Anything else?" Helena pauses, then reiterates when I say nothing. "Anything else you'd like to add to your summary?"

I lift a shoulder in a half shrug and resume making my way towards her.

"War. A lot of it." Probably the reason I've been having those terrifying dreams. All the blood and death replaying over and over again as I sleep.

The fairy sighs. Her hand reaches out and takes mine, guiding me towards her. Her touch sends a comforting warmth through me. I stand before her now, her breath warm on my forehead. She cups my face in soft hands and tilts my head back. "You mustn't ignore your past and heritage."

Her words startle me, shift something deep inside. My past? "It isn't my past, or any of ours. It isn't our present either, so I don't understand why I need to learn about this."

Helena's head dips down and her forehead presses against mine. Her lashes make a slight breeze that stings my eyes with every blink. "History has a habit of repeating itself. What may seem insignificant now will be vital soon enough."

My mind flashes back to my dream. My head rolling. How vivid it all was. How I *felt* the blade slice through my skin.

No. It was only a dream—my imagination taking all this brutal war talk and turning it into something disturbing.

Helena releases my face and takes a step back, giving me room to breathe. When did the library start to feel so small? The ceiling is hundreds of feet tall, yet I'm somehow convinced I'll hit my head off it. The bookshelves line the far walls, but they seem to be closing in. My sense of special awareness dwindles.

"Akantha," Helena's soft voice brings me back. The room is tall and wide, a void of empty space. "Please consider listening to the next lecture. It's about the conflict with Wayfro. It's important information for you to learn before getting married to one of their princes."

My stomach tightens, and the room squeezes me again, caving in on itself to wrap me in a dire hug. "Right ... the prince."

The prince I'm being forced to marry. My blood chills, moving through my body slowly. This may be the only lesson that actually has some impact on my present.

She sighs, the book lands on a table. "On second thought, the lesson can wait. Let's check in with the seamstress. Your mother is throwing a ball to welcome the prince and announce your sister's suitors." She reaches for me and touches my upper arm, guiding me out of the maze of a room.

A ball? We had one less than a month ago. "She couldn't have combined it with the festivities for Dracula's hibernation anniversary?" The day that the first vampire went into hibernation. Callisora used to scare me with stories about how he was sleeping underneath the castle and that if we were bad Father would feed us to him. Whenever she told me those stories, she'd sneak into my room during daylight, when everyone else was sleeping, so she could sleep with me. Turns out she had scared herself more than me with that silly story.

"Of course not. Your mother enjoys celebrating events separately. Plus, it means you get to wear another luxurious gown."

I lower my head. Which also means I'd have to wear a corset and shoes. Who needs to be able to see and breathe anyways?

Helena links her arm with mine. "Besides, Princess Callisora's suitors being chosen as well as a werewolf entering our kingdom at the same time? What better reason to throw a party? I'm sure it'll be fun and relieve some tension."

Relieve some tension? It might do the opposite and turn everything upside down.

I inhale deeply through my nose. I shouldn't think so negatively. Who knows, maybe my fairy handmaiden is right. This might not be so bad. Inconvenient, yes, but terrible?

Chapter Seven

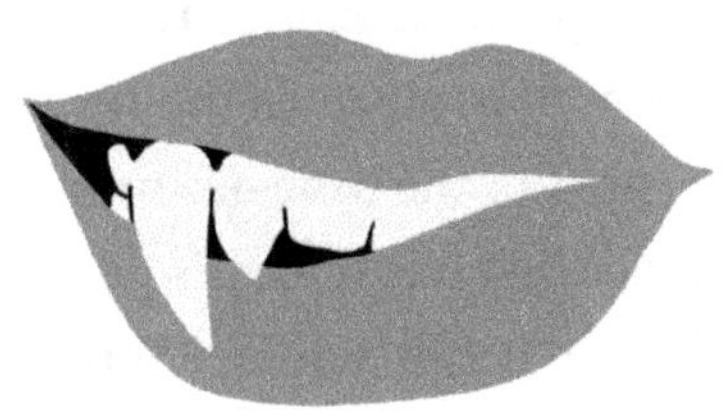

Farran

The smooth stone walls stand tall on either side of us. The halls curve and break off at many points during our walk, exposing the vast amount of corridors in this labyrinth. It won't take long for me to get lost in here.

My wrists itch and I scratch at the flaky skin. My new burns are nearly healed, and since they aren't healing while I'm still wearing the silver, the skin isn't scarring. Though, the old scars still remain.

Hungry.

I cringe, my gaze glancing at the fairies around me. The glittery skin of my fellow captives isn't healing as quickly as mine. Their blistered necks, ankles, and wrists make my mouth water.

One of the King's pre-existing fairy servants, one with lime skin and blue hair, stops at the front of the group and turns to face us. I stumble to a halt. Her bright green eyes travel over all of us; they linger on me for a moment longer than the others, then continue on. "You will all be staying in this room with the rest of us. You'll have a bunk assigned to you."

A vampire dressed in silver armour approaches us. The leech stops next to the lime-skinned fairy, careful not to brush up against her with his poisoned armour.

The fairy offers a gentle smile. "You will all be following me. I'll show you where to get cleaned up and dressed," her eyes land on me again. "The wolf will be going with Sir Vladimir," she gestures to the vampire next to her.

The mob of fairies walk off, leaving the vampire and me alone.

Kill him before he kills us.

I swallow. Could she be right? Could the princess have bought me just to kill me?

Sir Vladimir's brown eyes travel over me, surely taking in every inch of my battered, dirty body. He finally makes eye contact with me. "You'll be staying with the fairies at night, but you'll be getting cleaned up in our showers," he turns his back to me and begins to walk down the hall, "Let's go, wolf. I don't have all day."

His dry tone makes my stomach clench tighter. I follow.

We head down more twisting corridors and past a thick door with a rectangle cut in it. It's barred.

Inside appears to be dark. The stench of body odour and metal oozes out of the small window.

"That's the dungeon," Sir Vladimir explains, seeming to know what I'm looking at without looking back at me. His black locks brush against his shoulders, thick with sweat.

I nod having heard of dungeons from the Slave Keepers. They'd often taunt the fairies, threatening that they'd be thrown into the fairy dungeon, because they were turned without the permission of their monarch. That the fairies' wings would be ripped from their bodies and pinned to a wall. Or that the dungeon masters would cut and burn their wings, slowly torturing the fairy.

Humans are cruel. However, if those stories are true, then perhaps all creatures are.

Sir Vladimir stops in front of a door and I nearly bump into him. He glances over his shoulder at me before pulling the door open. He leads me inside to what appears to be a tavern. A bar is set up along the far wall, lined with stools. Booths litter the rest of the room. The aroma of alcohol-injected blood, along with sweat and other body fluids, hangs thick in the air. No one else is in here, most likely all on patrol or resting for the day shift.

I follow the leech through the room and down another hall, this one lined with doors. Possibly sleeping chambers? At the end of the hall is a communal shower. My stomach drops. Is he going to watch me bathe?

Sir Vladimir enters the open space.

"Get cleaned up. There are clothes right here," he gestures to the pile of fabric heaped on a stool that matches the ones by the bar. "I'll be down the hall. Join me when you're done. I'll be sure to see that you get fed before seeing the princess."

My stomach growls in approval, and my wolf howls happily in my mind, the sound echoing. I hold back a cringe and nod, "Thank you."

He nods in return and heads down the hall. "Leave your clothes wherever. They'll be discarded later."

I wait until he's down the hall and out of sight.

The stone room is damp. Condensation sticks to the smooth rocks, slithering down the walls and dripping from the ceiling. Small spouts stick out of gaps in the stonework. A brass handle resides a few inches below. After peeling my poor excuse for clothes off my body, I go to one of the handles and turn it. Water pours out of the spout. It's cold at first, but quickly warms up. Clumps of dirt chip off my body without protest. Running my fingers through my thick locks, I try to get as much of the matted hair wet as I can. Two bottles sit on the floor—one for body and the other for hair. A cloth sits next to them, folded into the shape of a thick square. My hair gets washed twice, then my body a few extra times. I scrub at the skin until it's raw and red, then rinse.

By the time I'm done, my skin tingles, and my scalp feels less irritated. Walking across the room, I grab a towel and pat my body dry. Then I reach for the clothes. The fabric is soft, but the colors are muted.

Pulling on the outfit, I struggle to find the proper holes for my arms and head to go through.

After it's taken me far too long to slip into what I now realize is a dress, I add the belted accessories and the shoes to my new look. Smoothing my hands over the long, tanned skirt of the dress, I step out of the shower room and head down the hall.

A mirror catches my eye. Stopping halfway down the hall, I peer into the doorway of the empty bedroom. Quietly, I tiptoe inside to the head-to-toe mirror that leans against one of the walls. I haven't seen my reflection in so long, possibly since I was a child.

A woman with messy brown hair and orange eyes stares at me. Orange eyes? They're supposed to be brown.

Hungry.

Right. I need to feed. The orange of my eyes matches that of the sheer orange shawl draped over my shoulders and dips down to my navel. The grey dress has no straps and dips down between my breasts. It hugs my hips and falls down to my lower calves in the front and back, but covers nothing along the sides. If it weren't for the tan ankle-length skirt under it, my entire legs would be exposed.

My head tilts. The colors compliment my skin tone, but imagining this outfit on a brightly colored fairy? My heart aches. There's no way they'd enjoy having the sparkle of their skin hidden under such bland colors.

"Enjoying yourself?" a deep voice asks.

Instead of looking in the mirror to see who's speaking, I growl, and spin, my teeth sharp and nails turned into claws.

The leech in the doorway seems unfazed and unamused. Sir Vladimir looks me over: "You done? I have work to do, you know."

My body relaxes and I clear my throat. My teeth smoothen, and claws retract. "Yes, I'm sorry."

He nods and turns away, leading me out of the room and down the hall. I adjust the straps of leather that cover my body, securing a pouch to my hip as well as a blue cloth to my waist. We walk through the bar, where a few vampire guards now reside, drinking tall glasses of a thick reddish brown liquid. The stench of blood and booze hits my nose again, and I don't protest when Sir Vladimir opens the door for me to leave.

Stepping into the hall, I'm already lost.

Sir Vladimir doesn't wait for me as he marches down the hall. I follow.

The door to the dungeon comes into view. We pass it, and I calm my inner wolf as well as myself. He's not taking me somewhere to die. At least, not yet.

After turning down a couple of halls, we arrive at a set of double doors. One of them flies open. A female fairy rushes out, wearing the same outfit as mine. Her yellow eyes lock with mine for the shortest of seconds before she dashes past us. My gaze doesn't follow her down the hall, though; it fixates on the doors. A mix of delectable scents fills the air, but fades away as the door swings shut.

Frozen in place, all I can do is watch. Thankfully, Sir Vladimir catches the door and opens it wide, allowing the smells of fried beef, steamed vegetables, and baked potatoes to dance their way up my nose. My stomach grumbles as I enter the busy kitchen.

Seven male fairies rush around the kitchen. They gather ingredients, do prep work, and bring food out the door we had just entered. Another fairy stands in front of the ovens, watching over multiple boiling pots.

Sir Vladimir walks me to the island that stands in the middle of the space. He clears his throat.

The male fairy by the oven lets out an aggressive sigh. "I already told you, Megan, lunch is almost ready. And if you ask me again, I'm going to *accidentally* drop your food on the ..." he turns around, his body stiffening at the sight of the leech next to me. The last word in his sentence slips out, "... floor."

I glance up at Sir Vladimir. His dark brow is arched, and is that the hint of a smirk? His eyes meet mine and then shift back to the male fairy. "New recruit," he states, gesturing to me.

The fairy rolls his dark eyes. It's strange; I've never seen a fairy with hair that doesn't match his skin. Black locks fall just above his ears, but his eyes and skin are an off red. "Yes, I know. I'm making meals for all the new servants. Send her to the dining hall to be served." He turns his back to us.

"She's a werewolf. I doubt the meal you're preparing would satisfy her."

The fairy's body visibly tenses. He gazes over his shoulder at me. Those dark red eyes of his look me over.

"Oh?" He spins around, a large grin spread across his lips. "In that case, I will personally make sure she eats."

He may be smiling, but his tone and twitching eyebrow give away his annoyance.

Sir Vladimir nods. "I'll leave her with you, then. I have more important things to do."

"So do I," the fairy grumbles.

The leech turns and walks back the way we came. "She's Princess Callisora's new pet, so treat her well," he calls without looking back, and then he's gone.

Silence engulfs the space. The pots boil over, but the red-skinned fairy doesn't look away from me. He clears his throat, his eyes travelling up and down my body. "So, werewolf, what are you hungry for?"

My mouth waters. "Meat." The word comes out deep and husky, the voice belonging to my wolf.

He seems unfazed by the voice and walks to the freezer. The fact that humans so willingly share their technology with the creatures of the Dark Forest is surprising to me. I'd overheard some of the Slave Keepers talking about a peace treaty that humans had formed with us monsters. Humans share technology and we don't eat them. Of course, there's still the odd monster who breaks the rules, but the humans aren't extinct.

Dante opens it to reveal a stockpile of frozen beef, pork, and chicken.

My stomach tightens. I clear my throat. "Do you have anything ..."

Alive.

"... fresher?" Eating a living creature will help me gain my strength. The fresher the muscle, the better. And if I can sink my teeth into a still beating heart—my mouth waters at the thought alone.

His gaze flickers over me again, then he nods. "Follow me." He leads me out a back door.

"I didn't know vampires ate human food," I say, attempting to spark a conversation.

"They don't. They drink blood. We don't normally feed off human food either. It's not filling. But we aren't able to sustain our natural food source here."

I shoot him a side-eye. I'd never actually seen the fairies at the Slave Camp feed. Sure, the Slave Tamer had fed us all food, but human food was never enough to satisfy. "What do you normally eat?"

He gestures to a barn. "We're here."

Frowning, I follow him into the small red barn. He slides the door open, and as if by magic, it looks three times bigger on the inside. Sheep, pigs, cows, deer, horses, and the odd chicken all reside within the structure. My stomach rumbles, and my wolf howls within my head, ready to feed. My feet travel down an aisle of their own accord. I stop in front of a pen with a doe lying in some hay. Reaching over the door, I unlatch It.

The fairy's hand touches mine, stopping my movements. He locks the gate again, shaking his head. "Not her, she's expecting."

I swallow the lump that's formed in my throat. My hand tingles from the brief contact with his. "I understand."

"Good!" He nods once, then turns. "Follow me," we walk to the back of the stable. "We mainly use the animals as a blood supply for the royal vampires. Whenever one gets too old or sick, we kill it and use the meat for our own meals."

He stops in front of a stall that houses a cow.

The black and white creature lays on its side, its breaths slow and deep.

"She's nearing the end of her road. You can eat her."

I don't have to be told twice. My fingers work the latch, flicking the small rusty hook out of the loop. The door creaks open, and the animal doesn't move, but its eyes watch me. Dark voids meet my orange ones. The cow snorts at me and looks away.

She's ready.

I've never fed off a living animal before. Will it cry out? Will it try to resist? Will the other animals panic?

Kneeling next to the cow, I take notice of her deep breaths. She's not afraid of me. Does she know what I am? What's about to happen to her? Though, based on what this fairy has said, she's probably accustomed to creatures coming into her pen and taking from her.

Black eyes look at me again. They seem impatient like she has better things to do than lay here and wait for death. A low *moo* escapes her.

I take a breath and place a hand on her tight skin. She closes her eyes in response.

Allowing my wolf to come free hurts. My teeth stretch to a point, jaw pops out of its socket and grows before reconnecting. My fingers crack and expand as nails become claws. My throat widens, the bones popping and cracking as it does. I don't allow the wolf to emerge fully, only enough, so I have the power and ability to kill this poor creature.

Before the cow has a chance to open its eyes and glare at me again, I strike. My teeth dig into its windpipe, cutting off its air intake. Apart from the body tensing, there's no reaction. The animal lets me kill her.

The body goes limp, and I can't hold back. My wolf takes the reins and bites down harder on the cow's throat. My head jerks away. Flesh and muscle tear, and I sit there with the animal's esophagus hanging from my mouth. Devouring it is easy. My claws then dig into the chest cavity, searching for the main source of sustenance.

The fairy shifts on his feet behind me. I glance at him. He's covering his mouth and nose with a handkerchief. Is he disgusted? Probably.

"You don't have to watch."

His dark brows pinch together. "And leave a werewolf with my livestock? An un-housebroken one at that? Definitely not."

I refocus on the chest cavity and all the stringy chunks of flesh. "I have a name." Breaking the ribcage is easier than I expected.

"Most do." His calmness sends a chill down my back.

Digging into the lifeless animal's body, I grip the organ I've been searching for. I use my nails to cut the arteries that hold it secure, then remove it from the cow. The heart sits still in my hand, small veins covering it. I imagine how it must have looked while it was still beating. How it moved, squeezing, and releasing. "I'm Farran."

"Dante."

I nod once, then take a bite of the heart. Its tender and just the rich taste of it alone is enough to lull my wolf into submission. I swallow. A chunk of ventricle remains lodged in my teeth, but I dig it out with the tip of my tongue and swallow it whole. I take another bite.

One of the wooden pillars creaks. Glancing out the corner of my eye, I see Dante leaning on it with his arms crossed. He doesn't seem disgusted after all. He's staring at the body. His already red eyes seem somehow brighter. As if feeling me watch him, he looks away. "So, you've been taken in by the princess?"

My stomach tightens, but I force another chewed-up chunk of aorta down my throat. With a nod for confirmation, I consider what my new Master would be like. Would she be as heartless as my old one? Would she torture me? So far, I've been allowed a full animal as feed, but what about after this? How often would I be fed?

"May I offer a bit of advice?"

I turn towards him, the half-eaten heart clenched in my hands, "Please."

Less desperate.

I clear my throat and try again, "Of course you may."

The corner of his mouth lifts. I barely see it due to the angle at which he's standing, but the smile lines are clear on his cheek. "The Princess is a fan of finer things. Animal blood isn't to her taste. Human blood, however, is. She's practically addicted to it. If you can feed her, she may be kind to you." He glances at me a moment. "I don't know what she has planned for you, but it may be best to be in her good graces."

I swallow the lump that's formed in my throat. *Her good graces?* "Thank you for the advice, Dante."

CHAPTER EIGHT

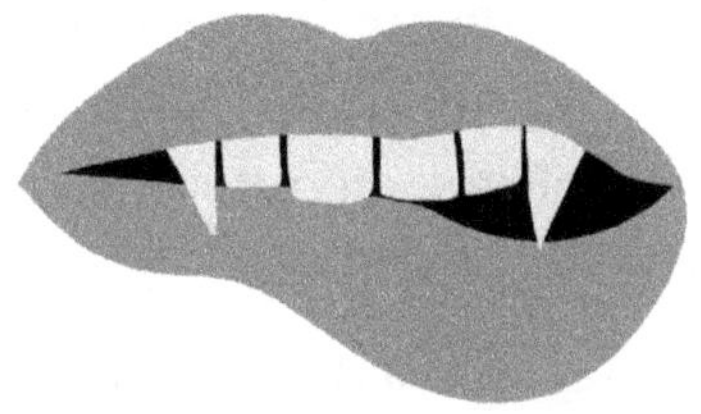

Callisora

MY DRESS FALLS TO the floor. I step out of the fabric heap and kick it to the side.

I snatch the white dress shirt and black pants from the back of my wardrobe. The shirt fits nicely over my corset, and the pants hug my hips. My fingers comb through long chunks of waved hair, lifting it up at the back of my head to be tied with an elastic. The long curls come together and spiral down my back. I pull on a pair of knee-high black boots and tie the laces.

Opening the thick black curtains that shield my room from the morning's sun, I look out at the Dark Forest. A thin layer of mist hugs the ground, filling the spaces between trees and hiding the worn-out pathways that lead to cottages and beloved meadows.

My hand presses against the thick glass, and I lean into it. The window opens slowly, welcoming the warming breeze into my chambers. I take a deep breath. I'm often awoken by the evening air, but find the mornings delightful. Not many of us get to enjoy the feel of the sun on our skin and a warm breeze through our hair. I peek my head out the window and down at the distant ground. I push myself up onto the window ledge. The wind lifts my bangs, allowing them to dance across my forehead. A deep breath of air enters my lungs. I hold it and then jump.

As I fall, I tuck my right leg up under my butt while extending the left. I've found doing this aids in my landing and allows my descent to be more graceful. My body cuts through the air. The ground gets closer and closer.

My left foot hits the ground, followed by my right and then my hands. While regaining my balance, I grit my teeth at the pain shooting up my left leg. My eyes close, breathing slows. I don't move as the bones reform, clicking back together in their proper places.

The pain eases, and I stand, eyes open. I'd learnt long ago that putting all the shock of my landing on one leg hurts less and took less time to heal than it did for both legs. It would take even longer if I didn't feed in a long while, which I also know from experience.

I've also learned not to leave by the main gates at sunrise. My bodyguard is notified and hunts me down much quicker that way.

My legs move quickly though I hobble at first. By the time my pace is regulated, I'm at the wall that surrounds Valdama. I'd found a hole in the wall when Akantha and I were younger. We used to sneak through it and pick flowers that bloomed on the other side. We are grown now, and she has a garden filled with flowers, so we no longer pass through the opening together. I, on the other hand, still use it, though it's a tight fit.

I squeeze my body through the opening. Jagged stone scrapes against my bodice, but doesn't cut through my clothes or skin.

Emerging from the other side, I smooth the fabric of my top. There's a bit of dirt stuck to it, but I pay it no mind. Where I'm going, the company is filthier than my clothes could ever be.

I take slow, careful steps as if any broken twig or odd rustle of leaves could notify the kingdom of my departure. But honestly, I do this every dawn and hardly ever get caught. The thrill of being free and hunting my own kill is exciting. The restraints are gone and I can fuck who I want. Drink from who I want. I don't have to listen to the kingdom's rules or worry about marriage. I can breathe.

Once I've travelled far enough into the density of the Dark Forest, I break into a sprint. Though this daily outing is freeing, it also has a time limit. Knowing my personal guard, he'll be checking on me by mid-day. I need to be back before then.

Thanks to my natural speed, I zip through the weave of forestry. I slow and step out of the line of trees that shield me from sight. A mist-covered river separates the Dark Forest and all its monsters from the humans and their land. The only way to cross is an ancient bridge made of stone.

Slightly north of this bridge is the Zulmar—the Zombie Graveyard. Where many humans—and some creatures of the night—bring their loved ones who've died too soon. The Zombie King is known for resurrecting the dead, but I've heard that they don't always come back the same.

South of the bridge is Mermaid Lagoon. A body of water that is rumoured to house a colony of mermaids. I've never seen one myself, but I also don't have a death wish. Mermaids are said to be aggressive creatures who lure men and women alike. They sing their song, get you close to the water, have their way with you on the shore, then drag you underwater and eat you.

The sound of my boots tapping against the bridge's stone surface echoes in the darkness. The sky has lightened in color, but the sun has yet to show itself. The streets are paved with black asphalt, making the roads look like rivers of thick tar. The first step onto the substance always chills me, reminding me of my irrational fear that it will liquefy and I'll fall in.

Light illuminates the street. Tall poles with flickering flames that dance inside large glass lanterns stand along the edge of the road, guiding anyone caught out after dark.

Each of us live in a world of our own creation. As vampires, we like to feel we are above everyone else by dressing and living our lives as if we reside in the Middle Ages. Fairies lean into the more magical side of things; their clothes and lifestyle are more whimsical. The werewolves live in huts and cabins, but dress like the modern day human. Even though we all live such varying lifestyles, we live in the same world and somehow manage not to kill one another. The sharing of resources probably assists with that too.

Voices call out in the night, their words slurred. I follow them.

Two men stand outside a rundown pub, both sporting scruffy beards and round beer bellies. Their bulbous bodies stand on either side of the entrance, surely blocking it on purpose.

I step towards them, my jaw clenching, preparing to engage in whatever drunken advances they swing my way.

Their hearts beat slower than the average human, surely an effect of a lifetime of drinking. I know they've spotted me when those sluggish pumps of muscle quicken. I meet their eyes, which are as wide as an owl's, with reddened sclera.

One of the men, who's sporting a black long sleeve shirt and brown trousers, speaks first. "Hey beautiful," his words slur to the point where it sounds like a thick accent.

The other, who's wearing a red shirt under a grey jacket, speaks next. "What is a fine young lady like you doing out this late? Surely you know how dangerous it can be."

My teeth clench. I am that danger, you drunken fools. I force my lips to spread into a smile, "I am well aware. I'm merely here to have a good time."

Black shirt straightens, "In that case, perhaps you ..." he hiccups. “Perhaps you'd like to come back to my place? I can offer you the best of times."

Red shirt scowls, "Oh please, you're too drunk to walk home, let alone entertain the young lady," his dark eyes focus on me. "I, on the other hand–"

I raise my hand, cutting him off.

"It's very kind of you to offer, but you two aren't my type," my smile grows into a sneer. "Perhaps when I've lowered my standards."

Without giving the bumbling idiots a chance to respond, I push past them and enter the pub.

The door slams behind me. Voices and laugher hit me like a wave, only to be replaced by silence. The whiplash of tone makes me dizzy.

All eyes are on me as I approach the bar. Whispers replace the quiet. I take a seat next to a young man with blond hair and a grey jacket. He doesn’t look at me. Well, he doesn’t face me, but his eyes watch me from the corner of his vision.

I tap the top of the wooden bar. My stool’s thin cushion is worn out, causing the wood under it to dig into my bottom.

“Morning, doll face!” The bartender walks over, his beefy hand stuffed inside a glass along with a cloth. “What can I get ‘cha?” He rests the glass in front of me.

The foggy glass stares up at me. How many mouths have touched its rim? How many greasy fingers have wrapped around its girth? I fight the shudder that creeps over my body. "The strongest thing you have." Not that it'll affect me.

With a nod, he reaches under the counter and retrieves a dark bottle. With a twist of the cap and a tilt of the bottle, my small glass is filled.

"Thanks."

I curl my slender fingers around it, warming my skin to the touch. Lifting the glass to my lips, I down the liquid. The bland taste is underwhelming. Even the bitter undertone that nips at my tongue is hardly noticeable. It burns my throat for less than a second. I make a face, disappointed. How could anyone like the flavour? Or perhaps it's the side effects I don't feel that they enjoy.

The bartender watches me down it, then refills the glass and moves on to the next customer.

The man next to me sends another side-glance, then lifts his hand to flag the bartender. "I'll have what she's having. And you can add her drinks to my tab."

The bartender nods, grabbing my neighbour a new glass and pouring the brownish liquid.

He straightens his jacket before lifting the tiny glass to his mouth and taking a sip. His body shudders as he forces a swallow. He coughs and finally turns towards me. "Strong stuff you're drinking."

I shrug and down my second shot. Licking my lips, I give him a once-over—blond hair that's combed back, a red shirt pokes out from under his jacket. His pants aren't too tight or too loose. He doesn't seem to have a beer belly, but the jacket could be hiding the start of one.

Taking my challenge, he downs his own drink. The glass slams against the table, but doesn't break. He pants, his face twisting into a bitter expression. Pathetic.

"Wow," I rub his shoulder. "That was impressive." I force my eyes on his. Most well-fed vampires are capable of luring their prey, tricking them into doing as they wish. I'm not as skilled at it as my father, but I'm still able to get a drunken horny man to follow me home. Not that I'd have to try hard anyways.

He grins a set of straight, lightly yellowed teeth at me. "Want to get out of here?" He's not bad looking, but not as handsome as some of the men I've welcomed into my bed.

I stand without hesitation. Blood is blood, and blood laced with alcohol is definitely a treat. I can already taste the dopamine-laced bitterness washing over my tongue. "I'd love to."

Now standing too, he takes his wallet from his pocket and removes a few bills. After placing them on the counter, he turns to me. He doesn't have a chance to say anything before a glass is thrown across the room and explodes off the back of his head. His pulse picks up for a moment, then stops. Body gone limp, the man falls to the floor, blood oozing from his scalp.

The bar goes silent.

My stomach tightens at the sight of my meal being spilt over the grimy wood floor. Anger swells in my chest, making it hard to breathe. My gaze snaps to a group of men who roar with laughter. I clench my teeth and stroll over to them. "Who threw that?"

The group of five humans are all seated at a round table. They look up at me, their dirty faces still painted in amusement. One of the men stands. He's well built, as are the others. Perhaps they work in the mines? Or are builders? It doesn't matter.

He crosses his arms over his broad chest. "I did," his eyes flicker over me. "A beautiful woman like you shouldn't be leaving with someone so ..." he pauses. "Inferior."

I manage a sweet smile, "Is that so?" I walk up to him, "and you think that you're a suitable match for me?" I taunt.

He puffs out his chest. "Of course. I could show you a good time."

Reaching out, I grab him by the shirt. Lifting him off the floor with ease, I dash across the bar and slam him into the wall. Napkins float up off the tables as we pass and drift onto the floor. My eyes burn, and I see the reflection of my red irises in his glossy eyes.

Those eyes widen, and his heart picks up in pace. "V-Vampire."

I sneer. "Still think you can handle me, tough guy?" Whispers spread through the bar. Surely other monsters visit the pubs around here, searching for a feed, but they don't normally announce their presence like this.

He doesn't speak, just shakes his head. The look of pure terror cloaks his face.

"You cost me my dinner," I hiss. "Perhaps you should take his place."

He finds his voice. It's shaky and stuttered, "P-please d-don't kill me. I-I have a wife and kids."

Disgust fills me. He's married and is in here hitting on women? I should save his wife from having to live with swine like him. I open my mouth to speak, but a scream cuts me off.

"Werewolf!"

People scatter, knocking over chairs and tables, scrambling, and bumping into each other, trying to flee out the back of the building. My eyebrow ticks, and I release my prey, preparing for a fight. The man stumbles to his feet and follows the others, no doubt grateful for the distraction.

I turn towards the entrance of the bar, rotating my shoulders and shaking my hands to loosen up my muscles.

Sure enough, a wolf stands in the doorway, although it seems smaller than I'd imagined. It's definitely larger than a wild wolf, but not the seven-foot human-wolf hybrid I expected. This one looks the part, but is smaller, maybe six feet. Its orange eyes lock with mine. A jolt of energy runs through my body as my muscles tense and then release. My brain throbs against my skull, feeling like it might burst out of the confined space before it settles back down.

The wolf blinks, breaking whatever electrifying state it'd shot through me. What was that?

"Master." Its mouth doesn't move, yet I still hear it. *"I'm sorry for scaring away your feed."*

I narrow my eyes, realizing who it is. The werewolf my father had purchased upon my request. She's already becoming an issue. I step towards her, "How dare you come here?"

The wolf's head tilts. *"You bought me as a guard dog, did you not?"*

My nose scrunches. "For the full moon. You don't have to come anywhere near me until then, you little–"

She lowers her head and whimpers, *"I apologize, but I only wanted to keep you safe. This is no place for a princess."*

My teeth clench. How is she even talking to me? Aren't werewolves only able to communicate with other werewolves in this form? Perhaps that's what that zap was? Was she creating some sort of bond with me?

"*Please,*" her voice is meeker now. "*Let me make it up to you with a meal. I know where there are plenty of humans who no longer deserve life.*"

I arch my brow. So, it's revenge she wants? I smirk. Perhaps this wolf's a good investment after all.

CHAPTER NINE

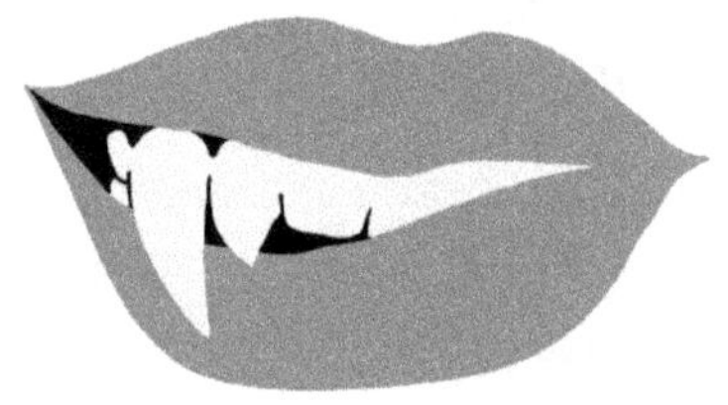

Farran

FOLLOWING THE FAMILIAR STENCH of sweat and burning wood, I track down the slave camp. My old home. Although, I suppose it was never a home, more of a place in which I'd lived. Perhaps someday, I'll find a true home for myself.

Once we've crossed the bridge and re-entered the Dark Forest, I shift back into my human form and slip back into the clothes I'd been wearing.

"How much further?" The princess demands from behind me. Her footsteps are heavy, crunching leaves as she walks. Is she getting tired? Or losing interest?

I look up. Spots of the purple sky are visible between the leaves of the tall trees. It's surely past the leech's bedtime. "We'll be there soon," my voice sounds more sure than I feel. I've never had to track anything before, but the scent of the camp is growing stronger, so that must mean we're getting closer.

She sighs, but says nothing else. We walk on.

Voices cut through the quiet dawn. We both stop to listen. The voices are deep, masculine.

The princess presses her back against a tree. I crouch behind a bush. We make brief eye contact. She presses her finger to her lips, ordering me to stay silent. I nod. We both peer out from our hiding spots.

Sure enough, we've found the camp. A dozen single-man tents stand amongst the clearing, surrounding the one large one that houses the slaves. The little fairy girl's face crosses my mind. I could free her. I could free all of them.

Focus.

Right. I need the princess on my side first. Then I could fantasize about ridiculous things like freeing slaves.

Guards walk the grounds—all of them men. Some dip into their tents to get some sleep during the day, others coming out for their shift. The day shift is the easiest since everyone is sleeping. I'd stayed up a few times throughout the day and could hear the guards fooling around with young women they'd taken home from the pubs or ones who'd wandered too far into the forest. Guards who weren't going to pound-town got to lounge around, whereas the night shift had to feed and tend to the slaves.

One of the guards walks towards us, heading for his tent. He runs a hand through his shaggy blond hair and yawns. Like most of the humans who work for my old master, he wears blue jeans and a grey top. His shirt is tight across his muscled chest, but that could be a sizing issue.

Callisora steps out from behind the tree.

“Wait—” Maybe this isn't a good idea. What if she gets hurt? Or killed?

The princess glares over her shoulder at me. “Stand guard.” She carefully walks towards a forest path and follows it closer to the camp.

The guard, who had turned towards the flap of his tent, stiffens when the princess steps on a twig. He spins on his heel to face her, his silver blade out and at the ready. But when his eyes land on her, he falters.

Her hips sway as she approaches him. She reaches out and touches his blade. "Careful, you could hurt someone with that." The princess's voice is soft and seductive. I'm almost tempted to come out from my hiding spot to hear her better.

He swallows, "I ... I apologize, miss. I thought you were ..." he trails off. "What are you doing out here? It's dangerous to be out here alone." He looks towards the trees as if to see if she's alone, which she's not.

She touches his chest, running her fingertips down it, "I came into the forest for a stroll and found myself lost. I'm so relieved to have come across your camp."

His gaze focuses on her again. His Adam's apple bobs. "You must be tired from the long walk. Please," he opens the fabric door to his tent, "come in and rest a moment."

"Well, aren't you just the sweetest!" She glances over her shoulder briefly, casting me a glance, then enters the tent. He doesn't seem to notice and follows her in.

I let out a breath and relax behind the bush. I rub my sweaty palms on the skirt of my dress. My fingers ache from being clenched into anxious fists. I didn't even know that was a thing I did when I was nervous. The princess' tone echoes through my mind. It's not long before her moans reach my ears. My eyes close. I take in the sweet scent of the morning dew and the distant sound of horse hooves hitting the ground.

Frowning, I open my eyes. Horse hooves? Sniffing the air, a familiar scent welcomes me, but I'm unsure who it belongs to. I stand and duck behind a tree, waiting for the stranger.

CHAPTER TEN

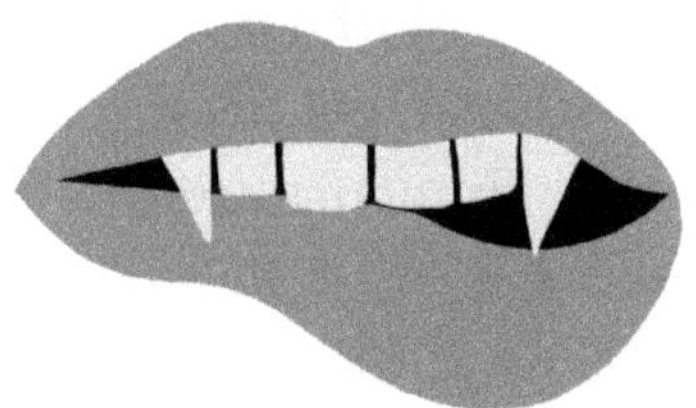

Callisora

THE PAVILION REEKS OF sweat and feet.

A thick blue sleeping bag lays across a cot, along with a worn-out sheet that seems to be substituting for a pillow. A nightstand stands next to the poor excuse for a bed. The blond haired guard lights the lantern that sits atop the wooden surface of the nightstand. Its light flickers, casting shadows across the fabric walls.

I'm lost in the movements of the flame. It dances freely, but is not truly free. Just like me. As long as it's trapped within the lantern, and I'm trapped under my father's rule, neither of us will ever be free to burn brighter.

An arm wraps around my waist and my body tenses. Thick fingers rest on my stomach, pulling me against a firm chest. His hard manhood pokes at my lower back. "What's your name, sweetheart?"

I turn to face him. My arms drape over his shoulders. "No names," I look at his lips. They're dry and cracked, but his pulse is steady. He seems to keep himself in good health. "Only sex." And then a feed.

His cheeks pinken. Without hesitation, his beefy hands cup my buttocks and lift me. I jump a little, giving myself enough momentum to wrap my legs around his waist. His lips collide against mine. His tongue breaks through the seal of my lips. Tongue grazing against my own, he carries me to the bed. Saliva drips down my chin, having escaped from the sloppy kiss he's leading me through.

My back presses against stiff fabric. The loose fibers scrape against my skin, making it itchy. He breaks the kiss, allowing me to surface for air. Kneeling over me, blondie lifts his shirt off over his head, exposing his bare chest and minimalistic abs. In response, I unbutton my blouse, taking my time to both teach him and preserve the shirt. I pull the fabric away, exposing what little visible skin can be seen. My corset earns me a disapproving grunt.

"Keep going," I order through gritted teeth. My body buzzes with need, though it's not his cock I desire. I'm hungry, but I can't bite him until his brain has released that glorious sex drug, tainting his blood, and making it more savoury than sweet.

With a nod, he moves off the bed to remove his jeans. I unbutton my black pants and lift my butt as I wiggle out of them. All too quickly, he climbs back onto the cot and makes himself at home between my legs.

His erection presses against my lower lips in anticipation. It throbs as he moves it along my slit. He reaches between us, using his fingers to spread me open. Clearly, this man has never heard of foreplay or has never had to warm a woman up before. He lines his tip-up with my entrance and forces his entire length inside me.

I cringe at the discomfort.

He thrusts, his hips moving to a rapid rhythm that slowly stimulates me. He groans, planting a hand on either side of my head, "You're so tight."

I roll my eyes. Of course, I'm tight; I'm a vampire. Our bodies are twisted pieces of sexual art. But seriously, another sex talker? Can't men just shut up during the act? It would be far more enjoyable.

He tilts his head back, eyes closed, moaning and groaning. I move my hips with his, holding back an annoyed sigh. The bottom of my corset digs into the flesh of my abdomen and breaks the skin. The scent of blood, even though it is my own, amplifies my pleasure and awakens my hunger. A moan escapes my own lips. I wrap my arms around him, and he shifts his upper body down.

He breaths heavily in my ear. The sound is annoying, and I close my eyes to ignore it, focusing on the movements of his hips as his cock glides in and out of me. I move my hands up and down his back, hoping he'll get the hint that I want him to move faster. He doesn't.

Moving his head to my neck, he plants small kisses along my flesh. I tilt my head to the side, giving him better access even though it does nothing for me. I've never understood the need for useless neck kisses.

He twitches inside me. "I'm close," he grunts. His body moves faster, thrusting into me harder. Perfect.

I grip him tighter, wrapping my legs around his waist, and pull him into me more. My fingers grip at his hair and shoulder, exposing his neck to me. My mouth waters at the sight of the veins that rise up against his skin. I lick his neck, allowing some of the venom that fills my mouth access to his skin. My fangs stretch out from my itching gums. His moans grow louder. I wait for the right moment, watching his vein as it rises and falls with every thrust, then bite.

He freezes, "Wh-what?" Perhaps I waited too long, and the numbing is wearing off?

I move my legs, forcing him to keep moving. He doesn't hesitate. His hips resume their rough thrusts. My fangs retract, and the blood flows. A desperate moan echoes through me. A needy, hungry moan. I swallow mouthfuls of blood. The thick liquid heightens everything I'm feeling. My eyes roll back. My core tightens, and I cry out in pleasure. Body tense and twitching, a wave of ecstasy flows over me.

He pulls out and releases himself onto the bedding below us. His body relaxes.

I regain my composure and lick the wound. Listening to his heartbeat, I confirm he isn't dead. He might be by dusk, but for now, he lives. Rolling him off me, I stand and pull my shirt closed. The dainty buttons refastening with ease. I pull on my pants and stretch my arms over my head.

With a sigh, I take the vial of blood that hangs around my neck and empty it of the now spoiled blood. If I were to step out into the sunlight with blood that isn't from my most recent feed, the magic wouldn't work, and I'd burn to a crisp. Holding the vial to the man's slowly healing wound, I capture enough blood to fill it.

Stepping out of the tent and into the light of dawn, I catch sight of my werewolf in the dense trees. She seems to be speaking with someone.

As if sensing me watching, my wolf's gaze snaps to mine. Her brows pinch together, and a frown tugs at her lips.

Glancing around, I make sure no one is coming. Surely someone had heard us, but maybe not? Maybe they didn't want to interrupt?

The coast seems clear. I rush back into the thicket and to her.

I hear it before I see it. The light thudding of an impatient horse's hooves as they beat the ground, but seeing the black stallion and its rider still startles me. Hadn't I been careful when leaving Valdama? Yes, I had been. Had the wolf?

The werewolf rushes to me and opens her mouth to speak, but I cut her off with a raise of my hand. The guard atop the steed looks down at me, his eyes glowing red with irritation.

I smirk in amusement, "Don't you ever get tired of fetching me, Sir Vladimir? I'm sure you have better things to do with your time." Yes, I despise him constantly hunting me down, but seeing how annoyed it makes him does bring me a small amount of joy. This is his own fault. If he hadn't found Akantha and me one evening while we were playing outside the kingdom walls, he wouldn't have been assigned as my personal guard.

His lips curl into a sneer. "Not at all. It's a pleasure to be pulled from my duties and hunt you down as the sun rises nearly every morning," he demounts his horse and offers me his hand. "Now, I suggest we return home before your father thinks me incapable of my job."

"Oh, we wouldn't want that," I taunt, accepting his hand. He pulls me close, but not too close. My heart pounds in my ears. The feel of his hand around mine sends shivers down my spine. It feels so comforting, so protective. Removing his hand from mine all too quickly, he lifts me by the waist and helps me mount the horse, gliding my body through the air in a swift motion.

He rises onto the horse. His chest pressing against my back. Even though he's covered in armour, I can feel his strong chest as it rises and falls, and hear the pounding of his heart as his muscular arms wrap around me to retrieve the reins. How would his chest feel without all the armour? I shake my head at the thought.

The horse begins its journey through the Dark Forest and my werewolf follows behind us. My mind drifts, thoughts of tonight's event flooding in. I push them aside, only to have them replaced by another thought. *The ball.* I'll be meeting my suitors at the ball. I lean back against my guard, allowing the swaying of our bodies atop the horse to lull me into a false sense of security. I'll never be free, but at least I can enjoy this a little longer.

Chapter Eleven

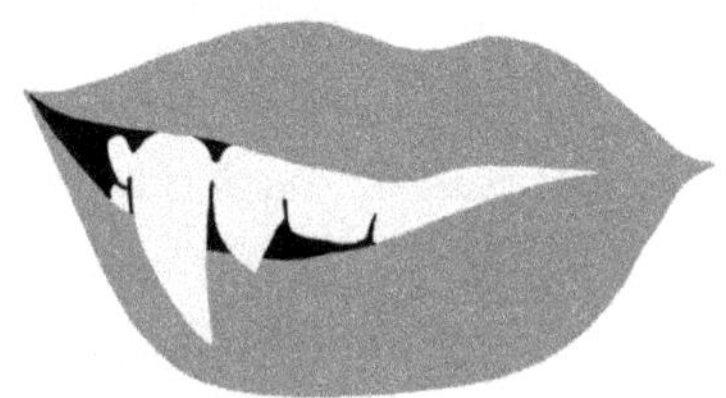

Farran

Princess Callisora acts strange around this leech. She talks to him, teases him, and he does the same back. She seems very comfortable around him.

I follow behind the horse, my eyes trained on Sir Vladimir. My fingers drag along the scarred skin on my wrists.

The walk feels longer than it is. Perhaps the horse is taking its time? Or Sir Vladimir is?

Saying I am surprised to see this leech in particular come to retrieve the princess and myself would be an understatement. Perhaps that's why he was the one who'd escorted me to the showers, because we both are tied to the princess' safety. Or rather, he fetches her when she runs off, and I was purchased to act as her guard dog during full moons. But what am I to do when it's not a full moon? Do Sir Vladimir and I share the responsibility of protecting her? Possibly.

We arrive at the gates of Valdama. Two large wooden-plank doors open for us. Two guards are stationed in lookouts at the tops of the stone walls, whereas six others work the ground. They watch us, smirks of amusement across their lips. Do they see this often? Sir Vladimir rushing out at the dead of day to retrieve the eldest princess?

The sun's light brightens the gloomy gothic kingdom. Small houses stand amongst the shops and streets, all looking worn down and neglected. How can a kingdom so large and seemingly well off, look so barren and dead?

Guards roam the streets, their armour shimmering violet. Surely a spell had been cast upon their gear so that they wouldn't roast in the daylight.

We approach the front steps to the castle, steps I had climbed only hours ago. The horse stops, and Sir Vladimir whispers gentle words into the princess' ear. She stirs, her body pulling away from his and sitting up on its own.

The two get down from the steed. Sir Vladimir helps her down by lifting her by the waist. She doesn't thank him. Her rudeness doesn't seen to bother him, but instead makes him smile.

Callisora turns away from him and climbs the steps.

I bow my head to Sir Vladimir, thanking him silently, then rush up the steps after her.

The princess pauses at the doors to the castle. She glances at me from the corner of her eye. "What was your name again?"

My throat tightens. She wants to know my name? That's a good sign, right? My heart pounds against my constricting chest.

"You don't have to get so excited. I'm merely asking your name. Or do you want me to forever address you as wolf?"

I swallow, "Of course not, Master. My name is Farran."

"Never call me that again. 'Princess' is fine," she frowns.

With a nod, I reach for the door and open it for her.

Callisora walks ahead of me, leading the way down the long corridor and into the throne room, where the king sits upon his throne, waiting.

His red eyes land on us, and he stands. The princess and king walk towards each other without exchanging a single word. I keep close to the princess, sensing the tension in the air. It's clear by his deep frown and narrowed eyes that Callisora's little adventure outside the kingdom is not something he approves of.

The two meet in the center of the room. The king raises his hand. My stomach twists and my heart thumps in my ears. I've seen this stance before. That look. This scene.

Stop.

Without a second thought, I pull the princess out of the way. The king's hand cuts through the air and collides with my face. Bones shatter on impact. The force of his assault sends me flying into a pillar. My back cracks. I fall to the floor in a heap of pain. Bile rises in my throat, but I swallow it down. The room spins. My ears are ringing.

My spine pops back into place, but isn't healing fast enough for me to stand or even sit up. Sound returns to the room.

"Wretched creature," the king hisses in my direction, his red eyes drilling into me. "You are meant to keep an eye on her, not go gallivanting through the forest as you please. Disappoint me again, and you won't live to see the next moon." His threat sends my head spinning again.

"O-Of course, your majesty," I squeeze my eyes shut, trying to ease the pressure in my head, "My apologies."

He shifts his attention off me, and my head feels light again. "Take her away!"

At first, I think he's talking about the princess, but then I'm being lifted by two fairy servants and carried out of the throne room.

I'm carried down a series of halls. They all look the same, yet I somehow know where I'm headed. A door creaks open, and the smell of freshly washed linen overwhelms my nose. I rub at it, but the scent burns even more and my eyes water.

My back sinks into the squishy fabric of a cot. Another hangs overtop me. My vision blurs again. I close my eyes, trying to relax as my body heals itself.

Footsteps approach me. The cot sinks as someone sits next to me. Opening my eyes again, a golden-skinned fairy with silver eyes and hair comes into clarity. "Name?" She places a hand on my slowly healing cheek.

"Farran," my voice shakes.

She nods. Her hand warms my cheek, then burns. I pull away, but she increases the pressure of her touch, "Don't move, Farran."

My gut clenches. I can't breathe.

By the time her hand starts to cool down, I'm panting. She lifts a wooden bowl up off the ground and rests it in her lap. Clear liquid swishes over the edge as she does.

I crane my neck, trying to see in as she dips a rag. "What's that?"

"Water," she rings the cloth, then wipes it against my numb cheek. "To wash away the blood."

She returns the fabric to the bowl. I touch my cheek with a shaky hand. It's smooth. No signs of broken bones. No pain.

"How did you ...? "

"I healed you. It's a gift." She stands and waves her hand through the air. "Now, roll over. Let me see your spine."

I frown. "I can heal myself."

She shakes her head at me: "You are malnourished. Your healing is slow and insufficient. Now, roll."

With a sigh, I do as she says. Shifting onto my side, I grit my teeth as she presses another burning hand to my back.

The fairies who'd carried me in speak, but I don't understand them. The one healing me responds. I focus harder on their words, but it's no use. They're speaking another language entirely. Perhaps their native tongue? But how would servant fairies know it?

I swallow.

"What's your name?" I ask when she pulls her hand away.

"Helena," she answers in a soft tone. I move to sit up, and she places a hand on my shoulder. "Rest. Your body needs it. Her highness won't need you until dusk." She stands and walks across the room to what I assume is her cot.

The room is filled with at least fifty bunks. There are two doors, one that I was carried in through, and the other—I assume—opens to a washroom?

Other fairies climb into their beds. I stare at the bed above me. When no one climbs into it, I find myself strangely at ease. My eyes close. My body aches, but the pain is a dull one. The warm pain is enough to remind me I'm still alive as I drift into darkness.

CHAPTER TWELVE

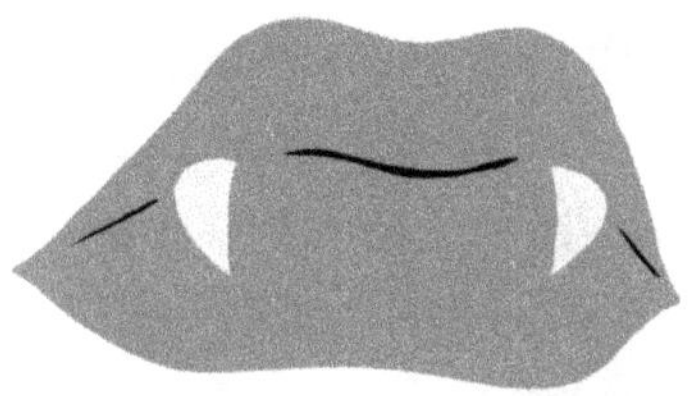

Akantha

MY HEAD RESTS ON the edge of the tub. Water covers my body. I shift and water spills over the rim, drizzling onto the floor. I'd awoken extra early this evening and took it upon myself to draw my own bath. The task was surprisingly simple.

A soft knock, then the door to my room creaks open. "Lady Akantha?"

"In here," I call.

The tip-tap of her shoes echoes through the room as she crosses it. Once around the privacy divider, she sighs, "What are you doing?" Bony fingers dig into my underarms and lift me. More water hits the floor, but then the liquid sinks deep into the tub. "You could drown," her voice falters.

I shiver as water drips from my body. My feet touch the floor and I regain my balance. Sometimes her strength is alarming. "I'm not a child. I can run my own baths, Helena."

"It's my duty to keep you safe, well dressed, and clean."

She moves to the left, then returns. I'm wrapped in soft fabric. Her hands move up and down my sides, drying my damp skin. "Have you thought about what accessories you'll be wearing tonight?"

I inhale a deep breath through my nose. Ahh, yes, what am I going to wear to the ball? What would I be seen in when my fiancé spots me? The seamstress had allowed me to choose what I wear with my dress, which Helena called *simply gorgeous*. Which means it is precisely that—simple. But the opportunity to decide for myself is appreciated.

Callisora enters my mind. What would my sister do in this situation? A smirk spreads across my lips. I cross the room and pull open my wardrobe. "I'm engaged to the youngest son of the Werewolf King. I should be dressed in something natural."

"Natural?" I can hear her frown. "I'm not sure I understand what you mean."

Fingers gliding along stiff fabrics, I stop on one. A gift one of the guards had acquired for me for my two hundredth birthday. A shawl made of bear fur.

Helena gasps when I remove the shawl from its spot amongst the rest of my clothes. "Where did that come from?" She takes it from my hands. "I thought I threw this ugly thing away."

She had, but I'd managed to get it back. It wasn't a traditional gift for a princess. Despite that I'd kept it, because it was the only gift any of the staff had given me. Someone had thought of me, apart from Helena.

"I think it's perfect. Wayfro has plenty of bears," which is probably where the shapeshifting tradesmen had got it from. "And if I wear this, then it'll show that I've accepted the arrangement," which I haven't, but that's beside the point.

"Your parents won't like this," Helena protests.

My lips press together. Mother's blue aura comes to mind, along with father's grey. Unease settles in my chest, will they be upset? "They won't be looking at me. They'll be focused on Callisora," one of the perks of my older sister being so rebellious.

The bear fur shifts in her hands; she sighs, "You're going to be the death of me, child."

With that, we work at getting me dressed. "Is there any way I can get out of wearing the corset?"

"My Lady ..." It comes out as a sigh, "You may not think your parents will be watching you, but they will be. As will others. It's not appropriate."

I pout my lips and widen my eyes. The lack of blinking makes them water. "Please?" I'd discovered at a young age that Helena struggles to say no to me when I'm on the verge of tears.

She lets out a small grunt, "Fine! But If anyone asks–"

"I'll take full responsibility," I insist, stepping into the gown. Helena pulls the fabric up my body. My arms slide into the sleeves, and I'm tied into it. The shawl is draped over my shoulders, the rough fur tickling my cheek. Helena brushes and braids my hair.

She takes a step back: "Beautiful!"

Chapter Thirteen

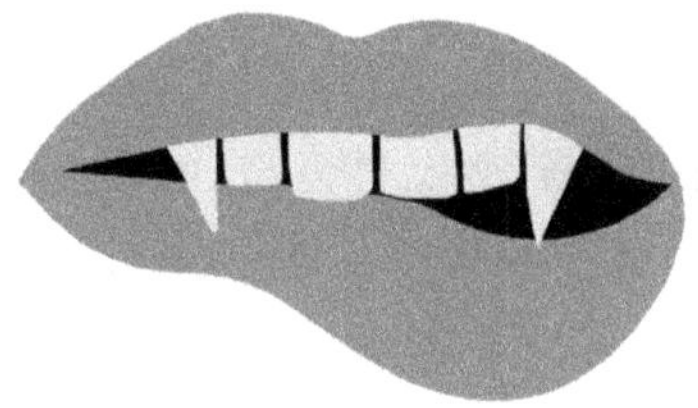

Callisora

A knock comes from my bedchamber door.

"Enter!" I place my hairbrush on the vanity.

A green skinned, blue haired fairy walks in. "Your highness," she dips down into a curtsey. "I have come to fetch you for the ball."

I wave a hand over my shoulder. "You may rise."

She does, the straw blue curls that frame her face bouncing. The majority of her hair is in a tight bun, but those few strands seemed to escape somehow.

"Do you mind?" I glance at my hair in the enchanted mirror. The spiraling waves have been brushed, but not yet styled. I don't mind the look, but Mother wouldn't approve.

"Oh, but your highness, it looks so lovely down!"

I glare at her through the mirror, annoyed.

"You dare tell me what looks best?"

I'd much rather go to the ball like this, but I'd rather not be punished by Father in front of an audience.

She lowers her gaze to the floor. "I apologize. It won't happen again."

"Best not!"

I hold my chin up high. She approaches and ties my hair up into an intricate style that requires bobby pins to be slipped between the locks. It's heavy, but maybe an over-the-top hairstyle will deter any suitors from pursuing me. It's doubtful, but appearing to be high maintenance could work.

When she finishes, I stand and exit my bedchambers.

The heels of my shoes pound the floor as I walk down the long halls with the green fairy next to me. We approach the tall oak doors that stand between me and the ballroom. Butterflies nest and breed in my stomach. The doormen pull the slabs of oak open as I near. Their heartbeats fill my ears. I glance over one of the men and his heart flutters.

Stepping inside, I'm reminded of why mother loves this room so much. Tall cathedral ceilings, floor-to-ceiling windows that overlook the glowing blue floral in the garden, and all the assortment of colors that our guests wear. It's not hard to depict the kingdoms; fairies dress in bright pastel colors, vampires wear darker gothic colors, and werewolves are dressed in neutral. It's not often that the Zombie King and his princess join our balls, but even they dress up as best they can.

When I was younger, the crystal chandelier that hangs low in the room used to awe me. The way it reflected the light and colors from the dance floor onto the tall white walls would take my breath away. But now, the decoration seems pointless. Why hang something that no one pays attention to? No one here is watching the aurora borealis dance across the room.

Mother strolls over. Her tight black dress shows off her wide hips, plump buttocks, and enlarged chest while also paying tribute to her small waist and narrowing thighs. Her dark hair flows over her shoulder like a rippling waterfall. Small jewels intertwine with thick locks. Nothing but perfection.

She stretches her arms out to me. "Callisora, you look gorgeous," her hands rest on my shoulders, and she leans in to kiss my cheek. "Don't embarrass me," she hisses in my ear, then pulls back. Mother links her arm with mine and walks me towards the refreshments, a pleasant smile plastered across her thin lips.

I scan the room, searching for a familiar heartbeat, one slow and boring. "Where's Father?"

"Speaking with the guards," she answers all too quickly.

Not believing the lie, I nod. I'm unsure if she believes it herself or if she just doesn't want to let her perfect appearance be tainted by the fact that my father is probably in a broom closet with a fairy wrapped around his cock.

Mother walks me towards a tall vampire with long blond hair: "He is the son of Duke Harris. So be nice."

Not giving me time to respond, she clears her throat loudly enough for the handsome gentleman to turn around.

His brown eyes land on Mother first. A charming smile crosses his lips and he takes her hand. "Your majesty, you look ravishing this evening!" His lips press against her knuckles.

A strange sound escapes my mother. A giggle, and her cheeks pinken. "Oh, why, thank you, young man. Aren't you too kind?"

"I only speak the truth, your highness."

The pink spreads to her ears. Mother glances at me, an annoyed glint in her eye, but then it vanishes. As if she's remembered, I'm here and that he is my suitor.

She looks back at him. "This is my daughter, Callisora." She gestures at me. I'd much rather be ignored while the two flirt shamelessly in public, but alas, this is my fate.

His smile grows into a grin, "Princess," he bows his head to me. "I've heard such wonderful things about you."

Liar.

Taking my hand in his, he draws close and kisses my knuckles. How original. "Princess, my name is Viscount Carlos," long white blond strands of hair fall over his shoulder.

I'm tempted to keep him bent down like this. How long until he grows impatient and straightens without his princess' blessing? His eyes look up at me, the brown orbs a massive contrast to his pale lashes. Between his look and my mother clearing her throat, I know it's time to allow him to stand straight.

I force a smile, though it's only a small one. "Your Grace, I've heard such wonderful things of your father. He serves the King's Council very well."

I don't actually know this. Father has only ever spoken poorly of his Council, but it should be enough to please Mother and hopefully get me out of this conversation faster. "Aren't you next in line for his seat?" Another fact that I'm guessing. Most upper-class wouldn't dare pair their second born with the eldest princess.

He rises, a grin across his face, his ego lifted. "Please, Carlos is fine. And indeed I am. But the chance to meet you is a far greater blessing."

I seriously doubt that.

"Yes, well, it was nice meeting you," I turn to leave, but Mother grabs my arm and turns me to face him again.

"Why don't the two of you go dance? I'll send your second suitor your way when he arrives."

I grit my teeth and play it off as a smile. "What a lovely idea!"

Carlos seems to agree, as his smile appears to be growing brighter. He takes my arm and walks me to the dance floor. People part, making room for us. He turns, facing me, and rests a hand on my hip. Securing my right hand in his left, he takes the lead.

"So, your grace–"

"Carlos."

I ignore his interruption. "Does your father enjoy being a part of the Council?"

"I believe so. He hasn't spoken poorly of it, to my knowledge."

He's not looking at me. His gaze is focused on something—or someone—behind me. It's rude, but I do my best to ignore it.

I focus on his words, doubting that what he's saying is true. My father isn't the easiest to get along with. "And are you excited to take his seat?"

His nostrils flare, and his eyes meet mine. "I suppose I haven't thought much about it, to be honest."

"I would suppose not," given how he is here to marry me and become king. We dance in silence, swaying to the music. He twirls me around, then draws me back in. "Do you happen to know anything of my other suitor?"

His eyes glance up as if the ceiling or massive chandelier had the answers he was searching for. "I've heard that his father is part of the King's Council, just like my own."

That doesn't surprise me. Where else would my father find strapping young men to take over his throne?

"I'm afraid I don't know much else. Suppose it'll be a surprise to us both." Carlos grins at me again. That charming grin of his makes me sick. My stomach turns, and anger levels rise. I want to punch him in his pretty little mouth and watch as his jaw heals out of alignment. "You must feel quite privileged, princess; two men pining for your hand in marriage. What a blessing."

More like two spoiled snobs fighting for my father's throne and power. "I don't have much of an opinion on the matter."

"Pity! It is your future being gambled, is it not?" His hand moves to the small of my back, and he dips me. Brightly colored fabrics move around, swaying and twirling. I'm brought back up. He presses me close to him, my chest against his.

His lips are now near my ear. "Whom you'll be bound to for eternity."

I pull my head back, retracting away from him. I look his face over. A face that is still far too close to mine. "I never agreed to being bound to anyone."

The bonding ceremony takes place during the wedding of two vampires. It's a ceremony where they drink one another's blood in order to bind their souls together so that they can find one another even after death, when they're reincarnated.

"It's tradition," his eyes aren't on mine. They're focused lower. On my lips or cleavage, it's hard to tell.

"No, it's tradition for me to marry."

A light chuckle escapes him, "It's tradition to bond with someone you love."

I frown at that. "Love is not part of this arrangement."

His eyes meet mine, then look beyond me, then meet mine again; a devilish smirk plays at his lips. "We'll see," he releases me and bows. "It seems our time is up, princess. I look forward to our next dance." I nearly fall over from lack of support, but regain my footing quickly enough.

I curtsy in response, glad to rid myself of this arrogant buffoon. I will not fall in love with him or my other suitor. I will not bond my soul to another and give up even more of my freedom.

Carlos walks past me, headed back towards my mother. I watch him as he strolls over and makes conversation with her, making her laugh and blush. How embarrassing.

"Careful, people might take that scowl as jealousy," a familiar deep voice ripples through me. I turn to find Vladimir standing before me. He's wearing a suit that's as dark as his hair and a red button-up shirt instead of his guard uniform. I almost don't recognize him. If it had been any other guard, I probably wouldn't have.

I clench my jaw, looking him over more. His shoulder-length hair is slicked back and proper-looking, exposing his chiselled jaw. The top few buttons of his shirt are undone, showing off his toned chest and giving me high blood pressure. "Don't you just look all clean and tidy?"

Vladimir chuckles. He offers a hand out to me. "May I have this dance?"

Giving him a skeptical once over, I accept his outstretched hand. He draws me in, one strong hand planted on the small of my back and the other cradling my own daintier hand. He lets me lead the dance. I swallow. "So, are you my mysterious second suitor?"

He takes the lead, speeding up our steps and gliding me across the dance floor to make room for a new couple who've arrived. "I suppose I am." He doesn't look at me. His eyes seem to move around the room, as if looking for danger. His body is strangely tense. Is he still in guard-mode? Does he ever relax?

"I didn't take you as the marrying type. Or as a Duke's son."

His eyes meet mine for a moment, then break away again. "I chose to turn my back on my position as his successor so I could be a guard. I felt it was a more active way to protect the kingdom. But I'm still his eldest son."

I nod, understanding the responsibilities that come with being the first born. "So, you're being forced into this situation just as I am." It's good to know that my father isn't the only controlling one.

He nods. "Only difference is ..." the hand on my back releases me. I spin away from him, then return into his arms. "Only difference is that I won't be married by the end of this."

I arch my brow. He's forfeiting so soon? Is that why Carlos had seemed so cocky? He knew Vladimir's his competition and had no fear of him fighting for the crown. I can't allow that to happen. Call me self-centerd, but I want to be fought over. "I suppose you're right. You're a guard—a warrior—not a king."

A fire lights in his eyes. Too easy. "And what's wrong with a strong king?" He presses his hand harder against my back, pressing me up against him more fully. I feel every muscle through the fabric of our clothing. And the lump between his legs. It leaves me breathless.

I swallow. "An aggressive king is not a strong one." I take a breath, calm my nerves. It's just Vladimir. I've known him since I was young. He is not someone I should be taking this much notice of.

His face gets closer to mine. "Hmm, is that so?"

My core begs for more. For him to be closer, but that isn't possible with all these clothes on. I clear my throat, "Let's focus on getting this dance over with," I reclaim the lead.

He dips his head down, his lips close to my ear, "What's wrong, princess? In need of another feed so soon?"

I shiver. No, but I am in need of release. That human from the slave camp was useless. I can't tell him that, though. "My feeding schedule is none of your business, guard."

"Oh, but your majesty, it is!" His smooth words tickle my ear, his breath warm against the exposed skin of my neck. "I've watched over you since you were a mere two hundred. Who you devour is my business," his hand moves up my back, causing a chill to rise up my spine faster than his fingers ever could. "And who you sleep with is my business too, as your suitor."

I close my eyes, enjoying his closeness and touch. I hadn't expected him to feel so sturdy against me. I'd fantasized a few times, but that was it. I never thought

I'd be in his arms like this. My eyes open. No, I can't let him win me over this easily.

"It's only your business if you're on the list of those being bedded and devoured."

A heartbeat pounds in my ears. Is it mine? Or his? "Well then, I suppose I'll have to get myself onto that list." Without warning, he pulls back.

My eyes widen, and I look upon the face of the creature that holds only one of my hands now. I sway, but he doesn't fully release me until my head has drifted back down from the clouds and re-entered my body. "P-pardon?"

He says nothing, just smiles. Now that we aren't pressed against one another, I can tell that it's his heart racing. Though mine is doing some strange backflips as well. His eyes dart away towards a servant's entrance. "That's probably your best chance at escaping tonight." He winks at me before pulling away to vanish into the crowd.

I stand there a moment, the sudden separation from him leaving me feeling tattered. He wants to be on my list. He wants me to bed and kill him? That can't be right. Surely, he's teasing me. He just said he wasn't interested in pursuing me. Or is he only not interested in marrying me?

Laughter fills my ears. I look over my shoulder to find Mother still chatting with Carlos. Father is still nowhere to be seen. This really is my chance to leave early.

I weave through the mob of guests, heading towards the door Vladimir's eyes had guided me to.

Once out of the ballroom, I lean against the wall. My hand rests over my pounding heart. What was that? Had teasing him about not wanting to be king really led to that?

Heat radiates from between my legs. When had I ever felt this aroused without hunger being tied to it?

One of my hands moves up my stomach to my breast. I squeeze and massage it. My other hand drifts lower. I struggle to press it between my legs. Lifting the gown would be too much of a hassle, but feeling nothing through the layers is agonizing.

A male fairy walks down the hall. Judging by the bright green dress shirt and matching pants, he's not one of our staff. His orange eyes land on me, and a blush crosses his already pink-glittered cheeks. He quickly averts his eyes.

"You, come here. What's your name?"

He stops walking and swallows. "Anthony, your highness. I am one of the Fairy Princess' successors."

"So, you're a prince." I arch my brow.

The fairy looks at me confused, then understanding seems to strike him. He nods, "In your culture, yes."

Right, the monarch of the fairies is the Prince or Princess. They don't have a title that surpasses that. Their heirs are known as successors or just heirs. Strange group of monsters. "Well, how about you put that mouth of yours to good use and get over here." He hesitates, but walks over. He must not be very high on the successor list if he's this willing to follow orders. "On your knees."

He falls to one knee before me, his eyes focused on my skirt in a way I know all too well. The lust that fills his eyes blooms in my core with far greater intensity.

I grip a handful of fabric and lift it. He aids me and dips under the fabrics. Soft hands touch my thighs and I quiver. His breaths are heavy, as is his heartbeat. Has he ever done this before? He doesn't make it very far before we're stumbled upon.

Vladimir—tall, dark, and annoying. He walks over with his arms crossed over his chest, "I didn't think someone like the princess could be shaken to the point of grovelling for attention."

The fairy below me flees from the shelter of my skirt, dashing down the hall and sending me off balance. Vladimir catches me and draws me into his chest.

My throat tightens. My tongue is too big for my mouth. I glare up at him, but don't pull away. His touch sends waves of heat through me, each one crashing into my core and making my need for a man—any man—stronger.

His heart beats a steady, strong beat as if my touch doesn't affect him in the same way. So, what was that in the ballroom? Was it really only my own heart pounding in my ears? Shame.

Vladimir guides me to the wall and sandwiches me between him and it. His brown eyes look me up and down. "You should be careful, or others might think you're easy."

My chest tightens. A rib jabs at my heart. Easy? How dare he. "And so, what if I am?"

He smirks at my challenge and leans in closer. His nose brushes mine. His eyes focus on my lips, and I look to his own mouth as he speaks. "I know you better than that. Yes, you throw yourself at men, but you carefully choose who you sleep with."

I laugh, but the sound gets lodged in my throat as he presses himself against me more. His firm chest and the hardness between his legs make my head spin. Normally I'm the one in control; how had he become the dominant one in this dynamic? When did the tables turn? "I'd appreciate it if you didn't make judgments of me."

The truth is, I choose men based on necessity. The disgusting Slave Keeper was proof of that.

One of his hands trails down the side of my body. I want to grab his hand and show him where I want to be touched, but I don't. Not only because he's pinned against me, but also because—well—I'm not quite sure. He's my guard. I shouldn't be feeling these things for him. Plus, that would only encourage his behaviour. "You should go before someone sees us like this."

He smirks and moves his face. His breath mixes with mine. His lips whisper a touch to mine, but they don't actually meet.

"If you get another urge to order someone onto their knees to pleasure you, you know where I'll be." With that, he pulls away from me. He clears his throat and repositions the bulge in his pants.

If I weren't already breathless, the bulge would surely take my breath away. Why'd I waste my time with humans if vampires were so well hung?

The reason is simple—I don't want to get pregnant. Being a female vampire of Dracula's bloodline, I can only be impregnated by another of the same species, which is exactly why I choose humans, and why I spoke to the fairy. Vladimir and Carlos are dangers to my womb. Mainly Vladimir. Carlos seems to be more interested in wooing my mother.

"You should head back into the ball. Your parents will be looking for you."

I frown. So, he's going to tease me and then send me back in there? "Or you could escort me to my room?" and then leave.

He chuckles and shakes his head, "I may be here as your suitor tonight, but it's still my duty to look after you. And I'm not escorting anyone to any bedrooms tonight." He gestures back to the ball.

I cross my arms over my chest and march back into the ballroom. Carlos appears out of thin air, "Ahh, so Sir Vladimir found you," he grinned, "Come, let's dance." He takes my arm. So, Vladimir had been asked to find me? No wonder he recoiled his tip on my escape. I get a glance at Vladimir before I'm dragged back to the dance floor. I barely hear Vladimir's heart again, but I do. A smirk spreads across my lips at what I hear.

He's jealous.

CHAPTER FOURTEEN

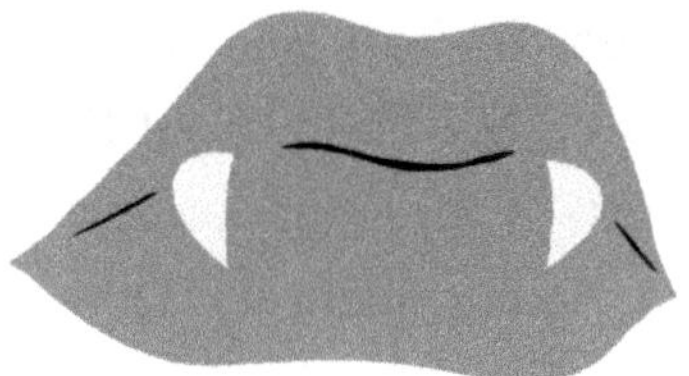

Akantha

"WE'RE SO VERY LATE," Helena pants as she rushes ahead of me, the tapping of her shoes echoing off the stone walls. She pauses a moment to wait for me to catch up, then rushes ahead again.

I don't hurry, which seems to panic her more. "You act like the ball will end before we arrive." As much as I'd like it to. "I'm meeting my future husband; Mother won't let it end until that happens. Even if it carries over into daylight."

"Oh, the ballroom would look lovely drowned in sunlight," she sighs with contentment. Her shoe catches on something and she stumbles. "Oh, my Lady, please watch your step." She reaches out and takes my arm, carefully walking me past whatever she had tripped on. "And about your Mother, though I'm sure it's true that she'd keep the ball going, I don't think it's polite of you to make her and your fiancé wait so long."

I let out a heavy sigh, trying to ease the nervous knots in my chest. "Yes, I suppose you're right."

Helena pauses a moment, halting her urgent mission of getting me to the ball. She takes both my hands in hers, facing me. "My Lady, about the marriage ..." her voice trails off.

I tilt my head, "What about it?" Does she think it's a breach of my freedom too? Will she offer to take me away from here? We could live in hiding. She could teach me how to do things. What a simple life we could have. I'd miss my family, but I'm being forced to leave them either way.

"I may be incorrect, but I don't believe I'll be accompanying you to Wayfro."

My heart stops. The lack of blood flow makes me lightheaded. No. This can't be happening. Not only am I losing all freedom, but I'm also being forced to leave without Helena? "What do you mean? I can't go without you."

Who will read to me? Anchor me to the ground when my head is lost in the clouds?

"Wayfro doesn't keep slaves, and they don't hire fairies. I'll most likely be assigned a new task here." She speaks slowly, her voice quivering.

I shake my head. "No. I'll speak with my fiancé. Surely he'll allow you to come with me." Perhaps I should butter him up before requesting such a large favour. I don't give her time to protest. My decision has been made. I resume walking towards the ballroom, now with more purpose and determination.

Helena follows after me, now struggling to keep up. "Open the doors!" She calls.

The doors open, the only sound being the grunts of the doormen pulling.

Music and conversation mix to make a roaring clatter of sound, assaulting my ears. I barely register the doors closing right behind us.

Helena links arms with me and escorts me down the twenty steps. I glide my free hand along the railing as I descend, counting every stair until I've reached the floor. "Are you alright?"

I nod.

Someone says my name, but it mixes with the other noise, bouncing off the walls and hitting me from all directions. Multiple auras mix together all around me, some vibrant and lovely, others dark and wary. Helena leads me towards an aura I recognize—my mother's. The ocean of blue ripples as glints of yellow swim in random directions.

My ears are ringing. I strain to hear what she's saying, but it's no use. Between her excited fast-talking and the gazes that are slowly drawing towards me, I can't focus. The eyes of so many others, all of them unseeable to me, graze over my body in one fell swoop They assess me. Judge me.

Finally, a sound of mother's does reach my ears. A gasp. She touches the fur shawl, "What is this?"

"It's bear fur, your majesty," Helena speaks softly. "Lady Akantha insisted that it would show the Wayfro Prince that she has accepted his hand in marriage."

Mother makes a disgusted noise.

"I think it's genius," Father's voice booms. He's not louder than the music, but loud enough that I can fully hear him. One of his heavy hands moves to my shoulder. "Such a wise choice, my dear."

I offer a smile. Helena releases my arm and my father takes my other. He glides me across the dance floor.

"Your Mother suggested that we have you meet the prince somewhere less overwhelming. I disagreed until I saw you walk In."

Is that why people were staring? Did my face give away my discomfort?

"I've asked him to meet you in the garden. But do not fear, there will be eyes on the two of you, assuring he does not harm you and vice versa."

What harm could I cause? It's amusing that he could think so little of my ability to take care of myself, while at the same time be worried that I'd hurt someone. Or perhaps he's only humouring me.

He opens a door and leans in, whispering in my ear, "And don't think your mother missed that you aren't wearing a corset. She definitely did. Try to hide your little acts of rebellion better. She's watching for them."

I smirk and am handed off to the arm of a guard. Stepping out of the ballroom, I'm engulfed in the refreshing scents of bloomed flowers. A chilling breeze kisses my face, carrying with it the smell of the woods. A scent I don't often encounter.

I'm led down one of the many garden paths. This one is filled with extremely strong scented flowers. Helena often complains that their colors aren't as bright, but I like them more for their noticeable perfume.

The guard stops, "Helena will be out shortly," he whispers, "If you need us, just call." I nod and release his arm. We walks back the way we came.

I swallow the lump in my throat and step forward. I round a corner, the smell of trees and earth becomes stronger.

"Hello!" A man's voice cuts through the darkness. My heart jumps into my throat, making it hard to breathe. I step into the opening, where the flowers circle around a canopy. I've explored the garden enough to know where I am based off the smell of the flowers alone. Sure enough, standing near the only bench is a tall man with a green aura. Brown waves twist their way through the green, almost like vines growing in grass. He continues speaking, his deep voice shaking me to my core, "I'm Liam, youngest of the Wayfro Princes."

I curtsy and bow my head, "It's a pleasure, your highness. I am Akantha."

"Princess Akantha," he corrects, though it sounds more like a question.

"Yes—well—I'm the second born, so I'm not addressed by such a title."

"You are daughter to the king and queen, correct?"

My body tenses, "Well, yes ..."

"Then you are a princess. Simple as that." He approaches. A large hand takes my own, "Come, sit!" He tugs me forward gently. I'm guided forward to the bench. We sit, the warmth of his body wrapping around me. He drags his fingertip over my knuckles. "So, I've heard some very interesting rumours about the second princess of Valdama."

"Oh?" I look up at him, trying to make out what his facial features would look like. Does he have a crooked nose? Broken countless times from wrestling with his brothers. A strong jaw? One that complements the brilliant glow of his eyes, what color do they have? All vampires have brown. Do all werewolves have one set color as well?

He leans in; his breath tickles my cheeks. My nose wrinkles from the sensation. He lifts a strand of my hair and toys with it. "Of course, there is talk of your beauty." Is he flirting with me? "But the rumour that I find much more interesting is the one about your sight. Is it true? Can you not see?"

My throat constricts. I look away; the chunk of hair he was playing with tugs at my scalp. I nod once. I'm so used to everyone knowing. Having to admit it to a stranger feels strange. Unnatural.

Prince Liam stands. He moves in front of me, kneeling before me. He parts my legs and moves between them. I gasp, pulling back and squeezing my legs together. My heart pounds in my chest. Where are the guards? How are they allowing this? He doesn't seem phased as he moves my legs to the side. His hands reach up and cup my face, guiding my gaze back to him. "Don't be ashamed of who you are. You may think it's a weakness, but I think it's a strength. People will underestimate you. Use that to your advantage."

My brows pinch together. He speaks with such certainty. Like he's sure I'll have to face some big threat. But I won't; I'm not next in line to the throne, and neither is he. If anything, our life together should be peaceful. Pre-determined and boring.

He sighs. The breeze carries his scent. "I'm sorry if I made you uncomfortable. Werewolves aren't known for beating around the bush."

I frown, "Pardon?"

The prince clears his throat. "It's a figure of speech. It means that we are direct with our questions. It's an idiom slang we picked up from the humans."

I blink, surprised by the cultural differences. How he's able to be called a prince even though he isn't first in line for the throne. How his kind welcomes the tongue of humans. If Father heard anyone speaking like a human—even the vampires who were born human—he'd have their tongue cut off. Is that really a cultural difference, though? Or just the cruelty of power?

No. Father isn't like that. It's his duty, not pleasure.

"I think I understand," I slowly reach out, wanting to touch him. My fingers make contact with blazing skin. Is he made of pure fire?

"That's my peck, Princess," he whispers, leaning closer. My hand slips deeper down his shirt. My face heats, and I withdraw with hyper speed. A small chuckle rumbles out of Prince Liam. "Do you feel up every man you meet?"

My face growing hotter, I hug my hand to my chest and turn away, though the action isn't as effective with him kneeling before me. "No, you're the first man I've ever met." Somehow the admission makes this all that much more embarrassing. And it's not technically true. "I see auras, so I can see you in a way, but I don't know what you look like ... S-So I wanted to touch your face to see ..." my voice stutters and shakes before finally fading.

Without warning, he takes my cradled hand, fingers brushing against my chest. He pauses at the feeling of the firm, perky breasts against his fingers, but then he resumes his task. Why did I insist on not wearing a corset? "What does my aura look like?" Taking my hand, he guides my fingers to his face.

I swallow, "Like moss and vines." It's a simplistic description, but not a lie.

"What does my aura say about me?" My smooth skin meets rough stubble along his narrow jaw.

"I-I don't know. I don't fully understand what it means." But his aura doesn't make me feel uncomfortable. It is welcoming and nurturing.

He releases my hand, and I carefully drag my fingers along his features. Smooth cheekbones, well-kept eyebrows, and a strong nose, maybe broken once, but it's barely noticeable.

"What color are your eyes?" My voice is barely above a whisper.

"All werewolves have brown eyes," his rough voice whispers back. I wait for him to mention my unnatural blue eyes, but he doesn't. "Our eyes turn orange when we're angered or feeding. Much like a vampire's turns red."

I nod and swallow. My heart races. My fingers glide through his hair, "And your hair?"

He moves closer, planting a hand on either side of me—the bench creaks from the weight. "Blond," husky doesn't begin to describe his tone. It's deep and raw, sending pleasant shivers down my spine.

I lean forward, bringing my face closer to his. My other hand glides through his shaggy locks. "Is this okay?"

He lets out a soft purr and nods, barely moving his head. "That's perfect."

The intimacy is overwhelming. I don't even know this man, but the soft sound of his purr draws me in. I fight it and pull back, moving my face away from his and bringing my hands back to his jaw for a moment longer before dropping them into my lap. "What does your wolf look like?"

The purring slowly dulls and I feel like I can breathe again. "He's a brown color. Stands around six-foot-nine on his hind legs."

I nod. "Can I see your wolf some time?" The words come out slow, unsure, but even. Is it rude to ask a werewolf to see them in wolf form?

He chuckles, "I'd have to get naked first. Wouldn't want to ruin my suit."

My face burns. Yes, I wouldn't see him naked, but knowing he was would still be very inappropriate. "What? Oh, no, please don't. That's okay. I don't have to see it."

The prince lets out a deep laugh. "I wasn't planning on stripping right here and now, Princess."

I'm both relieved and horrified. Had I really thought he would?

His voice is cheerful, "I'm sure you'll get to see my wolf soon enough. I'll even let you pet me. It's an honour not many get to experience."

Pet him? What does his fur feel like? Is it soft like his hair? Or as rough as bear fur?

"When I show you my wolf, maybe you could show me your fangs? I've always wanted to see a vampire's fangs, but I'm not stupid enough to anger one into having them attack me!" He chuckles.

My throat tightens and tongue swells. I'm quiet for a long moment, trying to find my words. "I'd show you if I had any. They haven't come yet. Mother says I'm a late bloomer." Another thing wrong with me.

Liam cups my cheek. "That's okay," his tone is soft and reassuring. "They'll come in when they're ready.

Someone clears their throat.

Prince Liam jumps to his feet and steps away from me. My back sinks deeper into the wooden back of the bench. I take a breath and look towards our intruder.

Helena stands there, the ember in her yellow aura glowing brightly. "Sorry to interrupt, but I believe it's time for Lady Akantha to turn in for the night."

The prince clears his throat and nods. "Yes, of course." He steps towards me again, takes my hand and bends down as he kisses it, "I shall see you again soon, Princess."

I stand, smiling lightly, "See you again soon, Prince Liam."

"Just Liam," he says, releasing my hand.

"Well, I shall see you again soon, Just Liam," I bow my head to him.

The chuckle he tries to hide beneath a cough does not escape me. I smirk and raise my head.

Helena swiftly walks me through the garden. The dull playing of music fades into nothingness. "That was extremely irresponsible. What If someone saw you? What If I hadn't come along and that rascal took advantage of you?"

"That rascal is my fiancé. And we weren't doing anything wrong. Just talking."

She groans in protest. "He was kneeling in front of you."

Thankfully she hadn't shown up earlier when I was feeling up his chest.

A twig snaps, and we both stiffen. I turn towards the intruder. "Who's there?" My body trembles.

"Show yourself," Helena orders in a tone I don't quite recognize.

I don't see him at first. His dark purple aura blends into the dark void, but the pink speckles bring him to my attention. His presence makes me uneasy. Something about him seems off-putting.

"I apologize for startling you. I am Jeharad. A guest of the party. I seem to have gotten lost."

"You aren't supposed to be out here, human. Leave," Helena's firm voice sets me on edge.

Human? Who would bring a human?

"Of course. Again, I apologize."

He wanders off.

Helena huffs and we resume our march inside, "I'll have to inform the guards. Possibly the queen too."

I nod, my mind drifting back to the prince and all his mysteries.

CHAPTER FIFTEEN

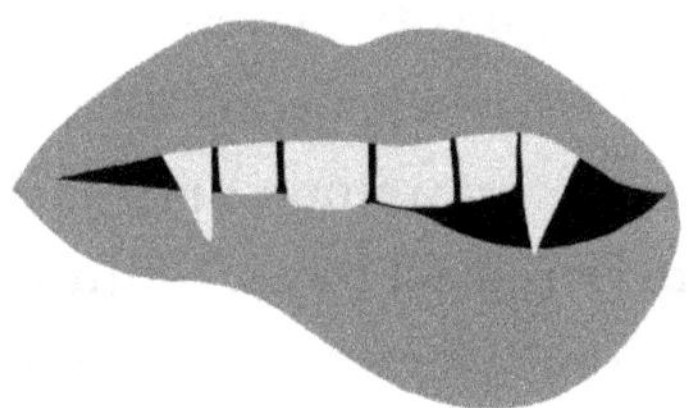

Callisora

THE CUSHION OF MY throne hugs my bottom. My body is still pulsating from the encounter with Vladimir last night. What right does he have to treat me like a toy? I am not to be played with. The nerve of him.

"Callisora," Mother snaps. "Pay attention. How are you to lead the people if you do not know the people?"

"She won't have to lead a soul. Just sit there and look lovely," Father corrects, a forced smile across his lips. It almost looks as though he's cringing at his own words.

Mother raises her chin, her long locks swaying as she does. "The people will look to her for guidance. Do not belittle a queen's duties."

I ignore their argument. It's not like Father even listens to the lower classes' complaints, only the nobles. I've never even seen a vampire who isn't related to Dracula enter the castle. Sighing, I focus on my parents' heartbeats. Although the two of them are bickering, their hearts beat with a slow rhythm. Fighting must not be as exciting after a few thousand years.

Another set of heartbeats joins us. I refocus on the real world and notice a woman in ragged dull-colored clothes walk in. Her heart races. I smirk, she's scared. She should be, no one ever steps before the king looking like that.

I catch a whiff of her. She smells human—dirty, unwashed human. Father despises humans. Well, he hates all creatures that aren't vampires. He believes that vampires are the superior race, even though we're on equal levels with the fairies, zombies, and werewolves economically. It doesn't help that he encourages the slavery of fairies and werewolves either.

The lad by her side appears calmer and more well-dressed. A bright blue tux jacket tightly hugs his body. Black pants do the same to his thighs. His heart beats slower than the woman's, but still quick for a human. His scent, unlike the woman's, makes my mouth water. I haven't gotten off for a few nights, so my body longs for him. It's been wanting most men I lay my eyes on lately, but I know how to restrain myself. I'll just sneak out at dawn again and embrace what little freedom I have left.

Although, the human before me could be a tasty snack. I wouldn't have to travel outside the castle for a quick fuck and meal. He's sexy enough to put Vladimir in his place, too. However, the magic J under his left eye is a tad off-putting. What kind of curse would leave such a mark?

I lean back in my seat, smirking and waiting for the show to begin. This should be interesting.

The ragged woman clears her throat, interrupting my parents and their bickering. Her first mistake.

Father straightens in his seat. His eyes glow red when they land on the humans.

"What?" His voice is cold and rigid. I'm surprised he hasn't killed them on the spot. Perhaps the rumours about his cruelty are a tad exaggerated. Or is he waiting for an excuse to rip them apart?

The woman bows her head, "Your majesties. I am Zahaya. I have travelled very far. I believe I could be of assistance to you."

Second mistake, thinking she is important enough to have meaning to my father.

Father lets out a dry laugh, "And what use would I have for a witch? And a poorly dressed one at that."

One of his long fingers taps the arm of his throne with a slow rhythm, probably itching to tear into her.

Witches and wizards age slower than humans. They can live up to two thousand years, thanks to the magic that plagues their blood, but they are just as easy to kill as any other human. Sickness, heart attack, being drained of their blood; all things that can end their lives.

Mother scoffs, "Pay no attention to him, madam. What have you travelled the distance to achieve?"

Now Mother is playing with fire. Will father rip her apart as well? It would be more difficult, but I'm sure he'd enjoy it. Would she fight back? Would he make me watch? My stomach turns at the thought. Yes, I'm not a fan of my mother or her favouritism, but watching her die would be agony. She's still my mother, after all.

I pull my thoughts away from my father's temper and look the wizard over. He's looking tastier by the second.

The witch bows her head to Mother, silently thanking her. She raises her head, her gaze shifting between the King and Queen as she speaks. "Word of your youngest daughter, Akantha, is spreading. Before, they were rumours, but now—after many witnessing her appearance at the ball—word is travelling that your majesties have a weak spot in their kingdom."

Akantha isn't allowed to leave castle grounds, and she normally doesn't go to the balls where we have outside species attend, so it doesn't surprise me that this is only spreading now. Father probably couldn't scare everyone into silence.

Father stands, his pulse spiking. Strike three, little witch. "Lies. We are feared."

Mother also stands and grips his arm. Good choice; I doubt the fairies will enjoy cleaning up that mess. Blood isn't easy to get out of rugs, even red ones.

"What do you suggest we do?"

I rub my forehead. Why is she entertaining this human? Maybe Father is right; a queen should sit silently. But what will become of me if I follow that philosophy?

Zahaya moves a strand of matted dark hair from her face, seemingly not threatened by my father and his murderous tendencies. "I believe I can cure her," she explains. "My assistant and I can cure her blindness and restore your rank in the monster world."

Cure her? What does she think she can do that we haven't already tried? Father had an Elder injure Akantha's eyes when she was too young to even walk, hoping her vampiric healing would restore her sight, but that didn't work. It didn't work when Father did it himself, either, an additional six times before Mother eventually stopped him. Akantha's infant cries still haunt me at the dead of dawn. I shiver at the memories.

Father's face twists into a scowl, "A vampire taking assistance from a witch? What malarkey. I'd much rather drown myself in the mermaid lagoon." The image fills my mind; Father walking into the murky water, a set of hands reaching up to the surface and dragging him under. I'm not upset by the image, but it still makes me uneasy.

"I can make a potion. Use magic. Spells and potions have evolved over the centuries," The witch insists.

"When can you start?" Mother offers a smile, ignoring Father's aggressive hiss, bared fangs, and red eyes. She's not scared of you, Father.

"You are free to stay the night. You day-walkers must be exhausted."

Ugh, what an ugly word. *Day-walkers*. Just call them mortal, Mother.

Zahaya shakes her head: "I left the human world a long time ago. I no longer sleep when the moon is up." She glances over her shoulder at the lad, then at me. "I would like to meet Akantha, however, and see how much magic will be involved."

I slowly rise, eager to leave the room before Father starts handing out punishments. My butt throbs from sitting on the stiff throne for so long. "Follow me."

Chapter Sixteen

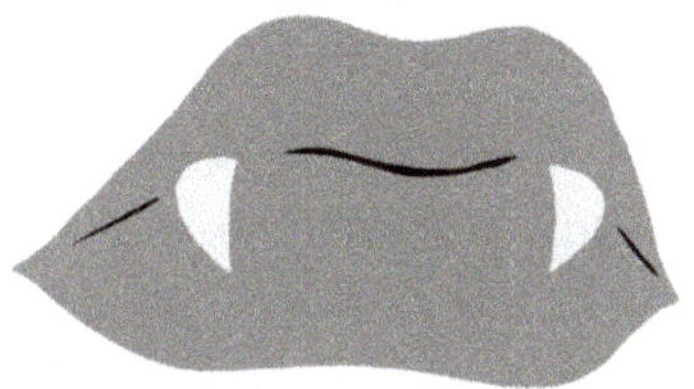

Akantha

Callisora's blood-floral scent penetrates my door. It's less blood and more flowers today. "Come in!"

I call, not giving her a chance to knock. There're two others with her. Two strange smells. Curiosity mixes with fear. I've never met so many new people in one week before.

The door creaks open, and Callisora walks in first, her strides long and powerful, followed by a greyness, then a familiar aura. Both make me uneasy.

"Zahaya, this is my sister, Lady Akantha. Akantha, this is a witch who goes by the name Zahaya, and her assistant. They are here to aid you in gaining your sight."

Callisora's words are dull. She doesn't sound like she fully believes what she's saying.

I don't either. A frown tugs at my lips, "I don't understand."

The greyness steps forward. "Using magic, I may be able to create an elixir or cream that can cure you of your blindness."

Anger swells in my stomach. Cure me? Am I sick? How dare they. How dare they assume what I want. Yes, seeing my family's faces would be wonderful, as would seeing the flowers that bloom in the garden, but then I'd also have to see the things that haunt my nightmares. Blood is easier to drink when I don't have to look at it. People are easier to face when I can't see the looks on their faces. "What are mother and father's thoughts?" I ask, keeping my tone flat.

"They are discussing it. Mother has invited them to spend the night." Her tone tells me otherwise. I wouldn't be meeting these two if it's not happening.

I nod slowly. "Well then, it looks as if I haven't a choice. I shall allow you to create whatever you wish and test it on me. But if it hurts, then that will be the end of you both." An empty threat bound to make them watch their steps. Maybe I could have Callisora or one of the guards fulfill it for me.

"Of course," Zahaya clears her throat. "Jeharad, come closer!" She orders. They both move directly in front of me.

Jeharad? From the garden? He's a wizard? What was he doing at the ball?

I don't give away that I know him. I sit perfectly still. Had he run into me on purpose? To inspect my blindness for himself before risking his and Zahaya's lives by presenting themselves in front of my parents?

Zahaya reeks of many things mushed together—toadstool, swamp gas, and what smells like urine. The stench doesn't seem to bother anyone else, but it makes my stomach recoil.

Jeharad, on the other hand, smells fine. Like fresh grass and pine tree needles. If he's her assistant, shouldn't he smell as dreadful as her?

"Now, write this all down," a bony, bridle finger presses into my left temple. Her touch stings, like the tip of her finger is doused in holy water. "Two hairs from the tail of a unicorn, a tear from a dragon, four frogs' warts, three mermaid scales, and a zombie's eyes."

"Zombie's eye? Are you sure?" he asks in the same soft tone as last night. A tone that belies he's playing at being naive. What could he possibly know? Be thinking? I shiver.

"Of course, I'm sure. Now write it down," she presses another finger into my right temple. The burning stops and is replaced by a rapidly building pressure behind my eyes. "Add willow bark as well."

He lets out the smallest of sighs. I seem to be the only one who hears it, or perhaps the other two in the room have no reason to respond to it.

"Very good. I'll see what I can gather tonight." Zahaya removes her fingers from my temples, but the throbbing lingers.

I give a nod, and the two take their leave.

Callisora comes over and sits next to me on the bed.

"What an odd woman!" She strokes my hair.

"She smells dreadful."

I lean into her. My head throbs. I don't like that woman. Why would she and her assistant be coming here now? Why wouldn't they have come when I was younger? How long do humans live? Surely witches and wizards live longer due to the magic in their veins.

She snorts. "I thought I'd imagined it. How can someone smell so disgusting? Perhaps it is a witch thing?"

A smile plays on my lips. I shake my head. "The other one didn't smell like her."

"You mean Jeharad? I don't doubt he smells good. He's pretty sexy."

Her voice shakes my insides and my stomach tightens. The smooth tone of his voice plays over in my mind. He didn't sound sexy. Attractive, maybe, but sexy?

Lifting my hand, I wiggle my finger back and forth. "Ahh ahh, you mustn't get distracted from your suitors."

She huffs dramatically, "I suppose you're right. Speaking of them, I should get going. Mother is most likely planning something for me to do with them," she stands. "Are you coming?"

I shrug, "Perhaps later. I'm quite content here."

Plus, I now have a headache that needs caring for. Perhaps a nap will suffice.

"As you wish!" Callisora walks towards the door, but pauses. "I almost forgot to ask. How was your meeting with the Wayfro Prince?"

Prince Liam's aura pops into my mind, along with the dream I'd had about him. We were getting a little too intimate on that bench, and Helena hadn't been around to stop us.

My face heats and my throat feels tight, "I-It was good," my voice sounds rough and flustered.

She lets out a small breath of laughter, "Well, I hope to hear all about it later."

She leaves, closing the door quietly behind her.

I lay back and let out a sigh.

Chapter Seventeen

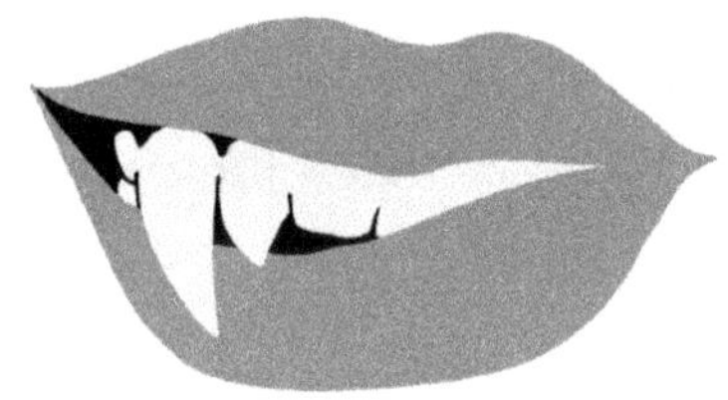

Farran

Entering the kitchen, I'm struck by the smell of frying meat and boiling vegetables. It's similar to the scent of the first time I came here, but not the same. Perhaps it's the absence of potatoes? Or maybe different spices are being used? I walk towards a small table and sit.

Dante steps away from the stove. He quickly washes his hands, then grabs a towel. He walks over while drying his hands. "Weren't you just in here for breakfast?" A small smirk tugs at the corner of his lips.

I shrug. "It's lunch now."

He tilts his head back and laughs. "Lunch? What do I look like?"

"A cook," I reply with an amused smile. "A very good one at that."

His eyes sparkle when he smiles. His skin seems strangely pale for a fairy. Sure, he sparkles like one, but normally fairies are more vibrant. The red of his skin is muted, as if he'd laid out in the sun too long and it bleached away.

"How long have you been here?"

Dante's smile falls, and he sits across from me. His dark eyes meet mine. They're red, like his skin, but they seem off. I'd never met a fairy with red skin or red eyes, so it could be normal, but my gut tells me otherwise. "My whole life. I was born here."

I nod slowly. I shouldn't be judging him; I haven't travelled to Frayus and seen all the fairy colors. Perhaps I'm just used to the traditional pastel colored ones. "Do your parents work here too?"

Dante hesitates, shifting in his seat. "My mother died when I was young. She was the cook. I replaced her."

My gut tightens. I reach across the table and place my hand on his. His skin is cooler than I expected. "I'm so sorry. How ..." I clear my throat. "How did she die?"

"The king killed her." His tone is flat, emotionless. "She was pregnant with a Youngling." He looks away, but doesn't remove his hand from under mine.

He's hiding something.

I ignore my wolf. My heart hurts for him. The Vampire King had murdered his mother? I rattle my brain, trying to find a new topic for us to discuss. "Can I see your wings?" I blurt. Many of the fairies at the slave camp didn't even know how to summon their wings. No one had taught them when they were turned. I'd always wanted to see fairy wings, though.

He blinks once, clearly surprised by my request. He looks at me again, "The king doesn't let us stretch our wings."

My brows pull together, "Does he not let you speak your native tongue either?"

I'd noticed the fairies would only speak it in the dorm. The fairies that were bought with me are being taught the language by the others who've been here longer. Perhaps with the hope that they'd some day be free to go to Frayus and speak to other fairies with ease?

He shrugs a shoulder, "He and every king before him. I think they're paranoid. Like we're making fun of them or planning an uprising."

I let out a breath. I'd be more worried about the second. "Well, I suppose I'd be paranoid too."

"It doesn't matter. I don't know much fea anyways." Fea must be the name of the fairy language.

"What? But it's who you are."

How could he not have learnt with the other fairies literally giving lessons before bed each morning?

Dante shifts in his seat again, "Yeah, well, that's what happens when you are raised in captivity."

Liar.

Leaning forward, I caress the side of his hand with my thumb. "I know how you feel. I was practically raised in the slave camp." Images flash before my eyes of when I was small and still human.

His eyes meet mine. "I'm sorry. That must have been awful. Never knowing what was going to happen or where you were going to go."

"It was hard at first. I constantly plotted how I would kill my master. But after watching my wolf-mother die trying, I decided to go along with it and obey him. And wait for my chance." Her screams still haunt me, I was so young. She'd tried to kill a guard so we could both escape. They'd killed her right in front of me. Her body had stayed chained to the post with me for weeks. The smell was so intense that I couldn't sleep or eat. Finally, they removed her when the Slave Tamer at the time came in and saw the body. He had scolded the men who'd killed and left her, but that was all.

Dante's eyes glide over my face, sympathy emanating from them. "My mother used to tell me stories about how the Slave Keepers would beat the creatures." His hand twitches as if he's going to reach out and take mine again, but he doesn't.

I smile at his concern. "I'm alive to tell the tale." I lower my hand, not denying the beatings I and the fairies had to endure over the years. I want to ask more questions about his mom. Why did the king kill her?

Dante in return strains a smile. He leans back in his chair and takes a breath. I retract my hand and lean back in my chair too. "I heard you brought the princess to the slave camp. How'd that go?"

"Good, actually. She fed, and I'm hoping that she'll want to go back and free the slaves with me."

I'd thought about it while I watched her twirl on the dance floor during the ball. Princess Callisora would be the perfect one to help take down the Slave Camp. Her elegant beauty would allow her to enter the camp and her bloodlust would destroy it.

Dante arches his brow and crosses his arms over his chest: "That's a tall order. Are you sure her feeding was good enough to convince her of that?"

"I also took a beating from the king in her place."

Both his brows are now raised, "Wow. Brave. Foolish, but still brave."

"Thank you."

"I'm almost tempted to make your lunch due to your bravery."

I straighten my back, "I think you should. Then I can gush about how delicious it is."

Dante chuckles, "Alright, alright. But only because I like the compliments." He winks. The action sends butterflies swarming through my stomach. Dante stands and goes back to the stove. "Steak?"

The fluttering insects eat at the walls of my stomach, clearly as hungry as I am. "You know me so well."

Chapter Eighteen

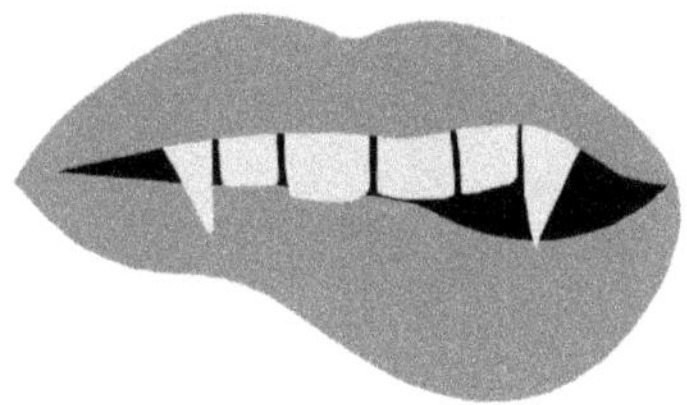

Callisora

The heels of my shoes make a *clack* sound that echoes off the stone walls of the long hall.

The throne room comes into view. I'm aiming to avoid it and whatever blood spill Father's tantrum had most definitely caused. A linking hall comes into view, but I stop. Two people sit in the throne room, huddled together on the floor. I pass the opening to the hall that had been my original goal and peek into the throne room. Sure enough, my mother is hunched over on the floor, her back to me. It rises and falls rapidly. There're slices in the fabric of her dress. Her bare back is exposed through the cuts, but there are no gashes. They've probably healed by now. Another person is in there with her. Surely, it's not Father. He never sticks around after dishing out punishments. I know from experience, as does Mother.

I bend down to remove my shoes and place them on the ground. The stonework is cold against the soles of my feet. Careful not to make a sound, I enter the room. Thankfully there are long strips of fabric that hang from the pillars. I hide behind one of them and peek out to get a better view.

Carlos kneels in front of my mother, moving strands of hair from her face as she cries. Sure enough, the floor in front of her is red, marred by her blood. That's going to be a pain to clean.

Carlos cups my mother's face and tilts it up to look at him. He speaks soft words that I can't hear, and she responds. There's a sparkle in her eye—something foreign. Hope? Happiness?

"It's love," a voice whispers from behind me.

I open my mouth to scream, but a hand covers it. Drawing my fangs, I bite. Sweet blood glides across my tongue. I don't swallow. Don't dream of becoming that much of a monster.

The hand doesn't move, so I do. I turn to face the man who's intruding on my spying. Vladimir offers me a smile.

Of course, it's him.

He finally removes his hand. He licks the blood. His tongue gliding across the rough skin all too slowly.

My throat tightens. My core burns at the thought of that tongue exploring me, gliding across my soft skin, lingering over the sensitive parts of my body. My nipples harden as a tingling sensation runs through me.

No. I can't let him get in my head.

"What are you doing here?" I whisper, my brows pinching together.

Vladimir shrugs a shoulder. "Same as you? To see a romance bloom?"

I scowl, "That's my mother. She's married."

"Not happily," His eyes drift over my shoulder. "Either that, or it would seem your father isn't the only one who takes on mistresses. What would a male one be called? A mister?"

I clench my teeth together, "I don't know."

He arches his brow, "Really? I thought you would."

My face heats, heart pounds. My hands curl into fists, "Excuse me?"

He rests a finger against his lips, "Careful, we wouldn't want to get caught."

My nostrils flare, "If my father—your king—sees them like this, he'll–"

Vladimir leans in close, his face inches from mine. "Your father cowers behind his throne at the sign of danger. He forces his daughters to wed without choice and gives no explanation as to why. And he lays in bed with women who are not his wife or his species." His eyes move up and down. "He is no king of mine." He pulls back. "I do not blame my queen for appreciating the attention of another, but she must be careful. As must you."

My breathing is laboured. My corset feels too tight, restricting the air from getting to my lungs. I plant my hands firmly on my hips, "I don't need the likes of you informing me of what I must and mustn't do."

Vladimir closes his eyes and takes a breath. He then opens them again. "Enjoy your day, your highness." He carefully slips out of our hiding spot and leaves the throne room.

I grind my teeth. Why must he irritate me so? I leave the spot next and go to the hall. Slipping on my shoes, I take a breath before re-entering the throne room in a more announced manner.

Mother and Carlos are standing now. They move away from one another at the sight of me. I pretend not to notice.

I approach them and wrap my arms around Carlos' left one, pressing my breasts against his bicep. He glances down at my chest, then at me. I shift my attention to Mother, "I hope I am not interrupting. I was planning to escort Carlos around the kingdom." It would be good for me to get to know him a bit better. Plus, it would allow Mother to change into nicer clothes and keep them both away from each other before a servant spots them together and reports it back to Father.

Mother nods, folding her hands in front of herself. "Of course. Have a pleasant time." She turns and leaves. Her steps are slow. I listen to her racing heart. She may look calm and collected, but she's panicking on the inside. Does she think I'll tell Father? Mother and I may not get along, but I'm not cruel enough to do that.

I turn to Carlos.

He's watching Mother. His eyes give everything away. There's no lust there, only pure admiration and affection. Perhaps Vladimir was correct. I tug his arm, and he looks down at me again.

He clears his throat, "Shall we go?"

I nod once and walk him out of the castle.

Once outside, I descend the castle steps. My shoes sink into the gravel-covered ground. Heels were not the best idea for this terrain.

I haven't left the castle to walk around Valdama since I was young. Mother would bring me on strolls to the Elder's, but I haven't gone in centuries. I only exit the castle now to escape the kingdom, and I don't take the main streets, I sneak out the back of the castle grounds.

Carlos leads me to the right, avoiding the entirety of the kingdom and leading me to a gated, posh community. The houses are tall, and the landscape is well kept and beautiful. This must be where the upper class lives.

"It's lovely, isn't it? So many beautiful families and content faces. Your father has done well," he gestures to a tall grey building with a black roof. "That one is my family's."

I clench my jaw. Of course, he thinks this small part of the kingdom is lovely; he lives in it. But what about the lower classes? They're the ones who are leaving. The ones who are starving. My mind retreads to Vladimir's words, "Some find him to be a coward."

Carlos chokes out a laugh, "Vampires are still at the top of the social ladder. We're the most feared.

The deadliest. It takes many brave and strong kings to accomplish and keep a title like that."

I bite my tongue. Most deadly? Most feared? The humans in the pub the other night didn't run screaming when they saw I was a vampire. No. They went running when they saw my wolf in her fur. And even if any of what he's saying were true, the council handles most of it. They make sure our image is maintained. If things start going south, they make a plan to fix things. "I'd like to go walk around the rest of the kingdom. I've honestly never seen it."

Carlos visually hesitates, "I'm not sure that's any place for a princess."

My brows raise, "All visitors from outside these walls have to walk through the main part of the kingdom to get to the castle steps. Why do outsiders get to see it, but I don't?"

He lets out a heavy sigh. "Very well, but don't say that I didn't try to protect you from those horrors." Placing a hand on the small of my back, he leads me back down the path we'd taken. The front steps of the castle come into view again, but we don't go to them. Instead, Carlos loops his arm with mine and walks me into the heart of the lower class' sector.

People of all ages walk down the gravel streets. They turn to watch us, their red eyes wide in awe. I avoid their gazes and focus on my steps upon the loose ground. The paths in the upper class were more well packed, here it is another story.

I cast a glance Carlos' way. He's looking straight ahead, seemingly oblivious to all the rundown buildings and starved-looking vampires around us.

Something burnt catches my eye. I release Carlos' arm and approach the remnants of a structure.

What was surely a tall landmark is now crumpled and decayed. The ceiling has fallen in at some point. The walls are brittle looking with graffiti and black stains. Charred wood and remnants of fabric are enough proof that a fire did indeed happen here. "What is this?"

Carlos huffs. "An eye sore. This will be the first thing to go when I become king."

I glance at him from the corner of my eye. What high expectations he must have. And he really believes he'll be my king as well as my mother's? Interesting.

I turn and get the attention of a young female vampire, "Pardon me. Can you tell me what this building was?"

Her round eyes focus on me. She must be truly starved to have such deep redness in her eyes. But even starved, she appears lovely. Her brown waves hug her beautiful, though dirty, face, "It was the school. It burnt down two kings ago."

My heart sinks. *The* school? Not *a* school? "How do the young ones learn about their heritage?"

She shakes her head.

"I'm afraid they don't. Parents teach their children the best they can," she looks up at the sky, then back at me. "I'm sorry. I must go. My young need feeding."

I nod, "Of course! Thank you."

I turn back to the building. Images of children running outside fills my mind. Teachers yell at students to listen to their lessons. Young vampires showing each other their fangs that just grew in. "How could my father allow this?"

"Weren't you taught about vampire history?"

"Of course, I was."

I look up at him, my brows pinched together. What does my learning have to do with this?

Carlos smiles. "Then who cares if these peasants know? They're lucky to be breathing the same air as such a beauty as yourself."

I clench my fists, my nails digging into my palms. How could Mother be swooned by this man attached to such a tongue? How could Father think I would be? Surly Vladimir is only a suitor to please the high-ranked Duke, but Carlos is here as per requested by my father. I'm sure of it. "I suggest we head back. I grow tired of all this fresh air."

"Right." Carlos reclaims my arm, escorting me inside and all the way to my bedroom. I'd expected him to leave me when we entered the castle, but apparently, he's a gentleman. Or maybe he's expecting me to invite him in? That's definitely not happening. "I had a splendid time. I look forward to our next meeting." He takes my hand and kisses it.

I straighten my back and grit my teeth in an attempted smile. "As do I."

He leans in and plants a delicate kiss on my cheek. I'm tempted to slap him, but don't. He walks off down the hall.

Swinging the heavy door open, I get a whiff of dog. I walk in and spot my wolf standing by my vanity, examining her own features as if she'd never seen them before.

"What are you doing in here?" My tone is harsh, mainly from the annoying events that had just transpired.

"I'm your handmaiden or your guard ... I'm not quite sure," she says in an almost cynical tone, then adds, "Master."

"You are going to stink up my room. I wouldn't appreciate the stench of wet mutt on my curtains."

"I'm sorry, Master, but I needed to speak with you."

I approach my bed and sit. "Stop calling me Master. Princess is fine. I've already told you this."

She swallows. Her heart thuds in her chest.

"What was your name again?" I ask, my voice peaking.

Air fills her lungs in one sharp breath. "Farran, Ma- Princess," she corrects herself.

I nod slowly, then walk towards my wardrobe to find a suitable nightdress.

Farran scampers behind me. "Princess? I wanted to speak with you about something." She takes my hand and lowers to one knee.

My head snaps to look down at her. "What are you doing? Proposing? Get up!"

Farran doesn't respond to my order. My frustrations burn into a fiery rage. I pinch the bridge of my nose with my free hand, massaging between my eyes to try and ease the pressure.

"Of course not, Princess. I simply want to ask a favour."

My hand lowers. I arch a brow. The tightness in my muscles eases. My anger dulls into boredom. I take my other hand away from her and return to my clothes. "I don't do favours." Though she did take a beating on my behalf from Father, so I might actually owe her.

Farran stands quickly, "Please, Princess, hear me out," Oh, how I loathe begging! "You'll be getting a hefty feeding. At least a dozen human men."

I glance at her from the corner of my eye. Where would she know so many men?

Oh.

I smirk. "You still want revenge on the Slave Tamer?" How entertaining. Was killing one of his keepers not enough for her? No, I killed him. She must want to taste the Tamer's blood herself. "I will consider it."

Plucking a nightdress from my wardrobe, I hand it to her, "Now, dress me."

Chapter Ninteen

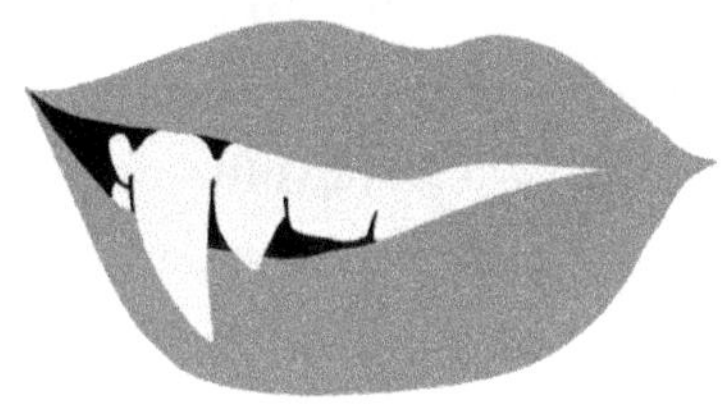

Farran

Watching Dante order the other fairies around is strangely arousing.

It could just be an effect of the approaching full moon, though. The moon's power and beauty have a way of affecting my wolf and me.

"Let's get this kitchen cleaned up so we can turn in for the night. Come on," Dante claps his hands together as he barks—more like hisses—orders.

Fairies move around the kitchen, washing dishes, putting pots and pans away, sweeping the floor, and sanitizing counters. Dante helps where needed, speeding the process up.

I watch from my seat. I've sat here enough times that it has officially become 'my seat,' though only Dante and I address it as such.

He walks over and sits across from me. "Thanks for waiting. You wanted to chat?"

Glancing at his still buzzing kitchen, I don't feel right taking him away from his work. "Don't you have to help with cleanup?"

He shrugs, "They've done this hundreds of times. It's what we do every dawn." Dante stands and offers his hand out to me, "Let's step outside for a bit."

I take his hand without hesitation and follow him through the door that leads outside and to the barn. Instead of going towards the building, we walk away from it and the castle. Dante stops and takes a seat in the grass. I look at him, then at the horizon.

"Farran?" He looks up at me, "Are you going to stand there all day? Or are you going to join me?"

I sigh and sit next to him.

He doesn't speak. His gaze is focused on the Dark Forest off in the distance.

The sun rises over the treetops. The castle and kingdom settle down for the day, but we don't.

When the sun is all but peeking over the treetops, painting the sky with shades of pinks and purples, something touches my hand. I glance down to find Dante's hand touching mine, his pinky finger slowly moving over mine. He speaks, "So, did she agree to do it?"

My cheeks heat up. I nod. "Yes, but we need a plan."

My wolf purrs in my head, but thankfully not out loud. I need a way to burn this moon-induced energy. "I'm thinking of going into the Dark Forest and scouting out the slave camp. They probably moved after Callisora, and I were there last." They don't move the camp often, but if one of the humans showed up dead, that would be more than enough of a reason to relocate.

Dante nods. "That's a good idea. Are you going to wait until tomorrow night?"

"No. I think I'll do it during daylight. Callisora won't need me, and the Slave Keepers won't expect a night creature stalking them during the day."

"I don't know. That doesn't sound safe. They might spot you and re-capture you." Dante's gaze is on the side of my face. "Plus, won't you be tired? Being up all night, then all day and all night again."

"I can handle it. I used to do it all the time when I was in the camp." Most of us would be kept up by the crying of newly turned fairies.

I turn to face him, smiling genuinely, "Don't worry."

Sighing, he nods, "Alright, just be careful.

"I will be. Promise."

I leave the castle when the sun is high above the trees. Even though Valdama is well hidden from the sun, light still seeps in through the leaves of the tall trees, spotting the dark area with blotches of light.

I walk through the empty streets of the city.

The gates of the kingdom come into view, as do the guards.

Two tall leeches in silver uniforms stand between me and the Dark Forest. One of them locks eyes with me. "Has the princess escaped again?" His tone is dull, emotionless.

I shake my head, "No. She's in her room. I'm actually going out for a run."

The guards look at one another, then at me.

"Are you authorized?" The other guard asks.

I shift on my feet, "Oh, well, no. But I'm not planning on going far ..." my voice fades. Should I have gotten permission beforehand? Who would I even get permission from? The princess?

The second guard sighs. "It is close to a full moon," he looks at the first guard, "She probably needs to stretch her legs. I doubt she's had a chance in a long time."

The first guard hesitates before sighing and stepping aside. "Fine. But you stay close to the kingdom walls and don't stay out all day."

I bob my head. "Yes, sir, thank you, sir." Slipping out the gate. I'm hit by a burst of freshness. The air is crisper, the trees smell stronger, and even the grass is more vibrant. When I last left Valdama to go after the princess, I hadn't noticed the beauty of the Dark Forest. Yet now that I'm not racing to get the runaway back home, I have time to take it all in.

I enter the line of thick trees, taking my time as I head towards the sound of flowing water. The stream isn't far, which is nice. It's wider than I expected, though. I'd have to run to be able to jump and cross it without getting my feet wet.

Instead of crossing it, I stretch my arms over my head, taking a deep breath.

Shift.

"Soon," I whisper the promise. I strip away my clothes, struggling with the belts, before removing the muted articles of cloth with ease. Once naked, I neatly hang everything on the branch of a tree.

My mouth goes dry. Apart from when I shifted at the bar, I haven't done it in years.

Shift!

I shake my head in an attempt to ease the voice inside.

Without permission, she claws her way to the surface, fighting against the cage I've locked her up in. She flails, scratches, and bites at the lock until it gives way.

I fall to my knees, gasping as she jumps out of the steel structure and takes over, forcing my body to shift to match hers. The hairs on my skin grow longer and thicker, muscles expand, bones pop out of place and back into different formations. My spine grows longer, forming a tail. Pain races through my body, using my veins as a highway.

Finally, the pain subsides. The transformation is over and I'm left panting on the forest floor.

Rising on all fours, I shake my body.

Stepping towards the stream, I get a look at the brown fluff of fur that I've changed into. A long snout and dark eyes are the first things I notice. Pointed ears stand tall, though the tip of my right one flops a tad. Shiny dirt-colored fur runs along my body, longer on my tail and shorter on my face.

I dip down and lap up some of the fresh stream water. Though the sun is out and the day is warm, the water is surprisingly cool.

A twig snaps across the stream. I jump back, and my wolf growls.

Another wolf, nearly twice my size with grey fur, steps out of the trees. His eyes narrow on me, and he snarls.

My wolf whimpers, and I lower my head in submission. "S-Sorry, your majesty."

I'm unsure how—maybe it's his smell or the way he carries himself—but I recognize who he is. I haven't interacted with him personally, but I've seen him with Lady Akantha and around the castle.

Prince Liam lets a breath of air out through his nose, then turns to where he'd hung his own clothes up on a tree branch.

Intending to give the prince his privacy, I turn away and head into the thicket.

Following the river, my mind wanders. Why was the prince out during the day? Was Akantha not allowing him to feed in front of her? Was he out hunting? He didn't smell like blood or fresh kill. Maybe he just needed a run? That doesn't seem to fit right, either. Something's off about him.

Shaking my head, I decide to focus on the reason I'm out here. With a snort, I break into a run.

Feet pounding against the ground, I weave through the forest. Trees fly past, their brown trunks and green leaves digging up a memory from long ago.

I ran with another wolf back then. She was older, but mostly everyone was. I had just been turned, and it was my first run in wolf form. My only run in wolf form. She'd galloped ahead of me, but not too far ahead, due to the chains that wrapped around both our necks to connect us. I'd thought of running off, but she discouraged it. "Master would hunt and kill us before we find any refuge," she'd stated while drinking from a stream.

How could I have forgotten that? How long has it been now? How long since that first run? Since I've seen my adopted mother's face?

I slow my steps, coming up to the camp. It's abandoned.

Dead fire pits, flattened grass, and the stench of blood is all that's left. They must have moved after finding the guard Callisora killed.

Sniffing the ground, I search for a scent. Thankfully, the slave camp isn't good at covering their tracks. The smell of sweaty humans and dirty fairies is thick and easy to follow.

Walking back into the long grass, I don't look up as I walk, worried the stench might be less potent if I take my nose from the earth.

A new scent enters my nose. I stop. Rotten flesh.

I snort and shake my head. Pawing at my snout, I try to get the smell out.

"Puppy?"

I stiffen.

The small voice speaks again. "Help."

The plea causes me to gasp. Sniffing around, I walk toward a bush. "Hello? Is someone there?" My throat tightens. What if it's a trap? Rogues hunt during daylight. What if it's a rogue wolf? Luring me in to trap, kill, and eat me?

Sniffles come from the bush. "Are you with the bad men?"

Bad men? "Do you mean the Slave Keepers? No, I'm not with them." I move closer, but hesitate when I notice the thorns on the bush. "You can come out. I won't hurt you," I attempt a soft tone, though I'm unsure if it sounds as genuine as I'd like.

The bush shifts. Someone rustles leaves within, clearly trying to follow whatever path they took to get into the prickly hiding place. Out steps a little girl, no older than five. My heart drops. Another memory plays in my mind.

I'd been walking in the forest with my mom, picking flowers. There was growling, and then everything went black. I woke up at the slave camp, covered in blood. My new mother sat with me, protecting me from the Slave Tamer and his keepers.

The overwhelming stench of decomposing flesh attacks my nose, bringing me back to the little girl. I take a step back.

She whimpers, glancing at our surroundings. "What's wrong?"

I shake my head. "Nothing," I say. Wait, how can she understand me in this form? Maybe she was bitten by a werewolf?

I do my best to ignore the odour by breathing through my mouth. Ignoring the smell somehow enables me to get a better look at her. I realize something. She's the one who stinks. She's dead. A zombie.

Grey skin covered in protruding brown veins cloaks her body. Her right eye is missing, her left cheek had been torn away, revealing yellow teeth. She wears a purple dress and white shoes. The two pigtails do little to contain the mats in her long brown hair. Chunks of flesh on her arms and legs are missing or hanging from the bone.

I make eye contact with her, creating a bond like I did with Princess Callisora, just encase the girl's only guessing what I was saying the entire time and couldn't actually understand me. "Wh-what's your name?" I ask between gulps of air, which does little to ease my turning stomach. "What are you doing away from the graveyard during sun-up?"

She sways a bit, but regains her balance. "I'm Princess Julia. I heard kids at night and wanted to play. I left the Graveyard and found them. They were scared and ran away ... I dunno how to get home." She sniffles, tears of black blood stream down her young face. "Those scary men came, and I had to hide. I wanna go home."

I nod. Princess? How could there be a princess? Zombies can't reproduce. How did the Zombie King manage this? "How about you climb onto my back, and I'll get you home?" My wolf whimpers even as the words come.

Princess Julia looks me over with her one eye. "Puppy won't hurt me, right?"

I shake my head. "Of course not." My wolf would rather run far away, as would I. But I can't just leave her here. Princess or not, she's alone, scared, and in need of my help.

The girl hesitates further. I lay down, welcoming her to come. She does. The princess climbs on and grips two fistfuls of fur.

I rise and walk away from the trail I was following, abandoning it.

CHAPTER TWENTY

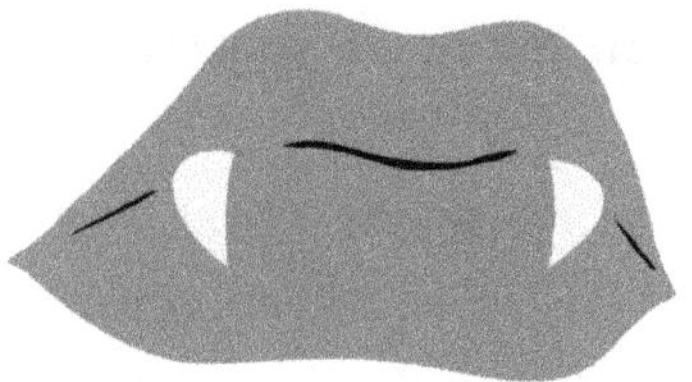

Akantha

AWAKE AGAIN. BIRDS CHIRP outside my window, but they aren't the reason I was jarred awake. No. My latest nightmare is the culprit. The brief break from them was nice, temporarily replaced with sweet fantasies of romance. But all good things must eventually come to an end.

The nightmares always end the same way—my head no longer connected to my body, rolling along a smooth marble floor—but this time, there's more. I saw my killer's face. Dark hair slicked away from his face, thin lips surrounding a devilish smirk, red eyes glowing bright. Red eyes. A vampire killed me? But who? I haven't met many noble vampires in my life. But the man's face isn't one I recognize. He's familiar, but I don't know him.

A floorboard creaks, and I stiffen in my bed. I grip the blanket tight around my chin. "Who's there?" I demand, my voice wavering.

When no answer comes, I sniff the air. The musty scent of the room mixes with another. One I recognize, but am unfamiliar with. One I've smelt countless times in my room, but never spoken to the owner of.

Cinnamon.

My heart beats against my chest. I sit up, my movements slow. "Why do you keep coming here?" The scent is strong. I know they're here, even though all I see is darkness. "Why can't I see your aura?" Is it one of their gifts? Perhaps they can hide themself? But how would they know to hide their aura?

Whoever is standing in my room, motionless, quiet, and unseen, has been visiting me for as long as I can remember. I have a memory of being still in a crib and feeling them brush a strand of hair out of my face. They probably thought I was sleeping, but their scent had awoken me. When had I become so used to them that their smell no longer dragged me out of my slumber? When had I stopped telling Helena and my parents about the strange figure who'd break into my room to watch me sleep?

Probably after the sixth or seventh time, they'd dismissed my claims.

Though I was a child when I first started mentioning it, I doubt they'd believe me even now.

"No one can get past the guards," Father had assured me. "It's probably something her young mind has created to make her feel more at ease at night,"

Helena had once assured my worried mother. Even Callisora never believed me. She'd slept in my room a few times to try and catch a glimpse of my daily visitor, but never saw them. She never shut down my claims; she'd say, "Some things are better off left alone. Whoever it is hasn't hurt you, so they're probably harmless," though the uncertainty in her voice was evident.

I stand from the bed and reach out, navigating my room, listening for them trying to flee. They don't. They stay completely still, so I don't hear them. My ears strain to hear their breathing. Are they holding their breath? Or am I actually insane? Could this really be all in my head? A figment of my imagination? Something—or someone—I've created so I feel less afraid after a nightmare?

My outstretched hand touches something. Fabric. I almost move past it, thinking at first that it's the dress Helena had hung from the tub divider for tonight's walk in the garden with the prince. But I pause. I'm not near the tub or its divider. Slowly, I turn towards the thing—or person.

That's when I hear it. A breath. Is it mine or theirs? Surly whoever has been visiting me is living, right? What if it's a ghost? That would explain why it has no aura, but not why it has enough weight to creak the floorboards.

Swallowing my fear, I reach out. My hand comes into contact with something firm. Warm. A chest. A man's chest. A man who probably stands over a head taller than me, based on the fact that my hand is directly in front of my face, and it's sitting between what I assume is his pecks. Color shoots out from my hand, revealing his green aura. Multiple shades of green swirl around one another, always touching, but never mixing into a new solid color.

He inhales sharply, surely aware that I can see him. How much does he know about me? About my gift? He doesn't pull away. He stands here, with me, motionless. A chill runs through me. What if he's the man from my dream? Could it be a warning? A premonition? Perhaps another extension of my sight?

No.

It's just a nightmare. But this man is real. And he's been breaking into my room since I was at least a toddler. Watching me. Part of me somehow knows him. Knows he's here to watch over and protect me. It's a strange feeling. I can't explain it. It's as if touching him has made me more accepting of him and his constant presence in my life. "Who are you?"

No answer.

"I can see you. I know you're here. There's no point in staying silent."

He still doesn't speak.

I swallow. Is something wrong? Am I not supposed to confront him? Will he stop visiting me now? What if my intuition is wrong and he really is here to cause me harm?

No. He would have done so by now. "Why are you here? What do you want from me?"

Still no answer.

My fingers spread over his chest. Perhaps getting a better look at him would help ease my whirling mind. He doesn't stop me as I move my fingers down. His clothes are tight against his broad chest, leaving little to the imagination. The fabric of his shirt ripples over his muscles. He doesn't appear to be overly muscular, not nearly as much as the prince seems to be. It's hard not to compare the two since they're the only two men who've ever let me touch them like this. The only men I've ever met, really.

My hand glides back up his torso, joined by the other. All ten of my fingers trace his collarbone. It protrudes from his skin, leaving a shallow divot at the base of his throat. I take mental notes of every aspect of him. He doesn't smell of death, so he couldn't be a zombie. He isn't muscular enough to be a werewolf, but again I'm basing that solely off the prince's physical structure. He could still be a vampire or fairy. Wouldn't his skin be colder to the touch if he's a vampire, though? Not as warm? So, he's a fairy? Is he tall enough to be a fairy?

I sigh. He doesn't seem to fit into any category. This would be so much easier if I could see him. This is probably the first time I've actually wanted nothing more than to see.

My hands move to his face. A pointed chin and clenched jaw greet me. He doesn't stop me as I step closer—in fact, he rests his hands gently on my hips—my fingers carefully explore his high cheekbones and tall forehead. His ears are pointed like a fairy, which aids in my discovery of his species, but they're too long to be a fairy's ears. "What are you?" The words slip past my lips.

He steps back, his aura slowly fading as soon as the warmth leaves my fingertips. Without hesitation, he dashes out of my room.

Gasping, I chase after him, "Wait!"

Colors pass by in a blur as I focus on the fading green aura. Why is no one stopping him? Voices call out to me, asking where I'm going and what I'm doing up in the dead of day, but I don't respond. Turning down hall after hall, I focus on the light footsteps ahead of me, ignoring the heavy ones chasing after me.

I run through a door and into the fresh air. My skin burns. I ignore the prickles of pain. The aura is gone. He'd vanished a while ago, but I had relied on his small sounds to lead me. Only now, he's completely disappeared. Vanished into thin air.

"Princess!" A voice calls. A green and brown aura comes into view. His familiar earthy scent fills my nostrils.

I bow my head, the motion painful. "Prince Liam." What is he doing up at this hour?

"Princess, you're smoking!" His hands touch my arm gently, and I wince. He guides me back inside. "You shouldn't be out in the sunlight."

The stench of burning flesh hits me like a fallen tree. I hold in a gag. My skin bubbles like boiling water.

"I'll be fine."

My voice is pained and shallow. I'm escorted back into the castle. The darkness of the building caresses my body with its chilled atmosphere. My skin will take a few hours to heal, but the sunburns are proof that Cinnamon is real. That this isn't some sort of strange dream. Or perhaps it's proof that I've gone completely insane and willingly ran out into the sun to burn myself alive.

"What were you doing out there?" The prince's voice is strained. He's panting, though it's easy to miss if you weren't listening closely. Had he been running? Hunting maybe? That would explain why the smell of the woods is so strong. He must be used to being in them.

I swallow. "Did you see anyone out there?"

"Pardon?" His voice cracks.

"A man," I clarify, "I was chasing a man. Did you see him?"

He's silent for a moment. Had he not heard me? Maybe I'd asked too quietly? Finally, he sighs, "I only saw you. No one else."

I nod. It's probably safe to assume that no one else saw him running past them, otherwise someone would have called the guards.

"Is something wrong? Why were you chasing a man? Did he hurt you?" His gentle hands cup my cheek.

I cringe at both the sting his touch brings to my open wounds, as well as the fact that I've admitted to Cinnamon being real. "No. I just thought I heard something. It's nothing to worry about."

"You heard a man? When? Where?" His voice deepens. I imagine an orange glow in his eyes. His face leans in closer to mine. He inhales through his nose. Is he smelling me? My heart stops. Can he smell Cinnamon on me? "Was someone in your room?"

What a guess. However, given the time of day and the fact that I'm awake and chasing after a mysterious man, it's to be expected. "No. I thought I heard someone in the hall. They sounded lost, and I wanted to help them. But by the time I stepped out of my room, they were gone." It's a clumsy story, but hopefully believable enough.

There is silence. Is he surveying me? Mentally analysing my story? The prince sighs in frustration, "I'll notify the guards that there may be someone wandering in the castle, lost," he assures me, though I know they'll find no one.

"Thank you," I bow my head again and turn to find my way back to my room.

The prince catches my elbow, "Wait, Princess, since you're up, might I offer to accompany you to a feeding?"

I pause. A feeding would help me heal faster, and I doubt I'll be going back to sleep anytime soon. I turn to face him again, a small smile painted across my lips, "I'd love that. Thank you."

His hands guide mine to his arm. We walk, me hugging his thick bicep. My bare feet pat against the floor. Yeah, Cinnamon is definitely not as muscular as a werewolf.

"About last night," he clears his throat. "In the garden."

My face heats and chest feels tight.

"I'm sorry. It's my fault you acted the way you did."

My brows pinch together. "What do you mean?" I keep my gaze fixed forward and my voice low.

He swallows. "When a werewolf purrs, it attracts potential mates," he explains, "you weren't in control of your actions or feelings, and I'm truly sorry. I'll make sure that it doesn't happen again."

I nod, relieved that there's an explanation for whatever had happened. But is he really the one that needs to apologize? "It's my fault too. I shouldn't have gotten so touchy."

The prince chuckles, "You don't ever have to apologize for touching me. I was surprised you were able to fight it, though."

My throat tightens. The hallway feels too small. He's taking up too much space. I take deep breaths through my nose, hoping he doesn't notice.

He does.

"Princess?" his voice oozes concern, but I brush it off.

I look up at him with an innocent smile, "Yes?"

He takes a small breath, "I must admit, I have just recently gotten out of a long-term relationship. So, if I seem off at times, I do apologize. I don't want to hurt you."

A relationship? "What happened?" Somehow this knowledge allows the walls to ease back a bit. I can breathe. Maybe it's the fact that he won't be expecting too much from me too soon?

"It's complicated, and I'd rather not talk about it. But I want to be open with you. So perhaps I can tell you another time."

I nod, accepting that he needs his heart to heal before he can talk. I just hope he isn't hurting too badly. I've never loved someone, but I can't imagine heartbreak is easy. "Since we're being open and honest, my father has welcomed a witch into the castle."

"Oh?" He doesn't sound surprised, more curious. "And why has he done that?"

I shrug a shoulder, then hiss at the pain that nips at my burnt flesh.

"She's going to hex my eyes. She claims to be able to grant me sight." I don't know much about magic, but if it can truly do this, then I'll never doubt it again.

"Do you think it'll work? No offence, but I'd think that if your sight could be returned, it would have been by now."

My jaw clenches. He doesn't seem to be trying to upset me, but his skepticism causes my stomach to twist and bile to rise up my throat. I swallow it down. Maybe I should have pried into his ex more. "It's true that nothing else my parents and the Elder have done has worked thus far, but having an open mind isn't something to be looked down upon."

"I never said it was."

I Inhale through my nose. The sharp air stings my nostrils. Now he's just being infuriating.

"My father just wants me to be stronger. There's nothing wrong with that. Besides, I'd rather not be known as the weakest link."

We stop walking, and the prince turns me to face him. His warm hands cup my face. I expect the contact to hurt—and it does—but it's only a light sting compared to the agonizing burn I was expecting.

"You are not weak," I feel his eyes on mine. "You were born this way for a reason. You should embrace it, not try to change it."

A frown tugs at my lips, "Your highness-"

"Please, call me Liam," he requests, then gets back on topic. "I don't think you should change who you are. You're a beautiful creature with more strengths than you realize."

My stomach twists again. What does he know of my strengths? He barely knows me. We just met. I barely know myself.

He releases my face with a sigh, "Please, just agree that you'll consider what I'm saying."

I swallow and nod. "I will take your concerns into consideration." Though I still want to try. Even if I didn't want to, I'd have no choice, because Mother and Father want me to try. "But I do wish I could see things like everyone else does. The glowing moon, the colors that a sunset paints across the sky ..." Cinnamon.

A soft chuckle escapes him. "Just remember, Princess-"

"Akantha," I correct, "If I'm to call you by your name, then you should call me by mine." Plus, I could get into a lot of trouble if someone were to hear him address me as princess.

"Of course, Akantha," he clears his throat. My cheeks heat at the sound of my name on his lips. "Keep in mind that no matter how beautiful the world seems, there will always be ugliness. If you want to see the colors of light in the sky, you also have to witness the shades of darkness that engulfs the ground."

My brows draw close together. “What does that even mean?”

“Without darkness, there is no light. I’m just warning you, seeing isn’t all it's made out to be. I wish I could see the world as you do."

I shake my head. I don't see the world at all. It's a bit insensitive for him to talk as if being blind has been easy. I've had to work very hard to be able to navigate my way through life thus far. “Surely it isn’t that bad.” However, I do have fears of the world being dark and miserable.

He sighs. “If you’re that set on this, then I support you.” He sounds defeated.

I nod once, and we head to the dining hall.

CHAPTER TWENTY-ONE

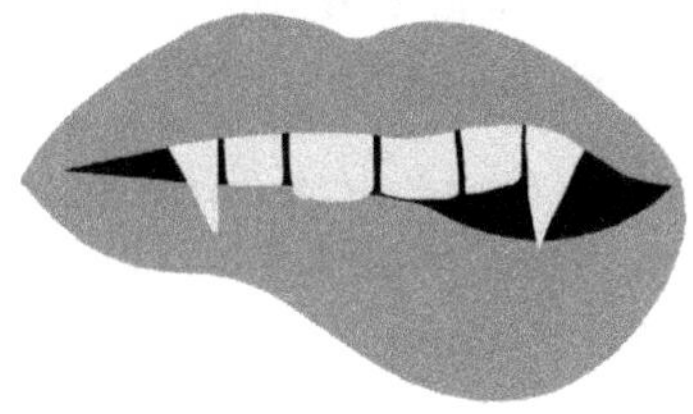

Callisora

I TIGHTEN THE ELASTIC around my hair, restricting it into a high ponytail. The confined spiral falls down my back. My blouse and black pants are freshly cleaned, courtesy of the maids. The fabrics hug my body. The window opens, and I jump out.

With two feet on the ground. I need to get out of here. Out of Valdama to clear my head. My thoughts keep drifting back to Vladimir and how good he'd look under me. I need to get laid. Get myself off and have a feeding.

I take my usual path, through the hole in the stone wall, and out into the Dark Forest. The fat crescent moon hangs above the trees, illuminating slivers of darkness. Animals hide in the shadows, but they dare not approach me. They may be predators, but I am the beast that will tear them to pieces without a second thought.

I plant my hand on a fallen log and pole vault over it. The moss-covered surface is fuzzy and damp. Some of it pulls away from the bark when I remove my hand.

My feet pound the earth as air whips at my face, lifting hair off my back. Pumping my arms, crumbs of moss chip off my hand.

The forest opens, and I slow, panting.

Two humans cross over the arched bridge in the distance and head towards the graveyard. They walk through the open gates and past headstones, heading towards the massive tree atop a hill, where a tall, lean man waits.

I shiver. The Kingdom of Zulmar—also known as the Zombie Graveyard—is one of the creepiest places I've ever seen. The smell alone is almost enough to detour me from going to the human world. Almost.

I hold my breath as I walk past, rushing towards the bridge that separates me from my next meal. My shoes tap against the stone surface of the bridge. I reach the halfway point.

A hand grips my arm. I spin around, prepared to snap at the humans who'd just been crossing, or possibly a zombie. To my surprise, a set of red eyes look back at me.

My mouth dries when the moon illuminates enough of the vampire's face for me to realize who is touching me. Whose hand is sending tingles up my arm.

My heart tremors. I narrow my eyes. "What are you doing here?" I demand, pulling my arm free of his grasp.

Vladimir's brow arches. "Stopping you from causing another pub scene."

My arms cross over my chest. How did he know I'd made a scene? Did the wolf tell him that? "Leave. Now. You have no business here."

"No business?" He takes my hand and examines it. Picking away chunks of dirt and moss. His touch drives me crazy. Such rough hands, yet they hold my own so gently. He continues. "You are in the midst of being married. And I am your guard, which makes your outings my business."

"You never cared before."

His gaze shifts up to my face. There's something in his eyes. Anger? Hurt? "I am one of your suitors now. I can't be as lenient anymore."

"This is ridiculous," I glare harder. "Let me go and go wander in the woods for an hour."

"So, you can run around to sleep with and feed off these low lives? They don't even know how to properly pleasure you."

My muscles tighten in my arms and chest. I scowl and pull my hand away from him again. "Oh? And what do you know of pleasure? How many wenches have you been with?" I challenge, my mouth tingles as my fangs come out to play.

His lips curl, "Princess," he leans forward. With a small gasp, I step back, my lower back presses against the wood railing of the bridge. He leans in, bringing his lips to my ear, his armoured chest just inches from my bosom. "I've brought more women pleasure in the past two hundred years than you have orgasmed in your entire lifetime."

My core tightens. Chills run up and down my spine. "It must be hard to have slept with so many men and only climaxed so few times."

My breath catches. How dare he speak to me like that. And how dare I like it. My body feels like it's on fire.

"Oh really?" My nostrils flare. My head tilts so I can narrow my eyes at him. His smooth features look dark and dangerous. The sun rises behind him, painting the sky a dark violet. "Why don't you prove yourself?"

A small chuckle escapes him. "You best run along home, Princess."

My jaw clenches, and I lean into him now. He stumbles back a moment, seemingly startled, but then pushes back. Chest to chest, I rest my hands on his shoulders, "And if I don't?"

"I'll have to punish you." His tone is playful, his eyes glowing with red hot desire. Or perhaps that's the reflection of my own.

Scenes of our naked bodies pressed against each other plays through my mind. Calloused hands running over smooth skin. Angry kisses and deep nail markings in skin. "And If I want to be punished?" My head tilts.

Vladimir's Adam's apple bobs as he swallows, his eyes trained on my neck. "You won't be able to handle all the things I could do to you. The things I could make you feel."

My thighs squeeze together. Heat radiates from my core and spreads throughout my entire body. "Someone thinks highly of themselves."

He shrugs a shoulder and leans back, pulling away and leaving me to be devoured by my own lust. "I should get you home before your father realizes you're missing."

I bite my inner cheek. "I don't need you to escort me. I can handle myself," I wave a hand, shooing him. His presence is making this feed even more dire. "Leave." I turn away from him.

"Never."

The word slips from his lips effortlessly, but leaves me frozen in place. That single word causes my stomach to twist. The heat between my legs intensifies. Never? He'll never leave me? Even if I don't choose him? I look over my shoulder at him in disbelief. Surely, he doesn't mean that.

His heart quickens, but he watches me with calm, caring eyes. How have I never noticed that look before? Has he always looked at me with such fondness?

I step towards him, reaching out and grab his shirt. I pull him down to my level. Our lips are inches apart, "If you betray me, I will end you."

"Never," he whispers in response, his hands moving to my lips and sending waves of shivers over my skin.

That word again. I press my lips against his. Moving his tongue along the seam of my mouth, I welcome him. He slides into my mouth and grazes against my inner cheeks. His lips are hard as rock, yet as gentle as silk. He tastes of steel. His hands move from my hips, strong arms wrap around me and pull me against him. Is his chest as hard as his armour? I'm determined to find out.

With my hands on his shoulders, I break the kiss. Staying close to him, our short pants of breath entangle together. I look into his now red eyes. "I'm so hungry." But not for blood. Hungry for him. Hungry for everything he can make me feel.

He presses me against the bridge's handrail, and something presses against my lower abdomen. Something hard and bulging. My breath catches, and he smirks, "I'm hungry too."

I swallow, ignoring the small voice that screams, *this is a bad idea.* That sleeping with another vampire could be my downfall. "Devour me."

He cocks a brow, "Is that an order, princess?"

I can only nod. My throat is as tight as my chest. How am I even able to breathe?

Taking me into his arms, he carries me towards the Dark Forest.

I gasp as my feet leave the ground, but instantly relax in his arms. "Where are we going?" I'd expected him to take me to the human town and book a room or something.

As if hearing my thoughts, he replies, "I don't want to break the poor innkeepers' beds."

Heat spreads across my face. He thinks he'll break the bed. How big is this guy's ego?

I close my eyes. Feet pound the ground, twigs snap, leaves rustle, but nothing is as thunderous as the heart beating next to my eardrum. It races faster than its owner, who carries me as if I weigh nothing. *Ba-dum, ba-dum, ba-dum.* Each heavy beat of adrenaline matches my own excited one.

Excited?

What do I have to be excited about? It's just sex. It's just Vladimir.

Tomorrow it'll be like nothing happened. Just a one-time thing. I'll get him out of my system and be done with it.

But what if I'm not?

His bedroom door flies open. When did we get to his room? No, when did we walk through the guards' pub? Or even get to the castle? To the kingdom? What if someone saw us?

I'm placed on my feet. He shuts the door. The room is dark. It has a damp atmosphere, but there's no water in sight, just a bed, dresser, mirror, desk, and a random plant. Who keeps a plant in their room?

Vladimir grunts, catching my attention.

We stand there, eyeing one another. His eyes trail over me, making me feel naked, but also not naked enough. I look him over more thoroughly as well. Wide shoulders, shoulder-length black hair. What's under his armour? Does he have washboard abs? Muscles on top of muscles? And what about lower? What treasure does he hide in his pants?

He steps toward me. His fingertips glide across my jaw and his gaze meets mine. "May I?"

Amused by his sudden cowardice, I smirk, "May you what?"

He leans in, his lips too close and yet too far from my own, "May I take care of you?" His words move across my lips and dance over my face, leaving heat in their wake. The heat washes down to my heart, urging it to skip and scamper about in my chest.

My body and mind scream two different answers. I go with my body, "Yes."

His lips crash against mine like an ocean's angry waves. Hands—both his and my own—work at removing clothing. Strings and buttons undo, articles of fabric are practically ripped from one another's bodies.

My blouse is gone, and my pants drop to the floor. Vladimir doesn't even hesitate. His fingers untie the back of my corset with ease. Maybe he has done this a few times before. I, on the other hand, struggle to figure out the clasps of his armour, but still manage to get it off him.

The damp air hugs my body. I break the kiss and take a step back, wanting to take in the sight of him. Vladimir doesn't allow it. He reaches for me and lifts me up. I'm pinned against the wall. Unpolished bumps and edges dig into my back. My legs wrap around his waist. His already hard shaft presses against my entrance. His hips move, grinding himself along my soaked slit.

I swallow.

My hands have perched themselves on his shoulders. Slowly, I glide them down, allowing my fingertips to roam over his pecks and every muscle they find after that.

One of his hands is planted against the wall, while the other cups my ass.

Long strokes of him pressing against me quickly become not enough. I bite my lip. I want him inside me. "Vladimir, please," I beg. I haven't had relief in days. I need this. Need him.

He keeps grinding his delicious cock against my wetness. "Not yet."

I bite my tongue to stop from hissing demands at him. He had said he'd punish me. And what's better punishment than sexual torment?

Vladimir tilts his head to the side. "Feed."

I frown. "What? No. I'm not a Rogue."

I don't feed on my own kind. The thought of even doing so is appalling. What if I become addicted like those monsters? What if I feed off my own people as a result?

"Trust me, you won't become a Rogue."

He steals another kiss, his hard cock rubbing against my clit as he grinds. I groan. He breaks the kiss, his breathing slightly laboured. "Bite me."

Maybe it's the hunger or the lightheaded feeling caused by his grinding, but I do. I lean forward, summon my fangs, and bite him. I don't numb the skin with my saliva. I don't warn him. I just do it. My fangs puncture his flesh, and sweetness fills my mouth. Thick liquid pours down my throat. My body burns hotter. Pleasure fills me. My hips move with his, eager to reach the upcoming climax caused by the taste of his blood alone. He says something, but I don't hear. He swallows, the skin moving around my lips. This feeling is at least two times as intense as dopamine tainted human blood.

With a single movement, I gasp, releasing his neck.

Panting, Vladimir smirks at me with two small streams of blood running down his neck. "We need to work on your self-control."

I swallow the last bit of blood in my mouth. Guilt and panic mix in my full stomach. "Did I take too much?"

He moves his hips, and I gasp again. He's inside me. His thickness, reaching deep inside me. "Nothing I can't handle." Vladimir's hips move rhythmically. His cock glides nearly all the way out of me, then plunges back in. Slow but intoxicating.

My insides shift with every thrust. The inner walls of my pussy hug his erection, begging him to stay. I lean my head back, resting it against the rough wall. I can barely feel the scratches my back and scalp are receiving. He's too overwhelming and a soft moan escapes my lips. I look at him, my cheeks ablaze.

He groans and rests his forehead against mine. "Fuck, I've wanted to do this for so long."

"You have?" The words come out much softer than I intended.

His eyes meet mine, and he tilts his head. Hungry lips cover mine. My lips move against his, tongues dancing with each other. My body tingles from the contact. Fingers move into his hair, getting lost in the thick strands of black.

His steel-flavoured mouth leaves mine all too soon. I whimper, but he doesn't return. Vladimir kisses a trail down my neck, an act I never understood until now. Each kiss he plants upon my flesh leaves a tingling sensation. I swallow. Is he going to bite me back? Do I want him to?

Yes. Yes, I do.

I tilt my head, exposing my neck for him, but he keeps kissing lower. The lower he moves, the less of his cock penetrates me. Soon enough, it's just the head that's entering me repeatedly.

Moving his hand from the wall, he cups one of my breasts. Without hesitation, he draws my nipple into his mouth. The sucking and the sensation of his tongue gliding over the perky nub releases another moan from my lips. I look down at him, watching as he treasures my body. My arms drape over his shoulders. My nails drag gently along his back.

He takes more of my breast in his mouth. Then I feel it. His fangs growing against my skin. He releases my breast, then kisses up my skin. He sinks his teeth into my cleavage. I gasp. My nails dig into his flesh.

A sting emanates from the puncture wound and spreads throughout my body. Wetness covers that area of my skin. He sucks and swallows deeply. His lips part from my skin. He glides his tongue over the incision, but it doesn't stop bleeding right away.

He plunges himself deep inside me again. I let out a gasped moan. His hips move faster, our bodies making wet slapping noises every time they collide.

The stinging from my wound turns into a tingle. Warmth envelops my body.

Both of his hands move to my ass, cupping it and holding me steady. His cock throbs within me, pulsating to show his pleasure. "How are you feeling?" His voice is strained.

I nod, all blood rushing from my head and down to our joined genitals. I never want this to end. I open my mouth to speak, but only moans escape.

He makes an animalistic growl, which sends my body into high alert. He pounds into me harder, rougher, "Louder. I want to hear you."

I tilt my head back, my hands on his shoulders again, and let out a series of moans.

"Princess, I'm almost-"

"It's okay," I close my eyes.

My words seem to send him over the edge. He thrusts as deep as he can, pumping his seed deep inside me. Panting, he rests his forehead against mine. Our breaths, heartbeats, everything intertwines.

My eyes open to find his looking at me. He's a bit sweaty. We both are. "You didn't finish."

I shrug, "It's alright."

Vladimir shakes his head. He pulls me away from the wall and carries me towards the bed. I'm carefully laid atop it. The mattress isn't as soft as mine, but it's still much more comfortable than the wall.

His cock is removed from me, still semi-erect. His cum along with my own arousal, ooze out of me. Vladimir climbs over top of me, claiming his dominance over me. I should feel challenged, but I don't. A warmth fills my chest and squeezes at my heart. This man who's always protected me is currently shielding me in his bed.

And here I thought he'd be under me.

A lopsided smirk crosses his lips, "Careful Princess, or I might think you've fallen for me."

I frown, wiping whatever goofy expression from my face and growing more serious. "Never."

He chuckles. A large, calloused hand runs down my stomach.

I shiver, "What are you doing?"

Vladimir's hand passes my navel: "What do you think?"

I shake my head, at a loss, "I don't–"

I'm cut off by my own gasp as one of his fingers moves over my lower lips. His thumb circles my sensitive spot.

"Has anyone ever done this to you?"

My brows pinch together. I shake my head. It's always been sex, feed, and leave. If I got off, then great. If not, then better luck next time.

He slips a finger inside me and curls it. My back arches, and my mouth opens wide with a soundless gasp. "Well then, you're in for a treat." Vladimir leans in and claims my mouth. His finger thrusts inside me while his thumb glides over my sensitive clit.

My hands move to his hair, tangling themselves in his thick locks. My hips move with his hand, bucking as his fingers work me.

Another finger enters. I moan, the sound lost against his lips. His free hand loses itself in my hair, tugging it gently.

Something hard presses against my outer thigh. I don't have to guess what it is. He's ready again. I remove a hand from his locks and down his rippling chest, heading towards his cock, but he grunts. Breaking the kiss, he shakes his head, "This is about you." He kisses along my jaw to my ear. Taking my earlobe in his mouth, he sucks it. His fingers curl and uncurl, his thumb toying with me like a joystick.

Heat spreads across my cheeks. A fire within grows, starting from my core and consuming every inch of me. I'm getting close again, just like when I'd been drinking his blood. I tilt my head back, my back arches. I allow myself to be embraced by the wave of pleasure. My body tenses, twitches. My pussy tightens around his fingers, restricting his movements, but not entirely stopping them. Breathing becomes more difficult. I try to take a breath, but instead release a series of moans, gasps, and other sounds. Time slows as ecstasy envelops me, carries me away from my body to a warmer, brighter place. Then I fall, coming back down from that high in a swift yet natural motion.

I work to catch my breath and open eyes, which have closed on their own. My chest rises and falls in rapid breaths. I swallow the alarming amount of saliva from my mouth. "Again," I pant.

Vladimir arches his brow. He wraps an arm around my waist and tugs me against him, "Let's rest first, then we can go for another round." He rests his closed mouth against my forehead.

My breaths keep coming in heavy waves. What am I doing? I shouldn't be here. Going around sleeping with humans and other monsters is one thing, but sleeping with a vampire? And Vladimir of all vampires? I've known him for as long as I can remember. He's annoying and bossy.

"Vladimir?" My voice takes me by surprise. Why am I talking? He had just said to rest.

"Mhmm?"

I swallow the lump forming in my throat. "There's something I've wanted to know for a while." I might as well ask since I have him here.

Vladimir looks down at me. His brown eyes move as he takes in my expression, possibly trying to figure out what I want to ask. "What is it?"

"Why are you here?"

He smirks. "This is my room."

My chest tightens. Damn him and that smirk. "No, I mean." I slice my eyes as I take another breath, calming myself and the millions of thoughts running through my mind. I open my eyes again. "Why are you here? Among the guards? Why did you find me that day? Why weren't you studying to take your father's place with the council?"

His jaw clenches. "I have never wanted to be part of the council." He cups my cheek, brushing a strand of sweaty hair away from my cheek. "I wanted to do more than just sit around. I wanted to help in some way."

My tongue feels too big for my mouth. I force the words to come. "So, you stepped away from the council so you could protect me?"

He chuckles softly. "Well, not only you. I was supposed to be a city guard. I was going to guard the people in case of an attack." My stomach twists, as I know where this is going. "But then you and Akantha went missing. I was able to find you, thanks to my hunting gift."

I gasp. My lungs feel too full, and yet not full enough. "And that's how you always find me? You can hunt?"

"With ease." He shrugs a shoulder.

I bite my lip. "I'm sorry. You're stuck constantly hunting me, because of that day."

"Hey," he angles my face to him when I try to look away. "I wouldn't have chosen a better outcome."

My eyes water. What is this feeling? My heart feels heavy. It's pressing down on everything else. I can't breathe. "But I'm not what you wanted. You wanted to guard everyone, not one stupid princess. And now you're stuck in this betrothal nonsense."

"Smart? Yes. Beautiful, absolutely." He shifts so he's propped up on his elbow again. His expression soft. "Annoying? Without a doubt. But you aren't stupid." His hand brushes against my face and trails down my neck. "Besides, looking out for you is my way of looking out for the vampires here in Valdama."

Except he's still in this betrothal and he doesn't want to be king. "Why don't you want to be king?"

He tilts his head. "I won't marry anyone I don't love. I don't think it's fare to force you to do it." And yet, he's forcing me to marry Carlos by saying he won't be king. "I want you to be a good queen, which I know you will be. You just need the right king by your side." He leans down and kisses my forehead. "Now, enough of this business talk. Rest."

Sighing, I close my eyes. There's no point in arguing with him.

Being here with him is pointless. Apart from living out a sex-fantasy, this would never happen again.

It's a one-time thing.

I won't let it happen again.

Chapter Twenty-Two

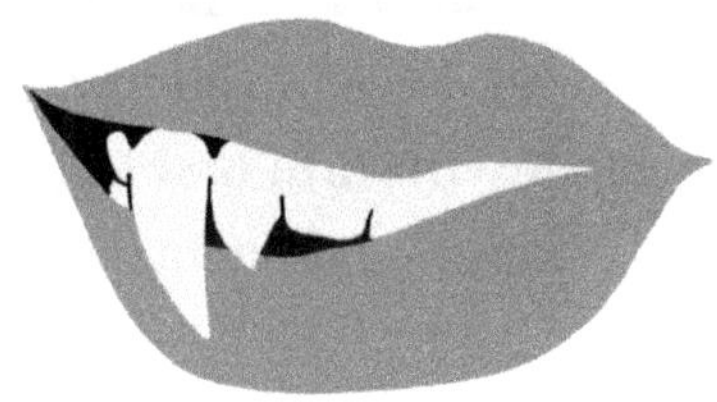

Farran

Zulmar is close to the bridge of the human world. Some of the Slave Keepers would tease us, saying that the Zombie King didn't release the fairies he bought. Instead, he'd turn them into zombies too.

It gave me nightmares for years.

I smell the graveyard before I see it. It smells like Julia, but far worse. I hold my breath.

Rude.

I breathe through my mouth again.

A black metal fence surrounds the land. Tombstones line the rolling hills. A large tree stands in the middle of everything. I enter the gates, and the princess instantly slides off my back.

"Daddy!" She cries out, running with her arms wide open.

A man steps out from behind the large tree. He approaches us, limping. He doesn't smell as bad as the princess, but he looks worse. More decomposed, yet at the same time, he seems well preserved.

Julia rushes over and hugs the tall zombie.

He smiles his rotten teeth at me, patting the girl's back with a hand that is more bone and tendons than it is flesh. "Thank you. I am in your debt."

I make eye contact with him and feel a zap. Did he just make a bond with me? I thought only wolves could do that.

"Oh no, don't worry about it. It's the least I could do," I look him over curiously. "Are you the Zombie King?"

I've heard the Zombie King is the one who single-handedly brings people to life and is able to transfer life forces from suicidal people into the terminally ill, allowing them to live longer.

His smile grows, "Indeed, I am him."

I bow my head, "It's an honor to meet you, sir."

"There is no need to bow, hero."

I raise my head.

"I'm sorry, I'm just used to–"

"I know. But there is no need for that here."

Princess Julia yawns.

The Zombie King looks down at the girl, then at me.

"I apologize, but it is late in the day. I should be getting her to bed."

"Oh, of course." Do zombies even have beds? Do they even sleep? I smile at the girl. "Sleep well, princess."

The girl runs over and wraps her arms around my neck. "Night, puppy." She rushes off, jumping into an open grave.

No, I don't think they have beds at all.

"Safe travels," Zombie King turns and follows the princess.

I stand there for a long moment before leaving the holy grounds. I rush away, inhaling the sweet smells of the forest.

I stop as soon as I spot smoke.

I nearly rush out of the thick trees and into a clearing. The smell of blood follows with the sounds of people yelling and crying.

My skin crawls. I had found it. Why is the camp so close to the zombies? Were they hoping the smell would hide them better? Well, I doubt I would have been able to follow their trail if I got too close to the graveyard. This location makes the most sense; they're closer to their two trading partners—the Vampire King and the Zombie King.

I peek through the branches of a bush and watch as men walk around, yelling at the still captive fairies. The small girl I'd spoken to before leaving is lying on the ground, not moving. Had the transformation not taken? Or had she starved?

A few men gather by a fire, their voices mixing together. Daylight is often when they hunt for innocent children and capture them with the intention of turning them into a monster.

I blink and back away. This needs to end. Too many have lost their humanity and lives to the Slave Tamer. I sneak away.

Stopping by the river, I change back into human form, get dressed, and head back to the Valdama. The sun is starting to set. Vampires aren't roaming the streets yet, but I still hurry across the village and into one of the castle's servant entrances.

I head to the slave chambers, where fairies are getting ready for the day. I approach Helena, who's lounging in her cot. "Good evening Helena. Do you know where Dante would be?"

She looks up at me from her bed. Her golden hair is combed and braided over her shoulder; a style I've seen her make with the princess' hair. "He has his own room in the south wing. He occasionally sleeps in here, but I think he was in his room last night."

I nod my thanks and rush back out. His own room? Why would he have his own room?

Rounding a corner, I bump into someone, knocking them—and almost myself—to the floor. I regain my balance. "I'm so sorry." I offer my hand, stiffening when I realize who I've just plowed into.

Dante looks up at me and laughs. The sound sends butterflies through my stomach. "I'm glad you're alright." He takes my hand and stands. "I was worried all day. Couldn't sleep."

I grin. He was worried? "I found it. I found the camp. I also met the Zombie King. It was so strange. I found his daughter and brought her back. It was almost like he was expecting me ..." I shake my head. "Anyways, I found the camp."

"That's amazing!" His eyes look me over, the exhaustion and relief not matching the grin on his lips. "I was worried you wouldn't come back."

"I told you I would."

I raise my chin high, hands on my hips.

He lets out a soft sigh, "I know, I know. Come on; you must be starved."

With a small smile, I follow him to the kitchen.

Chapter Twenty-Three

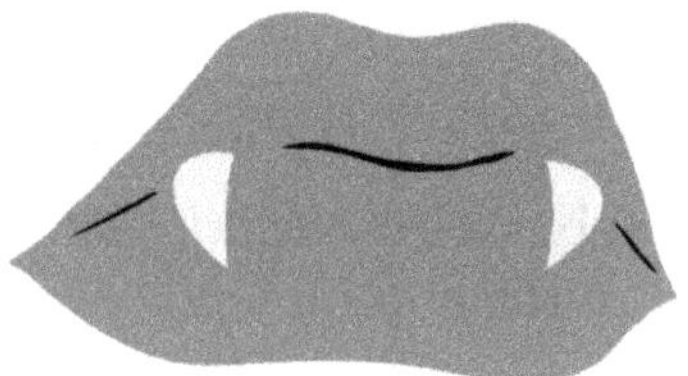

Akantha

BLOOD PASSES MY LIPS and drowns my tongue. My stomach recoils, but I force a swallow. My feeding with Prince Liam four hours ago had been rather filling. He'd devoured part of a pig, and I drank about eight litres of blood. It had helped with my healing, but left me overly full.

"Akantha, you've hardly eaten."

Mother's hand touches my arm. Her fingers are as gentle as always, caressing the fabric of my gown. Her touch—much like Helena's—sends warmth and calmness through my body.

"Stop worrying, Adora. She is no longer a child. If she doesn't wish to eat, then she won't."

Father's tone is stern yet uninterested like his thoughts are elsewhere, and Mother's voice is interrupting. If it were Callisora not feeding, I'm sure he'd say otherwise. I'll never understand why he's so hard on her.

My parents bicker for a few moments. I try to focus on the blood, how its thickness moves around as I teeter the glass, the center of gravity changing. The topic changes.

"Where is Callisora?" Father demands, his fist landing on the table with a *thud.* "That blasted girl better not be off in the human lands again."

She's not even here, and he's already upset with her. I feel sorry for my older sister. She has so much on her plate with being the next queen and all, and Father is only adding to her stress. As well as stressing himself out.

"She's probably just enjoying her freedom whilst she has the chance." Where was Mother's compassion the other evening? What's going on with her? She seems more cheerful than usual.

Father huffs, "She is disgracing the crown."

I bite my tongue. If Callisora were here, she'd mutter that she'd learnt from the best. I've heard the rumours and she no doubt has too. Her observing our father and mimicking his behaviour shouldn't be surprising.

I place my glass on the table, careful not to spill any of the blood so Father can drink it. "I wish to return to my room." I need to get away from all these harsh vibes. They're making my stomach turn.

As I rise, Father interjects. "You are to meet with Zahaya in the library."

A frown tugs at my lips. I bow my head. "Of course, Father. I shall head right over." My chest feels tight. She's made an elixir already? I'm not ready.

Helena takes my arm and leads me out of the dining hall. We walk down familiar halls and stop when we've reached the library. Helena lets go of me so she can open the large double doors. They moan open, and I enter without assistance.

"Ahh, your highness. So glad you could make it." Zahaya's cheerful tone sounds forced. Did she hope I wouldn't come? Maybe I shouldn't have. "Please, come have a seat."

Helena takes my arm again and guides me towards Zahaya's greyness. I narrowly avoid the corner of a table with my thigh. Of course, the witch had rearranged the furniture. I sit.

"Jeharad, get me the potion," Zahaya orders.

I don't see him until he moves, his dark aura hiding from sight. A shimmer pulsates through the purpleness, making me aware of his every move. His hidden aura reminds me of Cinnamon, but having an aura that camouflages with the void and having one that hides itself completely are two very different things. The longer I sit in the same room as Jeharad, the more I'm unsure if I can trust him. Jeharad grabs something from a table and swiftly returns.

"Thank you." Zahaya takes it, and her nails tap against glass. Perhaps a jar? She steps forward, closing the distance between us. "Keep your eyes open; this may sting."

I wait, eyes wide, head tilted back.

The sound of a finger dipping into slush-like liquid sends a shiver down my spine. She brings it to my face and holds it over my eye. I sit there, waiting for what feels like minutes. Finally, a thick serum drips into my eye. I struggle to keep my eyes open. She does the same to my other eye. When she pulls back, I struggle not to blink.

My eyes burn. Tears rise, but don't fall. The moisture doesn't help the burn; in fact, it makes it worse. My hands clench into fists, nails digging into the skin.

Zahaya clears her throat. "You may blink now."

I do. My eyelids flutter. The gel spreads over my eyes, and the tears fall down my cheeks.

The darkness starts to fade, splashes of color hit me all at once. My mind races, trying to process everything. My heart swells and rises into my throat. Colors. I can see colors. I try squinting to make out what I'm staring at. Maybe a window? Is the garden outside it? "It's blurry," I state, voice shaky. I try blinking again in hopes that it'll clear things up rapidly. The light and colors fade away, and I'm dropped back into darkness. My heart sinks and shrivels. I lower my head.

Helena places a hand on my shoulder knowingly. "It didn't work." Her fingers flex around my shoulder, an attempt at comforting me. Her touch does little to nurse the feelings mixing inside me—hopelessness, loneliness, brokenness.

"Hmm." Zahaya returns to where Jeharad had gotten the jar of goo. "Perhaps they need to be fresher," she mumbles. "Yes!" She agrees with herself. "I must get fresh ingredients for it to work."

"The king won't be pleased," Jeharad whispers, now by Zahaya. Does he not think I could hear him?

Zahaya takes a breath, planting her hands on the table. "I'm sorry, princess. I need more time. I hope I didn't cause you too much trouble this evening."

I take a breath, gathering the pieces of self-hatred I didn't realize I had, and stand. "Not at all. Please, take your time." I grab for Helena, and we leave the library, eager to get away from this crazy woman and her sidekick. I don't need them reminding me I'm broken. The rest of the world already does, but at least the world knows enough to do it behind my back.

Helena stops me in the hall. "My lady, are you alright? You don't look very well."

I rub my sweating forehead. I now wish I'd drank my breakfast. "Just a headache. The light and colors I saw were very overwhelming." It isn't a lie, but also not the entire truth. I'm angry. Angry at myself for thinking this might work.

"I understand. You should relax. Come!"

Helena walks me back to my room.

CHAPTER TWENTY-FOUR

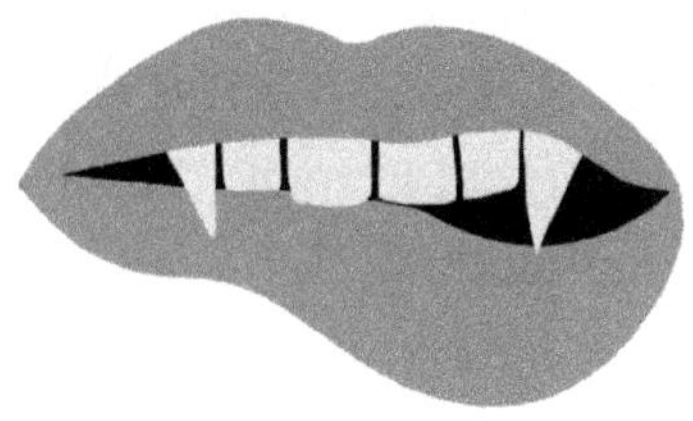

Callisora

STEALING ONE LAST KISS before Vladimir opens the door, we exit his bedroom.

I hold my head high as he leads me down the hall. There are more guards here now compared to when we arrived. They watch me. Most of them wear devilish smirks and one even winks at me.

They must have heard us.

Vladimir clears his throat, and the others all look away, continuing with their nightly routines. We step into the hall of the castle.

"That was awkward," I whisper.

He chuckles, "I warned you not to be so loud!"

Yeah, after the third round.

I lift my chin higher, "Perhaps I wanted them to hear."

More chuckles escape him as he shakes his head. "Just be glad you're the princess." He wraps his arm around me, resting a hand on my hip, and walks me down the long hall. "If it were anyone else, they'd be whistling and calling out profanities."

I look up at him, "I've been to a human bar. I know how men are." I glance behind us, the door to the guards' barracks is closed, but the men's voices leak through as if it were wide open. "I'm disappointed in your men. Degrading their own kind in such a way."

"That is life, your majesty. Now come, I'm positive you have other affairs to attend to this evening."

I nod, holding in a sigh.

"Wish I didn't, but you are correct," We continue walking. "I've decided to speak with the council about building a school."

"Really?"

"Of course. It isn't right that only we get to learn about our heritage."

He lets out a grunt. "That's surprisingly kind of you. What a shame that I can't take you back to my bed right now."

I laugh. Surprisingly kind? "Meet me in my bed chambers at sunrise, and I might let you touch me again." Just one more time couldn't hurt.

"Let me?" He chuckles, shaking his head again. "Of course, your majesty."

Smiling, I walk with him to the throne room. Before entering, I wrap my arms around the back of his neck and press my lips to his. He groans. The sound vibrates through me. He presses me to the wall, his body hard against mine. My body buzzes with anticipation. Burns with longing for more. Another taste of his lips, skin, and blood.

Shoes tap against the floor in the distance. We pull away from one another as a maid rounds the corner.

"Thank you for the escort. I shall see you again at a later time."

Vladimir bows his head. "As you wish."

He turns and heads back the way we came.

I watch him until he's out of sight, his movements hypnotizing—long strides, firm shoulders, strong hips. My core tightens just watching him. He turns down a hall, and I snap back into reality. Entering the throne room, I find Mother and Father are waiting.

"Where have you been?" Father demands with a loose hiss in his tone.

I bow. "My apologies, Father. I merely lost track of time whilst waking."

"I see that you did not bother to brush your hair or dress appropriately. Go get properly ready."

How could I forget to change out of my human-hunting clothes? I take a breath. "Of course, Father. After I do, may I speak with your council? I have a pressing matter that I wish to discuss."

"Absolutely not. Queens are not permitted in the council's meetings. Why would a princess be?"

"Because If I am not heard out, I shall never choose a husband," I threaten, head held high.

Father's face hardens. "You will do as you're told."

My hands clench at my sides, and I grit my teeth. I hold Father's glare far longer than I should. His fingers curl around the ends of the throne's armrests. He shifts his body as if he's about to stand. I bite my inner cheek, giving in. "Very well." Excusing myself, I retreat to my room to change.

It's no surprise that Father will not allow me to speak with his council. But maybe someone else will be able to grant me access. Someone who's desperate for their son to change career paths.

The gravel shifts beneath my feet.

I've changed into a purple gown with long sleeves, but the early evening breeze still nips at my skin. Normally the temperature doesn't bother me, but tonight it is.

Nobles walk the streets and chat outside their homes.

All happy chatter dulls to silence as I pass them. Are they surprised to see me? Maybe it's because I'm outside the castle? Where were they when Carlos and I were out for our walk the other night?

A familiar house comes into view. This is the right one, right? I hope so. Unless the library map of the kingdom is wrong, or the family had moved in the last fifty years.

My shoes make little noise as I climb the front steps of the home. Swallowing my nerves, I knock.

No one answers.

I knock again.

There's rustling inside. The door opens to reveal a man with slicked black hair and dark brown eyes. Darker than I thought possible.

I force a smile, "Good evening Duke Dorian."

His brows raise, "Princess? What a surprise! What can I do for you?"

Tilting my head, I look him over. He's dressed in black pants and a grey shirt. Not a wrinkle in sight. "May I come in? I'd like to speak with you about something."

He frowns and steps aside so I may enter. "I hope this isn't something about my son. Has he not been treating you well while courting you?"

Walking in, I shake my head. "It's not about Sir Vladimir. He's been treating me well," *very well indeed.*

He closes the door and walks me to the sitting room. We both take a seat at a small round table. A white cloth lays over the surface of the furnishing, a lamp atop it.

"So, Princess," the Duke folds his hands in his lap. "What can I do for you?"

His eyes travel over me, lingering a moment on my cleavage before carrying on.

I take a deep inhale through my nose. "I'd like to attend a council meeting."

His brow arches, and the edge of his mouth lifts ever so slightly. At least I know for certain who Vladimir gets that expression from now. "Whatever for?"

Straightening my back, I answer, my chin held high, and my chest puffed out. "I would like to arrange for the school to be rebuilt. Since I'm to be queen soon, I figured it would be fitting to make my first action be something to win the people over," even if I wasn't born with a penis. Why does that even matter?

His eyes drift down to my chest again before focusing on my face, "That's a sweet thought, but women aren't allowed in the council meetings."

"What about when I become queen?" My brows pinch together.

He shakes his head, "You're still a woman."

"I'm royal blood," My fists clench in my lap. "So, my husband will be allowed to attend the meetings, and I won't? That's hardly fair."

"Tradition is tradition. I'm sorry."

I bite my lip. There has to be some way of getting into that meeting. "What if I gather names of vampires who want the school? Please, Duke Dorian. This would mean so much to me." I lean forward, allowing a better view of my breasts and the small space they occupy.

The horn dog takes the bait, openly staring down my dress. And I thought Vladimir was a rascal for sleeping with his princess, his father is worse. Who ogles their son's betrothed? Although I doubt anyone expects Vladimir to win my hand, he was clearly chosen to make his father look good. Too bad Carlos is too busy wooing my mother to get into my bed. Perhaps in due time. "Perhaps if you get a few hundred names, then I could squeeze you into our meeting as the voice of the people." He looks my face over again, and I sit up, "We have a meeting later this evening. Have the names ready by then."

Only a few hours? How am I going to gather a few hundred names in that time? How many names would be needed to impress the council?

I give a firm nod and stand. "Thank you, Duke Dorian. I best be off, then. There's no time to waste."

His lips curl into a somewhat amused smile. He doesn't think I'll be able to do it, does he? "I hope to see you at the meeting. But only come if you get an adequate amount of names."

I leave, my teeth grinding as I storm away from the nobility section of the kingdom.

It had taken me far longer to get ready than I'd expected. Finding paper is easy; finding a quill and clipboard is not. I ended up asking one of the fairies to swipe what I needed from Father's office. They weren't a fan of the idea, but thankfully still did it for me.

Now I'm standing outside, unsure of how I'm going to do this. How am I going to convince these people to sign their names on a petition to rebuild this dilapidated pile of sadness?

A woman carrying her baby approaches. "Good evening, your highness. What are you doing outside the castle?" She looks fatigued. Is it from lack of blood? Or because she has a tiny child to tend to?

I offer the tired woman a smile. "I am gathering names to build a new school."

She looks me over, brows raised. "Really?"

I nod. "Indeed. I believe it would be good for the young ones, like your child. Our heritage is something to be remembered, not only by the nobility, but by everyone."

A grin crosses her lip. "I will sign."

She takes the quill and signs her name.

"Thank you. Please, tell others. I need a lot of names in order for this to even be considered."

"Of course, your highness." She rushes off.

My presence alone is enough to draw in more vampires. I urge them to spread the word, and it's not long before there's a small group of citizens surrounding me, willing to sign their names.

"If you are willing to help build, please write that next to your name," I announce, hoping they will hear me over their own chatter.

One man writes next to his name, then looks me over, "You'll be pitching this to the council?" when I nod, he continues, "I'd recommend getting the Elder's blessing on this. The council may take you more seriously."

What does this vampire know of the council? Upon closer inspection, I notice his family crest on his jacket. Is this a noble disguising himself as a peasant in order to sign? "I will take your suggestion into consideration."

He gives a single nod and walks into the crowd.

"Master?"

With a sigh, I glance over my shoulder to find Farran approaching, "I've told you not to call me that."

She swallows, "I apologize."

Handing the clipboard to another vampire to sign, I turn to her, "And where have you been?"

Farran's eyes shift to the crowd, then focus on me. "I've been looking into that thing we discussed."

Thing? My brows pinch together.

"I'm sorry that I haven't been around you as much. But I was out hunting for the ..." she looks at the group again. ":.. Can we speak more privately?"

I groan and look towards the woman currently holding the clipboard, "Do you mind continuing to collect names for me? My pet and I are going to pay the Elder a visit."

The vampire's eyes widen, and she nods, "It would be an honour."

She doesn't have to go that far.

I thank her and walk with Farran.

"What is it Farran? What's so important that you have been neglecting and avoiding me?" Not that I really needed her last night, but she was literally bought to stand by me in case of danger.

"I left Valdama during sunlight to track the Slave Camp. They've relocated since we last visited."

A sigh slips past my lips. "You're free of them now. Why must you be so insistent on torturing the Slave Tamer?"

She stops walking and I do the same. "I'm not free. I was bought. I'm still a slave." She shakes her head, "That man does terrible things. He turns young humans into monsters, then holds them in his camp until they're old enough to sell. Yes, he normally sells to your father and the Zombie King, but that's not all.

I've seen him sell to rogues. That's what happened to ..." Her words fade, eyes water. She blinks rapidly, so no tears fall. "I want to end the camp and free those trapped in it. No one deserves to be held against their will."

My chest tightens. Yes, I feed off humans, but I don't turn them into vampires. The transformation from a human into any creature is unbearably painful and deadly. And he also sells them to rogues? Cannibalistic monsters who are rumoured to eat their prey live? "I didn't know."

"How could you?" Farran looks away, staring off into the distance. "We should go see your Elder."

I nod, and we walk.

"I'll help you. It's not wise to go at night. Plus, I have a meeting soon. We'll leave at dawn."

Farran gasps. "Really? You're sure?"

I give a single nod. "But we shall never speak of this again."

"Agreed."

The old hut comes into view. It's located in an area that's out of the way from the rest of the peasant homes, but not so far away that it's a hassle to walk to. I walk up to the door and knock. It creaks open, but no one's there.

Farran and I share a look. I peek in. "Hello?"

"Enter."

I swallow. "Stay out here," I whisper to the wolf before stepping into the hut. The door closes behind me. The inside of the hut is cleaner than I'd expected. I had thought that there would be papers everywhere, perhaps some potions, and other strange things, but it looks like any other home. There's a wooden table and a kitchenette. Two doors lead off of the dining and kitchen area, one possibly being a bedroom and the other a washroom?

Words don't come when I try and speak. Clearing my throat, I try again, "I've come to ask for your assistance."

"What with?" The voice sounds older, scruffier in a way. I met the Elder when I was younger, he would come to the castle and try to heal Akantha's eyes. He isn't the type to openly walk about the kingdom and even if he did, I wouldn't have seen him due to being locked inside for centuries.

"I would like to rebuild the school in Valdama. My father won't allow me to sit in on a council meeting, but I spoke to Duke Dorian, and he agreed to allow my voice to be heard if I could gather enough names. One of the vampires I spoke to suggested speaking with you."

A man with white hair and slightly wrinkled skin steps into the room, exiting the darkness of what I assume is the bedroom. How old is he? Not many vampires have wrinkles. "Ahh, so you're here to request my blessing?"

I bow my head. "You are the wisest and oldest vampire in the kingdom. I wish to ask for your blessing. All the vampires in Valdama deserve to learn." I take a breath, "I also hope that this will encourage vampires to stay here and not migrate to the human world."

He looks me over. “You are very brave to take on your father in such a way.” He walks towards the dining table and gestures me over. “May I have your hand?”

I offer it out to him. His surprisingly smooth fingers wrap around my wrist. He closes his eyes. My arm burns as blood rushes away from the spot where he holds me. “I see the school. It will stand tall.”

My breath catches. Is he looking into my future? Is the Elder related to Dracula? How else would he have the gift of sight? Or is this magic?

“You will become quite close with the vampires here. You will be a good queen. Though, your reign will not last for long.”

Wait, what?

He releases my arm and opens his now red eyes; a smile crosses his lips. “I grant you my blessing,” he removes a piece of cloth from his pocket and holds it out to me. “Present this to the council. They’ll know you speak the truth.”

I take the piece of fabric and eye it. The red cloth seems simple enough, apart from the hand-stitched emblem on it.

“What do you mean? I won't rule for long. Will I ... Will I die?”

“You should go, or you’ll miss your meeting. I can’t tell you more,” he places a hand on my back and ushers me towards the door. “I look forward to seeing you again soon, Princess.”

The door shuts behind me. I spin around to protest, but it's too late. The inside of the building is dark.

Sighing, I slip the fabric into a hidden pocket of my dress' skirt, then turn to Farran, "We need to head back."

Farran grins. "How'd it go?"

"Don't act as if you heard nothing."

"You're right. I heard it all. This is so exciting." There's a skip in her step. "Why didn't you tell me that you wanted to rebuild the school? I didn't even know there was a school to start off with."

"I have no need for you today, Farran. Please go get some rest. We have a long day ahead of us. Meet me in my room at dawn."

Farran lowers her head: "Of course, your highness."

Chapter Twenty-Five

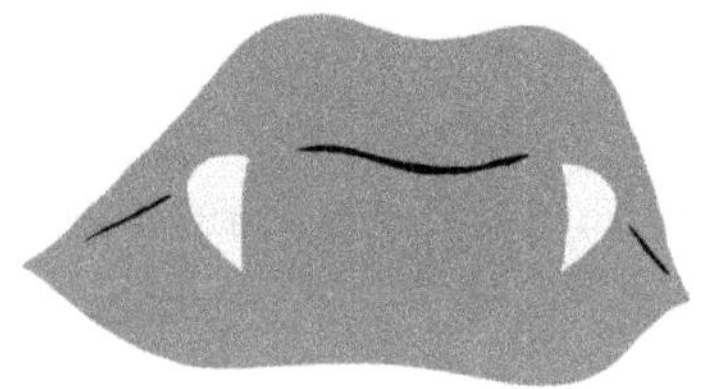

Akantha

"Akantha? Akantha, wake up!"

I groan, lifting my head off my arm and stretch. "What is it?" My head pulses faintly, but otherwise, I don't feel much of the effects from the dreadful goo that was dripped into my eyes.

"You fell asleep," Helena scolds. "I'm trying to read you your lesson. You can't keep falling asleep."

Another groan escapes me. "The text is all one-sided and boring. It glorifies the vampires. I want to know about the history of the other species." I slump back down, resting my head on my folded arms atop the table. "I grow tired of this war stricken-one-sided-vampire-orientated mumbo jumbo."

Helena sighs and places the book on the table. "My lady, these are the only history books we have. This is all that is in your lessons. Please pay attention."

"I've heard them over and over. I am sick of it. I want to know more."

"We don't have access to those kinds of resources."

I sit up, gasping, "Perhaps Prince Liam has access to werewolf history?"

That could be a refreshing point of view.

Helena lets out a breath. "Most likely. It's his history, after all."

"Well, he is going to be my husband, so perhaps it would be best for me to learn about his heritage too," I repeat the words she'd used on me during our last lesson.

"Of course," she doesn't sound pleased. "Shall I get a maid to fetch him for you? You could do a supervised lesson." No doubt she's worried that we'll repeat what happened in the garden the night of the ball or something more.

I stand, the chair scraping against the floor.

"That would be splendid. Please do that," I weave through the library, getting lost in the labyrinth of chairs and tables on my way to the door, "I think the garden would be the perfect place for the lesson. Some fresh air would do me some good."

Helena stands from the chair she had been sitting on, "One moment," she walks across the room and opens the door. There's mumbling, then Helena returns and takes my hand. "Let's go."

She leads me out of the library, down a few halls, then out into the garden.

We walk past the array of aromas. I stop and crouch down to sniff one of my favourites. Smiling lightly, I stand again.

Before I can continue walking, Helena steps in front of me. She moves a strand of hair from my face and tucks it behind my ear.

My cheeks heat and I swat her hand away, "Stop that."

"Your hair is a mess." She sighs and combs her fingers through my tangles, ignoring my protests to stop. I don't mind her brushing my hair in private, but anyone can see us out here. I don't need to give the staff and my family more of a reason to think I'm helpless. "I should have done your hair before coming out."

I huff, giving up on trying to stop her. She's nearly done anyway, draping the thick locks over my shoulder. "No one will see."

"Your fiancé will."

"Prince Liam will not care if my hair is out of place," I lift my chin in protest. A twig snaps and I jump.

"Sorry, I didn't want to interrupt." Liam's voice is soft.

"Your majesty." Helena pauses, her hands hovering in the hair above my head. She quickly retracts them. "Please, join us. Thank you for coming."

"It's the least I could do."

Leaves crunch beneath his feet as he walks over. Heat radiates off him. It's strongest when he's near me. His aroma sends shivers down my spine. The scent of trees and earth is stronger every time I see him.

Liam takes my arm and loops it with his. We walk down a path, Helena following close behind. "Where would you like to start?"

There's something about the way he speaks to me, it doesn't feel the way I'd imagine one would speak to their betrothed. It's not as flowery and smitten. His voice is softer, calmer, and collected.

I shrug a shoulder. "The beginning?" The earliest historical recording in our library is that of Dracula's second marriage, which was to the daughter of a human who'd killed his first wife with a stake through the heart.

"Alright."

He stops and plucks a flower from its bed. He glides the stem through my hair, tucking it behind my ear. His breath caresses my forehead, but doesn't affect me the way I'd expect. There's no rise in heartbeat or hitched breath. Is it because he isn't purring? Was my attraction to him the night of the ball really caused by him? Perhaps it's because I know he's hurting from his breakup? Could that be why I'm not overreacting to every little touch and action? He pulls away, and we resume walking. "Well, you know about Dracula, the first vampire. Peter Stubbe was the first werewolf. Aldock was the first fairy. And then there's the Zombie King. All four were created by Shri."

My brows pinch together. I'd heard of Peter and Dracula, but not Aldock. None of them interests me as much as that name. It sounds familiar, though I'm sure I'd never heard it before. It's as though I know it, deep down in my soul. The name nags at me, trying to tell me something, but it's too far away for me to hear. "Who's Shri?"

"Shri?" I can hear the grin in his voice. Is he happy I had asked about her specifically? "She was the Elf Empress—Empress of Monsters, actually. Dracula, your ancestor, killed her."

My heart stops. Mouth drops open. "That's impossible."

I try wrapping my head around everything he's said. "Our textbooks say he was bitten by a bat and froze to death. That he awoke as a vampire. They say nothing about him being created by an elf." What even is an elf? They don't exist in today's culture.

Prince Liam snorts. "You believe that?" He clears his throat. "I had heard that vampire history was altered, but I didn't think it was completely changed."

I bite my lip, slightly embarrassed for admitting I had indeed believed the origin story of my ancestor. Even though I had known that the texts were glamorized. "I want to know everything."

There is silence. We stop walking again. Prince Liam turns to face me. He doesn't move closer or wrap an arm around me. I look up at him. "Of course. I'll tell you all I know."

Helena clears her throat, "I'm not sure her father will like that you're altering her thought of vampire culture."

A small sound rumbles through his chest. It's not a purr. It sounds more like a faint growl. "Actually, I'm telling her what's in the werewolf and fairy textbooks."

My chest tightens. I let out a small gasp.

"How do you know what's in the fairy text?"

He reaches out and collects a lock of hair from my face and tucks it behind my ear. Unlike when Helena did it earlier, I don't find it bothersome. However, I do get the sense that he's trying too hard to act like he *likes* me. Could he? Or is he pushing himself too hard? "When Shri was alive, every Harvest Moon she and her creations would get together. The current leaders of each monster race still do this, apart from the vampires. Due to this, we share history with one another, too."

My lungs fill with sharp cold air so quickly, I swear it cuts them.

"Really? Why are vampires not welcome? Why have I never heard of this?"

"They are. Every time a new king takes the throne, they are offered a seat at the table, but because your history was altered, no king accepts the offer." He pauses. "Everything you and your sister hear and know is filtered through your father, and his father before him, and his father before him, all the way to Dracula."

Helena clears her throat. She's warning him.

I swallow, "Perhaps if I tell this to Callisora, she will accept, and we can all be united again. People will be able to speak freely."

History won't repeat itself. We can undo the wrongs of the past.

He's quiet for a moment. "You are amazing," I hear his smile. "You are truly one of a kind. It's a shame that you aren't the one becoming queen."

My heart aches. I'd never be a good enough queen. "I don't know if I'd be able to handle that much responsibility."

"I believe you'd be able to. It's in your blood and soul."

My brows pinch together. My soul? I pull away from him. "I'm not sure that is a good thing. It doesn't sound like vampires are the best rulers."

"My lady," Helena gasps. "Don't let your father hear you speak in such a way."

I sigh, hugging myself. "My apologies, Helena. Please do not report this to him."

"I won't. I just ... Please be careful who you speak around. I'll allow these lessons, but I won't allow you to speak poorly about your species, ancestry, or upbringing."

"I understand. Thank you, Helena."

I look Prince Liam's aura over, taking in how the shades of greens and browns move together both as separate parts as well as one. "Oh, I nearly forgot" I search for one of his hands and hold it in both of mine. "When we are married, and I come to live with you in

Wayfro, can Helena come? It would mean the world to me."

He dips down and rests his forehead against mine. Again, this action seems genuine, but not so much romantic. "Of course, she can come. I'd never take someone important away from you." He takes a breath. His exhale tickles. "I don't think we'll live in Wayfro, though. I thought we could live in the Dark Forest. In a cottage."

I pull back. "What? Why?"

He lets out a small chuckle. "I feel uncomfortable here, and I don't want you feeling uncomfortable around thousands of werewolves, so I think it would be best for us to live somewhere with common ground."

He probably doesn't want me around his ex and she around me. "I like that plan. Do you have a place already?"

"No, werewolves are known for building their own homes. So, I will build us the perfect home. I'm planning to leave tomorrow to scout a spot."

"That sounds amazing. I didn't know that you could do that."

"It's nothing."

A thought occurs to me. I swallow before asking, "Do you want children some day?"

There's a moment of silence. Dread hangs over me. Why would I ask that, knowing he is heartbroken and that we're taking things slow?

He takes a breath. "I know that we can't have any since you have royal blood, and I'm not the same species as you, but I would. Perhaps we could adopt or something. Maybe even get a young child from the Slave Camp."

I blink. I hadn't thought about getting a child from there. It would be nice to rescue a child or seven from the hands of those humans. "That would be perfect." It does sadden me to know that I'll never have my own children, though. My pure-blooded body will reject any seed that isn't a vampire's.

"But we have plenty of time for that. I want to get to know more about you before we add anyone else to the equation."

"Of course," I nod. "I look forward to it."

Helena mumbles under her breath, "Well, this lesson got off track quickly."

CHAPTER TWENTY-SIX

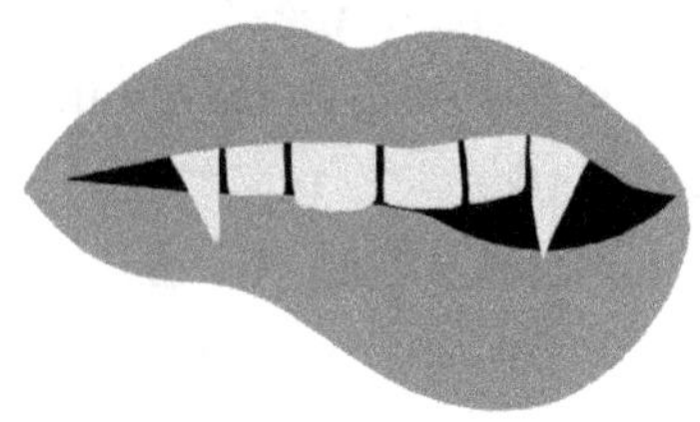

Callisora

MY FEET ACHE. PACING doesn't help.

Muffled voices leak through the thick door of the council room and into the hall, but they're just voices. No words seem to be attached.

The men speak for what feels like hours, leaving me stranded in the hall to wait. I'd been tempted to knock, but don't want to interrupt and risk jeopardizing the school. I can only hope that the Duke will somehow know I'm here and call me in. But what if he doesn't? What if he had no intention of letting me speak at all and was only trying to distract me? No, he wouldn't risk me taking my anger out on his son and possibly not choosing him as king.

The voices quiet down, allowing one to stand out amongst the rest. I recognize this one.

Footsteps approach the door. I smooth a hand over my long hair. Maybe I should have changed into something more flattering to woo the men. It's too late now.

Duke Dorian opens the door enough to see out into the hall. "Did you get the names?"

I nod, my tongue swelling in my mouth and making it impossible to speak.

The door opens, revealing the grinning Duke. He reaches out and wraps an arm around my shoulders, ushering me in. The movement is quick and leaves me light-headed.

My heart pounds as the doors close behind us. A long oval table with twelve men sitting around it resides in the center of the grey room. It—along with the vampires—are all that's in this blank room.

"Members of the council, your majesty, it has come to my attention that the lower class of Valdama wish to have the school rebuilt. The Princess has taken it upon herself to gather names of all those interested."

As the Duke speaks, all eyes are on me, glaring. I've invaded their private space. Their female-free zone.

Father's eyes hit me the hardest. Yes, the others make me uncomfortable, but he frightens me, twisting my stomach into knots. "Well then, show us these names," his voice is angry, yet uninterested. He doesn't care about this. He only cares that I'd found a way to disobey him.

I hold the papers out to one of the councilmen, but he doesn't take it. I frown.

Duke Dorian takes the papers from me, looks them over, then passes them on.

The councilman takes them from Dorian.

My jaw clenches. Seriously?

The papers are passed around, each member seeming to be genuinely impressed by the number of names.

"It won't cost much, just materials. Many vampires offered to help with the building," I try swaying them further

A couple of them nod in approval.

The papers reach my father last. He doesn't look at them. They fall onto the table in a heap, "We aren't wasting materials on a school. There are far more useful things we could be using it for."

My heart drops. "But father–"

"No buts. I told you that you weren't allowed to come to the meeting, and you went behind my back. A good queen listens to her king," he scolds.

I press my tongue to the roof of my mouth, trying to ease the pressure that is building behind my eyes. I won't cry in front of him. Not in front of any of them.

"Your majesty, if I may," Duke Dorian speaks in a calm voice, even though he's probably in as much trouble as I am, just for allowing me to walk through the door.

"Dorian," Father hisses, "I have half a mind to strip you of your title."

The Duke's body stiffens.

Can Father do that? Dorian has Dracula's blood raging through his veins just as Father does. He surely can't take that from the man.

One of the other members, probably another Duke, smirks. He has blond hair and a similar facial structure to Carlos. He takes a handkerchief out of his sleeve to wipe the edge of his mouth.

I gasp, a little too loudly, and remove the piece of fabric that the Elder gave me. "I also went to speak to the Elder. He thought the school was a good idea and gave his blessing. He gave this to me as proof."

Father rises to his feet and closes the distance between us with long strides. He snatches the cloth and inspects it. He hisses, baring his fangs. "It's the Elder's crest."

The council members mumble.

Father glares at me. "Very well, we will consider your school proposition." He turns to the members, "All those in favour?"

I frown. They're voting? But shouldn't the Elder giving his blessing be enough?

Nearly everyone raises a hand, avoiding eye contact with Father.

He scoffs. "And all those opposed?" His own hand raises along with two others.

"Very well. The school will be rebuilt." He glares at me, "Since the Princess insists on it being done, I grant her full responsibility for it."

His tone is enough to tell me that he hopes it blows up in my face. I bow deeply, "Thank you, your majesty and council. I will not disappoint you."

"You best not."

Dorian remains stiff next to me. "Thank you for your time, Princess."

I nod, fleeing from the room as swiftly as possible.

The doors shut behind me, but I'm already far down the hall. I turn the corner and lean into the wall. My lungs fill and empty. That went smoother than expected. No doubt I'll be punished later.

Once I gather myself, I go roam through the halls in the hopes of tracking down Vladimir and dragging him to my room to celebrate.

Chapter Twenty-Seven

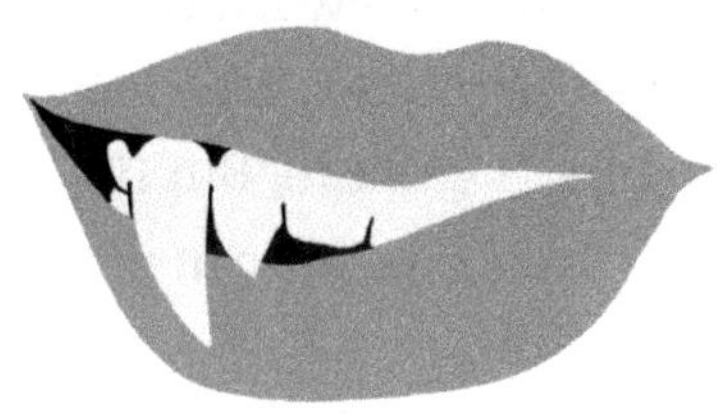

Farran

THE GRASS TICKLES MY legs. This seems to be my and Dante's new relaxation spot. Sitting outside the castle, watching the moon set and the sun rise. It's a beautiful sight.

A couple of cows stand out in the field, getting in one last grazing before Dante takes them back to the stable to sleep.

"I expected her to need me more than this. I've only had to go after her once, and even though I fed her, she's still cold to me." I lean back on my hands, looking up at the dark sky.

Dante sighs next to me. “She’s the princess, Farran. She needs to appear strong and heartless. Just be glad that she actually addresses you by name.”

“I suppose.”

“I should get back to the kitchen. I need to make sure everything is put away properly for the day.” He doesn’t move, though, just keeps sitting and watching the cows.

“Oh, come on,” I shift forward and tilt my head at him. “Can’t you sit with me a little longer?”

He smiles lightly, “I want to. But if someone leaves food out again, we might get mice in the kitchen. Those little pests eat anything.”

“You know, I just realized that I’ve never seen you eat.”

His red eyes flick over my face. He shrugs, “I don’t think what I eat would appetize you much.”

I cross my legs. “And what is it that you eat?”

“Souls.”

My brows raise. “What?”

He takes a breath. “Souls of the dying. We could take it from the living too, but it doesn’t taste as good when someone is struggling. Animal souls are the best. Fairies can last months on just eating one soul.”

I nod slowly and notice a pattern between all species. They all feed off animals instead of humans.

“Have you ever eaten a soul?”

“Once,” he nods, “When I was younger. But the King doesn’t let us hunt, so we have to sustain ourselves with human food.”

I nibble my inner cheek. "Perhaps we could hunt together some time."

He blinks a couple times.

"I know you aren't allowed, but maybe we could sneak off one day and do it while everyone's sleeping. It could be nice."

A soft smile spreads across his lips. "I'd like that. Thanks."

I smile back. We both turn our attention to the slowly rising sun. It changes the sky from dark blue to a soft purple.

"Hey," he gulps loudly. "Do you still want to see my wings?"

I gasp, jumping to my feet. "Yes! Of course, I do!"

Dante looks me over for a brief moment. He's smiling, but his brow is furrowed. He stands and closes his eyes. Dante removes his shirt to reveal a nicely toned chest that sparkles red. He turns, so his back is to me. There are two scars on his upper back, just shy of his shoulder blades.

The scars glow and then split open. His skin's sparkle intensifies. A set of transparent wings push themselves out of the open wounds. When they're fully out, they flap once. A red tint covers the wings, but is most noticeable in the intricate details of the wings. They remind me of a dragonfly, or a bumblebee.

The part of the wing that meets his back almost looks to be caked in blood. But how could that be? They are magical; they shouldn't be bloody.

"They're beautiful," I whisper, in awe.

He looks over his shoulder at me: "You think so?"

I nod, reaching out to glide my finger along them. They're so thin and brittle feeling. "I've never seen ones this color." Or any color.

A cautious cloud covers his face. "They aren't that common." His wings retract back into his body almost as fast as they came out. "I need to go." He grabs his shirt and flees back to the castle.

I stand there in the silence. What was that about?

Running a hand through my thick hair, I gather my thoughts. So many things about this handsome fairy are strange.

I take it upon myself to escort the cows back into the barn, guessing at which stall is theirs, then head inside.

Walking down the quiet halls, I head towards Callisora's bedchamber.

Once at the door, I knock, then walk in.

My eyes widen.

The princess is in bed with a man, which isn't that much of a surprise in itself. But he doesn't smell like her usual feed. He smells like a vampire. A familiar one. "Master–"

Callisora sits up quickly, holding her blanket to her chest. She frowns, her brows furrowed and eyes wide. "Farran! What are you doing? Get out!"

"But Master, I–"

"Now, Farran!"

I quickly close the door and wait in the hall.

I try my best not to listen in on the two as they bicker and rush around the room, assumingly gathering articles of clothing. Callisora orders him to jump out the window. He protests, but ends up doing as he's told. I wait a moment longer.

"Enter."

Approaching the door again, I push it open. Peeking in to double-check the leech is indeed gone. I walk inside and close the door behind me. "I'm sorry for walking in on you, Master."

Callisora stands in the middle of her room, wearing a sheer nightdress that hides nothing. What's the point of wearing something that's completely see-through? "You best be. And I won't tell you again, don't address me as Master." She crosses her arms over her chest, "Now, what is so important that you come barging into my room after sunrise?"

"Sorry, Princess. I'm trying." I shift from foot to foot. "You told me to come to your room at sunrise so we could sneak off to the Slave Camp." Had she forgotten?

Callisora rubs her forehead.

"I did, didn't I?" She sighs.

"Please, Princess, I will never ask you for anything else."

"You shouldn't be requesting my assistance with this, to begin with."

I bow. "I am aware. But there will be plenty of men for you to feed on," I offer, trying to entice her sexual hunger as well as her literal one.

"I am not hungry."

I frown and look at her. "You aren't?" Since when did the blood-addicted princess turn down a meal?

"But I did promise to help you." She sighs again. "Alright, let's get this over with so I can return to bed."

I nod, "Of course, princess. Thank you."

"Hush and help me dress. I wish to look acceptable for this slaughter."

"Yes, Princess."

Chapter Twenty-Eight

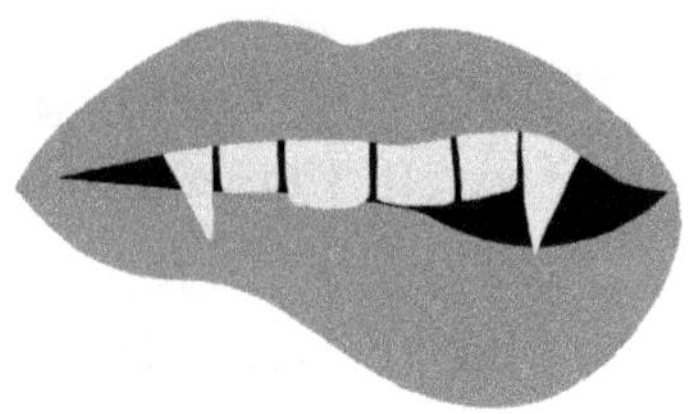

Callisora

I LEAD FARRAN TO my secret exit from Valdama, but she ends up taking the lead as soon as we step into the Dark Forest. We'd agreed not to take horses, partly so we don't attract attention to ourselves. Also, since we'd have to go through the front gates and there's no way we'd be allowed to leave.

We stay off any pre-made paths, but Farran seems to know what direction we need to go. The way is familiar to me too; it's the way I take to the human village. I've travelled this direction enough that I know when we enter the humans' part of the forest. The trees are less dense, berries are more scarce, and fewer animals travel here. It's like the mere existence of humans has drained the magic from the area and slowly destroyed the habitat.

"The camp is this way," Farran whispers, changing direction. She covers her mouth and nose with a handkerchief.

"What are you doing?" I scoff. This werewolf is so odd.

"They're camping close to the Zulmar. The smell is unbearable."

I sniff the air. "I don't smell anything."

"You aren't a werewolf. I have a more heightened sense of smell."

I grit my teeth at her response. How rude. Saying I'm inadequate. "Why would they camp so close to Zulmar if it smells so badly?"

"You're kidding, right? We infiltrated their camp and killed one of their humans." She clears her throat, clearly having noticed her tone. "My old master doesn't like uninvited visitors. He'd rather travel to the buyer. Apart from Rogues. He prefers Rogues come to him, so he's at a better advantage."

I shiver from the mention of those cannibalistic creatures. "You mentioned that earlier. He really sells slaves to rogues?"

Farran nods, the motion stiff, "Yes. I assume as food. The rogues only buy species of their own kind."

My muscles tighten in my arms, legs, and torso. If I hadn't been sure about killing this man before, I definitely am now. Who does that? Enables Rogues?

Farran crouches down and I follow her lead. She leads me through some shrubbery and stops abruptly, just before a small clearing. "There it is."

I stay low and peer through a small gap of leaves in the bush. The camp is smaller than I remember. Six two-people tents and one larger tent.

"The smaller tents will have Slave Keepers in them. The bigger one has the slaves."

I tilt my head, "At least they keep the slaves in a tent too." I cringe, realizing how condescending that sounds. Am I no better than my father?

I feel Farran's glare on the side of my face, but when I look at her, she's focused on the camp. "There will be people sleeping and others standing guard. They take shifts."

I nod, remembering from last time. "So, are we attacking at shift change, then?"

Farran shakes her head. "We should kill the sleeping ones first, then when the shift is over, they will be found, and we can kill the men getting off duty."

A frown tugs at the edge of my mouth. "Are you sure? Won't we be seen? It may be easier to kill the already awake guards and then release the slaves. The sleeping guards could be slaughtered after, possibly by the slaves." The less work I have to do, the happier I'll be.

Farran lets out a low growl, her usually brown eyes glowing a bright orange. "I don't care how we do it, as long as they're all dead."

She moves forward, and I grip her shoulder. "We need a well-thought-out plan. This isn't a plan. This is us running headfirst into our deaths."

"Well, Princess, if you don't want to go with me, then you don't have to. But I'm going in." Farran pulls away from me. She begins taking off her clothes, and I turn away. I'd heard that most werewolves strip before shifting to preserve their clothes. Do they have no shame? Or is it just this one who would get naked in front of someone without a second thought?

When I look back, Farran's no longer in her human form. That didn't take nearly as long as I thought it would. I'd expected the muscles contracting and bones reshaping would be painful and take a minute or two. Doesn't it hurt? Wasn't it agonizing? And even if it's not, even if she doesn't whimper from the pain, I thought I would at least hear bones or her heart racing from adrenaline.

I look Farran over. Her dark brown coat appears soft to the touch. My hand reaches out without my permission, fingers stroking the silk-like fur. How could fur feel so soft?

"Are you ready?" Farran's mouth doesn't move, yet I still heard her speak. Her orange wolf-eyes look up at me, unfazed by my petting her.

I swallow and step back. "Yes. Let's do this."

She snarls, but it's not aggressive. "You can stroke my fur more when we return to the castle, Princess." Then she is gone, slipping into the bushes.

I am taken aback for a brief moment. Pet her back home? What is she? A dog? A pet for me to play with? Well, I suppose that's part of it; she is mine to do whatever I'm pleased with. She is my guard. My handmaiden. *My slave.*

I shiver. Suddenly the thought of having slaves and servants leaves a bitter taste in my mouth. Perhaps when I became queen, I can form a peace treaty with the fairies and give them back their people. I could hire vampires to work in the castle. Maybe less would leave if there's work for them to do. What would Vladimir think of this plan?

Vladimir?

Since when do I see him as a king? Or maybe it is more than that. Maybe I really do see him as a partner. As my equal.

I shake my head. I need to focus. After taking a calming breath, I listen to the surrounding forest. Farran's heart is hard to find amidst all the others. One stands out, though. The beat is strong—healthy—nothing like when she first came to me. She's not scared.

She's angry.

Chapter Twenty-Nine

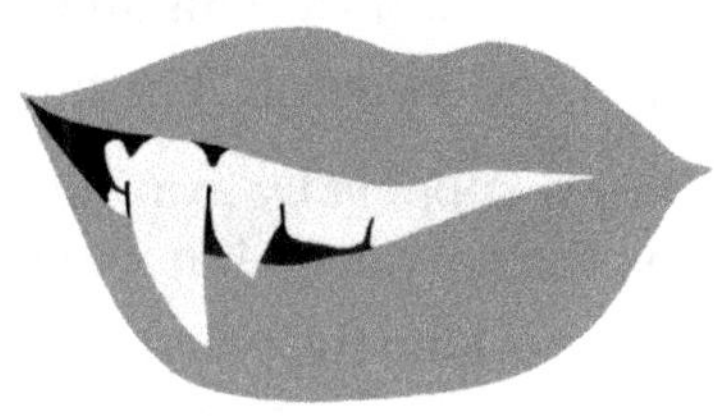

Farran

KILL.

I don't remember undressing or changing into my wolf form. My wolf must be as eager as I am.

Moving on all fours, I run out of the trees and towards the small clearing. I do my best to make as little noise as possible.

Where is Callisora? I sniff the air. I smell her, roses and blood. She isn't close, probably still hiding out in the same place I'd left her. That's perfect. I've made my way around the camp, and this means we can attack from opposite sides.

The sound of two men talking catches my attention. I slow my steps and listen. Staying close to one of the nearby tents, I strain to hear. The sun is slowly rising, and soon enough, there will be no dark shadows to hide in.

Words blend together as the two speak with drunken slurs. They seem to be walking in the opposite direction of me.

I peek around the edge of the tent and spot the men. They're stumbling and swaying. The taller of the two is using the other as support by leaning on him.

My gaze scans the darkness, but no one else seems to be in sight. I creep along the worn-in dirt path that leads to an overly large tent. The Slave Tent.

Guts twisting, I take a deep inhale through my nose. It wasn't long ago that I lived here. That I was chained up and abused by humans with electrified rods and silver pokers. I'll forever have the scars from those shackles. And forever remember the sounds of the cries that had filled that dirty tent.

The tanned fabric walls are stained with dirt and blood. Six large posts poke through the roof of the structure. Thick rope is nailed into the ground, keeping the tent sturdy. Two men guard the only entrance or exit of the structure. Both men are tall, but the one who's taller looks less built than the other, and they're both carrying long staffs. I swallow.

"What's wrong?"

I jump and look over my shoulder at Callisora. Her question is asked in the sweetest of whispers, but her face gives away her smug amusement. Does she think

I'm scared of those men? "The weapons they're carrying," I say with a growl, "They're electrified. And made of silver. They could stop your heart."

Callisora looks past me, straining her neck to see. There are two small puncture wounds at the base of her neck. Vampire bite? What has she been doing? She re-focuses on me with a smirk on her lips, "I guess we'll have to just not get hit by them." She winks at me playfully, then strolls off toward the men, a sway in her hips.

She's clearly trying to cause a distraction. What is up with her? She didn't want to be here a moment ago. Is she just trying to enjoy the kill? She had said she wasn't hungry. Maybe she just likes to torture people?

Stop stalling.

Callisora approaches the men, they're tense at first, but as she talks to them, they seem to visually relax. I seize the opportunity and take the long way around a couple of tents in order to get to the back of the Slave Tent.

Once I'm at the back of the tent, I listen. It's quiet, but I can't tell if there are any guards. I inhale deeply. Shifting to my hind legs, I lift my paws up. Mentally I count to three, then drag my claws through the fabric. The ripping sound tears through the dawn's calm air.

The fabric splits open. Thick air seeps out of the tent, reeking of sweat, blood, and urine. All familiar smells that strangely feel like home.

I peek inside. It's dark. Shadows of bodies huddled around posts fill the space. The memories come rushing back; the post I was shackled to, the hunger, the weeping, the sleepless nights. I fully enter the tent. Eyes are on me, but no one stands. No one seems to react at all. Not that they have much energy to. "It's okay. We're here to get you out of here," I know they can't understand me, but I still try. My voice is low, worried my growl will be detectable by the guards outside.

No one moves.

I approach a post and look at the four fairies chained up to it. Their faces seem familiar. They're young, so maybe they were changed around the same time as the young girl who I spoke with before leaving this place. The same girl I had saw dead outside just the other day.

Their frightened faces bring back another memory. One where I'm screaming and crying from the pain of changing to wolf form for the first time. I shake my head to erase the sound. "Let's make this quick." I slash my claws at the metal, ignoring the pain that shoots up my claws and vibrates through my bones. The silver shackles break away from the post.

CHAPTER THIRTY

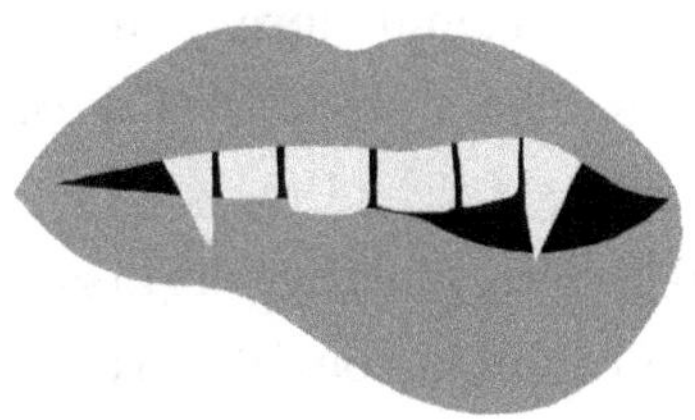

Callisora

MY CHEEKS HURT.

The men watch me, their hungry eyes moving over my body. Their racing hearts pound my eardrums. One of them reaches out and moves a strand of hair off my shoulder, "What's your name, beautiful?"

I force the smile to remain on my lips. "Do names really matter?" I tilt my head and step closer to him, my chest nearly touching his. "There are so many fun things we can do without ever needing to know each other's name."

The other man—the taller of the two—grunts out of what I assume is jealousy.

I move from the first man and over to the second. His breath catches when I step closer to him. "You want to go first?"

My tone is soft, yet playful. The warmth of the morning sun kisses my skin. Thankfully I'd remembered to refill my vile with Vladimir's blood; otherwise, I'd be burning right before their eyes.

His head bobs. Short strands of dark hair bounce over his wide eyes.

I smirk and lean in, placing soft kisses on his neck. His hands grip my hips roughly, drawing me closer. He forces me to sway, grinding into the bulge in his pants. A groan rises up his throat.

The clatter of breaking metal erupts from inside. The man pulls back from me slightly and looks to his partner, his brows pinched, "What was that?"

I take this as my chance and draw him towards me again, sinking my fangs into his jugular. He lets out a shocked gasp, stiffening. Blood fills my mouth. The normally sweet taste is replaced with a bitter one. The flavour I've loved so much is gone, and the longer it's in my mouth, the more revolting it tastes. What is happening to me? Why does it taste so dreadful?

I push him away and spit the liquid out of my mouth, gagging. The body falls to the ground.

"What the hell?"

I turn to the other guy, who's pointing his staff at me, his face a picture of shock. His heart races even faster now. The rhythm fuels me. Lunging toward him, I barely dodge the staff and knock him to the ground. I bend down and sink my teeth into him, just like I had with his friend, but this time I don't let the blood linger in my mouth. Instead, the red liquid flows down his neck and onto the grass beneath him. His limbs thrash before falling limp. I get off and open the entrance to the tent, fists clenched.

"What is going on in here? Do you even know how to be stealthy?"

Farran looks up from where she is. One of her paws is lifted into the air, ready to beat against the mettle shackles.

I roll my eyes. "If you would have waited a little longer," I rub my forehead and sigh, "I killed the guards. They probably have keys."

"We don't have time," she growls.

"We'll have more time if you stop making so much noise." I turn and peek outside before leaving the tent. Searching both guards, I retrieve a set of keys from the taller of the two. Keys in hand, I re-enter the tent and proceed to unlock the shackles as Farran steps aside and huffs.

Voices leak into the tent, coming from outside. My knees buckle.

"Leave out the back," Farran orders the freed slaves, "You can't stay here. They'll kill you."

They look at Farran, confused.

I sigh, "They don't understand you."

I translate and one of the fairies, a man with orange skin and hair, leads the women and children out the torn fabric. I smirk at the entrance Farran had made for herself. "Nice door."

The voices grow louder.

"We need to hurry," I hiss, working at the next set of shackles. My fingers fumble with the key. The fairy attached to the chains whimpers.

Farran moves past me, "I'll deal with them. You focus on getting everyone free." She walks out.

Chapter Thirty-One

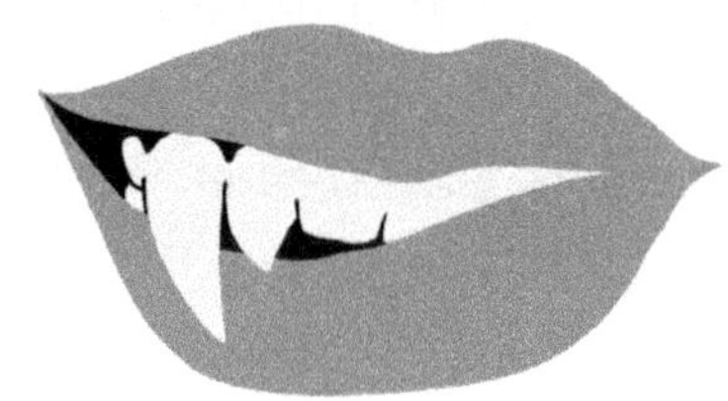

Farran

I STEP OUT INTO the fresh air. The sun peeks above the trees, lighting up the camp. The smell of blood hits my nostrils, and my mouth waters. The two dead men lay motionless on the ground; their faces are still frozen with their final expressions, pain and surprise.

A group of men come into view, all emerging from different tents. Some of them freeze when they see me, obviously not used to seeing a wolf who's strong enough to hold their non-human form. The others step towards me slowly.

"Hi there beautiful, are you lost?" One of the men asks, gripping a whip in his hands with a wicked smirk. Does he think I'm some weak werewolf who's wandered into their camp? No, not this wolf. He's the closest to me and the first one I should take down.

A shorter man steps out of his tent. His expression turns grim when he sees me. "Don't get close to her," he warns. Everyone freezes.

My fur stands, a knot forms in my gut. That voice. I know that voice.

The man approaches me slowly, passing his workers and giving them warning glances. "Farran, it's good to see you again."

My throat tightens. I can't speak. Can't growl. Even my wolf is whimpering in my head. I knew I'd have to see him again. I knew coming back meant I'd have to confront him. But that doesn't make this easier.

"Have you already forgotten me?"

"No," the word comes out as a whimper. My ears tilt back and my tail tucks between my legs.

He smirks, "Good girl!" He adjusts his fur cloak. "I'm surprised to see you here. And alive." His eyes flick past me. "Shame, those two were good men."

I find myself glancing at the two dead bodies on the ground. Does he think I killed them? They're too clean of kills to be done by my claws. My eyes travel back to *him*. He's closer now, nearly in front of me.

He crouches down to my level. My legs shake. Memories flood my mind—being taken from my mom, being bitten, standing completely naked in front of multiple humans as I changed for the first time, my adoptive wolf mother being dragged away. I used to believe that he cared for my well-being; that's why he'd hurt me when I stepped out of line. That's why he sold me to the vampires. But no, he had just wanted to get rid of me. He didn't expect me to survive there. He didn't expect me to come back.

A hand strokes my fur. I blink, realizing I'd lost myself down the rabbit hole of memories again. I back away.

"Oh, Farran, it's alright. I'm not going to hurt you. I'm your master, after all."

My stomach clenches. My tongue feels swollen, too big for my mouth. My legs start shaking and my heart races.

My master?

Callisora's face fills my mind.

No. She is my master. My friend. "You are no master." I regain my strength, strength he is trying to steal. My mouth opens and I lunge, locking my jaw shut around his throat. Cries of pain echo in my ears. I shake my head viciously.

The screams stop.

The now limp body falls to the ground. Time moves slowly. I watch as the other men yell out their battle cries and charge towards me. I howl in response and charge towards them.

Whips slash at my body, but the pain is hardly noticeable. Electrified staffs are lifted into the air, but I tear off the limbs of their owners before they can be thrown. Red splashes over my vision as I move. My teeth dig into multiple flashy surfaces, causing the powerful battle cry to become a muffled sound of pain and anguish.

Then, all is silent.

I pause to catch my breath, only to find that the deed is done. No one is left. I have no memory of knocking over tents or attacking people within them, but the evidence is there.

"Farran?" I turn toward Callisora's voice. She's standing outside the Slave Tent, looking unfazed by all the death surrounding her, but somehow she still seems off. Tired, perhaps?

A soft smile crosses her lips. She drops the keys in the grass and walks towards me. She strokes the top of my head. "Let's go home."

Chapter Thirty-Two

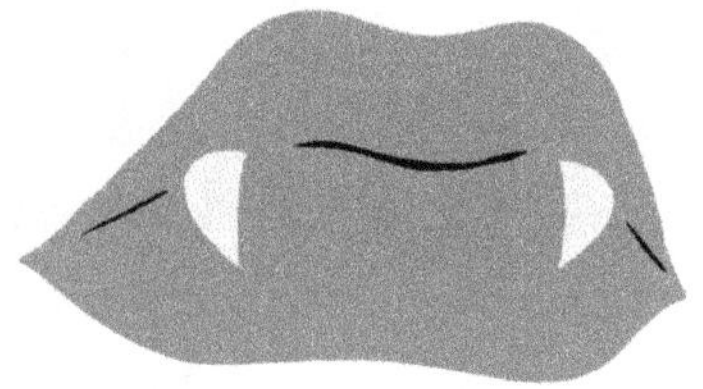

Akantha

I ROLL OVER. THE warm blankets hug my body. Why am I awake? What time is it?

Sitting up slowly, I move strands of hair from my face. The strands move back into place, brushing against my nose and cheeks. A yawn catches me off guard, and I stretch my arms over my head.

The room is quiet. Too quiet. A scent of Cinnamon hangs in the air. Twice in one week? I scan the room, but all is dark. Could the smell still be lingering from his last visit? Or is he hiding from me again? It's not often he visits me more than twice a month.

I listen to the silence. Waiting for a sign that I'm not alone. A sign that he's really here. But there's nothing;

no creaking floorboards, no soft breaths being taken. Nothing.

Then, what woke me up?

A scream echoes down the hall. My back stiffens, straightening my sleepy posture. The sound vanishes as quickly as it had come. My heart stops. I take a shaky breath before slowly removing the blanket from over the top of my legs. My feet move to the edge of the bed, hanging there for a moment.

My heart beats in my ears. I gather all my courage before forcing myself to stand. I walk towards my bedroom door, but am stopped by a hand grabbing my wrist. I inhale sharply and turn to look behind me. A familiar green aura stands there.

"I knew it," I whisper. I turn my wrist to grab onto him as well. "Why can't I see you all the time?" I demand. "Why are you invisible to me until we touch?"

No response.

I huff, frustration building inside me, consuming the fear I'd had moments ago. "I don't have time for this," I hiss. I pull away, but the aura doesn't vanish. *He* doesn't vanish. He stands in place, the hot stare of his eyes drilling into me. I force myself to look away from him. I need to find out who screamed.

I grab the doorknob. He wraps an arm around my waist, pulling me from the door and into his chest. Air escapes my lungs involuntarily. My heart pounds in my chest. I squeeze my eyes shut, doing my best to ignore all the parts of him I can feel. His chest, hips–

Opening my eyes, I gather myself. Something is going on and he's trying to keep me from it. "Let go."

He doesn't. If anything, his hold on me tightens.

"Sir," my voice is harder, firmer. I look over my shoulder at him. "Let go, or I'll scream."

I can practically feel his hesitation, the thoughts swirling in his mind. I know I should be afraid of this stranger. A stranger who constantly sneaks into my room. I should fear him, but I don't. I've never had reason to.

He releases a sigh, which tickles my ear. His grip on me loosens. As soon as his arms drop away, I long for them to return, to hold and protect me.

I push the thought away and walk from him to my door. It creaks open, and I step into the hallway. I feel him following me, though I don't hear his footsteps. I glance over my shoulder to see how far back he is. His aura is still there, but the colors are slowly fading away. He's close, but not so close that he's stepping on my heels.

I stop walking and listen. Everyone is asleep. Had no one heard that scream? Was it my imagination? I bite my inner cheek, then glance over my shoulder, "Do you know where it came from?"

All is silent. He takes my hand and walks me to my parents' room.

A frown tugs on my lips. That scream couldn't have come from there; Father never sleeps with Mother. There's no way he could have hurt her, because he wouldn't be there. Perhaps Mother had hurt someone? But she could never do that either. Maybe he's going to walk me past their room? I could be over exaggerating.

I arrive at a door. A door that opens to my parents—but mainly Mother's, since and Father spends his nights in the mistress suite—bedchambers.

The hand that's holding mine releases; I grab it again, "I'm scared," I whisper.

He squeezes my hand in response, his silence is almost reassuring. Like whatever is happening inside the room is nothing to concern myself with.

But I know better.

I know something is wrong. I know there was a scream. A scream of pain.

The air feels thick. My palms are sweating.

He lets go of my hand again and reaches past me to open the door. The door is much quieter than mine; it hardly makes any sound at all.

I step into the room and am greeted by silence. It's dark. There's no one here. But if it's empty, then why does it feel so stuffy? What am I not seeing?

I walk towards the bed and take a seat on my mother's side, then jump straight back up. The room isn't empty. The bed isn't empty.

Going to the head of the bed, I touch the edge of the pillow. My fingers move slowly across the fabric, only stopping when a strand of hair catches on my nail. I toy with it for a brief moment before proceeding further. My fingers glide over more strands of hair, then come into contact with a head.

I swallow a lump in my throat before bringing my other hand to the head. I map out the face; low hairline, thin eyebrows, wide eyes, a slender nose, and thin lips.

My heart stops.

"M-Mother?" Tears fill my eyes. How did I not see her sleeping here?

Cinnamon gently takes hold of my elbow and guides my hand to Mother's chest, where something is sticking out. It's thick and feels wooden. The wood burns my hand. I retract it quickly, holding it to my chest. Was the weapon doused in holy water?

My eyes burn worse than when I had that dreadful goo on them. Tears escape, streaming down my cheeks and dripping off my chin. I can't breathe. My lungs beg for air and I try to welcome it, causing me to hyperventilate.

I'm pulled into a hug. A flash of green resurfaces. I squeeze my eyes shut, burying my face into the comforting chest. Sobs rip out of me. My body shakes with uncontrollable tremors.

He strokes my hair. Tries to soothe me.

I get my breathing under control by the third stroke of my hair. I pull away from him. "You should go. I ... I need to call for help."

I want answers from him, but I doubt he'll give me any. Plus, I should handle Mother. Call for people so that her killer might be found before they could escape.

He steps towards me and kisses my forehead. Then, he's gone.

My face warms, in the spot where he kissed me it tingles. I feel different from when the prince has held me and been close to me. I've known of Cinnamon for a long time, and yet I'm still only now beginning to know him. There's something with him that isn't there with Liam.

I shake my head. *Focus.* I can compare the two later.

A stuttering breath enters my lungs. I try to regain my strength. I carefully walk towards the bedchamber door, unaware of any broken objects that might litter the floor.

Once at the doorway, I grip the doorframe, "Help!" I scream.

My voice echoes through the halls, "Help, please!"

In the distance, I hear voices. I call for help once more, then return to Mother's bedside.

The first to enter the room is one of the servants. She gasps and tells the others that she's going to find the king. Someone else retrieves Helena.

I sit by my mother's bedside until Father enters. Everyone steps aside so he can get to me. He grabs my shoulders in his rough hands, "What happened?" He demands, his tone hard and threatening.

My heart falters. He's never spoken to me like this. My mind goes blank. It's not until he repeats the question that I can think straight. I swallow another wave of sobs that are fighting to surface. "I–I heard a scream. It woke me up. I came to see Mother, to ask if I could stay with her, because I thought it had been a nightmare. When I got here ..."

"She was dead?" He finishes for me, and I nod. He lets go of me and walks away. "Get my daughter cleaned up and back to bed. And find whoever did this. I want them before me by midnight."

Helena rushes towards me and links arms with me, leading me out of the room as quickly as possible.

Once we are safely back in my room, she turns me to her and cups my face in her hands. "Are you alright?"

My lip quivers, heartache hitting me like a horse and carriage. "She's dead. Mother is dead."

My heart doesn't feel like it's beating anymore. My limbs just as numb.

Helena wraps me in her arms, and I cry yet again.

CHAPTER THIRTY-THREE

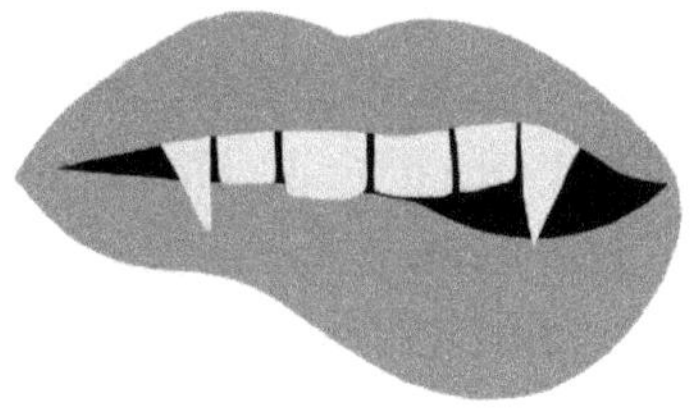

Callisora

AFTER FARRAN HAD FOUND her clothes, shifted back to human form, and got dressed, we travel home. It's quiet. We don't talk, just walk. Leaves crunch beneath our feet. The sun sets in the distance, though it's always dark in the thicket of the Dark Forest, so it's impossible to completely tell if it's day or night at any given time.

The gates come into view, but we head towards my secret entrance.

Something catches my eye, or rather someone. They're sneaking out of the kingdom, using my hole in the wall. I eye him up and down; he's tall and scrawny looking, but seems suspicious. I can hear his heartbeat from here; he's nervous. Scared. He's trying to run away from something. But there's no one following him.

"Farran?" I'm about to point him out to her, but she's two steps ahead of me.

Farran is in her wolf form again, running toward the guy. He spots her at the last possible moment and embraces himself for impact.

I rush over.

He struggles to push her off him and succeeds. Farran is flung off and into a bush. He stands and brushes himself off. His eyes meet mine, and he smirks, showing off his pointed vampire fangs. But his dark blue skin is glittery like a fairy.

"Who are you?" I demand, stepping closer, speaking loudly enough that I'll surely get the attention of the guards at the gate. What type of vampire could fight off a werewolf this close to a full moon? And why does he look like a fairy? A fairy wouldn't be strong enough to toss a werewolf like that either, right?

He chuckles. "Oh, princess, I'm your worst nightmare."

I roll my eyes, "That is the most cliché thing I've ever heard."

I proceed to walk towards him, holding eye contact. His eyes are silver, but there are strains of both red and blue in them. The sight of the mixed colors sends chills down my spine.

Farran, now free from the bush, pounces again. She knocks him over. Guards rush over—one of them being Vladimir—to help restrain him. He doesn't seem to fight anymore. His eyes are glued to me.

Vladimir pulls the man to his feet. I walk up to him. "Who are you?" I ask again, struggling to keep my voice stern.

He laughs in my face. "Oh, darling, you should be asking *what* I am."

"That's enough," Vladimir hisses. He and another guard drag the man back to the castle. Farran and I follow, but are also flanked by guards. Farran stays in her wolf form, her eyes trained on the man who is strong enough to shove her off him with ease.

We climb the steps to the castle doors and walk in when they're opened. Father is waiting in the throne room.

Vladimir forces the man to his knees. "He was caught sneaking around, your majesty."

Father walks over. He bends down slightly and grabs the man's face, tilting it up. The man offers a grin as if aggravating Father will get him far. Father hisses in response. "He's a Youngling."

He steps back and wipes his hand on his jacket as if being a half-breed is contagious. "How can this be? Younglings are killed at birth," He narrows his eyes. "How is this possible?" His voice is harder, more intimidating.

The man laughs. "Oh please, not everyone is as heartless as you. My mother is a vampire, father a fairy. If they wanted me dead, they wouldn't have had me." He glances towards me, then back at Father, "Us Younglings are tired of you vampires, acting like you're so high and mighty. We'll kill all of you, just like how you've killed so many of us."

Father raises his chin, looking down his nose at the man even more. "You killed her, didn't you?"

The man laughs, "Guilty as charged."

Father bares his teeth.

"Take him to the dungeon!" He orders, his aggressive tone seemingly affecting me more than the Youngling.

The criminal laughs, whereas I feel like vomiting. This man had killed someone. Who? How is he not scared of what will happen to him? Younglings are hard to kill, but they still feel pain, right? Father could easily torture the man just for fun.

Vladimir and the other guard drag the man away.

Father walks towards me. From the corner of my eye, I see a couple of guards grabbing Farran, restraining her with silver ropes. Father approaches me and grabs my throat. "Where have you been?" He demands.

I swallow against his hand, "I-I was out. We were at the Slave Camp and-"

His grip tightens, cutting me off mid-sentence. "Your mother is dead, and you were out playing?" Bones crack from his grip.

What? Pain shoots through my body, starting at my throat and dispersing everywhere else. My ears ring.

He lifts me off the floor. "I should kill you for being so thoughtless. So irresponsible. So clueless."

My windpipe closes. My hands paw at his, silently begging him to let go. To let me breathe. To let me live. Tears of pain and panic dampen my cheeks.

Finally, he releases me. I fall to the floor, gasping for air.

"You're lucky. Akantha would be a useless queen." He turns from me. The bones in my throat pop back into place one by one.

Farran is suddenly at my side, her head nuzzling into my shoulder. Is she trying to comfort me? Well, it's not working.

My throat opens, and air floods into my lungs. I cough lightly before standing. "Farran, I need to be alone."

Farran's eyes look up at me. The concern is there, but she says nothing. She nods, then walks off.

I head to my room, mind whirling, head heavy, and chest aching. My heart hurts, but not enough. Numbness eases in.

The halls echo with silence. The occasional maid rushes past, but even they seem to not make a sound.

Once in my room, I close the door and head over to my bed. Curling up under the blankets, I replay the evening over in my head.

Farran and I went to the Slave Camp.

We freed the slaves.

Farran killed some humans.

Mother died.

That last event feels odd. So unnatural. Why would someone kill Mother? If it had been Father, I would understand; he's a brute. But no, it was a Youngling who'd killed Mother. Father is the one who slaughters Youngling babies, as did every vampire king before him, so why would they attack Mother? What are they planning?

So many questions, but no answers. Nausea sets in. I squeeze my eyes shut, hoping it'll somehow help.

A knock comes from my door.

"Enter!"

I call out, expecting it to be a maid, asking me if I'm hungry. Surprisingly, I feel full. Even though I hadn't fed on those humans—even though their blood tasted like oil—I'm not hungry.

The door opens, and I force my eyes open, prepared to ask the maid to get something to help with my nausea. Instead, I see a tall silhouette entering my room. He approaches my bed and sits on the edge. His long dark hair brushes against the shoulders of his uniform.

I sigh and close my eyes again, anticipating a lecture. There is no way he isn't disappointed. He probably thinks I slept with one of the humans. Like what we had isn't special.

Is it?

To me, yes.

His hand takes mine

"Are you alright?"

I sit up too fast and look at him.

"What?" The room spins, but he stays stationary.

His expression is soft, "Are you alright? You just lost your mother–"

"Oh, right." I take a deep breath. "I'm alright. I think I'm still processing the news." I pause for a moment, "I thought you were here to scold me for sneaking out and rampaging a human Slave Camp."

Vladimir smiles lightly, "I think what you did was brave. You put your life on the line to save those who couldn't save themselves. Plus, I doubt my scolding would ever live up to what your father did."

I sit up. So, someone had told him. Or maybe he's guessing. It's not the first time Father's physically punished me and probably won't be the last. "To be honest, Farran annoyed me about the topic until I agreed to go with her. I didn't do much."

He reaches out and caresses my cheek. "Even so, I believe that this event is evidence of your potential as queen." I look into his eyes; they're soft and filled with emotion. Emotions I've never seen, but somehow, I can feel them within myself. "Even though the odds weren't in your favour, and it didn't benefit you, you took a stand, and you told them that you aren't okay with what they were doing."

My throat tightens. Stomach turns. Nausea rising again, reminding me of its presence. "Speaking of which ... I was actually thinking of," I pause. He waits silently for me to continue. "I was thinking of releasing the fairy slaves that we have and hiring people from our kingdom."

A grin spreads across his lips. "You want to make jobs for your people?"

I nod, the movement feeling stiff. How can I smile at a time like this? Mother had just died. Where are my tears? My guilt. It's all hidden somewhere inside me. "Yes."

Vladimir leans over and kisses my forehead, "You truly will be an excellent queen. You're already planning a brighter future."

I roll my eyes. He's so cheesy. I pull away a bit and take another breath. The nausea and dizziness settle for the moment. "Who found her? My mother ..."

Vladimir shifts, seeming to be physically uncomfortable by the question. He doesn't respond.

I continue waiting. The room is quiet. He really isn't going to give me an answer? I start prying. "Was it one of the servants? Father?"

"Akantha," His voice is so low I almost don't hear him, "Akantha found her. She said the scream awoke her. But no one else seemed to hear it. So perhaps she woke up just at the right moment."

He avoids my gaze, "Your father snapped at her, having thought Akantha was involved somehow, but now that we know a Youngling did it, I'm not sure if he still believes that."

My heart sinks. Mother and Akantha had been so close. Mother used to spend as much time with Akantha as she could when she was younger before Helena was taken on. "Is ... is she okay?" Who am I kidding? I'm not even sure I'm okay; there's no way she is.

Vladimir hesitates, "I don't know. She was taken back to her room right after."

I move out of my bed, ignoring the spinning room. "I'm sorry, but I have to see her."

He nods and stands, taking my arm to steady my swaying posture.

"I'll walk you to her room."

We walk in silence. Akantha's room isn't far from mine, but I have a feeling Vladimir is a bit on edge. Who wouldn't be?

He delivers me to Akantha's room, then walks off.

I knock on the bedroom door and Akantha's muffled voice answers, "Who is it?"

I don't respond. I enter the room, closing the door behind me.

Akantha is curled up on her bed, hugging her pillow to her chest. She sniffles, muffling her cries into her mattress.

I walk across the room and climb into bed with her. I cover myself in her blanket and wrap my arms around her waist. She sniffles again and rolls over, burying her face in my collar bone. I hold her until she cries herself to sleep. I don't have the heart to leave her. My heart aches, and the tears finally fall. My body shakes, and she nuzzles me in her sleep. It's hard to breathe as my throat constricts with each silent sob.

The tears ease, and I take a deep breath, closing my eyes and begging for sleep to take me too.

Chapter Thirty-Four

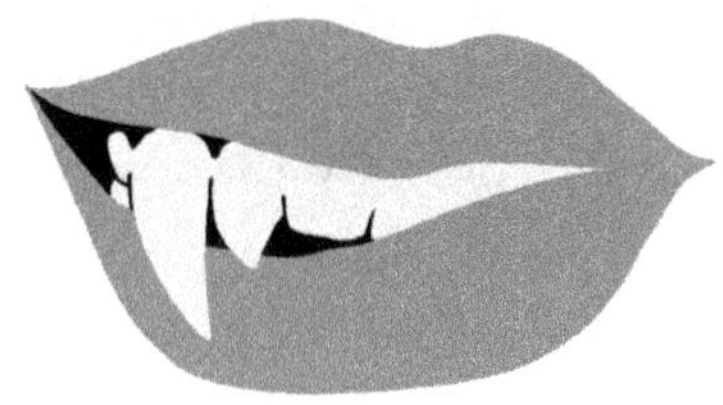

Farran

I walk down the narrow halls that lead to the servants' quarters. My muscles ache from all of tonight's activities. All the mauling. All the ripping apart of flesh.

I want to see Dante, want to tell him that everything had went well and that I'm okay, but I'm tired. I'd ripped my clothes when I shifted before pouncing on that Youngling, so I'm in wolf form until I get some clothes.

Something about that Youngling seemed familiar, though I've never met him before. His pale skin sparkled like a diamond, a mix of vampire and fairy traits. He had fangs like a vampire. Did he have wings too? What color were they? Would they be a regular fairy color?

Or red as blood?

I stop dead in my tracks. Pale glittery skin. Blood red wings.

I run down the halls and into the bed chambers. Thankfully there's no one here. I shift back into my human skin and find a clean uniform.

After dressing, I make my way to the kitchen.

I walk in. He's not here. I offer a smile to the chef that is taking Dante's place for the day. "Hi, I'm looking for Dante. Do you happen to know where he is?"

The bright yellow-orange-eyed fairy looks back at me. There's fear in her eyes. Does she fear were-wolves? She clears her throat and moves a strand of orange from her face. "He should be in his room. For some reason, the King insisted he not work today."

I nod slowly. That's odd. But if I'm right about this, then I understand why. "Okay, thanks." I turn and leave the kitchen. I make a beeline for Dante's room and knock on the door.

"I'm not allowed visitors." He calls.

"Why not?" I demand, the answer screaming in my head. I want to hear him say it.

There's a moment of silence before the door opens. Dante looks down at me, his expression unreadable. He inhales deeply, then exhales. After peeking out into the hall to assumingly be sure there's no one else around, he steps back, "Come in."

I storm into the room, my arms crossed over my chest. The door closes behind me.

He steps around me, keeping his head held high. He's facing me, his deep eyes looking into mine. "Why are you here?"

My jaw clenches. How did I not notice before? His skin is as pale as a vampire's, yet glittery like a fairy's. His ears are pointed like a fairy, but not elongated the necessary inch. And his wings. Those blood-red wings that no fairy should have. The clues were all there, but I hadn't seen them, or maybe I'd ignored them. "The queen was killed," I finally answer.

Dante nods and walks to his bed to sit on it. "I heard. Everyone has. But that doesn't answer my question. You've been out all day. You're probably exhausted."

"Why didn't you tell me?" I demand.

His brow arches. "Tell you what?"

"What you are." My fingernails dig into the palms of my hands.

Kill him.

Dante takes a deep breath. He looks like he's thinking. Is he debating on lying to me?

"The guy who killed the queen," I pause, trying to organize my thoughts. "He was half vampire, half fairy, right? Is that what you are? Are you a Youngling?"

He doesn't look at me.

"Tell me!"

My chest tightens, throat constricts. My eyes burn with tears that threaten to fall.

After another deep breath, Dante nods, his eyes focused on the floor, unblinking.

"Why didn't you tell me?"

I hear him swallow. "Because I'm not supposed to exist. I'm an abomination. The King said that if anyone ever found out what I am, he'd make me wish I was dead."

"What do you mean?" My words come out slow. I'm not sure I want to know the answer.

"I ..." He pauses a moment. "I was the Youngling my mother was pregnant with. I'm the reason she's dead. The king had found out about my existence when I was already a few hundred years old, so I guess killing me would have been more difficult," his voice trembles. "He killed her in front of me, promising that if I ever stepped out of line, he would make me wish I was never born," his head drops into his hands. "I'm so sorry, Farran. I never meant to lie to you. Maybe he's right. I'm an abomination."

My heart drops. I take a step towards him and crouch down. I move his hands away from his face. He looks at me. Fear clouds his expression. "I don't think you're an abomination. I think you're a kind man, no matter your species."

He looks at me, his eyes wide with surprise, "Really?"

I nod and offer a soft smile. "Yes, you lied, but you did it in order to protect yourself, so I understand."

He shifts so he's sitting up a bit more, "Does this mean you aren't mad at me?"

"Oh, no, I'm pissed and hurt," I cup his cheek. "But you mean a lot to me. Just ..." I take a breath, "no more secrets, okay?"

He takes my arms and pulls me into a tight hug, "I promise."

Chapter Thirty-Five

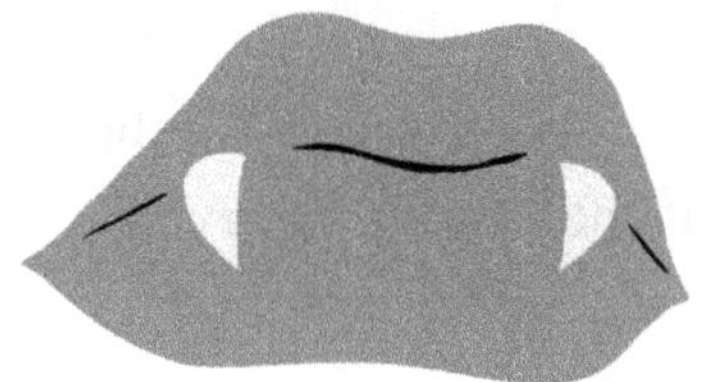

Akantha

LIAM AND I WALK through the garden, Helena trailing a fair distance behind us, the sweet scent of flowers easing my fatigue. I haven't been sleeping well; my regular nightmares have been replaced by the haunting images of Mother's lifeless body. And if a lack of sleep isn't bad enough, the full moon is approaching.

The full moon causes me—as well as other vampires—to feel drained, groggy, and weak, whereas it gives the werewolves strength, stamina, and power. One would think that would help me sleep, but it's been doing the opposite.

Liam's hand moves gently down my back as we walk. I clear my throat when it drifts too low. He moves it up again. He's been acting strange since Mother's death, too. Though it probably has more to do with the moon. He's been all handsy, wanting to hold my hand, touch my face, rub my back. It feels wrong.

I clear my throat again. His hand moves higher.

"How's your dad been taking everything? And Callisora?"

I inhale deeply, then release. "Father seems fine, a bit agitated, but that's nothing new. He's been getting things ready for Callisora to take over." I honestly haven't spoken to him much since finding Mother's body. Mainly because of how busy everyone has been, but also because of the tone he'd used with me.

"So soon?"

I nod. "A king can't rule without his queen. Though he makes all the laws and enforces them and seems to do everything, she is important too. She is meant to be the voice of the people, the one who keeps the king grounded in times of distress. We have a history of kings going mad with power." My chest tightens. "Without her here, the people, and council, won't listen to his orders."

Liam makes a noise, something sounding like part scoff and part laugh. "In Wayfro, the head alpha is often a woman—Like my mom—and her beta is her husband—my dad."

I bite my lip, trying to imagine Callisora as the more dominant ruler. She'd fit the role well. "And the people listen to her?"

He chuckles. "Of course. Have you ever heard a female wolf getting ready for a hunt? They're terrifying." His hand drifts lower. "But she is also more compassionate. She takes care of her pack before herself."

I hesitate. "What about the fairies?"

"The fairies?" the confused tone tells me that he's taken aback by my question.

I nod. "You said you'd teach me about the other species. Who is the more dominant ruler of the fairies?"

"Ahh, well," He was quiet for a moment. I clear my throat, and his hand retreats up my back again. "I believe the Fairy Prince and Princess rule equally."

My brows pinch together. "The Prince and Princess?"

"Yeah. They don't have kings and queens, just Princesses and Princes. I'm not sure why, but I believe their children are referred to as Heirs until they take the throne and receive whatever title."

Nodding slowly, I try to take that information in. It is definitely a different way of doing things. "And the Zombies?"

Liam clears his throat. "The king and princess take turns ruling. Currently, the Zombie King is ruling, but whenever he's stricken down, the Princess will take over, then when the king has fully resurrected again, he will reclaim his title. Normally they switch every few thousand years." His shoulder moves against mine as he shrugs.

Stricken down? Resurrected?

Liam stops walking and I follow suit. He turns towards me, moving his hands to cup my face. "Not that this lesson isn't fun and all, but I'm worried about you."

I tilt my head to look up at him. His aura is so bright. So powerful. "Worried?" My brows pinch together, hearing the waver in my voice.

His breath tickles my face. It's warm and smells like smoked meat. "Your mom died two nights ago. Any time someone talks about her, you change the subject."

My throat closes, making it hard to breathe. My chest cavity rattles from the impact of my beating heart. We're outside, and yet it's like the world around us is closing in. Plants rub against my legs. The breeze doesn't come, leaving me without fresh air.

"It's okay to be hurting. To be scared. I'm here for you."

Against your will.

The thought makes me stiffen. The world opens again. It's true, he's being forced into this marriage just like I am. He's nice, because he has to be. "I'm fine."

He sighs and leans in, pressing his forehead against mine. "You aren't. But it's okay. I'm here when you're ready to talk."

A bitter taste fills my mouth. Maybe I'm overreacting. He's right; I'm hurting. Mother is dead and I found her. Callisora found the killer—a youngling. "Liam?"

"Hmm?" There's a low purr in the air, coming from his vocals.

I force myself to step back. The sound vanishes. "The man who ... who killed her. He was a Youngling, right?" I'd overheard my parents talking about Younglings and Rogues, but I never paid much attention to those topics.

He's quiet. The air thickens.

"What is-"

"No," He cuts me off, his voice sounds more animal-like. "Younglings are very dangerous."

"I wasn't going to go talk to him."

He lets out a huff. Does he think I'm lying?

"Besides, he's locked up. He can't hurt me from inside his cell."

Liam steps toward me, grabbing my arms. His grip is tight, I don't think he's aware of just how rough he's being. "Younglings are more dangerous than anyone gives them credit for. They're half breeds. Overpowered and very dangerous. They have strengths from both parents and very few weaknesses."

My stomach knots. "Then why-"

"Vampire kings have been killing them off since forever. Your father himself has probably killed hundreds. They are extremely dangerous, and I don't want you to ever go near them. Do you understand? Never."

There's something in his voice. Something that says I'll someday have to confront a Youngling.

I nod. "I won't. I promise."

He sighs a breath of relief. His hands loosen from around my arms. "Thank you, princess."

Why's he acting so weird? "Right, well, I should go check on Zahaya and Jeharad. See how that sight remedy is progressing. They said it would be ready before Mother's funeral."

"I'll come with you."

"No," I blurt, my hand reaching out to stop him from approaching. I clear my throat, "I'll be fine. I have Helena. Besides, I'm sure you have things to do in preparation for us leaving after the full moon."

He takes a deep breath. "You're right, there's still a lot to do." He takes my hand and brings it to his lips, "I'll see you soon."

I offer a small smile. Relief washes over me as he leaves.

"He seems to be quite handsy today," Helena whispers when she approaches.

"I noticed that too. Do you think it's moon related?"

"Most definitely. Werewolves get more physically stimulated around a full moon." My cheeks warm. What would have happened if Helena wasn't here? Would he have tried something more than a kiss of my knuckles? The fairy links her arm with mine to guide me. "Enough about horny werewolves, though, where are we headed?"

I clear my throat. "I want to check on the witch and wizard."

"As you wish."

Chapter Thirty-Six

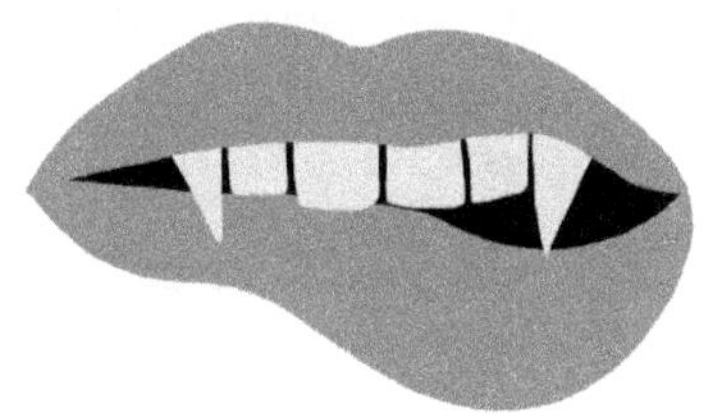

Callisora

Carlos follows me down the front steps of the castle. He reminds me of a lost puppy, or Farran. Speaking of which, Farran still owes me time to pet her fur.

The image of her blood-soaked wolf fur flashes before my eyes. The sight makes me both sick and hungry.

"What are you thinking about?" Carlos asks, his voice small. He's been acting the most depressed out of everyone. He and Mother must have had quite the connection. I wonder how deep that connection was. Had they kissed? Slept together? Though Father didn't seem sexually interested in Mother anymore, she was still his queen. Telling him that I suspected her and Carlos of canoodling would definitely anger him enough to have Carlos no longer be one of my possible suitors, but it would also most likely get him killed.

Since when did I not want Carlos as a suitor?

He is smart and a good match for me. Vladimir had even pointed that out.

Vladimir's face comes to view, his hungry eyes, dark hair, the smell of his sweat, the taste of his blood on my lips.

"Callisora?" Carlos' annoyed voice rings out, cutting my train of thought off.

I turn my attention to him, offering a sweet smile or at least attempting one. "Yes?"

"I said, what are you thinking about?"

You. Vladimir. "My mother."

His body tenses.

"You two were pretty close," I observe. "I saw the two of you joking around the other evening." I gaze off into the distance. "I hadn't seen her smile like that before."

He clears his throat, "She was a kind queen. She'll be missed dearly by everyone."

"I'm not so sure. Yes, many are saddened by her death, but she didn't do anything for the people. She sat by while my father ruled the kingdom into the ground."

Without warning, a hand strikes my cheek. I stop. What was that? My attention is drawn to Carlos. Did he hit me?

His watery eyes glow red. "How dare you. Adora was beautiful and kind."

So, they were on a first-name basis.

I want to slap him back, rip him into tiny pieces and throw the shreds at his father, but I don't. Instead, I rotate my jaw, easing the sting in my cheek. "And yet, someone killed her. There's more to being a leader than just smiling pretty. My mother had no backbone. She didn't stand up to my father. She didn't try to change anything." All she did was look down on me and baby my sister.

The red in his eyes dulls. "And what are you going to do? Build a school? That's hardly going to change anything."

"I want my people to be able to live comfortably here, to feel safe, and to learn about their history."

"Learning history isn't the same as changing things."

"That may be true, but if I start, then it could cause a butterfly effect. The Queens that follow me could make small changes, one at a time, and in a few thousand years, Valdama could be as strong and powerful as Father makes us appear to be."

Carlos grows silent, his jaw muscles clenching.

We proceed to walk toward where the new school will be built. There are people crowded around, organizing who's doing what jobs. It brings a smile to my face. They want this; they want a queen who will lead them to a bright future.

My gaze travels back to Carlos, who's also watching the group of vampires. What does he think of the lower classes? He's a nobleman; his father is part of the council. Does he look down on them? "What do you think of the fairy slaves?"

He shrugged, "I think they're fine. They do their jobs."

"Right." That isn't a lie; the fairies are very good at what they do, but they had to be, or Father would kill them. "What if I wanted to set them free? What would you think of that?"

His expression changes from slightly annoyed to confused. "Why would you do that?"

I shrug, "I think it would be good for our economy if we hired our own kind. The other kingdoms have eliminated slavery; why shouldn't we? We could pay them and boost the economy. Less vampires would want to leave. Even if we just pay them in blood to start with, it could help them all so much."

"I don't think that amount of change so soon is wise."

Disappointment tugs at my chest. "You aren't serious. As queen, I should do what's best for the people I'm ruling over." This conversation is moving around in a circle.

"No, as queen, you should listen to your king and birth children."

My teeth clench. This sexist pig. Am I just a baby-maker to him? Someone who'd obey him without question? And is he really addressing himself as my king already? "I have very important business to attend to. Please, do excuse me." I turn my back on him and walk toward the group of vampires, not looking back.

Chapter Thirty-Seven

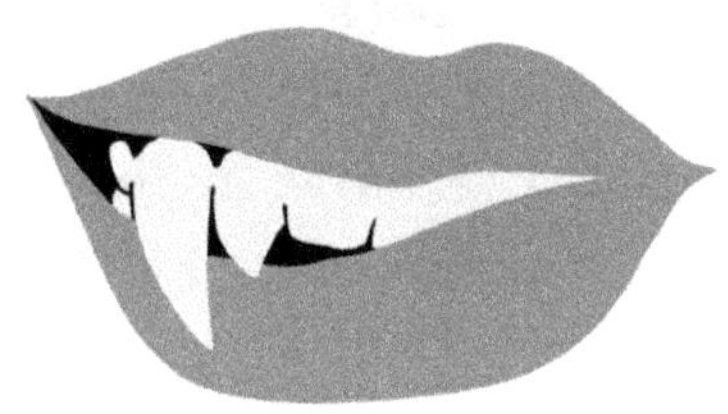

Farran

THIS IS SUCH A bad idea.

Very bad.

My wolf paces inside my mind as I stroll down the hall. My steps are overly confident. I'm trying too hard to look normal. To look like I'm not about to do something very dangerous.

I stop at Dante's door, holding a black cloak close to my chest and glancing down the hall to be sure no one is near. I haven't seen him since our conversation yesterday. Going from talking multiple times a night to only once is far harder than I'd expected.

I lift my hand to the door and hesitate. What if he says no? Taking a breath, I knock.

The door opens a crack, then wider. A hand reaches out and takes my arm, pulling me into the room.

I gasp.

I'm pinned against the door, a hand pressed next to either side of my head. Dante looks me over. "What are you doing here?" He doesn't sound annoyed. More worried. "I told you, I'm not supposed to have visitors. What if someone saw you?" His brows pinch together.

I offer a reassuring smile, my heart fluttering. "Everyone is too busy preparing for the late queen's funeral. No one saw me."

He doesn't seem convinced. "What are you doing here?" he repeats, his hands dropping from the door. He steps back.

I unfold the cloak, "I figured you could use some fresh air."

His wide, fearful eyes look in mine.

"We won't get caught. Besides, you didn't do anything. You don't deserve to be punished for what that guy did to the queen. The only person who should get to punish you is me."

A sly smile spread across his lips. "Careful of your wording, or I might think you want to punish me."

My face grows hot. My core clenches. I toss the cloak at him. It hits his face, then starts to fall down. He catches it in the air. "Put this on." I thought only werewolves got horny near a full moon. Is he part wolf too and didn't tell me?

Without further argument, he obeys, wrapping the dark fabric around his body and tying the string at his neck. "Where are we headed?"

"I thought we could go for a little hunt in the Dark Forest." I crack the door open to peek out into the hall. No one is around. Grabbing Dante's hand, I lead him out.

We slowly inch our way down the halls. I poke my head around each corner before we round it, being sure that no one is there. We're nearly out of the castle when I hear footsteps echoing behind us. I push Dante around a corner blindly and turn to see who's coming.

A pink-skinned fairy walks towards me. She glances around, clearly searching for my partner in crime.

I swallow a lump in my throat, "Hey!"

Her bright eyes land on me. A small smile spreads across her lips, causing my skin to crawl.

"Hello, Farran. It's so good to see you. How are you doing?"

"I'm doing alright," not that you care.

She leans over to one side, trying to see around the corner. "Who are you sneaking around with?"

A shiver rises up my spine. I need to think quickly. "Who? Oh, he's no one." I try to find a suitable name, but no one comes to mind. "It's one of Prince Liam's guards." He has guards, right? He has to.

Her pink eyes sparkle almost as bright as her skin, "Really?" She grins genuinely, "Good for you. Some of us were starting to worry that you and Dante had a thing going."

I frown and cross my arms over my chest. "And what exactly do you mean by that?"

She twirls a strand of hair innocently, "Oh, nothing. Just that he's a fairy, and you're not. It would never work out."

But he's not a Fairy. He's a Youngling.

"Right. Well, as you can see, I have a date to get to."

The fairy giggles. "Sorry to interrupt. Have fun." She winks before walking back in the direction she came.

I wait until she's out of sight before rounding the corner and grabbing Dante.

He keeps up with me easily. "That was close."

"We aren't home free just yet," I mutter, "we still need to get outside."

Rushing down countless halls, I'm pleasantly surprised by how well I've learnt the layout of this labyrinth. The servant door finally comes into view. One of the other fairies calls after me, but I ignore them.

The door flies open and we step outside. We don't stop, though. Instead, we break into a run, only slowing down when we've slipped through Callisora's secret hole in the kingdom wall and are a safe distance from Valdama.

Dante hunches over and rests his hands on his knees. "You're going to be the death of me," he pants.

I plant my hands on my lower back and lean back with a laugh. Facing towards the sky, I also pant. "You know you loved it."

"I didn't say that."

"You don't have to. I can tell by how fast you ran alongside me."

He grunts in protest, but doesn't verbally argue. He looks around. "So, what are we hunting for?"

"Deer?" I offer, though I don't hear any nearby. But judging by how loudly our feet had hit the ground as we ran, we probably scared off all the animals. "We'll have to be quieter, though." I look him over, "Do you know how to hunt?"

He shifts back and forth on his feet. "I hunted with my mother when I was young, but I haven't for a long time. I'm not sure I really know how."

His honesty makes my chest tighten. His mom? Questions swirl around in my head again. Maybe this is a bad idea? But maybe it's not. "This is my first hunt," I decide to admit. Tracking the camp isn't exactly the same as hunting moving prey.

He chuckles under his breath, "Guess we should get started, then."

Chapter Thirty-Eight

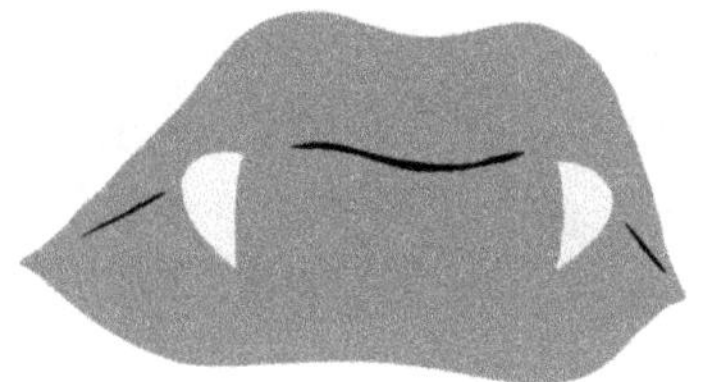

Akantha

Helena knocks on the thick wooden door. The sound echoes down the empty halls. We wait.

"I wonder if they're getting ready for the funeral," the fairy thinks out loud, her voice dripping with disappointment. But why would she be disappointed? Shouldn't the two come to the funeral? They were here, because of Mother's hospitality, right?

The door opens, the motion causing Helena to gasp quietly.

"Princess," Zahaya greets me, excited. "I'm so happy you're here!"

She walks past Helena and takes my hand in both of hers. "We've had a breakthrough." She leads me inside. Helena follows, closing the door behind us.

Being addressed as princess takes me off guard. I follow her, slightly dazed. But when the door clicks shut, I shake my head.

"You can call me Lady Akantha," I whisper, though I figure this strange woman won't change how she addresses me. Hopefully, she'll be leaving soon. She and her assistant's scents are too intense today, they're making my head pulse.

"Jeharad," Zahaya calls out. As per usual, I almost don't see him, but his small movements give him away, his dark aura glittering to life. "Lady Akantha is here. Can you fetch me the cream?"

She leads me to a chair, and I sit.

She'd actually heard me? Well, at least she's not addressing me as princess.

The room is small, considering that there are two people dwelling in it. "How have you been keeping? Do you need a larger room? Separate rooms, perhaps?" Would they be staying long enough to even enjoy a larger room or two?

Zahaya gasps, "Oh, no, that's quite alright. We're used to sharing a space, and we've lived in tiny apartments. This is more than enough."

I press my lips together and nod. That shouldn't bother me, but it does. My bedroom is small for a princess, but it could surely fit two people comfortably. This one is a third the size.

Jeharad returns and hands something over to the witch. She thanks him then steps closer to me. "Now, close your eyes." I do as I'm told. This potion must be different from the eye drops from last time.

Her fingers are rough as they slide over my eyelids. The thick cream smears with difficulty. I clench my teeth together as the potion seeps in through my eyelids, burning the surfaces of my eyes.

"Does it hurt?" Jeharad's words cut through the pain. His voice sounds strong, but I can tell he's worried.

"A little," I admit. "About the same as before."

"This is a different potion. I'm not as confident that it'll work, but the ingredients were easier to find than the last," Zahaya stands farther away, "I want you to open your eyes. Try not to blink too much; we want the cream to absorb into your eyes."

I swallow. My eyes open slowly. My eyelids are sticky, but it's the surface of my eyeballs that sting. The potion is seeping through my flesh and into my naked eyes. Raising my hand, I attempt to shield myself from the emerging brightness, but it's not as bright here as it was in the library. Browns, blacks, and greys blur together. Lines are fuzzy.

"Your majesty?"

Zahaya gets close to me again, but even though her face is inches from mine, it's a blur. I can tell she has brown hair and tanned skin. Her clothes are baggy, and her hat sits crooked on her head. "Can you see me?"

I nod, the motion feeling forced. "Kind of," my voice is low as if talking too loud might scare what little vision I have away. It's somehow more blurry than last time. Could it be, because of the softer colors?

A flash of white teeth startles me. "That's better than a no. How well can you see?" she holds up her hand, "How many fingers?"

"Three," I answer without hesitations. "Everything is fuzzy. It's all blurring together."

"How long will it last?" Helena asks, interrupting whatever happy moment Zahaya was leading up to.

The witch sighs and moves away from me.

"I'm not sure. It's a strong potion, so it should be permanent–"

"But it was also supposed to bring back her full vision," adds Jeharad, stepping towards me next. His bright green eyes stand out in the blurry mass of dark colors. His skin is a lighter tone than Zahaya's. His hair is darker, though. I can smell cabbage on his breath. "It should buy us time to get the fresh ingredients for the first potion." He turns away from me and returns to a table where Zahaya is standing.

"Those ingredients aren't easy to come by." Zahaya lets out a heavy sigh. "I suppose it's worth a try, though."

Helena rests her hand on my shoulder, then walks around in front of me. Her golden eyes meet mine. "How do you feel?" She reaches out and cups my face in her hand. Her skin is golden, and it sparkles like her aura. Her hair is braided and slung over her shoulder, silver and golden strands twirled around each other.

My eyes water, heart swells: "Helena," I gasp. "You're so beautiful!"

It's the first time I've ever actually seen the fairy who's helped raise me. The woman who's been by my side for as long as I can remember. Somehow, she is more radiant than I ever could have imagined.

I don't see her lips move, but her voice gives away her smile, "You can see me?"

"A bit. Mostly colors and rough shapes."

I reach out and touch her hair; hair I had once imagined was made of velvet, because of how soft it was.

Helena moves closer and wraps her arms around me. Her silent sobs of joy vibrate through me. I hug her back, squeezing her. I hadn't realized how important my seeing is to Helena. I hadn't realized how badly I'd wanted to see her, either.

The fairy sniffles before pulling away. "We should get you to your mother's funeral. I don't want this wearing off before you get to see your mother."

Her words cause my heart to ache. This would be the first and last time I ever get to see Mother.

Helena holds my arm as she guides me through the castle. Normally I'd protest against needing this heavy of assistance, but given how bright the lights and colors are, the help is greatly appreciated.

We walk along the smooth brown floors. I reach out my free hand, grazing it against the stone walls. The feeling is familiar, but the grey is foreign. Small bumps and crevices scrape against my fingertips. The dark shadows of the gaps where stones meet, but don't quite fit tighter blends with the polished rocks' surfaces.

The hallway opens to a large room with high ceilings, three large chairs, and red decor everywhere. A rug that starts at the chairs and leads to a pair of dark wooden double doors, the tapestry that hangs from the walls and even the cushions on the chairs are bright red.

I sniff. The stiff air is unfamiliar. "Where are we?"

"The throne room," Helena whispers as if the empty room will scold her for speaking.

Thrones, not chairs. No wonder this room is not familiar; I don't belong in it. This is where the king, queen, and heir to the throne belong. I belong in my room, the garden, and the library. I used to belong with the Elder, but even that is no longer a possibility. I only belong with Liam now. But do I? Do I even belong with or to him?

Without another word, Helena leads me towards the large dark doors. Two vampires in shining armour open them. Cold air rushes into the castle, embracing me in a way I didn't know was possible. It's like seeing is adding to my other senses instead of taking away from them. I could smell better, feel more, could I hear farther too?

We walk down the stone stairs, and I hesitate before taking my first step off the castle steps.

The gravel digs into my bare feet. I whimper, jumping back onto the last step.

Helena gasps. "Are you alright? I forgot about the gravel. I can get you shoes."

I shake my head. Where would she even find shoes? "I'm fine." The words sound less assuring than I mean them to.

"Please, princess, it won't take long," she insists.

A pair of hands rest on my waist, causing me to release a small yelp. "I'll keep her feet off the ground," Liam's voice exclaims. He carefully lifts me, then rests my feet on top of his. My toes hang over the edge, and his footwear is uncomfortable to stand on, but not as bad as the gravel.

"Liam?" I glance over my shoulder, taking in his dark eyes, tanned skin, and light-colored hair. "Aren't I heavy?"

He offers me a smile, though he doesn't know I can see it, "Not at all."

Helena sighs, "Very well." She steps aside, giving us some amount of privacy.

I look straight ahead, watching as a handful of guards carry a plank of wood with Mother's body on it. I catch a glimpse of her pale face. Her eyes are closed, lips blue. Her long black hair is laced with glowing blue flowers. Are those from the garden? The guards place the plank on a large stone oven, which is used solely for cremation ceremonies. It looks heavy. How many people did it take to bring it to the castle?

Liam rests his chin on my shoulder.

"How are you holding up?" His voice is low, his breath warm on my neck. I resist the tremble that threatens to work its way up my body.

I take his hands from my hips and guide them, wrapping his arms around my waist.

"I don't know."

I want to be held and comforted. I want the ache in my heart to ease and fade.

His arms tighten around me. "It'll be okay. They got the guy. He'll be punished."

I nod. Though, having the Youngling killed won't bring Mother back. Nothing will.

Father and Callisora walk up to the stone structure. I recognize the auras they admit, each outshining the ones around them and fighting with each other's for dominance. Callisora's seems off, though. There's a glimmer of aqua in her midsection. Head held high, but her eyes focus on the ground, my sister avoids looking at the body laying before her. She's thinner than I'd imagined. Taller too. Her hair, though blurry, shines in the moonlight.

Father seems to be forcing himself to look at Mother. His gaze is harder than I'd expected and surprisingly clear to me; he's giving the body an almost hateful glare. Father looks up from Mother and straight at me. I stiffen. I've never realized how intimidating his gaze is. How angry. Does he still think I had something to do with Mother's death?

"We are gathered to honour the memory of my wife, your queen, Adora," Father announces, turning his attention away from me and looking off toward the vampires who've come to pay their respects.

"Her time was cut short, but Valdama will not fall with her," he gestures to Callisora. "The princess has been preparing to inherit the throne for some time now, and though it's sudden, I'm sure that she and her desired partner will be ready to take their places on the throne as soon as the full moon passes."

My heart falls. How could Father turn Mother's funeral into a method of promoting Callisora's coronation?

Father's smirking face looks towards me again as if checking up on me. Does he know I can see him? He then grabs a flaming torch from one of the servants, as does Callisora. They each walk to opposite ends of the body. Callisora at Mother's head, Father at her feet. Father shoves his torch under the board Mother is on and lights the oven. Callisora is more delicate with her lighting of the oven.

Grey smoke escapes from the gaps around Mother's body as the board slowly burns. Soon thick black smoke rises into the air, followed by a rancid smell. The smell of Mother's body burning.

"All of you are welcome to stay as long as you'd like, to pay your respects," Father informs the surrounding vampires.

The flames grow, reaching for the moon. The tightness in my chest worsens. My throat constricts, eyes burn, and head feels dizzy.

My surroundings blur together, but not because of my tears. Blackness creeps in from the edges of my vision. A high-pitched ringing cuts through the air. I cover my ears with the palms of my hands and clench my teeth, trying to block it out.

I force my eyes open, squinting in the hope of seeing better. No one seems to hear the ringing, or if they do, they aren't reacting to it. I turn my attention to Helena, who still seems focused on my mother's burning body.

"Helena," I whimper. "Something's happening."

She turns to me and gasps, "Your eyes are turning red!"

She cups my face in one of her hands. Her touch normally feels warm, but now it's freezing. "You have a temperature. Liam, we need to get her inside."

His hold on me tightens. My feet lift up off his, and he repositions me, so my legs are hanging over his one arm, and my body is being supported in his other.

"What's wrong? What's happening to her?"

"It could be a side effect of the potion Zahaya and Jeharad gave her earlier today," Helena's hand touches my shoulder. "What are you feeling?"

I cringe from the coolness of her touch. "My eyes hurt, so does my head, and there's this ringing in my ears."

"Can you still see?"

I blink my eyes in an attempt to make any of the darkening colors crisper.

"Barely ..." I feel like I'm being spun around in circles.

Helena says something, but I can't hear it. The ringing becomes more intense. I rest my head on Liam's chest as he walks. His heart beats beneath the skin, but it's surprisingly slow. Calm. His breath tickles my neck. Is he looking down at me? Is he trying to talk to me? Is either of them talking to me? Why can't I hear them?

The fresh outside air vanishes, replaced by the stiff air that fills the throne room. We head through it towards the staircase that leads to my room.

As we travel down the halls, something breaks through the ringing. A soft voice, whispering through the air, as gentle as a breeze. I try to listen, but the pain is too intense, too distracting. I squeeze my eyes shut, attempting to focus on just the one sense.

My mouth dries when I'm able to make out what I'm hearing. It's a voice calling out to me. A deep male voice. Can Helena hear him? Can Liam? Why can I hear this voice, but nothing else?

"Akantha."

I try to answer the call, but my mouth doesn't seem to work. None of my limbs do. I can't even open my eyes. What is happening?

CHAPTER THIRTY-NINE

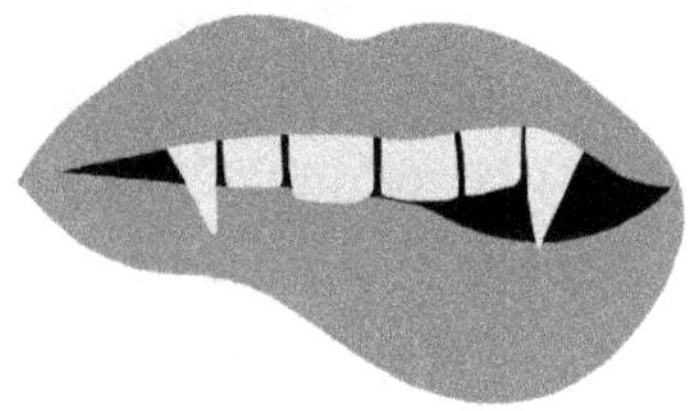

Callisora

AS MORE CITIZENS APPROACH, paying their silent respects to Mother, I get more anxious. Why would someone kill Mother? Why not Father? Maybe they wanted them both dead?

Some of the vampires speak to Father or me, consoling us on our loss. Father puts on a show, expressing emotions that a typical widow would, but they're fake. The glossy eyes, sad smile, all of it—fake

After a couple of hours, I can't bear to be here any longer. I'm worried about Akantha. Why did Liam carry her inside? Was this all too much for her? If something is wrong, her handmaiden would come get me, right? I take my leave, heading inside.

The castle is quieter than usual. All the servants must be either dealing with the funeral or hiding somewhere, slacking off.

I thought I had headed to Akantha's room, but I find myself heading in a different direction, to the dungeon. It's doubtful that the Youngling will answer any of my questions, but it's worth a try.

The door to the dungeon is surprisingly well-oiled. It opens easily, without a sound. The stairs spiral down into a dark, damp hall. Dim flickers of light cast moving shadows around the lanterns that house them. Cobwebs hug the walls as I walk along, peeking into each empty cell as I pass. When was the last time someone had cleaned down here?

"Hello, princess," a deep voice sings out from the dark corner of a cell.

I'd nearly walked past it, too distracted by the dust on the bars to see him sitting there. His heartbeat is so calm, so quiet.

I'm tempted to lean against the wall, but the thought of getting the back of my dress dirty detours me.

"I see you are making yourself comfortable."

He chuckles under his breath, "I'm simply reflecting on a job well done."

I clench my fists. "Why did you do it?" My voice is calm, though I want to scream; I want to rip him apart. Why did he have to kill the better of the two? Surely Father wouldn't have been much harder to find.

"Why? That's a good question. Why would I kill the Vampire Queen?"

"Don't mock me. Answer my questions, or I'll see to it that your life in this cell will be miserable and painful until the day you die."

He stretches out his hand, looking at his fingernails. "I knew the risks."

"And yet you still came," I mutter. "Why?"

He stands and walks towards the bars, towards me. He stops, careful not to get close enough so I can reach him. "You know what I am?"

I nod once, "A Youngling."

He sighs, shaking his head: "I'm half vampire. I am one of your people, even if my blood is mixed," he turns away, walking the length of his cell, dragging a finger against one of the walls, collecting dust as he moves. "But even though I'm half vampire, I'm not welcome here. I'm not welcome anywhere."

"You're dangerous," I repeat the words that I've been told so many times. "You're too powerful. All the strengths of a vampire and a fairy–"

"I'm aware. But killing us at birth isn't the answer."

He strides along the back of his cell, "Dracula, your ancestor, killed the first Youngling. He made it law that my kind weren't allowed to exist. And anyone who accepted us would be seen as the enemy," he pauses. I say nothing. "This tradition has gone on for too long. Passed down to the first-born son. But you're special; you're the first-born, but a daughter. You could break this cycle. You and your sister."

I rush towards the bars, grabbing them, squeezing them, "Leave my sister out of this. She's a helpless girl."

He chuckles, "Oh please, she's more important than you'll ever understand!" He watches me, walking along another wall, heading towards me slowly. "You asked me why I killed the Vampire Queen? Because we need you to be queen," he smirks lightly. "Times are changing, and if the leaders of the kingdoms don't welcome that change, then they will fall. And though I won't live long enough to see *the vampire's fall*, I know it will be a beautiful sight."

I grit my teeth. Every fibre of my being is screaming to rip him apart. To unlock the door and attack him. But something doesn't feel right. My stomach twists, and I feel a wave of nausea hit. Releasing the bars, I take a step back. I turn my back to the Youngling and take a couple of calming breaths. The nausea dissipates, and I glance over my shoulder at the man, who seems to be watching me. He's waiting. For what?

That's when it clicks. He wants me to open the door. *Wants* me to attack him out of rage. He's stronger than me, and he knows it. He can't escape without me. I straighten my back. "Well, thank you for the information. I'll be sure to pass it on to my father, who's still king." I make my way back down the hall, desperate to get out of this disgusting place.

Laughter echoes after me. "He won't be for long."

Chapter Forty

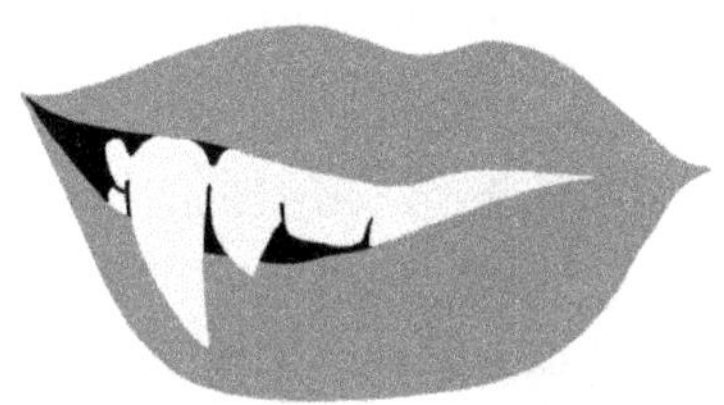

Farran

THE TREES STAND TALL, hiding the moon. But even without seeing it, I can feel it. Feel the strength it gives me. The power.

"Farran," Dante's voice draws me back to reality. Back to the forest. Back to him. His normally red eyes seem different. There's a tint of blue; the color of a hungry fairy or an angry fairy. "Are you alright?"

His tone doesn't match his gaze. The hunger in his eyes feels out of place when compared to the soft words.

I swallow and nod, "Yes, I'm fine. Just soaking in the moon. It's refreshing," I pause. "Does the moon affect you?"

He looks straight ahead, "Not the full moon. The Blood Moon and Harvest Moon do, though."

"The Blood Moon for your vampire half and the Harvest Moon for your fairy half?"

He looks at me out the corner of his eye. "That's correct. I don't draw as much power as a full blood, but I still feel it."

A twig snaps in the distance. We both freeze.

A doe walks into view, searching for a patch of grass to graze upon.

I glance at Dante, who's watching me.

"Are you going to shift and attack it?" He whispers so quietly I almost don't hear him.

I shake my head slightly, "No. It's too close to the full moon. If I shift, I could lose control and maul it so badly that you won't get to feed."

He smiles lightly, "Right." He refocuses on the doe. "In order for me to eat, it needs to still be alive. Even just barely."

I take a breath, nodding once. "Attack. Keep it alive. Sounds easy enough."

A light chuckle escapes his lips. "I'd appreciate it. So, do we have a plan?"

"I'm not really one for plans. They never go as expected." I stretch my arms over my head, "I'm thinking we charge, pin it down, wound it. Then eat."

"Sounds simple enough."

We separate. Dante walks off to the side, assumingly trying to hide himself amongst the thick tree trunks. I take a more direct route, weaving through the trees; my gaze focuses on the doe as it snacks on a few blades of grass. Its slender neck moves ever so slightly with every swallow, the muscles tensing and releasing with every chew. The rest of its body stands still, making as few movements as possible.

I crouch down, taking slow, careful steps. My body pulsates, muscles ache.

Shift!

Every morsel of my being screams in agreement with my wolf, but I don't. I keep a cool head. This is my first hunt with someone else. My first real hunt. My first hunt with Dante. I can't take all the glory.

A twig snaps, but it's not from Dante or me. The doe looks in the opposite direction of us. I follow its gaze, sniffing the air. A wolf. Not a werewolf, just a regular wolf. It stands on the opposite side of the doe, staring it down. It glances at me as if giving me a signal, then resumes eye contact with the deer.

Taking the distraction, I pounce. Running towards the doe, I prepare to attack, but a blur passes by and tackles it. The next snapping sound that erupts through the air is caused by the neck of the fragile creature breaking.

I rush to find Dante kneeling over the dying deer. Its eyes are locked on him, a fearful clouded gaze embedded in them. Its eyes start to flutter closed. Dante works quickly, leaning down to kiss the animal's forehead. He pulls back slowly. A string of translucent blue joins Dante's lips to the animal's skull. It moves slowly, like the current of a flowing river. A blue glob the size of a child's fist sprouts from the doe's head and moves along the translucent river and into Dante's mouth. The doe's body relaxes, limpening.

Dante sits up straighter.

I place a hand on his back: "Was that ...?"

"Its soul," he confirms with a nod.

I kneel down next to him, breathless. "It was beautiful."

He nods again, his eyes still on the body of the deer. Was he still hungry? He bends down again, opening his mouth. I catch a glimpse of a fang before it punctures the animal. The scent of blood fills the air, and I glance around for the wolf. I spot it, waiting in the shadows. Does it know what we are? It must be waiting for its turn. I make a mental note to leave enough flesh for the animal. It did cause a distraction for us, after all.

A moan catches my attention, and I realize it's Dante. He's still sucking on the doe's neck. Does it taste that good? Or is this his reaction to being fully satisfied for the first time since he was young?

I hunch over, open my mouth, and draw closer to the soft flesh of the mammal. Its earthy scent wafts up my nostrils. My mouth waters. Biting into the skin, I discover Dante is much slower at drinking blood than I had initially thought. The tangy fluid fills my mouth and runs down my throat. I pull a chunk of muscle free, sitting up to chew it.

The wolf approaches as I chew, its head low and tail between its legs. I watch it, whereas Dante seems oblivious. The wolf sniffs the body before nibbling at the hind end. I shift away slightly, giving the animal space. I'm not hungry enough to eat the entire thing anyway. Maybe I'll eat the heart, lungs, and a bit more body tissue before leaving the rest to this young wolf and his pack.

Dante sits up next to me. He looks over and arches his brow as the wolf starts chowing down on the deer. "Looks like we have company."

I'm tempted to point out that the wolf was here the entire time, but my mouth is still full. I finish chewing and swallow. "How was it?"

He nods, his gaze focused on my mouth. "Delicious."

A shiver runs down my spine. His eyes have their regular gentle tone to them, but they also look hungry. Not hungry for blood or souls, but hungry for something else. Something I can't quite place.

He leans over, closing the distance between my face and his. His nose brushes against mine, and I hold my breath. A tongue licks the edge of my lips. My stomach clenches. He licks the other side of my mouth. My palms sweat. He licks my chin. I clue into what he's doing. He's licking up the blood on my face. A heavy feeling rests in my stomach.

Dante's eyes meet mine. The glistening orbs pull me forward. Before I know what's happening, my lips touch his. The sweet taste of blood makes my chest tighten. Or maybe it's something else. I pull back. "I ... I'm sorry," I whisper, seeing the surprise on his face. What was that? Why'd I do that?

Dante smiles a small lopsided smile. "Don't be." He cups my face in both his hands and guides my lips back to his. His mouth moves against mine and my lips part for him. At first, it's just lips and heat, but then there's a tongue. His tongue. In my mouth. A hot sensation floods my body. My core tightens, sending pulsating heat throughout my body.

Dante shifts, and I move into his lap.

More!

My inner wolf cries out. I oblige by moving my hips, and he groans in pleasant agreement.

Dante moves his hands up and down the sides of my body. The fabric rubs against my skin. I want it off. I want to feel his touch on my bare body.

Finally, his hands move off of me and to his trousers. I follow his lead, doing my best to release myself from the confinement of my belts and the dress. I end up breaking the kiss to focus on the latches of the belts. Dante's hand carefully moves mine aside and aids me in undoing them. His expert fingers remove the belts and lift the dress over my head.

I swallow, fully naked atop him. My fingers glide under his shirt, lifting it as I feel up his chest, fingers moving over muscle. The shirt comes off, and Dante practically tackles me. My back lands in the lush grass. He's over me. His eyes are welcoming and affectionate. "May I?" He whispers.

My throat tightens. I doubt words will come, but then I respond in a breathless tone. "Of course."

He lowers himself onto me. His lips touch mine, and at first the kiss is gentle. He uses his hands to open my legs. His body fits perfectly against mine. Something stiff touches my inner thigh, and my stomach clenches. "Hm?" The sound vibrates against my mouth. He's asking permission again.

I nod against his lips, but he doesn't penetrate. Instead, one of his hands moves its way down my body and finds its way to my sex. His fingertips rub gently at my lips and then separate them to massage my clit. My breath catches, and I arch my back.

A finger enters me. It doesn't go deep. He moves the appendage in and out of me, wettening my entryway for him.

I raise my hands. My fingers move along his back. Nails drag along his skin. He groans. His body shifts slightly. He removes his fingers from inside me. He breaks the kiss and brings his fingers to his mouth, licking my juices off them. My core tightens.

Dante lines himself up and slowly thrusts into me. It's uncomfortable at first and he takes it slow. I whimper. He rests an arm on either side of me, supporting himself and creating a safe space for me. The pain eases. His thrusts glide more easily inside me. My whimpers become moans. His lips find mine again. The kiss deepens as the small, gentle thrusts become long and powerful. The pain that had emanated from my sex is now replaced by an overwhelming heat that swallows me whole.

His lips move from mine again and leave a trail of kisses across my jaw and down my neck. He licks and sucks my skin. It tickles more than anything. He then makes his way back up my neck and to my ear. Dante takes my earlobe in his mouth and sucks on it. I close my eyes. The rippling pleasure of him moving in and out of me, along with the hot sensation of his mouth on my ear, are too overwhelming. I turn my head to recapture his lips. His tangy taste delights my taste buds.

My body heats up. My core tightens. His cock is hitting all the right spots. Has he done this before? I don't care. We're doing it now.

My wolf pants in my head. Her moans mix with my own.

Dante's hips move at their own pace, rocking as they thrust into me. My hips move with his in response, causing ripples of pleasure to flow through me. The pleasure intensifies, building up inside me. I break the kiss and tilt my head back, my voice echoing into the darkness. Dante's lips move back to my neck, sucking and kissing until that buildup reaches its climax.

My back arches, body tenses and twitches. Everything tightens. My mind goes blank. I feel light and heavy all at once. All I can think about is the pleasure. The way he's gliding in and out of me.

The pleasure eases away almost as quickly as it came. I pant.

Dante pants in my ear. "I'm close."

I nod, panting heavily.

With the last few thrusts, Dante's body tenses next. The tension makes him shake slightly. Then, he relaxes. Heat fills me and I moan. His arms buckle under him, and he rests himself on top of me.

His forehead rests against mine. "How do you feel?"

I cup his face in my hands. "Like I need another round."

Dante chuckles between pants, "I just need five minutes. But then, we'll have to head back."

His voice is serious yet disappointed.

"Shh," I lift my head up to his, claiming his lips before he could speak more depressing truths.

Chapter Forty-One

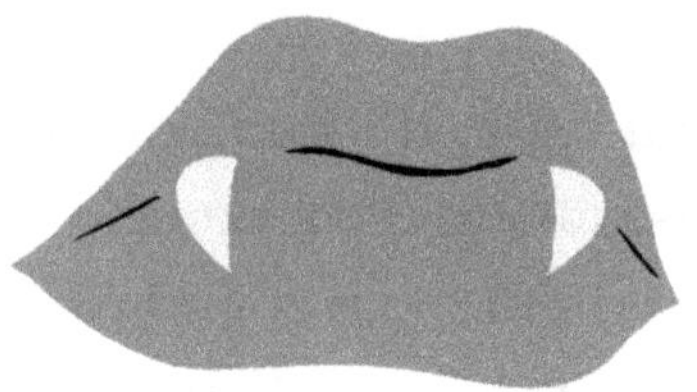

Akantha

All is dark. Black. Quiet. I'm alone. There are no smells to pick up on. No voices to hear.

Where am I? Who am I?

My stomach twists and turns, nausea playing with my body.

A creak from an opening door breaks through, and everything rushes back all at once. Voices whisper, carrying the thick scent of smoke and sweat into the room with them.

Footsteps approach me. They stop, and my body bows down. Am I lying down? A mental examination of my whereabouts confirms that I'm lying in a bed. A familiar bed.

"Akantha?" A soft female voice. Also, familiar. But why? "Akantha? Are you awake?" Akantha? Is that me? Am I who she's talking to? Akantha?

The room is quiet for a moment. The name repeats in my head. It sounds familiar too. Like I should know it. Like it's important to me. It must be mine.

"I'm awake," the words surprise me. I hadn't meant to speak. I swallow, easing the pain in my throat.

"Akantha."

I shiver. That voice. It's familiar too. But not as familiar as this woman or my name.

An ache forms at the back of my head. Events rush back to me. The man who smells of cinnamon. Mother's funeral. The blindness. The voice.

My eyes open, and I'm greeted by Helena's golden aura, glowing in the darkness. Of course, it's Helena. And I'm Akantha. And this is my room. My bed.

Liam is leaning against one of the walls. He seems off. I can't put my finger on why or how I know this, but I do. Something about him seems on edge, even if I can't see him properly.

I focus on Helena. "What happened?"

The fairy sighs. "You had a panic attack of sorts. Your father blamed Zahaya and Jeharad and sent them away. You've been asleep for a long time."

I rub my forehead. Then why do I feel so tired still? "How long?"

"Two nights. It's the full moon," she informs me, her voice tight. "But all is well. You're awake now, but you should stay in bed. An attack that strong surely took a lot out of you."

Two nights? It didn't feel like a panic attack. But could it have been a side effect of the seeing potion? "Yes, I will."

Helena leans forward to press her forehead against mine.

"Good girl. Now, I'm going to get something light prepared for you to eat," she pulls away and heads to the door. "Watch over her," she whispers.

"I will," Liam whispers in response.

The door closes after Helena. Liam walks over. He kneels next to my bed, taking my hand in both of his and holds it against the warmth of his face.

"You had us worried."

I inhale through my nose. "I'm sorry. I didn't mean to frighten you."

Liam lets out a soft sigh. I wouldn't have known if it weren't for the breath brushing against my hands.

"I was worried you wouldn't wake up. I was worried that being here with you would have been for nothing."

Here? Right, he's here to be with me. To get married. We are in an arranged marriage. "Do you want to marry me?"

He flinches, "What?"

I roll onto my side to face him. "Do you want to marry me?"

He's quiet for a long moment; then, he takes a deep breath, "At first? No. I was upset that my parents agreed to this. But I was reminded that it was my duty to aid my kingdom. Plus, you're a sweet and curious young vampire. I'm looking forward to spending my life with you."

I ignore the compliments, "Why were you upset?"

His honesty doesn't hurt. The thought of an arranged marriage had never occurred to me. And admittedly I am not excited to do this either. Though I've gotten to know him a little more, I'm still unsure if I am alright with the marriage. He's been nothing but kind and understanding, and yet I can't get past the fact that this isn't our choice.

He's quiet again. This time for a long while. I wait for him to find his voice. Or perhaps his courage! But his words still take me by surprise, "I was already engaged."

My stomach twists. Nausea hits, swirling through the twists and turns of my uneasy gut.

"What? With whom?" His ex comes to mind.

He speaks more freely now, "I had a mate. We were engaged, but then my parents arranged the alliance, and I was the only one out of my siblings who wasn't actually married yet, so I was assigned to the task of uniting the kingdoms on behalf of Wayfro," He pauses so he can take another breath. "Telling my mate was the hardest part."

My chest aches, not because he had truly loved someone before all this, but because this alliance had destroyed his happiness. I am the reason he'd ended his engagement. "I'm so sorry."

He shakes his head, "Don't be. This isn't your fault," he cups my cheek. "You're important to me. I care about you. Perhaps, with time, we could grow to love each other."

I open my mouth to protest, but a howl cuts me off; I frown, "Who was that?"

Liam stands, "Not who, what. I don't understand their accent. They aren't a werewolf. Or, at least, not a full one."

He walks towards the window, opens it, and sniffs the air.

I sit up. The cool breeze from the wind assaults the skin under my nightdress.

"Wait. If it's the full moon, why aren't you in your wolf form?"

He doesn't turn away from the window.

"I'm a descendant, like you. The original werewolf's blood runs through my veins. The full moon gives me power, but it doesn't command my shifting. Wolves who were created, or who don't have the blood of the Original, shift on a full moon without warning."

I let that soak in. Being a descendant of one of the Originals affects us? That explains why Father, myself, and Callisora all have a heightened sense, but Mother never did. I see auras, Callisora hears heartbeats, and Father can influence others. It's because of Dracula. "I see."

"Vampires, fairies, and werewolves who have the blood of their Original in them are born with a heightened ability. A zombie bitten directly by the Zombie King can be reborn countless times after dying a second time. The Originals give us power," he turns away from the window and walks back to me; he kneels and cups my face in both his hands, "and you are the–"

He's cut off by another howl. This time, it's closer. And it's followed by others.

"You need to stay here," Liam orders, pulling away and heading to the door. "I'm going to go make sure everything is alright." There's panic in his tone.

The door slams behind him. Silence fills the room. I stand and walk to the window, preparing to close it.

"Akantha. You must go."

The wind carries the voice into my room through the opened window. I close it, but the warning doesn't stop. It echoes in my head.

"I'm sorry," I whisper into the emptiness. I'm sorry that I can't stay here. I'm sorry that I'm blind. I'm sorry that I'm utterly useless. And I'm sorry that I can't sit here and wait for whatever comes next.

I grab a shawl out of my wardrobe and leave my room, following the servant halls to the outside of the castle.

Chapter Forty-Two

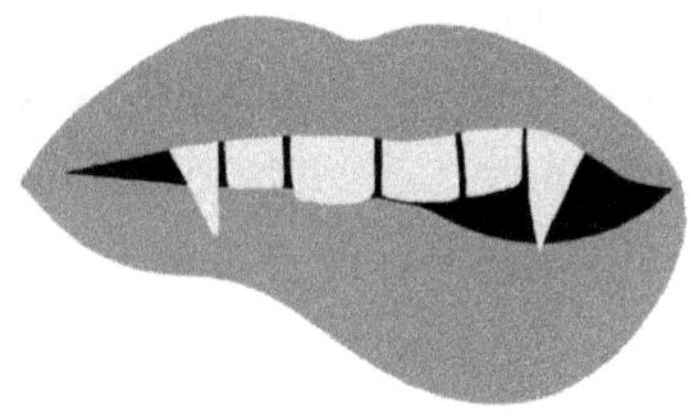

Callisora

THE FOUNDATION FOR THE school is finished. Men are building the framework while women review the blueprints. I supervise, feeling weaker than normal during a full moon.

I approach one of the young vampire women in charge of directing the others, "I can help with–"

She shakes her head, "Oh, no your highness. You being here is more than enough." Her smile assures me that her words are genuine, but I still feel like I could be doing more.

Another series of howls come from the distance, beyond the walls of the kingdom. Everyone freezes for a moment, listening, waiting. They then resume working.

They're probably reminding themselves the same thing I am; Liam is marrying Akantha, the werewolves have no reason to attack us. But unlike everyone else, I have the echoing words of a Youngling nagging at the back of my brain.

Times are changing.

Kingdoms will fall.

I shift uneasily. Perhaps I should head back to the castle. I'm not of much use right now. Actually, I may be serving as a distraction to most.

As I turn to leave, a series of guards walk over, moving past the working vampires without touching or disturbing them. They're led by Vladimir. His brows are drawn together, his eyes glancing around.

My chest tightens. This doesn't look good.

He steps closer, invading my personal space. His scent wafts up my nose, filling me. He leans in, but not for a kiss. His lips move next to my ear whispering, "We have a situation. It isn't safe for you to be out here."

My body tenses.

"What kind of situation?" I keep my voice low, taking note of the other guards. They're surrounding me, guarding me.

"Liam warned the King. He believes Younglings are coming this way."

My stomach twists. I fight the urge to gag. Younglings. Younglings are coming here to take down the Valdama.

I pull away from Vladimir and push my way past the other guards so I can get a good look at the kingdom. My kingdom. My people. The houses are built mainly of wood some brick. The people, most probably wouldn't be able to protect themselves or their families when their homes got destroyed. Swallowing, I look over my shoulder at Vladimir. "How much time do we have?"

"Not much," he watches me, his body standing straight. He's waiting for me to give him an order? The other men seem to be standing the same way, like soldiers ready to serve their queen.

I turn to face them fully. Taking a breath, I give my orders, "Vladimir will escort me to the castle. I want the rest of you to gather everyone and bring them to the castle too." The stone walls and heavy locked doors should keep us all protected. And if they can't, nothing can.

The men all nod before breaking off. They walk up to vampires, encouraging them that "The princess needs them to go to the castle." Their urgent tones don't leave room for argument.

I watch as the vampires quickly retrieve their families and head towards the castle gates. Vladimir and I follow.

Father emerges from the castle and stands in the open doorway, his red eyes scanning the crowd. "And where do you all think you're headed?"

I climb the steps. "Step aside, Father."

"How dare you invite these low lifes into our home," He hisses, glaring his blood-colored eyes at me, "It seems we need to have a talk."

"No," My voice cracks. I straighten my back and try again, "No. these are my people. You said it yourself; I am to be queen after the night of the full moon. Well, I'm starting a bit early." I walk up the last couple steps, so I'm in front of him. "Now, you either step aside, or I'll have to force you to."

He scoffs. Without being told to do so, Vladimir and two others take hold of the king and guide him off to the side. "How dare you lay your hands on your king."

Vladimir gives me a nod, assuring me that my father will be handled. I then turn to the growing crowd. Another series of howls boom through the air. Closer. I swallow the nauseating fear that rises up my throat and focus on the fear-filled faces. "Everyone," I finally announce, "Inside. There's more than enough room in the throne room for everyone." I step aside and watch as bodies rush past, some limping or carrying children, others rushing past with blurs of speed.

Liam slips outside, his eyes glowing orange. "You're bringing everyone inside. Good call." He doesn't look at me, his protective gaze is focused on the horizon.

I follow his gaze, "How's my sister?"

"She's awake. Tired and confused, but awake."

I let out a breath, and the tension in my chest lessons. She's alright. "What are you doing out here?"

"The howling," he answered simply.

"Anyone, you know?"

"No. I don't understand them. I suspect its-"

"Younglings," I interrupt, glancing at him from the corner of my eye to gauge his reaction.

He nods, his expression emotionless. "You should go inside. Take care of your people. I'll keep the intruders busy."

A frown tugs at my lips, "I can't let you do that. Who knows how many of them there are?"

"I can call for backup," he insists.

I shake my head. Akantha would never forgive me if I let her fiancé get himself killed.

A growl emanates from behind me. I spin around to find a wolf. Dark brown fur, golden-orange eyes. Her gaze softens on me. Her head tilts to the side.

"Farran?" I whisper, hesitant.

The wolf steps closer, brushing her head against my hand. I inhale sharply. Her fur is so soft. I stroke her head, glancing back at Liam. "I'll go inside, but Farran stays with you." His creased brow tells me he's not pleased by this, but he nods anyway. I focus on Farran again, "Be careful." I then head inside.

The doors shut behind me, and two guards lock them. My gaze travels around the throne room; vampires are huddling together with their families on the floor. I find my way to one of the servants and request that she and the other fairies find blankets for our guests and some blood. It's going to be a long night.

CHAPTER FORTY-THREE

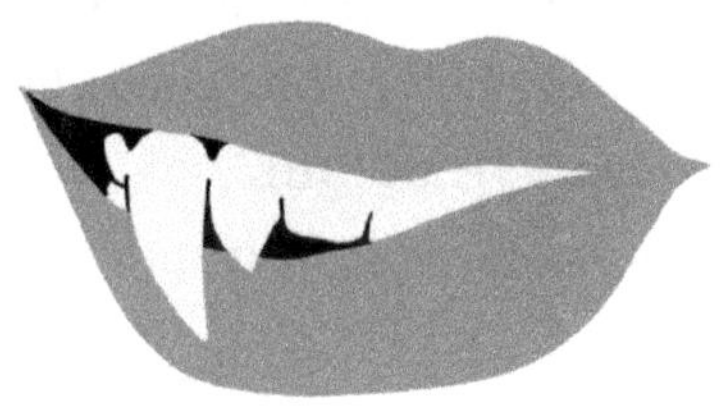

Farran

THE DOORS SHUT WITH a loud thud. I look at Liam, then towards the horizon. "How long until they're here?"

"I don't know," He begins undressing. "Hopefully long enough."

Long enough for what?

I want to ask, but don't. He's a prince; I shouldn't question him. At least everyone is safe in the castle. At least Dante is safe in the castle, hidden away in his room. When I look back at Liam, he's changed into his true wolf form.

Liam lifts his nose into the air and sniffs. A low growl sends shivers down my spine. He then raises his head higher and howls. The long howl is repeated three times until a faint response is heard in the far-off distance. Much farther away than the Younglings. "You called for backup?"

Liam rotates his shoulders and gives me a suspicious look, "Of course I did!" His tone insinuates that he doesn't like me. "Can you not howl?"

"I wasn't born a wolf. I was made into one, then raised by Slave Keepers. The only wolf I knew was taken away from me before she could teach me how to howl." I look away from him.

"That's unfortunate. It's an important skill. How do you call for help?"

He steps closer, then begins to circle me. He doesn't trust me.

"I don't." I've never had to. Who would help a slave?

He scoffs, then snarls. His snout wrinkles as he bares his teeth at me. Does he think I work with the enemy somehow? Is the moon messing with him? He's ready to pounce when something catches my attention, and I gasp. The sound causes him to look behind himself to see what's caught me off guard.

More than fifty silver glowing eyes peer through the darkness. Hints of orange catch the moon's light along with other hints of color. Some have a mix of orange and red. Others are orange and blue. No orange and black. The thought of zombies reproducing makes my skin crawl.

Liam moves to my side, his body double the size of my own, getting into an attack position; his head and body low to the ground, his legs bent, tail swaying slowly. I do my best to imitate his stance, only now realizing just how unprepared for a real battle I am.

No one moves. Even the air seems to stand still. The silence is deafening. My ears twitch at Liam's small breaths. How can he seem so calm? A howl cuts through the quiet, and Liam leaps into action, running towards the now-charging Younglings.

The lightly furred creatures emerge from the shadows. Some in wolf forms with short fur, others in human form. Some of the human forms are furry, others aren't. The variety of half-breeds leaves me breathless.

Liam collides with one of the Younglings. He knocks them over. Three others pile on top of him. More come towards me. I shake my body, preparing myself for impact. Mouths open, revealing large white teeth. I feel nothing at first, only see them make contact with my body and knock me to the ground. Then, the pain hits. It feels as if a wall has fallen on top of me. But no, it's one of them—a Youngling. I move around, avoiding the large teeth as they try to clamp down on my shoulders. My face. My throat.

Liam howls again. The pitch of which sounds more like a yelp. He's being mauled. I try to look at him, but there are too many bodies on top of him, and others blur past us to get to the castle.

The Youngling on top of me catches me off guard, digging his teeth into my shoulder. I cry out. His teeth are so deep that they scrape bone. He lets go, smiling down at me with a bloody smirk. He lunges for my other shoulder, then is gone.

The Youngling flies off into a nearby building. The home crumbles down around him as soon as he breaks through the wall. Dust rises from the rubble, followed by the confused Youngling. He sways in place, then makes his way out.

I look up to find Dante standing over me, his red wings out, fangs drawn. His eyes are still focused on the Youngling that had attacked me. Without warning, two others charge at Dante, and he lifts off into the air.

Sitting up slowly, I watch in awe as he moves over the crowd, then circles back. He tackles the two Younglings to the ground, causing a divot in the earth.

Dante lands before me. He holds his hand out and strokes my fur. "Are you alright?"

"No, but I'll live," I gesture to Liam. "Help him."

Dante rushes over to the pile of bodies, seeming to understand me without my having to create a bond. Is it because we had sex?

He links his fingers together, raises his arms over his head, then slams down on the back of one of the Younglings. The breaking of its spine is followed by an agonizing cry. Dante then proceeds to pull Youngling after Youngling off Liam, moving quickly as to keep the element of surprise as long as possible.

Once Liam is uncovered, I clamp my jaws around the back of his neck and pull his bloody body up. He leans on me as I help him back to the castle steps. He sits. "You'll be alright."

Liam scoffs. The left side of his face is bleeding from a wolf-like bite. Another more human-looking bite mark is on his neck. He's bleeding everywhere, and his fur is missing in spots.

A growl catches my attention. I turn around to find four Younglings surrounding us. Dante is farther away, fighting five more. A sixth jumps at him from behind, clasping his head in its mouth and taking him down.

"No!" I yell, running toward him, but I'm tackled again by a Youngling. I roll out of the way of their pounce and get back onto all fours. More Younglings catch my attention; these ones are climbing the castle walls, aiming to get in through the windows. My heart drops. "Callisora ..."

Dante lets out another cry, now being mauled as Liam had been before.

I look back and forth at Dante, then Liam—who's laying on the steps in pain, surrounded by another group of Younglings again—and the castle wall. I can't do it all.

More howling fills the night air. No, not more. We can't handle more.

Furry bodies flood into the gates of Valdama. The sheer number of them is enough to fill the courtyard. But they aren't Younglings. They're werewolves.

Three wolves rescue Dante, another four protect Liam. Twenty or more fish the Younglings off the castle walls.

A female wolf rushes to Liam's side, nuzzling his cheek in concern. I ignore them, working my way back to Dante. But the fight isn't over yet.

The Younglings keep attacking, even though they're outnumbered. Even though it's a full moon and the werewolves are at full strength. But even though the werewolves have more in numbers, the Younglings are stronger.

I stand, frozen in place, as bodies fall. Throats are ripped out. Howls from both sides echo under the full moon. For every Youngling that falls, six werewolves fall. The majority of werewolves are guarding Liam, others are guarding the castle alongside Dante. I'm standing in the rubble. No one attacks me. No one sees me. I'm worthless in this battle. Attacking a slave camp without a plan is one thing, but running head first into this war another. This time I'm the one being ambushed, but my enemy has a plan.

I swallow, glancing around, trying to think of something that could stop them. Half werewolves. There has to be something.

Silver.

Silver? That could work on the were-fairies. What about the were-leeches? I shake my head; one problem at a time.

I sniff the air and move through the streets of the crumbling kingdom. A scent seeps into my snout. Its familiar metal aroma burns my nostrils. I follow it, my eyes burning. Stopping at the remains of a small house, I dig. I need to find something. Anything. My paws graze something that instantly burns.

I yelp, pulling back, and lick the soft pad of my paw. "Silver," I whisper, relieved.

I rip off part of a curtain that is lying nearby and use it to wrap around the silver bar, which had clearly been crafted for self-defence against werewolves. I struggle to wrap the fabric, but I manage.

Taking the rod in my mouth, I make a beeline for Dante, whacking Younglings as I go. This draws a lot of attention, and more Younglings start charging at me again. I swing the bat-like weapon, and it cracks the shins of one of the creatures. I proceed to bash his skull in. I hit another, who seems only mildly inconvenienced by my actions.

An angry Youngling with red in its eyes manages to get the bar out of my mouth by grabbing it mid-swing. Its skin sizzles, but this doesn't seem to bother it much. It smirks at me, drawing the bar up over his head, preparing to swing it down on me and put me out of my misery.

"Stop!" A voice booms over the cries of war and pain.

My body stiffens. I can't move. No one can. Some of the others—both Youngling and werewolf—struggle against their newfound stiffness.

Akantha steps out of the shadows, her eyes glowing green, "That is enough," her voice isn't her own. It's feminine, but sounds older, wiser. Her gaze lands on Liam. The green fades away, and my body is my own again.

Breathless, I watch Akantha as she makes her way to her fiancé.

I shift my attention back to the Youngling standing over me. He's smirking. With a glance around, I confirm that the Younglings are no longer fighting. Except the pleased smirks on their faces don't escape me. Do they know what's going on?

The Youngling standing over me howls, and the group retreats. Why retreat when they clearly have the advantage?

What just happened?

CHAPTER FORTY-FOUR

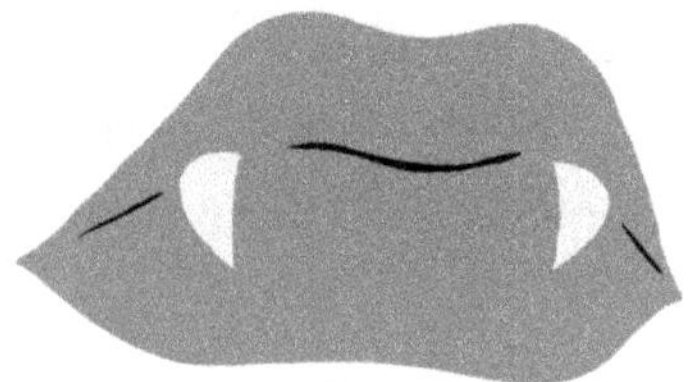

Akantha

I PUSH PAST THE werewolves that surround Liam. Feeling their eyes on me, I assume they hadn't expected a princess to be out on a battlefield. But why did the fighting stop? Everything is a bit fuzzy, including Liam's aura.

The werewolf next to him has a fiery aura; reds and oranges take turns flickering. A light blue emanates from her midsection. What does that mean? I've never seen someone have two auras before. Or maybe she doesn't have two auras, maybe there's someone growing inside her.

Looking away from the pregnant wolf, I kneel next to Liam. His breathing is uneven. The scent of blood both makes me hungry and sick.

"How bad is it?"

The feeling of her glaring eyes quickly fades. Did she realize that I can't evaluate this for myself?

"Not good. He's losing a lot of blood."

Liam takes my hand and squeezes it, "I'm sorry I couldn't protect you, Akantha."

My heart aches, my eyes water, "I'm safe. You protected me and everyone else. We'd all be dead by now if it wasn't for you."

I assume he'd called for backup, because otherwise, where would all these werewolves have come from?

He moves to get up. I stop him, placing a hand on his soft fur coat.

"You need to rest. Don't move."

He lets out a low growl, and I remove my hand from his side, realizing I was touching his wound. A gash as wide as my palm. "You should be the one resting. The moon will heal me."

"Don't be so stubborn and listen to your fiancé," the female wolf orders.

Liam tenses. "Amelia?"

I arch my brow, "Amelia?" Who's Amelia?

She clears her throat, "I'm sorry, where are my post-battle manners? I am Amelia; one of the Wayfro Wolf Knights."

She uses her most formal-sounding voice.

Liam lets out a grunt as he shifts his weight. His fluffy tail brushed against the skirt of my dress. He's standing on all fours now. "She's the one I told you about," he clarifies.

The one he'd told me about? As in, his ex-fiancé? I shift uncomfortably and focus on Amelia, "I'm so sorry that I ruined your engagement."

"It's fine," the cracking in her voice says otherwise. "I'm just happy that you two are safe and happy together."

There's a moment of silence before I finally speak again, "We aren't."

"What?" Liam and Amelia say in unison.

"We aren't happy. I can't live with myself knowing I stole my husband from someone else, and I know Liam misses you dearly," I stand. "I'm calling off the engagement, and I'll speak with my sister about organizing a different kind of treaty with the werewolves."

I climb the steps, only now noticing the pain in my feet. When had I stepped on gravel? When had I even left the castle?

"Akantha?" I stop, listening to what Liam has to say. "Thank you."

I smile lightly, then keep walking.

CHAPTER FORTY-FIVE

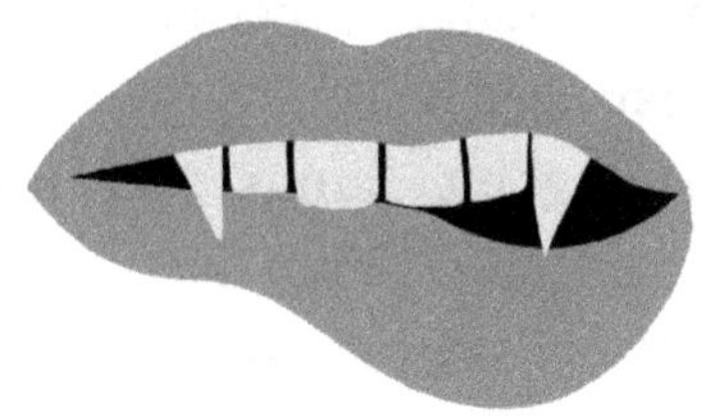

Callisora

KEEPING TO THE EDGES of the ballroom, I watch the vulnerable vampires curling up with their families as if that'll protect them from the oncoming threat. Howls have been echoing through the room all night, but now everything seems to be silent.

"Your highness," a voice whispers.

I tear my focus from the scared vampires to look at the Elder standing next to me. "Yes?"

The man is still looking at the people. "Allowing your people to take shelter here was very wise. It was brave to challenge the king, as well," he praises, his tone low and his words all-knowing. He takes a deep breath. "I hope you realize that your people will want you crowned immediately. They will not willingly serve under a king who refused to protect them."

I press my lips together. I hadn't thought of that. I hadn't thought past tonight. Even the guards were treating me more like their queen than their princess. They'd obeyed me over Father. "I don't have a husband chosen."

The Elder finally looks at me. "I believe you do," he gestured to my stomach, "perhaps the one who is father to your expected heir?"

I frown, placing my hands over my stomach. Father? Expected heir? That isn't possible, is it? Vladimir and I only slept together a couple of times. I couldn't be that fertile. And how did he even know I am expecting? Did he see it in my future when I requested his blessing for the school?

How am I going to balance ruling a kingdom and raising a child? I'm not ready. This is exactly what I'd wanted to avoid by sleeping with humans.

My shock causes the Elder to smile. He looks back to the crowded room. "Choose a husband who will stand by you as you rule. Who won't allow the title of king to go to their head? The war won't end tonight. Valdama needs a leader who will protect them as well as lead them." He pauses. "So, even if the father isn't the most ideal choice, you can easily choose who is best and make the baby appear to be his."

A small smirk crosses my lips. He knows me too well. I could choose Carlos and sleep with him as soon as possible. He'd believe the baby is his. A small laugh escapes me. As if I'd choose that toad.

"Trickery won't be necessary," I bow my head. "Thank you for your wisdom." I walk away, my eyes searching the crowd.

Even in a room filled with vampires, I can spot him easily. Even in his uniform, surrounded by others dressed the same, I know which one is him.

I go to him and hug his arm, "May I borrow you for a moment?"

Vladimir looks down at me, confused, "I don't think this is the time, princess."

I frown. Does he really take me for the type that would enjoy the company of a male suitor while there's a war going on? Well, he's probably right. "No, I want to talk to you. Not ... Do that."

His eyes shift, looking me over. Concern clouds his gaze. He nods and excuses himself from whatever conversation he was having with his fellow guards.

I escort him down a hall, so we're out of view. I lean against the chilled stone wall. Where to start?

"Callisora? What's wrong?"

I look up at him. His dark brows are pinched together. His forehead wrinkles.

I push off the wall and step towards him. He doesn't move. I grab onto the collar of his armour and tug him down to my level. He obliges. I press my lips against his. Heat overtakes me. The metallic taste of his lips embraces me. His arms wrap around my waist, pulling me closer. Our mouths move, moans getting lost in the space.

The kiss is broken. Vladimir rests his forehead against mine.

"Not that I'm not enjoying this, but is it really the time?"

"When this is all over, I'm going to get married and become queen."

He loosens his grip on me, "Oh," he fails at hiding the pain that my words cause. It's written all over his face. He must think I'm not going to pick him. Like he isn't worth the time we've shared.

I nod, my fingers toying with the fabric that's poking out from under his armour. "And I want you to be the one I marry," He's silent. I look up into his eyes. "I choose you."

Vladimir pulls away, "What? No. Carlos is the obvious choice. His father is of higher authority than mine. He's next in line to be on the council."

I step towards him again, pained by how little he truly thinks of himself. "He doesn't care about the citizens, though. He just wants to rule," plus, I'm pretty sure he was fucking my mother. I take one of his hands in both of mine. "Please, Vladimir. I need you."

He's quiet for a moment, gaze focused on nothing at all. I watch his face as he thinks over my words. Finally, he looks at me. "So, this isn't because you've fallen hopelessly in love with me?" A playful smirk toys with the corner of his mouth.

I roll my eyes, relief washing over me. I hadn't realized how tight my chest was beforehand. "Of course not!" Maybe a little. "It also just so happens that I am with child. Your child."

Vladimir's eyes widen at that. He looks down at my stomach. "Really?"

I move his hand to my stomach. There's no evidence of life just yet, but the motion seems to make him giddy. "So? Will you marry me?"

His eyes twinkle, "Of course I will." He moves both his hands to my face, cupping it gently as he draws me in for another deep kiss.

The sound of the castle door opening thrusts us both back into our *protect the kingdom* modes. We rush back to the throne room to find Akantha in the doorway. I gasp, rushing to her, "Akantha? What were you doing out there? You should be resting!"

She could have been hurt. I look her over, but she seems unscathed. And underdressed.

Akantha leans into me, practically falling into my arms. "I couldn't sleep with all that howling." I look past her. Destruction and bodies are the first things I see, then the werewolves that litter my courtyard, watching their prince limp into the castle.

I hold Akantha protectively.

"What happened to you?" I whisper, but she seems too disoriented to answer. I yell orders over my shoulder, "Guards, inspect the bodies for survivors and survey the area to be sure that the enemy is gone."

Vladimir joins me as everyone else springs into action. "What do you want me to do?"

"Take my sister to her room. She needs rest."

Vladimir plants a light kiss on my cheek before carefully taking Akantha and carrying her off.

I step outside to check the damage. Many homes and buildings have been destroyed. The earth is upturned in areas, and the scent of death hangs heavy in the air.

Even the small amount of progress on the school has been undone. We have so much work ahead of us.

Farran climbs the steps along with a male fairy by her side. Both looked injured, him more than her, but Farran's fur could be hiding a lot of the blood.

"Master, this is Dante," she introduces him. "He's a youngling. He works here in the castle."

I glare at him, prepared to call the guards, but Farran continues.

"He saved both Liam and me. He fought by our sides to protect the castle."

I bite my inner cheek. He's a Youngling, but he fought against his own kind? I sigh, rubbing my forehead. What a long night. "I'm assuming you're telling me this for a reason?"

Farran nods. "Let him stay? He could be useful. He might be able to help us understand more about Younglings."

This werewolf has a lot of favours to ask of me, apparently.

Dante speaks up next, "I'm not all-knowing, but allowing me to stay here would be greatly appreciated. I could be a strong ally. Plus, there's the fact of blood."

I scowl at that, "Pardon?"

Dante clears his throat nervously. Even Farran looks shocked. "I'm sure you know that traditionally the firstborn heir to Dracula's line is a son. Well, that's me. But because I'm half-fairy, the king refused to raise me as such, but he also couldn't bring himself to kill me."

He raises his hands in defeat, "Please understand, I don't wish to become king. I'm merely explaining myself. This is my home as much as it is yours."

I clench my jaw. I'm not someone special. Not the firstborn. I'm the second. But the throne is still mine. This is still my kingdom to rule over. I can either lead like the kings before me or change things. After taking a deep breath, I nod, "You may stay. But I want you working alongside the guards. Not whatever you were doing before. If you're going to help with war tactics, then that's the best place for you to be." He also wouldn't be able to cause any trouble without me knowing, with all the other guards practically on top of him. "But if you step out of line, even once, it'll be both your heads. Understood?"

Farran bobs her head. "Thank you, Princess."

Chapter Forty-Six

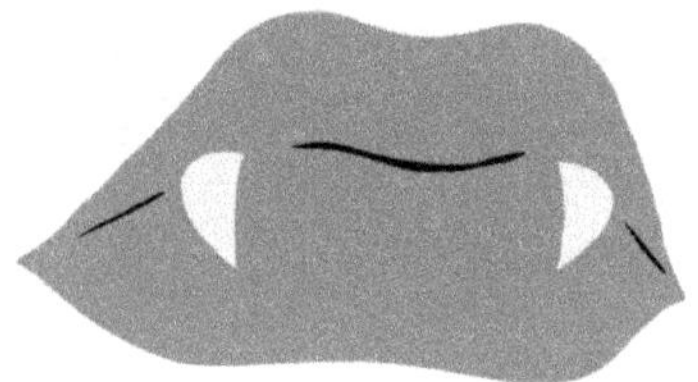

Akantha

I WALK DOWN THE halls with Helena, my arm wrapped around hers.

Nothing feels the same. It's like I've just woken up from an extremely long dream, but am still dazed by it. My body feels the same, but yet it also doesn't. I touch my arm, and it still feels like chilled skin. Unlike before, there's this fire inside me.

It's been two nights since the full moon, and things are starting to settle down. Callisora has been busy getting the civilians sorted out, Father has been getting everything prepared for Callisora's wedding and throning ceremony, and I've just been staying out of the way.

My nightmares have settled down since that voice started whispering my name. I'm not sure how, but I know the voice and Cinnamon are somehow connected. Could it be his voice?

There also seems to be this newfound sense of calmness that has engulfed me. I'm unsure if it's temporary or everlasting, but I'm going to enjoy it while it lasts. If listening to Helena's history lessons has taught me anything, there's always a calm before the storm. Though I'm not sure I want to head into that storm.

"Akantha?" Helena's soft voice brings me back to reality. When did we step out into the garden?

I lean into her as we walk.

"Yes?"

She slows her steps.

"Are you alright? You've been very quiet lately. I thought you'd be more excited about your upcoming marriage to the prince? Though I can understand that the past few days have been overwhelming."

I take a breath.

"I suppose now is as good a time as any to tell you."

Helena stops walking, as do I.

"Time to tell me what?" Her voice is inked with worry. What is she expecting me to say?

"I broke off the engagement. Liam was engaged before and had to end it, because of the alliance. I just ..." I take another breath. "I wouldn't be able to live with myself if I married him. I want to marry for love. I want to be in control of my life and what happens in it."

"Oh, my lady," she wraps me in her arms. "I admire your decision, but don't forget that you can't control everything in life. You'll never be one hundred percent in control of your destiny."

I rest my head on her shoulder. "I can try to be. I'm just ..." I search for the right words. "I'm ready to start living my life for me."

"I'm so proud of you. You've blossomed into such a brave young woman."

I laugh, tears forming in my eyes, "I'm not that brave."

Helena kisses the top of my head, "Why don't we go look for some flowers to pick for your sister's wedding? I'm sure she'd appreciate it."

Grinning, I nod. We resume walking through the garden, sniffing and gathering bundles of flowers.

CHAPTER FORTY-SEVEN

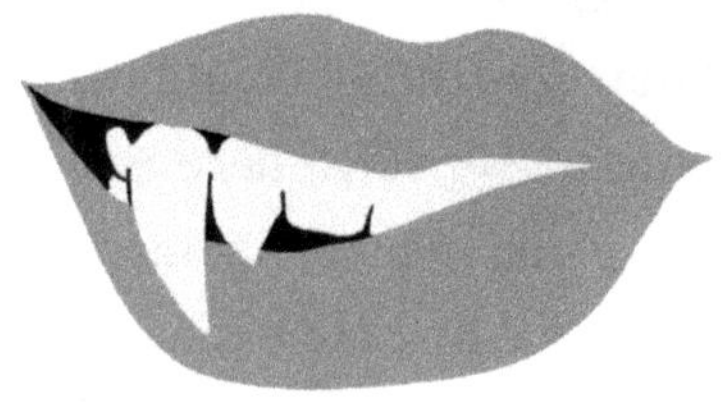

Farran

I SIT IN THE grass, watching the sunrise from my and Dante's favourite spot. I haven't seen Dante since the full moon. My chest aches. He had lied to me. He promised there would be no more secrets between us, but he kept the fact that his father was the king from me. The father who'd murdered his mother. I sigh and drop my head into my hands.

Footsteps cut through the dawn's calm silence. Someone sits next to me. I don't have to guess who it is. "Farran?" His voice is soft and warm. If I weren't upset with him, I'd be excited to have him here. "You've been avoiding me."

I uncover my face and glare up at him. "You promised we wouldn't have secrets, Dante."

His dark brows pinch together. "I know, I know. And I'm sorry that I didn't tell you everything. But it's not that I didn't want to. I couldn't. If anyone found out the king was my father ..." his voice trailed off.

I take a breath.

"I don't know what could have happened, but I get it. He let you live, even though he wasn't supposed to," I swallow. "Tell me everything. I want to know. No more secrets, or whatever we have here is over." I gesture between us as I speak, the words burning my tongue.

Dante turns to face me. He takes my hands in his. "She was a fairy. And I guess no female fairy is off limits to him, even the cook. He has gotten a few fairies pregnant over the centuries, and he always finds out and kills them before the child is born. I don't know how she kept me a secret, but she did," he takes a shaky breath, his hands are sweating.

"I was still young, barely old enough to cook without supervision. That day, I had wandered off into the depths of the castle, and he found me. I don't remember much of what happened, but I must have told him who my mother was. That, along with how I look, must have been enough for him to put two and two together. He was furious and lashed out at her, making her an example to the others. I don't know how many know about what I am, since he was able to convince everyone I was dead too, yet I wasn't," he sighed. "It was traumatising. I was given a new name, new identity. And the threat of being tortured on top of all that was too much for my young self to handle."

My lip trembles. I remove one of my hands from his so I can cup his cheek.

"I'm so sorry." I bite my lip. "I know how it feels to lose a mother. I've lost two."

My eyes water and I blink back the tears. "I don't remember much of it, but I remember walking through the forest with my mom. I think we were picking flowers, or herbs, or something like that. It was getting dark, and she'd wanted to go home, but I was having too much fun." My chest tightens, and throat restricts. "I remember hearing a wolf howling, then everything went black. When I woke up, I was in the slave camp. I asked for my mom, but I was told that I had a new mother. It wasn't until later that I realized my birth mother was probably dead." And given the amount of time that's passed since then, she definitely is by now.

Dante places his hand over mine, removing it from his cheek and kisses it.

I continue, "My new mother was a werewolf. I'm pretty sure she's the one who had turned me. I only changed into my wolf form a couple of times while I was at the slave camp. My first Master was nice and let the two of us go for runs in our wolf forms. We didn't even have to call him Master. It wasn't until my more recent Master took over—the one before the princess—that things went really bad. Life at the slave camp was never good, but he made it so much worse."

Dante moves closer to me and wraps his arms around me as I speak.

I lean into him.

"He beat us until we addressed him as Master. And if we ever addressed him as anything else, he'd hurt us. My adoptive mother stood up to the Slave Keepers one night, and they ..." My voice cracks, tears sting my eyes. "They killed her. They left her body at my post for so long ... When the Slave Tamer came to check on us, he ordered them to remove it, but never spoke to me. Never apologized or made sure I was okay."

My gut twists; my mouth fills with saliva. The tears finally fall.

Dante pulls me closer. I hide my face in his chest. His hand rubs my back. "I'm sorry you had to endure that. But you're safe now. I've got you." His lips brush the top of my head. "I'll protect you until the day I die."

Sniffling, I look up at him. "Really?"

He nods and brushes a tear off my cheek with his thumb. "Really."

Chapter Forty-Eight

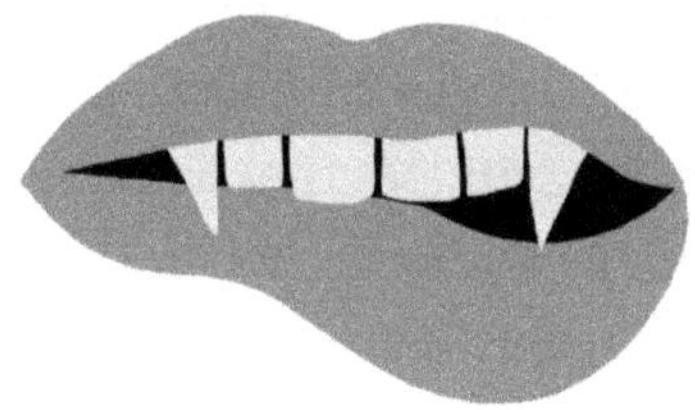

Callisora

THE DOORS TO THE throne room open before me. Walking in, I find Father sitting in his throne, members of the council standing in the center of the room, waiting. Vladimir and Carlos, along with their parents, reside at the base of the steps before Father.

It's time.

I swallow and cross the room, holding my chin high. I make eye contact with no one, my gazed focused on my throne. I climb the steps and sit. But I don't sit in my usual place; I take the Queen's Throne.

The room is silent. Everyone watches me. A smirk crosses one set of lips—Vladimir's. We make eye contact for the briefest of moments, causing the butterflies I'd just put at bay to attack my gut again.

"Callisora," Father's voice hisses. He speaks low, his body leaning my way. "That is not your throne yet."

I swallow the lump in my throat and look at him. "On the contrary, *that* is no longer *your* throne." I focus on the dukes and duchesses who've gathered to bear witness to my engagement announcement. Their expressions seem curious yet fearful. There's no doubt Father is fuming, but I pay him no mind. I won't allow him to hurt me again. Mother is dead. Father had tried to turn his people away when they needed him. The guards had listened to my order over Father's. I am already queen.

Tilting my head slightly, I offer a friendly smile to the group. "Welcome. I'm sorry if I kept you all waiting." I push up off the throne and caress the wrinkles in the skirt of my black dress. "I know why you're all here; to see who I've chosen as my husband and your king." I step back down the steps slowly. "It was an easy choice, honestly. One I denied for a while, but eventually accepted." Even if it weren't for the child growing inside me, I knew it would be him. "He cares for me and for the people of this kingdom. He is strong, brave, and not afraid to do what he believes in."

Carlos's face lights up. A smirk crosses his lips as he gives Vladimir a side-eye.

"I doubt he was put into the running for anything but courtesy, but it turns out he was the perfect candidate." I pass Carlos and take Vladimir's hand. My heart races from the touch of his skin. "Vladimir," I take a breath, "will you do me the honour of marrying me?" I look up into his eyes. Brown orbs look back at me, glossy and full of emotion.

Vladimir nods. He opens his mouth, but no sound comes. He clears his throat and tries again. "I will."

A bang sounds from behind me. I spin to face my Father. Vladimir's arms wrap around my torso and pull me close, protecting the baby and me.

Father stands atop the platform, his eyes glowing red and his fangs drawn. "How dare you," He hisses, "How dare you go against my wishes and choose this ..." He gestures towards the man holding me, "This is not the future I had planned for you. You were meant to be with Carlos. I promised you to him."

I arch my brow, glancing at Carlos, who's glaring at me with red eyes. My focus shifts back to my father. Somehow, I don't feel threatened or scared. I know Father alone could hurt me, but in Vladimir's arms, those fears have melted away. "Then you shouldn't have given me a choice."

Father's nose wrinkles. "Then I won't. You are to marry Carlos. He will become king."

"And he will raise Vladimir's child?" I challenge, causing Father's normally pale face to become the same color as his eyes. "I am marrying Vladimir. And that is final."

Carlos steps closer to me and touches my arm, "Princess, please reconsider."

Vladimir grabs Carlos, and I place a gentle hand over his. His grip relaxes.

I look Carlos in the eye, keeping my voice low. "Go against me, and I'll be sure everyone knows just how close you got to my mother."

Fear radiates in his eyes, and he steps back. He looks toward my father and speaks, his voice shaking. "I revoke my entry as the princess' potential suitor. I trust the princess' choices. Long live the queen."

The others are quiet for a moment. I glance around at the puzzled faces. Time seems to move more slowly. Finally, Carlos takes the initiative and bows, going down on one knee. One by one, the others follow.

Mine and Carlos' fathers stand tall, refusing to bow at first. It isn't until everyone else has bowed that Father lets out a gruff sound of frustration and walks down to us. He focuses on Vladimir. "May your ruling be long and victorious."

Long. If the elder is to be believed, we won't be ruling long at all.

Father storms out of the throne room.

Chapter Forty-Nine

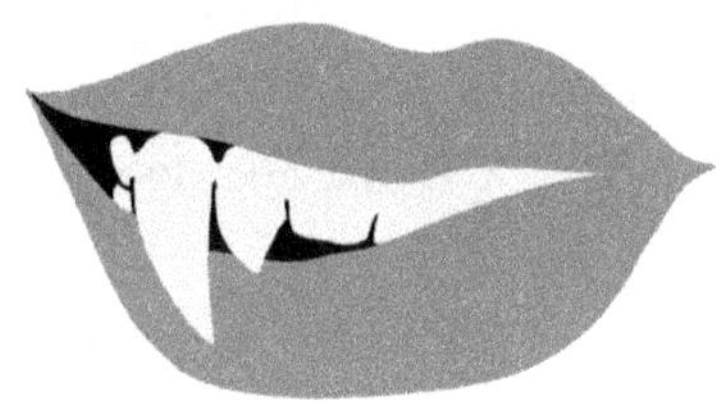

Farran

Callisora moves around her room with frantic speed. For someone expecting a child, she doesn't seem to care much for the *take it slow* orders that the Elder gave her. But considering it's her wedding day, I can't blame her for being a little all over the place.

It's been three days since Dante had asked me to move in with him, and though I feel overjoyed and giddy, I can't help but worry about Callisora. I clear my throat, "Why don't you sit down? Your wake-up call will be here soon."

Callisora sighs and sits on her bed, her messy waves bouncing even though she's no longer in motion.

"Are you okay?" I ask slowly, stepping towards her.

She rubs her forehead, "Yeah, I'm fine. Just a bit anxious," she tilts her head back, taking another deep inhale of air. "Tonight, I become queen. And a wife. Everything will be different."

I approach her with more meaning and take a seat next to her.

"But you'll still be you. And I believe that you will lead this kingdom into greatness."

"Or destruction," she murmurs, the words nearly slipping by me. I open my mouth to pry information from her, but a knock from the door cuts me off. I stand and go to open it.

Three fairies stand in the hall, massive grins plastered on their faces. They rush past me and over to Callisora.

"Good evening, Princess," One of the fairies—an orange-skinned woman with yellow hair—practically sings.

She heads to the wardrobe to retrieve Callisora's gown. She grabs the bundle of black and navy fabric and rushes over to where the others are grooming Callisora.

A green-skinned fairy sits behind the princess, brushing whatever remaining tangles are still in the long wavy mane. A silver-skinned fairy applies a light amount of makeup to Callisora's seemingly white face. If she weren't a vampire, I'd be worried about her complexion.

I stand on the sidelines, helping the fairies when ordered to. I watch Callisora; her eyes are avoiding all of us, her expression blank. What's she thinking about? Is it the wedding? The kingdom? Whatever it is, I can practically feel the turmoil radiating off her. While these fairies buzz around like humming-birds, feeding off the excitement of a grand event, their princess—and future queen—is in distress.

Without warning, the silver-skinned fairies squeals, "You look beautiful, your highness." She clasps her hands together and holds them in front of her face, her eyes watering. "You're so grown up."

Callisora scrunches her nose at that, "You three may go."

The fairies don't hesitate, they practically run out of the room. Was all that excitement just for show? Do they fear Callisora as much as they fear her father? After what Dante had told me and how I've seen Cal-lisora's father treat her, I don't blame them.

Callisora walks to her vanity and sits. She bites into one of her fingers before pressing it to the glass of the mirror. A reflection appears; Callisora's reflection. I inhale; I'd never seen an enchanted mirror before, I didn't know they actually existed.

Callisora tilts her head from side to side, examining the work the fairies have done. She reaches up and removes a bobby pin, allowing chunks of thick black hair to fall from the intricate up-do the fairies have made. The hair bounces as it resumes its rightful place, resting over Callisora's shoulders and against her back. She removes one pin at a time until they're all out. Her reflection's eyes meet mine, "Do you know how to braid?"

I grit my teeth and intake a sharp breath, "I have only done it once or twice," some of the younger fairies at the slave camp would ask the older slaves to do their hair as a distraction. I wasn't asked often, but when I was, I mostly copied what I saw others around me doing.

Callisora nods. She sits still, and I realize, after a long moment of silence, that she is waiting for me. I walk over and accept the brush when she hands it to me. The bristles glide through her hair with ease. The soft strands slip through without catching even once. I can't help but imagine the tables being turned and how rough my own hair would feel in Callisora's hands. How the short strands would catch on every bristle. How she would scold me for squirming from the pain.

"Farran?" Callisora's voice is small, like a child's. I focus on the reflection in the mirror and see just how small she looks, how fragile, how childish. Suddenly, the angry self-assured princess before me has melted away to reveal this exposed woman I've never met.

Her eyes avoid mine, "If you ..." she pauses, clearly struggling to find the right words, "If we had met under different circumstances, do you think we'd still ..." she trails off.

"Be friends?" I finish, unsure if that's even the right word. She is my master, and I, her bought slave.

She stiffens, then relaxes, "If I were to free you, would you leave?"

I arch my brow, trying to get a glimpse of the girl in the mirror, but her face is hidden by the darkness of her own self-doubt.

"Leave? Where would I even go?" I twist strands of hair around one another, "Of course I wouldn't leave. I have a home, a family," and Dante.

The room is silent. I finish the braid and add the hairpins Callisora had earlier taken out for decoration. The little gems at the ends of the pins add a sparkle that I never expected a vampire to be able to pull off. "All done."

Callisora slings the braid over her shoulder to inspect. "It looks good, thank you." She tosses it back over her shoulder before standing.

She turns to face me, "Thoughts?" She gestures to her gown.

I take in the sight of her. The off-shoulder neckline shows off Callisora's collar bones and neck, as well as a small bit of cleavage. The corset waist hugs her body, showing off her curves. And the bell-shaped ballgown skirt flows to the floor with effortless frills and lace.

The dress is mainly black with dark blue accents.

"You look great," I bow, holding out my hand, "Shall I walk you downstairs, Master?"

Callisora visually hesitates, "On one condition," She takes a breath, "You don't call me master anymore."

The words make me physically flinch. She's requested this of me many times. It's a hard habit to break. But there's something in her tone that feels different this time. Is she getting rid of me? Re-selling me?

She offers me a smile, a small thin-lipped, toothless smile. "I'm freeing you and all the fairies. You're welcome to stay, but that's your choice."

My chest tightens, stomach twists into knots. "I–I'm free?"

Callisora nods. She raises her chin, putting on that familiar Callisora-firmness, "Yes, but I have to become queen first. So, I have the authority to do so." She takes my arm, linking it with her own. "We should go. I don't want Vladimir to think I've gotten cold feet."

I nod and walk Callisora out of her bedroom, down the hall, and towards the throne room.

CHAPTER FIFTY

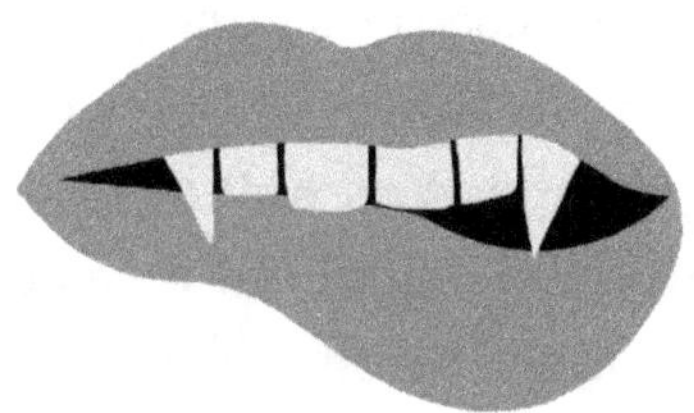

Callisora

THE WALK IS LONG. It feels like it's taking hours. The nausea that had made its home in my stomach when I awoke this morning is still refusing to leave. The pressure on my shoulders from the impending weight of leading a kingdom is intensifying the closer I come to the throne room.

We arrive at the end of the hall, which has some black fabric hanging in the doorway, shielding me from the eyes of onlookers, separating me from my destiny. Within moments, the curtains will draw open, and I will be presented to Vladimir.

Farran takes a breath next to me. "Alright, I'm going to head in. Don't run off or anything, okay?" She teases before slipping through the fabric, disappearing.

Time seems to be frozen; though people are moving around and talking on the other side of the fabric wall, my side stands still. I wipe my sweaty palms on the skirt of my dress. Maybe just a peek? I step closer to the curtains and grip the soft fabric between my fingers. Swallowing, I carefully separate the two pieces from each other and peer through. The room is brightly lit. Rows of chairs are filled with high-ranking vampires as well as leaders from the other kingdoms. Black and red roses fill the room, somehow making the throne room seem less intimidating. Maybe I'll have fresh flowers fill the room at all times?

The Elder stands on the platform that normally holds the thrones. Where'd they move the thrones to? I didn't know they could even be removed. On the Elder's left is Vladimir, dressed in a black tux with blue tie and pocket square. The servants must have picked out his accent colors to match my dress. Father and Akantha are standing on the opposite side of the Elder. Father's brows are pinched together and he's tapping his foot. His frustrated glare is focused on Vladimir. Akantha's eyes are focused on the floor even though she can't see it. What's weighing so heavy on her mind? Is the room full of people overwhelming her? Perhaps I can organize some outings for her before she gets married and leaves. First, I'll have to get more details about what happened at the full moon. Things have been so crazy since then that I haven't had time to talk with her. Hopefully I can soon.

Farran is along the side lines of the room along with all the servants. She and Dante are standing close, hands locked, receiving side-glares from some of the other fairies. Is Dante that popular of a guy? Or is it because Farran is a werewolf? I hope she knows what she's getting herself into.

The curtain closes, and I take a step back. My hand rests on my stomach. So many things are changing. It would be pointless to try and run from it all. That wouldn't benefit anyone, not even me.

The fabric moves, and I straighten my posture, folding my hands in front of me. The curtains are pulled apart, exposing me to the room filled with strangers and familiar people alike. An organ plays, though I don't know where it is.

I take a step, and then another, each one bringing me closer to Vladimir. His eyes meet mine, and suddenly the rest of the room melts away. His smile welcomes me, draws me closer. Who could have guessed that the annoying guard who would follow me around and drag me home every time I snuck out would be the vampire I would someday marry and have a child with?

Before I know it, I'm climbing the three steps to join Vladimir and the Elder. I face Vladimir, and he takes my hands in his, drawing my right hand to his lips. He kisses my knuckles before lowering my hand again.

"Thank you, everyone, for joining Princess Callisora and Sir Vladimir as they bind themselves to one another in vow and blood," The Elder's voice booms over the empty room.

I glance away from Vladimir for a quick moment, taking in the faces of the monsters in the first row. The Zombie King and his princess sit at the far end of the front row. The Fairy Princess sits next to them, her blue and green hair pulled up into a loose hairstyle that appears much more elegant than the one my fairies had tried forcing my hair to do. Next is the Werewolf Queen and King, each dressed in fine furs, possibly attempting a statement that mirror's what Akantha wore the first time she'd met their son. The rows behind are filled with a few of the heirs of the other kingdoms, as well as the odd witch and shapeshifter.

The other side of the room is filled with vampires. Nobles in the front row, and everyone else behind. At least some of the lower classes were able to join. I don't see Carlos or his father.

The Elder's voice rings out again, catching my attention and drawing my gaze back to Vladimir, who is still looking out at our audience.

"This union was formed on mutual trust, affection," and sex, "and respect. The love these two share flows deeper than any river and is stronger than any mountain. No matter the challenges, these two will face them head-on, hand in hand. They will lead Valdama through times of riches and struggles, and though they will hold their people high, they will continuously lift each other higher."

Vladimir's eyes lock on mine again—they're wide. Did he not realize the amount of responsibility that came with being with me? His eyes soften, and he smiles at me again.

The Elder gestures to Vladimir, "Do you, Vladimir, swear to protect and love Callisora and stand by her as she leads the kingdom?"

His eyes soften, even more, appearing glossy, "I do."

"And do you swear to protect this kingdom until your dying breath?"

The glossiness in his eyes vanishes, and he turns his attention to the Elder, "I do."

"And Callisora; do you swear to love, protect, and stand by Vladimir as he learns how to, and continues to, lead the kingdom?"

I squeeze Vladimir's hands, "I do."

"And do you promise to lead this kingdom as your father did, and his father before him, and so on?"

I intend to lead better than they have. Nodding once, my chest tightens, "I do."

"I shall now guide you through the bonding ceremony," the Elder announces. "You may now draw your partner's wrist to your lips and taste the blood of your promise to one another."

Vladimir lets go of my hands. He then grasps my right wrist. I watch as he draws it to his mouth. His jaw relaxes as his lips part. He bites down into the soft flesh. It stings at first, but the pain is quickly followed by a wave of pleasure. He releases. My arms drop to my side. The Elder holds a bowl under Vladimir's mouth. Vladimir opens his mouth, allowing the blood to flow into the bowl like a thick red waterfall. He licks the remaining blood from his lips, then offers me his wrist.

My heart pounds in my chest, trying to escape the bone-based bars that imprison it. I take his wrist in both hands, cradling it as if it's treasure. To think, a few weeks ago, I didn't want to be bound to anyone. And now, here I am, offering Vladimir everything I am. My mouth waters as I bring his wrist close to my lips. Another heartbeat echoes mine, Vladimir's. I pierce my fangs into his flesh. The warm metallic-tasting liquid fills my mouth. I swallow. My stomach clenches; I wasn't supposed to swallow. I allow my mouth to fill again, but the heavenly taste causes me to swallow again instinctively.

It's only been seconds, but it feels like an eternity. Just me, Vladimir, and his blood. Vladimir's heartbeat brings me back to reality when it begins to slow. How much have I drunk?

My mouth fills again, and I force myself to pull away. I'm greeted by the bowl that contains my blood. I want to drink it too. I want to swallow what's in my mouth and down the blood in the bowl. My blood. But I don't. I force myself to drain the blood from my mouth into the bowl.

The Elder pulls the bowl away from me, and I nearly fallow, but a hard look from Vladimir tells me not to. Reminds me why I'm here. What's going on. And who's all watching. Everyone.

The bowl is rocked around, the blood within swishing together. The Elder then offers the bowl to Vladimir, who looks paler than he had before I bit him. He takes the bowl in two hands and takes a long deep drink, tilting his head back. My inner child wants to yell, remind him that some of that is for me, but I stay silent. I had taken too much blood from him.

Vladimir lowers the bowl and holds it out to me. It's still half full. I accept it and mimic his motions, tipping my head back as I drink it. I force myself to drink slowly, wanting to convince everyone that I'm not enjoying drinking my own blood mixed with another vampire's. When nearly all the blood is gone from the bowl, I hand it back to the Elder. Licking my lips, I watch as he mixes the last of the blood with his finger. He then brings the bloodied finger to my forehead, pressing it there for a moment, then he dips his finger back in the bowl before doing the same to Vladimir. The Elder then smiles at us both while handing the bowl to a fairy, off to his left. The fairy leaves with the empty dish. The Elder gestures for us to look down the aisle I had walked up moments ago.

Two vampires approach us, each carrying a crown on a velvet pillow. The king's crown is made of thick silver, imbedded with red bloodstones, while the queen's is a thinner silver with white bloodstones. They were made for Dracula and his first bride, though she never got to wear the crown, because she was torn to pieces by Peter; the first Werewolf. It's still a lovely crown, even if its story is tied with the beginning of the war between vampires and werewolves.

The Elder steps between Vladimir and me. He lifts the Queen's Crown first. Normally the king is crowned first, but because I'm the noble blood, I suppose it makes sense for me to be the first to wear the heavy jewelry. A servant removes my tiara. I bow my head, and the crown is placed on it. Its literal weight isn't much heavier than the tiaras Akantha and I wear, but the weight I feel being placed upon me, passed down to me from my late mother, weighs a ton.

I raise my head, and the Elder moves on to Vladimir. Vladimir bows, and the crown is placed upon his head. When he stands up straight again, he looks powerful and strong. The Elder turns to our audience, "I present to you, Queen Callisora and King Vladimir of Valdama." He then turns to us, grinning. "Well, kiss her," he whispers.

Vladimir smirks, "With pleasure." He reaches out for me, grabs me by the waist, and pulls me close. I cup his face in my hands, and our lips touch. It's gentle at first, but is quickly met with intense desire. A clearing of someone's throat—no doubt my father's—causes us to pull apart. The Elder has already retreated back down the aisle.

The Fairy Princess stands and approaches us; she bows her head, "May you rule for ten thousand years in peace and prosperity."

I bow in return, "Thank you."

The princess turns to leave, followed by her heirs.

"Wait!" I blurt. The Fairy Princess looks over her shoulder at me, her green brow arched. I clear my throat, now is as good of a time as any.

"I'm freeing my servants," I announce. "Will you stay behind a while longer, so whomever doesn't wish to stay here has an escort home."

The fairy turns to me, her eyes wide. The look of shock passes, and she offers a genuine smile, not one out of courtesy this time. "I'd be delighted."

The Werewolf King and Queen approach us next, bowing and blessing us with hopeful futures, followed by the Zombie King.

"May you fight strong and live long enough to see the peace that follows."

My heart drops into my stomach. What does that mean? What does he know? What gifts does he have? Reincarnation? How could he predict a war coming? Millions of questions buzz through my mind, but no words come out.

Vladimir bows, "Thank you. We hope you will someday bless us with the wisdom you and your people possess."

The wisdom of the dead.

The Zombie King nods once, then looks to Akantha. Something twinkles in his eyes. Affection? Admiration? Whatever it is, it's gone within seconds, and so is he. Walking away as if his words hadn't just been nightmare fuel that will be feeding my dreams for centuries to come. If I even live that long.

CHAPTER FIFTY-ONE

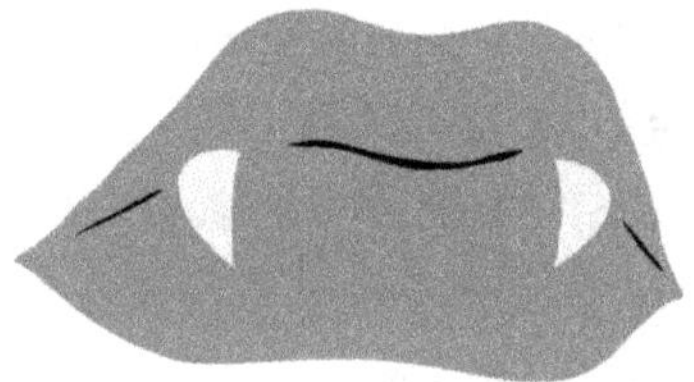

Akantha

THE ROOM IS FLOODED with voices and laughter. Colorful auras cover every inch of space. Callisora and Vladimir are making their rounds, talking to everyone, thanking them. Father had disappeared from my side a long time ago. Fairies are dissipating. I scan the auras, trying to find one in particular.

Finally, I spot who I'm looking for. They're leaning against a pillar. I approach them and offer a sad smile, "I guess this means you're leaving?"

They're silent.

"It would be selfish of me to ask you to stay. I know you're here against your will. I just hoped that your time here wasn't all bad."

"It wasn't."

My eyes burn. "S-so, you are leaving, then?"

"No," a soft hand reaches out and caresses my cheek. "I could never leave you, Akantha. You're like a daughter to me."

Helena pulls me into a hug, reminding me of the one we had just days ago.

I bury my face into the space where her neck meets her shoulder. "I don't know what I'd do without you."

"Or I, without you!" She kisses my temple, then lets me go. "Besides, if I left, who would teach the new servants how to clean the castle properly?" She takes a breath. "But I should go say my farewells to the others."

I nod, "Yes, you should." Helena walks away, vanishing into the merging blobs of color.

A shade of dark purple walks through the crowd, only now noticeable, because of the colors around it. I follow.

We leave through the throne room and walk down a hallway. Voices echo in the distance, almost undetectable. It's like we're entering a new world, and they're all being left behind. I clear my throat, "Jeharad?" He stops. "What are you doing here?" Wasn't he told to leave by Father?

He turns to me.

"I heard there was a wedding." He walks towards me, "Plus, I wanted to check on you. How are you feeling?"

I tilt my head to look towards his face. It's hard to remember what his face looks like; all I remember is Helena's. "I'm alright. Much better now that I've gotten rest."

He's quiet for a moment, "Can you tell me what happened?"

I shift my body weight from one leg to the other. "I got light-headed. I couldn't hear anything. Well, that's not true; I heard a voice saying my name. One I didn't recognize, but then I blacked out."

Thinking back to it still gives me shivers.

His breath hitches, "You heard a voice? Can you still hear it?"

"I heard it the night of the full moon," I admit, but then decide not to tell him about the few odd times I've heard it since then. It had been so soft that I could have imagined it. "I don't remember much after that, though. I remember seeing a battle, and Liam hurt. Then, suddenly, I was by Liam, and the fighting stopped, and the Younglings were leaving."

He reaches out and grasps my shoulders, "Really? That's amazing. Zahaya was right; you're the one." His voice is high-pitched. He's talking too quickly for me to understand.

"The one? The one for what?"

"The one to end the war that's coming. The one to fix everything!" He takes my hand and starts walking, dragging me along with him. "Come on, I need to get you out of here."

I stop and take my hand from him.

"I'm not going anywhere. My sister just became queen. I'm needed here." I don't know what I could be needed for, but Jeharad sounds crazy, and I don't like it. Plus, I'd vowed to make my own choices in life, and I'm not making running away one of them.

He sighs, "Are you sure?"

I nod, "Quite," I turn to walk away. I take two steps, but then I'm stopped.

A set of arms wrap around me, capturing me. A piece of cloth is held over my mouth and nose. I squirm my body, try to elbow my attacker, kick, scream, but my body isn't responding as fast as I need it to.

"I'm sorry, but I really wanted to do this the nice way," Jeharad's voice is the last thing I hear before everything goes silent.

Chapter Fifty-Two

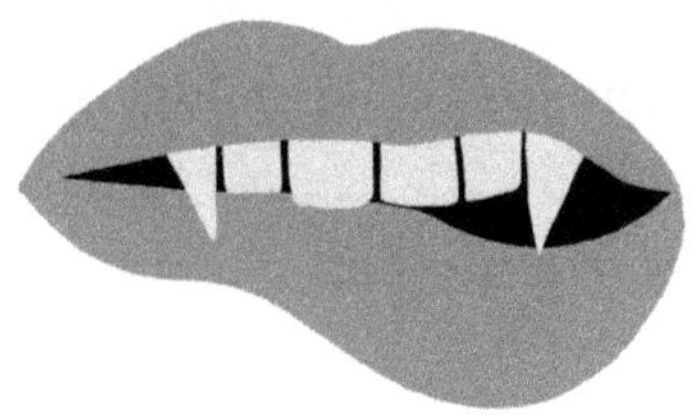

Callisora

A GREEN-SKINNED FAIRY CRIES before me, "Thank you so much, your majesty."

My cheeks ache from all this, smiling, "You're welcome, now go, before the others leave without you."

The fairy's eyes widen with worry. She bows again before rushing off.

Vladimir chuckles next to me, "What was that? The tenth?"

"Fourteenth," I correct.

He nods, looking out into the crowd. Most of the vampires have left the castle, same with the werewolves and zombies. All that's left is the Fairy

Princess and her new subjects. "It seems like we're losing all our staff."

"That's alright. We can bring in vampires and pay them to clean up after us."

He laughs again, "Well, we better not make too big of messes, to begin with, otherwise, they might think we're slobs."

I place a hand over my heart, "Excuse you; I'm a queen. I don't make messes."

Vladimir turns to me, wrapping an arm around my waist and holding me against him. "Only because your king is good at keeping you out of messy situations."

I laugh. If only he knew what type of situation the two of us were headed for. I don't even know what we're heading into. "Right. Well, I'm going to be an even bigger handful now that we're married."

His smile falls, and he groans, resting his forehead against mine, "Must you?"

I grin, "I must."

"Pardon me," a voice interrupts.

I push Vladimir back and spot Helena. Has she come to say her thanks too? I turn to her, giving her my undivided attention, even as Vladimir moves behind me. He wraps his arms around me and nuzzles his face into my neck. My jaw clenches, fighting the urge to squirm and giggle. "Yes, Helena?" I've finally remembered the fairy's name, and now she's leaving.

The golden fairy straightens her back, "Thank you for this chance at freedom, your majesty, but I would like to stay in your employment and continue to watch over Akantha."

Something inside me shifts. My chest tightens, heart stops. Akantha. She's getting married soon.

"Of course. And am I to assume you will follow her to the Wayfro once she marries?"

Helena frowns, "Hasn't she told you? She called off her engagement to the prince."

My gut twists. "No, she hasn't yet." What's going to happen to her now? And what about the alliance? I'll have to get into contact with the werewolves as soon as possible.

Helena nods, "Well, she has." The fairy looks around the quickly emptying room, possibly searching for my sister, "I intend to stand by her as long as she needs me."

The knot in my stomach loosens. I reach out and take the fairy's hand. "Thank you. I appreciate you looking out for her."

She gives my hand a squeeze. "It's my pleasure."

We exchange smiles, then look away from one another. I scan the room for Akantha, but don't see her.

"Speaking of my sister, do you know where she's run off to?"

"I'm afraid not. I left her momentarily to say farewell to my fellow fairies as they packed."

Something's wrong. I can feel it deep inside my bones. "Go check her bed chambers," my voice is sterner than I intend, but Helena is already off heading that way before I speak.

I spot Farran and Dante, who are chatting in the shadows. Looks like they're both staying. I pull away from Vladimir, and the two of us walk over.

Farran spots me first and grins, "Hello, Queen Callisora. What do we owe this pleasure?" Her taunting tone is annoying. Maybe I should have only set the fairies free.

"It's probably nothing, but have you seen my sister?"

Farran looks puzzled for a moment, then looks at Dante, who shakes his head. She looks back at me, "We haven't seen her for a while. Not since shortly after the ceremony."

That's what I was worried of. "Could you two do a quick search around?"

They both nod and walk in separate directions.

Vladimir places a hand on my shoulder, turning me to face him, "I'm sure she just went for a walk and got lost."

"Maybe."

But probably not. It's not like Akantha to explore unknown areas without someone being with her.

I pace the throne room until the others return. Farran gets back first, having found nothing.

Helena returns next with a note.

Dear King and Queen,

I've taken your sister somewhere safe where she can learn who she really is. Don't worry; I do not intend to hurt her. And I will return her home safely when everything is over.

Jeharad

I crumple the note in my fist. Blinking back tears, I can't speak. Why would Jeharad want Akantha? What is he planning?

"I don't get it."

Helena shakes her head, also unsure.

Dante rushes in with Liam and a female wolf.

"Liam?" I arch my brow at him.

"Dante said you were looking for Akantha."

I nod and hold out the note. Liam takes it, uncrumples it, and reads it over.

He frowns, "I was worried something like this might happen."

The female wolf looks at Liam with a worried expression.

He holds the note back out for me, but I don't take it. "There's a rebellion starting."

"I know about the rebellion," I snap. I've heard rumours, but Father never seemed worried about it, so I never cared much either. Could this have something to do with the Youngling in the dungeon?

He arches his brow.

"Do you? Because if you did, you would have guarded your sister better."

"What do you mean?" Vladimir hisses.

Liam's brows furrow, "Wait, none of you know? I thought only Akantha didn't know, but no one here?"

He takes a breath. "I suppose that makes sense since you're all vampires."

My teeth grind against one another, "You better start explaining before I start biting."

Liam smiles a bit at that, flashing orange eyes at me, "You know of Dracula, correct?"

I nod.

"A being named Shri created him, along with the first monster of every species. Dracula turned on her, killing her. The Zombie King collected her soul so she could be reincarnated when the time was right. When your sister was born, and everyone discovered she was blind like Shri, they suspected that she was the reincarnation," he paused for a moment. "But there's no proof, because the Zombie King hid the box that Shri's soul was in so no one could find it."

He takes a deep breath before letting it out again, "The main reason my parents wanted me to marry her was to protect the possible reincarnated Monster Empress," He raises his hands in the air. "That's what my parents called her, not me," He lowers his hands. "My guess is that the Rebellion wants to use her to cause the downfall of all the kingdoms."

The Vampire's Fall. This is tied to the Younglings.

I bite my lip, "We need to find her. Get her back here where it's safe."

The female wolf nods, "We want to help."

Liam nods in agreement.

"We'll need a plan," Vladimir adds.

But how long will a plan take? How long will Akantha be lost?

I hope she's okay.

Chapter Fifty-Three

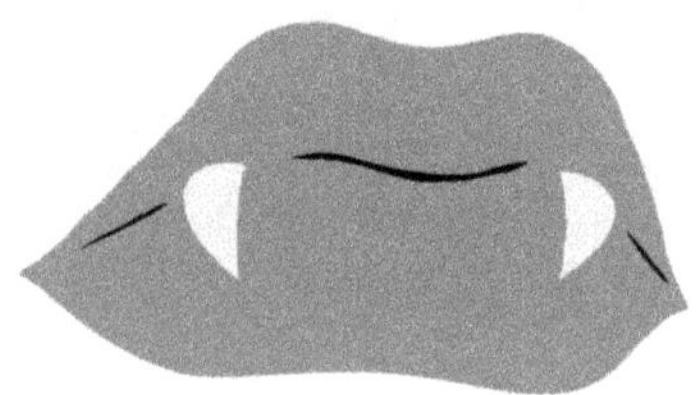

Akantha

MY HEAD HURTS.

I open my eyes and sit up. This isn't my bed; it's hard and lumpy. The room smells musty. It's smaller than my room. I stand and walk to the door, placing my hand on it. My fingers retract from the feeling of cold metal. Where am I? What happened?

Jerahad. Jerahad had happened. He'd put something over my face.

A window creaks open, and the scent of cinnamon fills the room.

Without thinking, I turn around and run towards the smell. I'm met by a tall, firm body. He wraps his arms around me. My cheeks are wet. Am I crying? His hand strokes my back.

"I'm scared," I whisper, my voice shaking. "Please don't leave me."

His chest moves. It takes me a moment, but I realize what just happened. He spoke. Only a single word, but it's the first word he's ever said to me.

"Never."

Akantha (A-Can-Th-A)
Species: Vampire
Age: 648 human years
Appearance: Strait black hair, blue/red eyes, pail skin.
Aura: Purple with blue waves.
Gift/Other: Sees auras. Blind

Callisora (Cal-I-Soar-A)
Species: Vampire
Age: 971 human years
Appearance: Wavy black hair, brown/red eyes, pail skin.
Aura: Red with silver swirls.
Gift/Other: Hears heartbeats. Has a blood addiction.

Queen Adora (Adore-A)
Species: Vampire
Age: 12,530 human years
Appearance: Wavy black hair, brown/red eyes, pail skin.
Aura: Blue and gold.

King Roderick (Rod-Rick)
Species: Vampire
Age: 15,694 human years
Appearance: Short black hair, brown/red eyes, pail skin.
Aura: Grey and red.
Gift/Other: Influence. Unfaithful.

Sir Vladimir (Vlad-I-Mirror)
Species: Vampire
Age: 1,654 human years
Appearance: Shaggy black hair, brown/red eyes, pail skin.
Aura: Red and orange.
Gift/Other: Speed. A Knight. One of Callisora's suitors.

Sir Carlos (Car-Los)
Species: Vampire
Age: 2,095 human years
Appearance: Wavy blond hair, brown/red eyes, pail skin.
Aura: Grey and blue.
Other: One of Callisora's suitors.

Farran (Fair-Ran)
Species: Werewolf
Age: 400 human years
Appearance: Brown hair, brown/orange eyes, tanned skin.
Aura: Orange and green.
Other: Can hear her wolf. Turned at a young age.

Prince Liam (Lee-Am)
Species: Werewolf
Age: 1,895 human years
Appearance: Blonde hair, brown/orange eyes, tanned skin.
Aura: Green and brown.
Gift: Speed.

Amelia (A-Me-Lee-A)
Species: Werewolf
Age: 1,340 human years
Appearance: Brown hair, brown/orange eyes, tanned skin.
Aura: Lavender and darker purple.
Other: A wolf knight. Was engaged to Liam.

Princess Erissa (Ear-Is-A)
Species: Fairy
Age: 2,967 human years
Appearance: Blue to green hair, blue eyes & skin.
Aura: Light blue and green.
Gift: Seeing the Future.

Helena (Hell-En-A)
Species: Fairy
Age: 2,702 human years
Appearance: Gold to silver hair, blue eyes, gold skin.
Aura: Yellow with glints of ember.
Gift/Other: Healing. Akantha's handmaiden

Dante (Don-T-Aie)
Species: Vampire/Fairy (Youngling)
Age: 1,227 human years
Appearance: Black hair, blue/grey eyes, red skin.
Aura: Red and black
Gift/Other: Fast flight. Bastered son of the vampire king.

Zombie King
Species: Zombie
Age: Unknown
Appearance: Black hair, black eyes, grey veiny skin.
Aura: Grey and silver.
Gift/Other: Resurrecting the dead. The First Zombie

Julia (Jewel-E-A)
Species: Zombie
Age: Unknown
Appearance: Brown hair, black eyes, grey veiny skin.
Aura: Pink and purple.
Gift/Other: Orical. The "Zombie Princess"

Zahaya (Z-A-Yeah)
Species: Witch (Human)
Age: 50 human years
Appearance: Grey-blonde hair, silver eyes, peach skin.
Aura: Blue and pink

Jeharad (Je-Har-Id)
Species: Wizard (Human)
Age: 16 human years
Appearance: Black hair, dark eyes, peach skin.
Aura: Dark purple and black

It Took a Village

Acknowledgements

Many say it takes a village to raise a child. Well, it's the same with writing a book. So many people go into helping with the book, be it critiquing, editing, or even just motivating the writer.

This story all started as a roleplay page I created on Goodreads, where Jordan Orchard and another member helped to create some moments that I re-wrote in this story. Without the two of them, The Vampire's Fall wouldn't have been the same.

I'm deeply indebted to Lauren Fontaine, who not only was the first person who sat by and listened to me gush about this story, but she also helped critique it and even offered some ideas. Amber Hobson, Hayley Kosikis, and my brother Andrew Duivenvoorde—who all were the first beta readers for this book—were all open to listening about the Creatures of the Night universe.

Mega thanks to my grandma, Brenda Marling, and my aunt, Evelyn Marling, who helped fund the editing of this book. Also, a big thank you to my husband, David Thompson, who supported me throughout my author journey.

The Vampire's Fall would not be what it is today without Evelyne Paniez, who created the beautiful cover of Callisora and the Valdama castle. Without Mari (cathrine6mirror) to do chapter art, The Vampire's Fall wouldn't have that extra bit of finesse that sets it apart from other novels.

I'd also like to recognize the other beta readers and critique partners such as Jessie Elliot, Neal Arbic, Marilyn Lamb, Bruce Hanson, Kelsey Sutton, Catherine Conners, Zara Chapman, and a few others listed already in this acknowledgement, who took the time to help work on this project. Each of them showed great enthusiasm while helping me on this book.

I also want to recognize the authors who inspired me to finally get this book done: Jenna Moreci, Meg LeTorre, Bethany Atazadeh, Brittany Wang, Jessi Elliot, Kristen Martin, Kristen Granata, and Sophie Jordan. Be it through YouTube videos or privet chats and emails, you have each inspired and motivated me in your own ways.

Another special author I'd like to recognize is Daniel Willcocks. Without him and his bootcamp, I wouldn't have gotten the kick in the butt I needed to find time in my day to write. Dan and the talented writers in his boot camp are endlessly supportive and uplifting.

Also, to you, the reader, for picking up this book and taking the time to read it

About the Author

Eliza Delmar

As a "Plantser", Liz creates her stories with little to no planning ahead of time, gathering inspiration from songs and images.

From short stories to full-length novels, Liz is most comfortable writing Fantasy, Paranormal, and Dystopian for New Adult, Young Adult, and Middle

Grade as well. She has begun to expand into Contemporary Romance under the pen name of Eliza Doe.

With the goals of producing her own graphic novels/comics as well as TV shows/films, Liz works hard to study the craft of scriptwriting for both mediums.

Being a mother of three, and married to an elevator mechanic, keeps her on her toes. Having a son with a severe heart defect, another with autism, and a daughter who is more adventurous and outgoing than both the boys put together, Liz still finds time to express herself.

https://elizabethduivenvoorde.ca

www.ingramcontent.com/pod-product-compliance
Lightning Source LLC
Chambersburg PA
CBHW070550310726
48982CB00011B/1537/J
9781777447823